Flashman and Madison's War

Robert Brightwell

Published in 2015 by FeedARead.com Publishing

First Edition

A CIP catalogue record for this title is available from the British
Library.

This book is dedicated to the memory of those of all nations
who fought in the now largely forgotten conflict known as
the War of 1812.

Introduction

This is the fifth instalment in the memoirs of the Georgian Englishman Thomas Flashman, which were recently discovered on a well-known auction website. Thomas is the uncle of the notorious Victorian rogue Harry Flashman, whose memoirs have already been published, edited by George MacDonald Fraser.

This book finds Thomas, a British army officer, landing on the shores of the United States at the worst possible moment – just when the United States has declared war with Britain! Having already endured enough with his earlier adventures, he desperately wants to go home but finds himself drawn inexorably into this new conflict. He is soon dodging musket balls, arrows and tomahawks as he desperately tries to keep his scalp intact and on his head.

It is an extraordinary tale of an almost forgotten war, with inspiring leaders, incompetent commanders, a future American president, terrifying warriors (and their equally intimidating women), brave sailors, trigger-happy madams and a girl in a wet dress who could have brought a city to a standstill. Flashman plays a central role and reveals that he was responsible for the disgrace of one British general, the capture of another and for one of the biggest debacles in British military history.

As editor I have restricted myself to checking the historical accuracy of the scarcely credible facts detailed in the book and adding a series of notes at the end to provide more information on the characters and events featured. Flashman often uses the term 'Indian' to refer to Native Americans/First Nation people, which I have not amended. To change to modern terminology would jar with the rest of the book and cause confusion, for example the Iroquois referred to themselves as the Six Nations and native peoples fought on both sides in this conflict.

The memoirs of Thomas' more famous nephew, Harry Flashman, edited by George MacDonald Fraser, are as always strongly recommended.

RDB

Lake Erie Map

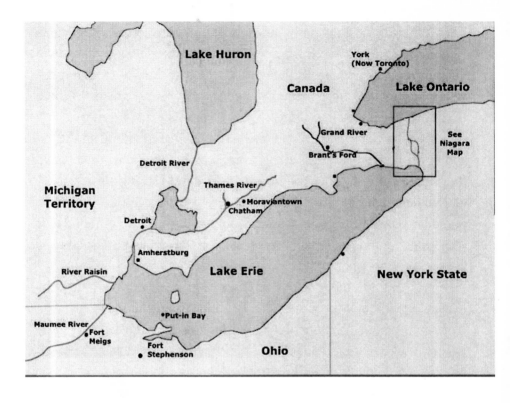

Niagara River Map

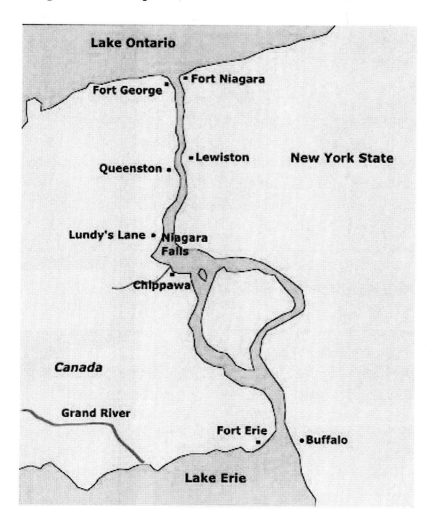

Chapter 1 – Queenston Canada, 13th of October 1812

I stumbled over a root. When I put my foot down a twig snapped with a sound that seemed as loud as a gunshot in the silent forest. The man to my right glanced over at me. It was probably a look of disapproval, but it was hard to tell in that nightmare of a face. Peering around, I saw dozens of the sinister figures flitting through the trees in absolute silence. Even though they were supposed to be on my side, they still made the hair on the back of my neck prickle in alarm. My companion gently grabbed my elbow and steered me towards a trail of moss patches that I could cross without making any further noise. He was naked but for a deerskin loin cloth and his tanned body was covered in painted patterns and swirls, but it was not his torso that drew your tremulous gaze. The skin over both jaws was painted black while another wide red stripe was coloured across his face from his eyebrows to the bridge of his nose. Above that his head was shaved apart from a tufted topknot, which was adorned with feathers, scraps of cloth and what looked like a silver hatpin.

The black part of his face split to reveal two smiling rows of yellow teeth. "We will soon be up to them," my companion whispered. "And then we will avenge the Great Father." The most incongruous thing was that the savage spoke in perfect English. His accent would not have been out of place in the English court. Indeed, I had just discovered that he had attended royalty in London and counted the Duke of Northumberland amongst his particular friends. Quite what His Grace would have made of the man's current appearance beggared belief; mind you they are wild sorts up in Northumberland.

The 'Great Father' he spoke off was Britain's best general in Canada, Isaac Brock, the man who had recently captured Detroit and proved that Britain could defend itself in this strange war against the United States. He was the man who had ordered me to stay with the savages and he was very clear that he did not trust my companion.

"Watch your back, Flashman," Brock had warned. "Even though they say that they are fighting on our side, I don't doubt that they would stick a knife in your back and scalp you if there was a profit in it." Oh he was a cheery motivator of men was General Brock, not that it did him any good. For at dawn that day the Americans had launched their invasion of Canada, crossing the River Niagara at Queenston. Initially the British had held most of them off, with a gun on the heights bombarding their boats. Brock had ordered the company of men guarding the battery on the heights to come down into the town to help with the hand to hand fighting against the invaders. He did not think that the Americans would find a way up the cliffs in the half-light, but he was wrong. Some wily American regulars ascended the steep slope and the British gun crew barely had time to spike the gun before they ran for their lives. The heights were the commanding position of the battlefield and had to be recaptured. As American reinforcements gathered on the hilltop, Brock personally led two hundred men from the town up the open ground facing the American position. The Yankee sharpshooters with their rifles were deadly and Brock was the obvious leader of the attack in his cocked hat and gold epaulets. He got nowhere near the American position before he was shot down and killed.

When I arrived on the scene two hours later with my new native comrades, they seemed genuinely puzzled as to why the Great Father would have charged headlong towards a large, well-entrenched enemy over ground with no cover. They shook their heads in dismay and muttered among themselves before starting to melt away into the nearby forest. It looked like they were going home already.

Brock had told me that when he had attacked Detroit, their war chief had demanded gifts and money for hundreds of warriors, but had only arrived with sixty. Of those, half had refused to fight and the rest had been of little use. He had been contemptuous of these Iroquois Indians, claiming that they were far inferior to the western Indian tribes led by their chief, Tecumseh.

"The Iroquois won't fight but we need them with the army," he had told me. "If they are left on their Grand River reservation then my militia soldiers will be worrying about the Indians raiding their homesteads while they are serving with their regiments." He gave a snort of disgust before adding, "You are an Indian man, you must understand."

It took me a moment to work out why Brock had thought I was an expert in Native American affairs. I had only just arrived for the first time in Canada and if someone had told me to look for a Mohawk I would have been searching the skies for a bird. But then I remembered that the letter of introduction I had carried from the governor general had mentioned, as well as my peninsular service, that I had also served in India. Perhaps Brock thought that all Indians were alike. I was about to correct him when I remembered his claim that the Indians would not fight. I had suffered enough for my country and had been looking forward to going home before I had been shanghaied into this new conflict. If my duties were going to be nurse-maiding a bunch of natives that were allowed to shirk away from every danger, well that was just nuts to me. I was no stranger to the art of shirking danger myself and if I could do it with official sanction, then so much the better.

"Well it has been a while since I served with Indian soldiers, sir," I told Brock, slapping my hand around the gold-hilted sword that I had won during a battle in India. "But I will do my best not to let you down."

Of course that was before I had even met an Iroquois warrior, and a damned alarming sight they were when I did clap eyes on them. I'll own that I did not feel that sorry to see them drifting off into the forest once they learned that Brock was dead. I know the war paint was designed to frighten their enemies but I can tell you that on brief acquaintance, it was more than a bit unnerving for their allies too.

Another relief force of British and Canadian militia was already on its way. They would try to dislodge the Americans from the heights, but it would be hot work. Once the Americans got a foothold on the Canadian shore, their militia would pour across. It looked like the doom mongers amongst the Canadian officials I had spoken to would be proved right: the Americans would easily invade Canada. Certainly one British officer would make no difference. With the general dead and the Indians apparently abandoning the scene, I was minded to follow their example. There was bound to be confusion over the coming hours, and in all probability a rout and retreat. It made sense to get a head start.

I felt no loyalty then to Canada and its arbitrarily drawn border and certainly none to those strange savages. I thought that if I could get back to Quebec without being overtaken by the American militia, I might still get a ship home. I was just walking back to my horse when I heard a voice call my name. It was the war chief, the Indian with the red and black stripes over his face. He had a long unpronounceable Indian name that started with a 'T'; mercifully he also had an English name: John Norton.

"Flashman," he called again. "Come on; leave your horse, we need to get moving."

"Where are you going?" I replied.

"Going?" repeated Norton and then he gestured with his musket up the hill towards the American position. "We are going to war!"

Chapter 2

It was one of the strangest conflicts that I have ever fought in. It is now known as the War of 1812, which is typically misleading as most of the fighting took place in 1813 and 1814. I started it as a prisoner of the United States and I am sure that that most Americans and Canadians did not want to fight. The citizens of New England and Nova Scotia certainly didn't. They largely managed to ignore the war completely and continued to trade with each other throughout the conflict. The Americans supplied grain that was used to feed Canadian and British forces, while in return the Canadians supplied manufactured goods including Sheffield steel blades. Merchants on both sides saw no reason to lose profits when there were ready markets to supply. Their representatives had not voted for the war and they did not want it.

"Even if we invade Canada we do not have the men to hold it," my Boston gaoler told me. "When the British war with France ends they will turn on us with all their veteran troops, and their ships will blockade our ports."

The American merchant captain who had rescued me from France and inadvertently delivered me to a new captivity agreed. Several times he visited me in prison and was adamant that the war would be a disaster for his country. "Even now the Royal Navy must have over fifty vessels in our waters compared to our navy of just five frigates fit for sea. They will be able to bankrupt the country by cutting off our trade."

When I eventually got into Canada on one of those trading ships I found that the British and Canadians were similarly pessimistic. There were just two British regiments of regular soldiers then in Canada, and they were demoralised as they had been due to return home. The rest of the Canadian forces were militia, more interested in farming than fighting. Many had moved to Canada from America and had no great loyalty to their new country. Against this meagre force the Americans had passed acts to increase their army first to thirty-five thousand and then fifty thousand men. In addition state governors were required to raise a further eighty thousand as militia.

Britain was already fighting France and that conflict would have the first call on available troops and ships. The Canadian authorities were told that they would simply have to manage with what they had. At any moment they expected swarms of American soldiers to come pouring over the border. To make matters worse the one area where the British had expected to do well, fighting at sea, had also gone against them. Early naval engagements had all been won by the Americans, with the USS Constitution smashing HMS Guerriere to matchwood.

But the strangest thing about the war was that no one seemed entirely clear on why the countries were fighting at all. The main grievance of the Americans was the way that the British navy intercepted their shipping and removed any crew that they judged were deserters from the Royal Navy. I'll admit that the British took a high handed approach here. In 1807 HMS Leopard even intercepted an American frigate in the middle of the Chesapeake Bay, and after a brief engagement, removed some of her crew. The Americans welcomed British deserters as United States citizens and issued thousands of protection papers, which were also forged and traded among British sailors awaiting the opportunity to jump ship. The British navy was not willing to let its prime seamen escape so easily and generally disregarded these identity documents. If a man looked like a Jack Tar and spoke like a Jack Tar, he was bound for a flogging and a hammock in one of His Majesty's ships.

Tragically the British parliament took a fraction too long to consider the American complaints. The ship from London carrying the message that various restrictions on US shipping had been repealed passed another ship in the Atlantic going in the opposite direction, containing the declaration of war. When news of the British concessions was announced even the American army commander thought that it was enough to end the war and a cessation to hostilities was agreed. That was when my Boston gaolers took the opportunity to rid themselves of their prisoner. I was put on a grain ship to the

Canadian port of Halifax, which carried papers protecting it from any action by the Royal Navy.

When I arrived on Canadian soil I had fully expected to be able to catch a passage back to Britain on the next available ship. After all I had not been home for over three years and had suffered enough in the Peninsular War, not to mention my recent exploits in Paris. No, a safe berth and a warm bed was what I deserved. Instead, I was told that no army officer of my experience could possibly be allowed home until the American president had ratified the end of hostilities. I fretted impatiently for several weeks waiting for confirmation that this brief war was over. The Americans had got most of what they wanted and their President Madison was being congratulated for his skill in forcing Britain to negotiate. Then to everyone's amazement, word came through that the daft bastard wanted to continue the fight.

There was much speculation as to the reasons why, what was then known as 'Madison's War,' would continue. To this day few make much sense. Some claimed that the British concessions over interference with American trade had not gone far enough. Other high minded northern liberals compared naval impressment with slavery and there was much rhetoric about lifting the fetters of oppression. Yet more suggested that it was opportunism; as Bonaparte would crush the British once he had defeated the Russians. But there were also claims that the British were supporting Indians in their raids on American citizens. Invade Canada, it was maintained, and you would cut off the Indians from their British support. Curiously though, it was the states from New York northwards, along the Canadian border, who voted against war. The vote was seventy-nine to forty-nine in favour of hostilities, with those from Pennsylvania southwards the most belligerent.

In the end it was probably politics that continued the conflict. Having announced the confrontation with much fanfare, those in favour of the war in Washington, known as the 'war hawks,' were reluctant to stop it. They knew that the British government's concessions had been granted before it even knew that the war had started. Perhaps more could be obtained once hostilities were underway. There were also American elections coming up; Madison needed the support of the war hawks and no one wanted to lose face.

The local merchants on both sides of the border were appalled at the decision, but their dismay was nothing to mine. I found myself embarked on a ship up the St Lawrence River, bound for Quebec, where I was to report for duty. It was a journey that led to that wooded hillside on the Queenston Heights.

The wood ran up the spine of the hill that approached the river and ended at the abandoned gun position. If I could have seen through the trees, the town of Queenston was to my left at the bottom of the hill on the river bank. Sporadic shooting indicated that this was still being contested by the British and American forces. To my right the strip of forest that we were walking through ended in more open ground facing the Americans. A sudden crash of cannon fire indicated that British guns in the town were still exchanging fire with the American guns across the river.

"Shouldn't we wait for the rest of the relief force before we go any further?" I had whispered the words to John Norton, but the burst of cannon fire had nearly drowned them out.

"No, we will fight them the Indian way, not like the white man's fighting." He grinned and added, "If we make the warriors wait they will drift off; their blood is up for a fight now." I still found that hideously painted face unnerving, but I nodded in understanding. In fact I did not really comprehend his meaning at all. I had no idea what the Indian way of fighting was, but I was about to find out.

We pressed on through the trees, the Iroquois advancing in six long files of men, well spaced out. There were over two hundred warriors in the group and they moved silently through the woodland. We must have covered several hundred yards when suddenly we heard something or someone crashing through the trees towards us. Norton grabbed my arm and pulled me down amongst the scrub. I lay listening to whatever was approaching. It was making far too much noise for an animal; it was human. Several running men, I guessed. We tensed for the ambush and then there was a partly muffled shriek and several thuds as bodies hit the floor. Norton got up and ran over to where

13

several men were struggling desperately against their Indian captors. One had already pissed himself in terror and looking at the nightmare figures holding them down, I did not blame him. As I appeared their wide eyes stared at my British officer's red coat in a mute appeal for clemency, while their captors kept hands firmly over their mouths.

"Be still and quiet," Norton whispered at the prisoners. Then he gestured to the warriors holding them, "Let them be." The Indians let go of the scared men and stood back, but several still waved tomahawks and knives threateningly.

"Please, mister," croaked one of the men to me, "we is on your side."

"Who are you?" demanded Norton quietly.

"We are from the York militia, with General Sheaffe. He sent us to scout how many Americans are on the heights." Sheaffe had been Brock's second-in-command and would now be leading the relief force.

"How many are there on the heights?" I asked.

"Thousands, sir," said the militia man, his gaze flickering between Norton and me as he tried to work out who was in charge. "I reckons at least six thousand, sir," he added firmly. I was appalled. From what we had heard they had certainly got that number of men on their side of the river and they would vastly outnumber any forces that the British and Canadians could bring together.

"Six thousand, that is ridiculous," exclaimed Norton. "They cannot possibly have got that many across. They don't have more than a dozen large boats and our guns must have sunk half of those."

"Well that is what we saw," insisted the militia man truculently, beginning to recover some of his composure.

"The more game, the better hunting," crowed one of the warriors and there was a chuckle at this from some of his comrades. But as the laughter died away I realised that amongst other Indians the news of the enemy numbers had caused consternation. They might have had their blood up for a fight before, but many clearly did not fancy the thirty-to-one odds that six thousand men would have on our meagre two hundred warrior war party. Some of the men at the back of the gathering were already turning round and going back the way we had come. I certainly did not blame them; in fact I was just about to edge back through the crowd to join them.

"Where are you going?" Norton challenged his retreating warriors.

"We have wives and children to look after," said one of the warriors at the back of the group.

Norton turned to the militia men, "You can go," he told them. He waited in silence as they scrambled to their feet and began running again down the hill, glancing nervously over their shoulders. Once they were out of earshot, Norton turned again to his warriors. "The women can look after the children and take them to safety if needed. The Americans cannot have that number on the hill." He raised his voice now so that all could hear him, apparently no longer caring if the distant Americans heard him as well. "You are warriors of the Iroquois, you are painted for war and our enemy awaits us. We will show the Americans how we can fight and the Great Spirit will decide who lives and who dies."

If Norton was expecting a rousing cheer at the end of this little speech he was to be disappointed. I was reminded of a similar oration given by my friend Cochrane when we had sailed into battle against what had seemed impossible odds. We had been on a small ship then and escape was impossible, but for the Indians here it was easy to slip away. While some picked up their weapons and moved forward to stand with Norton, others shook their heads in dismay at the odds and started to move back down the hill. I estimated that more than half were leaving.

"Let us climb the path," called Norton to those who were left, with what I thought was a rather fixed grin of encouragement. "With Captain Flashman here, we will bring confusion to our enemies so that General Sheaffe can sweep them into the river." He turned to me, "Is that not so, my friend?"

I was damned if I was going to take another step up that hill, but before I could reply a huge great Indian threw his arms about my shoulders and gave me a hug that would have suffocated a bear. As my face was pressed into his greasy skin the Indian pounded my back and declared loudly, "Fear not, Long Knife, the Mohawks of the Grand River will not let you down. We will help you avenge the Great Father." There was a cheer at that and as I extricated myself from the great oaf's embrace I found myself surrounded by Indians, patting me on the back as though I was General Brock's long lost son.

"That is very kind of you, I'm sure," I muttered as they moved away and started to stalk up the hillside. "John," I called to Norton, "Can I have a word with you?"

Norton held back until the other braves were out of earshot. "Don't worry about the warriors that slipped away, half of them will probably come back when they hear we are winning."

"Winning? Are you mad? I am more worried about the warriors that stayed. For God's sake, man, if there are six thousand Americans on that hilltop and you only have around eighty warriors left, they will all be slaughtered." I drew myself stiffly to attention. "As the British officer of this force I insist that we withdraw at once; we must let Sheaffe know what he is up against."

To my surprise Norton laughed. "I thought your orders were to encourage the Iroquois to fight and stay in the war, not to retreat." He patted me on the shoulder. "You are right, if there are six thousand men on that hillside then we should definitely let Sheaffe know. But first we should look for ourselves as I am sure that they have nothing like that number."

"But even if there are only two thousand men there, they will still outnumber your warriors by more than twenty to one; surely we should just send a single scout and wait here?"

"You do not understand the Iroquois way, Flashman. They are used to fighting against larger odds. They believe that the white man can be replaced in limitless numbers from across the sea, but for them several crushing defeats will see the extinction of their people. They will not stand toe to toe with the Americans. Each warrior fights according to his courage; there is no shame in retreat. They do as much damage to the enemy that they can, at least risk to themselves."

"You mean that they can run away whenever they want?" I was astounded and for the first time I felt some affinity for the Iroquois.

16

Many was the time I had desperately wanted to run from a battle, but fear of the resulting humiliation and ruin had kept me in line. Now I was with a force where I could run whenever I wanted. For a brief moment I was delighted. Then I thought on: the Iroquois force had already halved due to rumours of the enemy size. There were downsides in having allies that could melt away at a moment's notice. I would have to keep my eye on them; I did not want to be at the back of some headlong retreat with a pack of vengeful militia on my tail.

As if reading my mind, Norton added, "You will not find the Iroquois lacking in courage." Then he looked up the hill where the Indians were disappearing through the trees. "Come, we had better get on and I promise if there are anything close to six thousand we will retire to alert General Sheaffe."

We pressed on up the slope, the Iroquois now reduced to four shorter files of men. They moved so silently that the forward scouts surprised a deer, which ran through the trees between the line I was in and the one to my left. They went quickly too, and I was struggling to keep up. There did not seem any great need for silence now as there was the regular crash of cannon echoing through the trees, but knowing the warriors were all around me, the gaps between the artillery fire were eerily quiet.

"That big fellow," I whispered at Norton as I stepped around some fallen branches. "He said he was a Mohawk. Are there other tribes in your band, then, as well as Iroquois?"

"No, the Iroquois is a collective name for six tribes or Indian nations, of which the Mohawk is the largest. That was Black Eagle, a brave warrior if a bit impetuous." Before he could say any more there was a bird call and the Indians around me seemed to stiffen and become yet more vigilant. "Our scouts have reached the edge of the forest," Norton murmured. "Come on, let's find out how many men they really have."

We crept through the undergrowth, the last few yards crawling on our bellies, to emerge at the bottom of a bush that faced on to the clearing. Norton was right, there was nothing like six thousand men. It looked like there was just a sixth of that number, half regular soldiers and the rest militia. Most were arrayed over to our right, facing down the hill towards the clear ground alongside the forest where I guessed Sheaffe's men could be seen forming up. Ahead I could just make out the abandoned gun position that overlooked the river and to the right of that, across the clearing, was thick undergrowth that led down a steep slope to the river's edge. In the middle of the open space to our front sat four American militia soldiers. They had clearly been detailed to watch the forest edge, but lounged looking relaxed on one of the low grass banks.

"If we can get into that far undergrowth we can attack the Americans from behind," Norton whispered. "It would keep them disorganised and unsettled while Sheaffe approaches up the hill."

"But they would just chase the warriors off and anyway those militia guards would raise the alarm if we try to cross here." I was pleased to be able to spike his plan. The last thing I needed was to get involved in some death or glory charge with a bunch of savages; especially as they were prone to run away and were considerably faster over rough terrain than I was.

But Norton was not put off so easily. "The Americans would be foolish to chase our warriors into thick undergrowth and if they pursued us all the way down to the river bank, they would never get back in time to fight off Sheaffe." He paused before adding, "But you are right, the militia are a problem." With that he backed out of the bush and I heard him whispering to some of the other warriors. He returned a moment later, grinning, "Now you will see how Iroquois fight."

Well I sat and waited in that bush for five minutes and saw absolutely nothing. The regular soldiers and militia were still preparing for a British attack to our right and the four militia men spent most of their time watching their comrades rather than scanning the trees. For them it was a fatal mistake. As Norton had mentioned, Iroquois like to fight at little risk to themselves and these poor devils did not get a chance to cry out, never mind return fire. One moment they were relaxed, sitting on the grass and chewing tobacco, the next three of them were staring in shock at arrows protruding from their chests.

18

Only the fourth man looked as though he might manage to produce a shout of warning – he had been struck by an arrow in the shoulder. But as he tried to rise I saw the big Indian called Black Eagle spring up from a dip in the ground with his arm already drawn back. There was a glitter of metal and the fourth man was slumping back, with a tomahawk embedded deep in his chest.

There was giggling from the men about me as the militia slumped to the ground. As I was soon to learn, nothing cheers up an Indian more than doing the dirty to someone else. Without any further orders the Iroquois started to move forward down a shallow gully next to the bank the militia had sat on. They were all crouched down low, out of sight to the distant American forces. Norton was at their head and I had little choice but to follow. Without Norton nearby, and with Brock's warning ringing in my ears I was still not sure I would trust the Iroquois. On the other hand staying back alone in a British uniform with so many Americans about would also be a dangerous business.

By the time I passed where the militia had been killed, the four Indians had pulled their bodies into the ditch and were busy recovering their arrows. These archers also had muskets over their shoulders. As they crouched down over the corpses at first I did not realise what they were doing. Then I saw Black Eagle's knife carving around the head of one of the dead men and heard that awful suction and tearing sound as the scalp was torn from the skull. The Indian grinned at what must have been a look of stricken horror on my face and held up the bloody trophy.

"We will take many scalps today to avenge the Great Father," he told me while he cleaned his knife on a tuft of grass. I pressed on, feeling sickened. I had heard about the Indian habit of scalping since I had arrived in Canada, but hearing about it and seeing it are two very different things. I never got used to that sucking and ripping noise, which makes my skin crawl even now just thinking about it. Some Indians took scalps as trophies, believing that some of their enemy's martial spirit was in the warrior's decorated top knots. But scalping had been encouraged by both the French and the British during their wars in North America. Some whites even collected scalps. Later in

19

the war I came across a dying man from Kentucky who had several scalps tucked into his shirt. He asked for his own scalp to be sent on to his wife; Christ knows what she was expected to do with it!

We had to crawl on our hands and knees to cross the last part of the open ground as the bank had got shallower. But soon the entire war party had gained the shelter of the undergrowth at the top of the steep slope that ran down from the heights to the river bank. There, for the first time, I caught a glimpse of the American boats on the river. I saw six large cutters, but there may have been more. What surprised me was that the boats pulling back to the American shore were almost as full as the ones rowing towards Canada. Looking down at the shore by the village of Queenston I could see American militia queuing to get back in the vessels, loaded with booty. I remember two soldiers carrying a long case clock down to the beach; they seemed to view the venture more as a raid for profit than an invasion. A water spout appeared in the middle of the river near one of the boats – a distant British gun was still firing at the craft, but it would be lucky to hit one of the small targets at that range.

The Indians were already working their silent way south through the trees and bushes to get directly behind the American forces. There was an air of excitement amongst them now, grinning and whispering to each other as they pressed through the undergrowth. They did not seem to have the slightest concern that they would be hugely outnumbered. It was a warm day and the naked chests and legs of the natives blended in with the tree trunks and leaves that were a riot of autumnal colours. As well as deerskin breech cloths, the natives all had leather bags over their shoulders containing cartridges and spare flints. Just a handful had the traditional bows and arrows in addition to a musket; a few also had spears but all had knives and tomahawks or clubs, which were tucked into waistbands or hanging from cords.

With my new conspicuous scarlet coat I kept well back from the clearing, but through gaps in the foliage I could see the American soldiers moving to and fro. They were using a path further south to climb down to the river; it must have been their original route up to the heights. From the shouting and yelling coming from the distant track, they were now trying to haul up something heavy, probably a gun. It was obvious that they had no idea that hostile Iroquois warriors were just a few dozen yards away.

"I have sent a warrior to General Sheaffe," Norton whispered to me. "So he knows that we will distract the Americans while he makes his advance."

I nodded but I still did not believe that the Indians would provide much of a distraction. Outnumbered as they were, the Americans would soon have them pinned down … or so I thought. Nothing I had seen fighting in two continents had prepared me for the Iroquois style of warfare. In any conventional army they would have advanced in either line or column. Even light troops with their looser formations would still retain some structure so that their commanders could retain control. There was none of that with the Indians; indeed if there was even an order to attack I did not hear it. The whole war band had come to a silent halt in the undergrowth opposite the nearest American troops. They were a company of militia riflemen, around one hundred men, who were standing and sitting some eighty yards away, oblivious to the danger nearby. The American regulars, their professional soldiers, were some three hundred yards further on. Again, many of those were resting as any of Sheaffe's forces that they could see were still some distance off. All seemed peaceful.

The first I knew that an attack was imminent was when the Indians started to take aim. They were still in the trees out of sight of the Americans, many of them resting their guns against branches while they squinted carefully down the sights. I had heard people say that the American riflemen were sharpshooters, or as one New Yorker colourfully put it: 'they could shoot the teats off a sow.' Well the Iroquois were no slouches either, learning to hunt deer in the forest from boyhood. Some had rifles and others muskets, generally a lighter calibre than the army used. Now, in the stillness, they silently pressed their cheeks against their gun stocks and lined the barrels against their unsuspecting foe. Then all hell broke loose.

Chapter 3

I think it was one of the militia who unwittingly triggered the attack. As I peered at them through the leaves, one of the militia soldiers looking in my direction suddenly stiffened and started to raise his hand to point. He was just opening his mouth to shout when the first ball hit him, throwing him back into the dirt. Then the rest of the Indians opened fire. It was not a volley as I was used to, but a long ripple of well-aimed shots. Many of the militia started a grotesque dance as musket balls slashed through them and all around them. Before the fusillade had finished the first war cries had sounded and as the gunfire died away, the bushes became full of their deafening shrieks. It was the first time I had heard the sound; it was as though the tails of a troop of baboons had been slammed in a door. Wild angry howls and whoops that seemed utterly foreign to me, but the militia evidently knew all too well what they portended.

Even though I was with the Indians, my sympathies at that moment were with the militia. One minute they had been peaceably smoking and chewing tobacco and in a matter of seconds half of their number lay dead or wounded and through the musket smoke the first of the Iroquois could be seen charging towards them. While I had not heard of a Mohawk until a few days previously, these men had been brought up on tales of massacres, abductions and the torture and scalping of prisoners. The survivors managed a stuttering volley of their own, but these were rushed and snatched shots and I saw only two Indians go down. Then the militia were off running towards the safety of the lines of regular infantry, some dragging or half carrying wounded comrades with them.

I watched with fascinated horror as the first Iroquois reached the pile of bodies and injured men that the militia had left behind. While most of the Indians still had their muskets, some were armed just with hatchets and tomahawks and now these rose and fell, the victorious whoops of the Indians mixing with the terrible screams of the wounded. The retreating militia paused and those still loaded fired at the Indians butchering their comrades. Another Indian went down but the rest continued their gruesome work and in a matter of moments the first scalp was held aloft in triumph.

The effect of the Indian attack was out of all proportion to the numbers involved. Only half of the Indians had rushed forward to pillage the militia position. Norton I saw was amongst them, but he was encouraging the Indians to press on and pursue the surviving militia towards the line of the regular troops. I stepped out from the trees to better see what was happening in the clearing. Across the space there was frantic activity as though someone had dropped a fox into a hen coop, with a striking difference between the response of the militia and the regular soldiers.

The nearest regiment of uniformed troops was hurriedly reversing its facing to bring its guns to bear on this unexpected attack. Their officer was still standing in front of his troops and frantically gesturing to the retreating militia to get out of their line of fire. In contrast the militia regiments seemed to lose all cohesion, with soldiers running about in all directions. Some ran towards the attack, to stand alongside the regular troops or in small parties of their own. Many of the smaller groups opened fire at an impossible range, the noise and gun smoke causing confusion as people imagined that there were more Indians spreading amongst the clearing. I even saw a few pointing at me as they noticed that a British officer had emerged from the trees.

The most distinctive movement among the militia, though, was towards the south and the path back down to the river. It started as a trickle, with men pointing and shouting, but in moments it had turned into a stampede. Half of the Iroquois remained in the trees lining the river bank. They were still whooping and howling, to my mind making enough din for four hundred warriors, never mind the forty that were actually there. The militia were clearly worried that the Indians were about to cut off their one route of escape back down the river. The last thing they wanted was to be trapped on some foreign shore with a bunch of scalping savages and so they started to run. It only takes a few to start running before a panic sets in – heaven knows I have been enough of them – and within moments half of the militia, a full quarter of the American force on the heights, was fleeing the field.

I stood and watched in astonishment. Oh I didn't blame the militia for running. If I had been brought up on tales of Indian attacks then I would have hightailed it too when I saw those painted demons emerging from their own musket smoke.

I had watched the attack unfold almost as a spectator rather than a participant. It was not just that the Iroquois were allowed to sit out a fight if they felt like it; I did not feel that I belonged there at all. It was all just too strange and foreign, the war paint and body markings, the whooping and most of all the scalping. I had been sickened when I saw the first Indians reach the dead and injured Americans. I had seen worse atrocities in Spain, particularly between the Spanish partisans and the French, but this was a force that I was supposed to be a part of. Well, I thought, they will get their comeuppance now as the Americans were commencing their counter attack and thirty odd Indians, exposed in the middle of a clearing and surrounded by their enemies, was going to stand little chance.

The front rank of the American regulars opened fire on the Indians charging towards them. I listened almost with a feeling of nostalgia to the familiar shouted orders and crash of a musket volley. This was the type of warfare I knew and a handful of Iroquois were not going to succeed where French columns had failed. When I looked for Norton and his warriors they were all lying flat on the ground. For a second I thought they were dead but then they all rose to their feet, whooping again in triumph. They had clearly thrown themselves to the ground as the order to 'fire' had been given and the undulating ground had protected them. But now Norton raised his musket and pointed back the way they had come and the shrieking banshees started their retreat. The American officer knew his business and soon his troops were marching through the cloud of gun smoke from their volley towards the running Indians. I was already retreating back into cover when a second volley crashed out and some of the militia joined in with a fusillade of musket and rifle shots. Two Indians fell, but both were picked up by the others, one with just a leg wound. Before a third volley could be brought to bear, the Iroquois were out of range and heading into the relative safety of the trees and bushes on the river shore.

The Americans pursued the Indians towards the trees but as they got close they encountered a fusillade of shots and a handful of arrows from enemies that they could barely see. The Indians were still whooping and taunting them, but the Americans were reluctant to follow them into the undergrowth. I did not blame them; they had no idea how many warriors were hidden in the scrub. Eventually they pulled back to the edge of effective musket range where they contented themselves with firing volleys into the trees at any point they saw movement.

This musketry duel lasted for over an hour, the Iroquois unable to leave the trees and the Americans unwilling to advance into them. I used the time to go back to the river bank to see what reinforcements were being rowed over. To my surprise the boats going back to the far shore of the river were packed to the gunwales with soldiers, mostly militia, while those coming the other way were half full at best. It was then I heard another problem arrive for the Americans. The British had set up an artillery battery, which was firing the new-fangled shrapnel shells up onto the heights. These ideally exploded in the air above their target sending down a lethal hail of musket balls. Fortunately for the Americans, the British gunners were firing blind up the hill, unable to see how or where their charges hit. At least one landed in the undergrowth and from an increase in the amount of shrieking from the Indians I gathered that there were probably casualties. The rest landed at random across the clearing, most causing little damage, but when I went back to look several clusters of bodies showed that some had found their mark.

Eventually new crashes of gunfire announced the arrival of General Sheaffe. I had expected him to march his men up the cleared ground alongside the forest so that they could maintain their formations but he had chosen to take them through the same forest used by the Iroquois. They emerged, falling into their companies near where the bodies of the four scalped sentries lay. The Americans were now in a desperate position: a quarter of their force had deserted; no significant reinforcements were coming; they were being assailed by shrapnel shells from above and as they turned to face General Sheaffe's emerging army they had a hostile Indian force on their right flank.

Norton chose this moment to attack again. At least thirty warriors burst out from the undergrowth, charging the nearest American troops, howling their challenge and clearly expecting the soldiers to break like the militia before them. It was a mistake, for these were regular soldiers and the American commander decided that now was the time to deal with the Iroquois threat once and for all. His men let the Indians approach and then with no warning fired their volley. At least half a dozen Indians went down but all except one got up again and, helped by other warriors, they began a hasty retreat. Now it was time for the Americans to start a charge of their own. If the Iroquois thought that they would be safe again in the foliage they were wrong, for this time the Americans were not stopping. They withstood a withering fire of musket balls and arrows and pressed on to follow the Indians into the trees.

I pride myself in not being slow to decide that headlong flight is necessary. There were at least two hundred Americans charging into the trees. Against them were no more than eighty Indians, half of them blown by their own abortive attack and a good number wounded. I did not hesitate to start running; I was sure that the Iroquois would be overwhelmed with those numbers. This was confirmed a few moments later when an increased volume of war cries, hooting and whooping indicated that the Indians were also on the move. Some went south down the tree line until they reached the path that the Americans were using to bring up supplies from the river. There they attacked the few porters carrying equipment and pressed on. Others headed north like me, in the direction that Sheaffe's troops were just starting to appear.

I was going as fast as I could over the rough ground, but within a few seconds a dozen Iroquois had passed me. I glanced over my shoulder but none of the Americans were yet in sight. When I looked to my front again all of the Indians had disappeared, like phantoms into the woods. I ran forward a few more paces but then crashed to the ground as a hand gripped firmly round my ankle.

"Roll under here, Lobster," whispered a grinning young Iroquois warrior. He was lying under a thick bush surrounded by ferns. "Your red coat will stand out too much in the trees," he added as he wriggled back to make room for me.

"Thank you," I replied while crawling under the foliage. "Won't the Americans search the bushes?"

"No, they will not stay long, they will feel too..." he paused and seemed to be searching his memory for the right word. "Vulnerable," he said at last.

"You speak good English."

The Indian smiled, pleased at the compliment. "I learned at the church school," he whispered. "Now be quiet, they are coming." It was several seconds before I heard the sound of pursuit, a distant breaking of branches and murmur of voices as the Americans pushed through the trees.

"God damn it! Where the hell are they? I saw at least ten come this way."

"They will be hiding," called out a second voice. "Waiting for us to go past and then the bastards will shoot us in the back."

"Why don't we fire into the undergrowth?" shouted a third voice. "See if we can flush some of the critters out." I twitched in alarm at that for they were still moving forward and the speaker sounded like he was no more than ten yards from where I lay.

"Sure, you try that," jeered the second voice with a heavy note of sarcasm. "Leavin' yourself unloaded in a forest full of Injuns is just about the surest way I know of losing your hair." I heard some shouting in the distance but could not make out the words. Then the second voice yelled, "We're coming," in response and gradually the men moved away, back in the direction they had come.

"Are you going to shoot them in the back?" I whispered to my companion.

"No," he grinned. "I am unloaded and anyway it would be foolish to give away your position when there are so many enemies nearby." We waited, talking quietly for a few minutes as the Americans pulled slowly back to the clearing. He told me that his name was John Smoke

Johnson; it was the first battle he had been in. He asked me if I had been in other battles and when I told him a little of my experience he seemed impressed. "The Americans are snatching their shots and firing high," he told me as he reached into his pouch and pulled out a cartridge to start reloading his own gun while we still lay in the undergrowth. It was a small calibre musket and as he shifted it to make room for his ramrod I saw that he had carved out a shallow dip in the stock so that his aiming eye was right over the barrel.

"Have you shot any Americans?" I asked

"I think I got at least two."

"But no scalps?" I enquired looking at his belt where Indians tucked in the grisly things.

"Scalping is a brutal and useless custom," he stated firmly. "I am a Christian; I believe that God and the Great Spirit are the same thing. A man's soul cannot be held in his hair." He cautiously raised himself up, staring about him and then he gazed down at me. "Now, Lobster, it is time for us to return to the battle."

I raised my head above the level of the bush and could see several Indians walking back towards the clearing, grinning and chatting to each other. They were heading back down the tree line towards the spot closest to the American position from which they had been chased away minutes before. In my bright scarlet coat, fresh from the army store, I let them go ahead. The noise of battle coming through the trees was increasing as the British and Canadian troops appeared in the clearing. I guessed that the Americans would not have enough men for another charge through the trees as well as defending their line. I was right; when I finally got close enough to glimpse the American position through the trees I could see that they were in a precarious state.

The British had evidently got someone on the edge of the heights signalling to the guns below because now the shrapnel shells were landing much more consistently around the American position. I could hear the gun the British had originally placed on the heights to cover the river now banging away again, which would have made it hot work for anyone to cross by boat. As I crept to the edge of the undergrowth I

28

could see the British and Canadian troops to my right. They were arrayed in a line with a company of black troops nearest the trees. They looked fresh and business-like, which was more than could be said for their opposition.

The Americans had now been fighting on the heights for several hours. They were being assailed from the air by shrapnel shells exploding over their heads. As they organised themselves to face the British line their right flank was once more under sporadic but accurate fire from the Iroquois. A steady trickle of Americans, mostly militia, could be seen slipping away towards the path down to the river. The American commander was outnumbered, outgunned and outflanked, but still his men put up a stiff fight as the British line advanced. The Americans had more riflemen, which gave them accuracy and range, but these weapons were slower to reload and many were fouled with powder residue from earlier firing. The British, with muskets, could deliver a greater rate of fire and gradually this began to tell with the Americans edging back.

I advanced behind the black soldiers, Captain Raunchey's Company of Coloured Men, I discovered they were called. They seemed steady enough although the white officer Raunchey had brought a stone keg of liquor with him, which he supped from regularly as they marched. His men, like the rest of the militia troops, were all dressed in civilian clothes but had white armbands on their sleeves to show their allegiance. With so many soldiers on both sides in civilian clothes, any melee between the militia would have been a confused and deadly affair, with probably more than a few killed by their own side. Thankfully it did not come to that. The American fire was slowing down and we could hear a chorus of yelling from their ranks and see men running about.

Suddenly there was a greater movement to the path leading down to the river. A trickle of men became a flow and in a moment half of the force was running and pushing to get away. The rest huddled together with a white flag waving from a bayonet.

In the end it was not the British or the Iroquois that ultimately defeated the Americans: gradually more and more of their soldiers ran

29

out of ammunition. No supplies or reinforcements were getting across the river and many, particularly in the militia, had started the day with less than a score of cartridges in their pouches. These had quickly been used up and as men fell dead or wounded their pouches were searched in increasing desperation for the precious powder and ball.

As a bugle called a cease fire the entire British and Canadian line surged forward to secure the prisoners and to relieve them of any valuables, as was the way of war. The Iroquois, though, wanted more than loot; they wanted scalps too. Suddenly there seemed to be hundreds of Indians pouring through the trees. Christ knows where they had all come from. Some must have been those that had turned back in the forest, but there seemed to be more than the original war party. All too soon there were screams and shouts for help coming from the trees. Mercifully I could not see what was happening but I pitied any poor American that the Indians found there. It was bad enough to scalp the dead but from the sound of things they were despatching the wounded too. I pressed forward, searching for Norton. I thought he was the only man who would be able to make them stop. I was calling his name when a strange figure on three limbs came scrambling out of the trees.

It was a boy. He looked little older than fifteen but was dressed in a regular soldier's uniform and he had been shot in the leg. He held his bloodied leg up in the air and was trying to move as fast as he could on his hands and his one good leg, like a wounded dog. His eyes were wide in terror as he kept looking over his shoulder and he was nearly ten yards out of the trees when he noticed me standing nearby.

"Please, mister, help me," he implored. "They are killin' people and taking their hair."

Before I could reply another figure burst from the trees, it was the big warrior, Black Eagle, who came to a sudden stop when he saw me standing there. He pointed at the boy and declared, "That one is mine."

Normally I would not dream of standing between a big murderous warrior and whatever he wanted, but when I looked down at the lad I was struck by how similar he looked to a boy I had known in Spain. That youngster had been an ensign under my command. I had not been able to keep that soldier alive but suddenly I was damned if I was going to let this boy die as well.

"You will leave him alone," I commanded, watching as a look of rage crossed the Indian's face. "I hold a commission from King George, the great chief across the sea," I told him. "He is the man who is chief to the Great Father, and I command that you will leave this boy alone. The British do not allow prisoners to be killed or scalped." To further emphasise my point I reached down and drew my sword and with my left had I reached into my pocket and pulled out a pistol.

In response Black Eagle gave a low growl and came forward several paces towards me. It was only then that I began to realise that I had made a serious mistake. Until that moment I had fully expected Black Eagle to accept my authority. All that talk about General Brock being the 'Great Father', and gifts that they received from the British, had given me the impression that the Iroquois saw themselves as subservient, at least to white officers like me. It was then I remembered, too late, some advice that a wise sergeant called Ferguson had given me in India: never give an order that you do not know will be obeyed.

Well it was too late for that now. It was clear from Black Eagle's face that this proud warrior did not feel the least bit submissive to the white man in front of him. His dark eyes glittered dangerously in his hideously painted face and he started to balance on the balls of his feet, preparing to spring. I had seen him kill one militia soldier and he had three scalps hanging over his belt to show that he had killed more. I felt a prickle of fear run up the back of my neck as I wondered if in a minute or two my hair might also be hanging from that belt.

"Black Eagle, no!" It was Norton's voice to my right and I heard several other shouts in Iroquois to my left, but I dared not take my eyes of the big man in front of me. When he did move it was lightning fast. He lurched to his left and I swung my sword to my right. Surely, I thought, the long blade would give me a better reach than a man holding a tomahawk. My weapon was made from razor-sharp Damascus steel; I knew that if I managed to strike him the wound would be deep. But by God he was quick. No sooner had I flicked the

31

blade out to my right than he was bouncing to my left and now the hand holding the tomahawk was swinging down on my unprotected left side. I just managed to get the barrel of my pistol up in time to block the blow. The pistol caught the shaft of the axe just below the head and I felt the jar of the blow down my left arm. Already the Indian was twisting away, but now my sword was swinging around in an arc to catch him. I was aiming for his throat; I wanted to kill this bastard quickly, before he did for me. I thought I was going to get him, too, but at the last moment he started to twist and duck away. I tried to adjust my swing, but not fast enough and the blade swished over his head through empty air.

I sprang back a pace to give me more room and wondered fleetingly if I had time to cock the pistol. The spring was heavy and I would need to use my sword hand. Norton was still shouting at Black Eagle and out of the corner of my eye I could see the war chief was running towards us from the tree line, but another Indian got to Black Eagle first.

"No, Black Eagle, don't. It is not worth it for another scalp, they will hang you." It was Smoke Johnson, the young Indian who had helped to hide me in a bush. He tried to hold Black Eagle by the arms and they wrestled for a moment as I frantically pulled back the hammer on my pistol.

Smoke Johnson was only a slender boy and the great warrior threw him off but over balanced and fell down on one knee in the process. I was raising the pistol on him when the huge man suddenly dropped his tomahawk and gave a howl of agony. For a moment I thought one of the Indians had shot him in the back with an arrow, but he was staring at something in the grass at his feet. I did not recognise it but Smoke Johnson did.

"Ha, the Lobster has beaten you. He has fought in many battles, he told me so." The young man danced in front of his fallen comrade, blocking my shot. "See his skill, he could have killed you but instead he has shown you that a man's spirit is not in his hair." Norton was running up to us now and so I lowered the pistol while Smoke Johnson stood back so that the Iroquois war chief could see what Black Eagle

32

was staring forlornly at. In the grass I saw a tuft of long black hair, held together with a strip of red cloth and decorated with several feathers. It was only when Black Eagle slumped his head in defeat that I fully understood, for there on the crown of his head was a circle of very short black hair just half an inch long. It seemed that my sword had not entirely missed him after all.

Chapter 4

Black Eagle was being led away by several of the Indians, all of the
fight now gone out of him and a look of shock on his face, as though
he had lost a leg rather than a tuft of hair.

"That was very merciful of you, Captain Flashman," called Norton
as he came up to me. I bit back the retort that I had been trying to kill
the bastard as by now I was getting respectful looks from several of
the Indians present. Young Smoke Johnson was busy regaling all who
would listen that the 'Lobster' was a fearsome veteran of many battles
and had managed to shave Black Eagle's head while he twisted away.

"It shouldn't have been bloody necessary," I told Norton tartly.
"The British armies I have fought in do not butcher the wounded,
never mind scalp them."

"You are right; they should not be killing prisoners. Some of the
men who arrived late for the battle are trying to get scalps to prove
their courage."

"Black Eagle has been here from the start," I retorted. "Look at the
boy he was trying to kill – what courage is there in that?" We both
looked down. The young American soldier had apparently fainted
from either the pain or the fear of being scalped. His face, relaxed in
sleep, looked even more boyish and I doubted that he had even started
shaving.

Norton shifted uncomfortably. "I must return to my men and help
calm them down." As he turned to walk away I looked over his
shoulder and saw a very tall American officer striding purposefully
towards me. The American had a young British lieutenant in tow, who
was almost running to keep up. The boy at my feet was starting to stir,
which was just as well as I did not want the lanky soldier to think that I
had killed him. As I glanced down at the boy I noticed that Black
Eagle's tomahawk lay abandoned in the grass. I bent down to pick it
up. It was, I discovered later, quite a common design, but to me it
seemed extraordinary. Opposite the sharp steel blade of the axe was a
metal bowl, its bottom connected to a hole drilled the length of the
shaft: it was a pipe as well as a weapon. I wondered if perhaps once

34

you had hacked a man to death, you were expected to smoke a pipe of peace over his corpse. I shook my head in dismay and tucked the weapon into my belt as the American approached.

"Colonel Winfield Scott, sir," he introduced himself holding out his hand. "I saw what you did to save young Vanderbilt here and I am much obliged to you."

"I am only sorry it was necessary, sir," I responded. "I rather fear that the behaviour of our allies has dishonoured our victory."

"Colonel Scott is the commander of the American regular army force, sir," warned the British lieutenant as the colonel bent down and gripped the shoulder of the boy at our feet and whispered some words of comfort to him.

"What is to happen to the prisoners, Lieutenant?" I asked.

"The regular troops will be made prisoners of war, sir, and transported to Quebec, but the militia soldiers will be paroled and shipped back across the river."

I looked down at the boy, who was now struggling to sit up in the presence of his commanding officer. He was already starting to shake as shock set in. "I see," I murmured and then I turned to the colonel. "Sir, I don't know if you have ever had to travel a long distance with a hole in your leg? I have and it is not something that I would recommend. Perhaps this young soldier should be temporarily dismissed from the regular army and attached to the militia?"

Scott grinned conspiratorially. "I think that is an excellent suggestion." He bent down to the boy. "Son, I am going to have to relieve you of your army coat. I don't doubt you will get another in due course." As he spoke I walked over to one of the militia corpses and started to pull off its civilian coat. The collar was soaked in blood as its occupant had been scalped, but it would have to do. Once the boy was suitably dressed the lieutenant called over two soldiers and detailed them to carry the lad to join the group of militia soldiers held under guard. Scott turned to go but then hesitated and came back to me. "Sir, I do not believe I have yet had the honour of your name. I would like to commend you to your general."

"It is Flashman, sir, Captain Thomas Flashman, although I am not sure that General Sheaffe appreciates the blatant flouting of rules." Our British commander did not have the natural leadership skills of his predecessor, General Brock, who had been greatly admired by his men. Sheaffe was more a spit and polish, doing things by the regulations character, but he had at least won the battle whereas Brock had got himself killed in a reckless assault.

I have no idea what Scott said to Sheaffe, but a short while later I was summoned to the British commander. "Ah, Flashman, isn't it? I hear you saved one of their militia boys from a scalping," he called as I joined the crowd of officers around him receiving orders. "Colonel Scott was most impressed with your diplomatic handling of the matter. He has also given me a written note of commendation that should make you more welcome than most of us on the other side of the Niagara." He passed the note across to me before continuing. "I would be obliged if you would escort our prisoners back over the river and ensure that they are exchanged with any of our men that the Americans have taken."

The battle had finished at around four o'clock in the afternoon and by then it was getting on for six. There would not be daylight for much longer and so I hurried along the path that led down to the river. Several American bodies had been pushed into the surrounding bushes, some scalped and some with their hair intact. Halfway down, the track was blocked with a press of men, but some British soldiers guarding the prisoners ordered them to stand aside so that I could get through. A rough landing stage was at the bottom, made up of a partly submerged boat with some planks laid over the gunwales. To one side lay a group of wounded prisoners, including young Vanderbilt, the boy I had rescued. Someone had already bandaged and splinted his leg and he grinned and waved when he saw me.

A signal must have been sent to the Americans because two boats were already coming across from Lewiston, the town opposite on the American shore. They were rowing sharply upstream so that the current would bring them up to the makeshift jetty. I thought that they would load the wounded first but as the first boat tied on by the end of the planks a sudden stampede of desperate prisoners pressed forwards. They easily pushed the guards aside and charged up the fragile wharf, pulling and shoving at each other to get on the craft. Two men fell in, one was swept downstream but the other managed to catch a hold of the sunken boat. Within moments the first cutter that had been rowed across was dangerously overloaded, with the oarsmen punching those trying to board as they pushed off.

The jetty creaked dangerously as the men shouted for the next boat to approach but the crew on that were rowing hard against the current and holding off. They had seen the first boat pull away precariously low in the water and were worried about being swamped. I had seen enough and stopped the shouting with a pistol shot in the air.

"Everyone off that jetty! I am taking the wounded across first and the rest of you will wait your turn." I turned to the sergeant in charge of the guard. "Get them off the jetty and if anyone else jumps the queue, shoot them." Amid much grumbling there was a general movement off the wooden structure, but three men who were at the very end of it were reluctant to give up their prime position.

"I aint spendin' the night on this side of the river with those wild savages creepin' around the woods fixin' to take my hair." The spokesperson stuck his thumbs in the top of his trousers and leaned back. "So I reckon you is goin' to have to shoot me. Then we'll see what happens to you when they hear what you done on our side of the river." A self-satisfied smile crossed the man's face, which only diminished slightly when one of his companions spoke to him.

"Wait a minute, Clem, I've seen that fella before. He was fightin' with the Injuns on our flank. Look, he has one of their tommy hawks in his belt."

I sensed a growing hostility in the crowd as I reflected on the fact that this was the second time today I had given an order without knowing if it would be obeyed. But I thought I knew how to motivate these men to do my bidding. "You are right," I said calmly to the second man on the jetty. "I was with the Indians earlier; I am an honorary chief with them." I pulled the tomahawk out of my belt and slowly slapped the side of the blade on the palm of my hand. "Right

37

now," I continued, "I have persuaded them to leave the guarding of prisoners to the British soldiers. It was a tough job, as a lot of them really want more scalps, especially ginger hair like yours." I grinned at him while I tested the blade of the weapon with my thumb, it had been honed to a sharp edge. "Yes, they really like ginger hair and I only have to give my war whoop and hundreds of them will be pouring down that hillside hunting for some." The three men looked nervously at each other. "Now I thought," I continued in a very casual tone, "that you gentlemen would prefer to be guarded by British soldiers, but if I have got that wrong, do please tell me."

There was more muttering from the crowd of men on the shore while the three at the end of the planks shifted uncomfortably as they whispered among themselves.

"Clem," I looked up and big man in a red shirt was stepping forward from the crowd on shore. He sported a large ginger beard and long flowing ginger locks. "So help me, Clem, if you and your boys do not get over here right smartly I will damn well fix you myself." Clem and his two comrades stepped quickly off the jetty and took their place at the head of the queue of able-bodied men.

"Right, Sergeant," I turned to him. "Ask the boatmen how many they can carry and only allow that many onto the dock." I looked up to see the first boat being carried far downstream by the current. Several of its occupants were bailing with their hats. The second boat, seeing that order was restored, was now drifting down to tie up.

"Very good, sir," replied the soldier. "What about loading the wounded?"

"Oh I am sure we will get volunteers." I turned to the front of the queue. "Clem and Ginger, load three stretchers on that boat and you can travel with them." I went and helped young Vanderbilt aboard myself and a few minutes later a dozen wounded and a dozen able-bodied helpers, including your correspondent, were being rowed across the River Niagara towards the American shore.

"You really an Indian chief?" Clem asked me when we were halfway across the river.

"Oh yes," I told him, half for my own amusement and to avoid a mutiny mid-stream. "Tomahawk Thomas they call me." I winked at Vanderbilt before adding, "Scourge of the Piccadilly tribe, defiler of virgins and the meanest blade west of Bristol." I thought I had hammed it up for a joke but the fool Clem took me seriously. It seemed trivial at the time, but that joke may well have cost us a battle and changed the course of the war in the west.

"Have you taken many scalps, then?" asked Clem, licking his lips nervously.

"I have run out of room for them now in my hut so I don't bother," I replied, casually picking some dried blood off my coat.

"He stopped them scalping me," piped up Vanderbilt. "He killed a big warrior that was chasing after me."

"I didn't kill him," I corrected. "I cut off his hair with my sword," I said patting the weapon at my side. "Some of them believe that their spirit is in their hair."

Clem seemed to look at me with awe. "Well I ain't fightin' them again. I've heard stories and scalping is the least of it. We are militia; we are only s'posed to be deployed in the Republic of the United States to defend it against a British invasion.

"Well we are not invading you," I pointed out. "Your republic is raising a massive army to invade Canada."

"Your army captured Detroit," he pointed out truculently.

"I heard that was because your army crossed into Canada first. Remember *you* declared war on *us*. I have heard that you are raising an army of fifty thousand."

There was burst of laughter in the boat at that – even some of the wounded chuckled. "Our politicians might have *signed a paper* to raise fifty thousand," Clem explained, "but they sure don't have the money to pay for them. They are offering soldiers five dollars a month, but any good labourer can earn nearly double that amount. Only a fool will risk getting shot or scalped on army rations for half pay; that is assuming that they have the money to pay you at all. We haven't seen the pay chest for three months. That is why we went across, in the hope of getting some valuables."

"You wait until you see Lewiston," Ginger joined in. "It is a proper shit hole. Thousands of men all right, but hardly any rations. Most have used up their ammunition hunting game for the pot."

I looked across at the boy. Unlike the militia groups that were raised in their local communities and were obliged to serve, he had volunteered for this life. He looked tired now but he still managed a smile when he spoke. "I could not get a full labourer's wage and anyway I thought joining the army would be exciting."

"Well I think you have had enough excitement for now," I told him. The boat was pulling up at the American dock, where a crowd of men were waiting. We were the first boat to disembark as the previous craft had been swept well down river. Many of the spectators were keen to see the survivors of the battle and several were pointing to me in my conspicuous red coat. There was a company of regular troops guarding the quay and soon the wounded were being handed up to the dock. I climbed up with Vanderbilt to be met by the officer in charge.

"Captain Flashman," I said handing over the letter of commendation from Colonel Winfield Scott. I thought it might earn me some favour on this hostile shore. "I am here to collect any prisoners you have in exchange."

"Lieutenant Harker," replied the officer briefly scanning the note and handing it back. "The prisoners will be in the town gaol; you had better come with me." He looked across as Clem loudly regaled a group of men on the quay on how he had been nearly scalped by wild savages and that nothing would persuade him to cross the river again. "That is all we need," the lieutenant muttered. I did not say anything in reply but a cheer of support from those around Clem indicated that there would be quite a few who would be reluctant to tread on Canadian soil now.

We pressed through a large crowd. There certainly seemed enough militia in Lewiston to have reinforced their attack, but closer inspection showed that Ginger was right. Many of the men looked ill and thin. Some were dressed in little more than rags, with strips of cloth and rope holding together broken boots. There was a strong smell of human waste on the streets and I saw several soldiers crouched

40

pitifully in corners with their trousers around their ankles. A lot of men crammed into one place was bound to encourage disease. If the troops were also weakened with poor rations, things would only get worse. From the smell of the main street, dysentery was rife in the army.

I had expected to be jostled and shouted at, but most just stared at me with glassy eyes, evidently judging that abusing me was not worth the effort. We pushed on through the throng, watching carefully where we trod, until we reached a larger building. I guessed it was the courthouse, which presumably had the gaol attached. There I was handed over to a Major Cartwright, who seemed surprisingly genial.

"Come in, sir, come in, you will have a glass with me, surely?"

"I think I should probably be getting back, it is getting dark already."

"Ah, by the time we get the prisoners down to the docks it will be too late to row back. They will not row at night; too many boats have been sunk by logs coming down the river." He was steering me into an office and showing me to a chair as he added, "A truce has now been agreed between our armies, you will be quite safe here." He pressed a glass of brandy into my grateful hand and sat down beside me. "Where are your people from, sir?

"From? Oh you mean in England. My family home is in Leicestershire."

"Ahh," he breathed, smiling. "My parents came from Lincolnshire, some twenty-five years ago. I was only five at the time and barely remember the old country. We had relatives here already, you see, who helped my father set up in trade."

"And now you are at war with the old country," I prompted.

"Yes, it is strange that such a relatively short period of time should see us on different sides. Our ancestors could have stood side by side in the same ranks at, say, Agincourt or the Wars of the Roses, yet now we face each other." He paused to sip his drink and then brightened. "But from what I hear you fellows are standing side by side with some pretty rum fellows at the moment."

"We are?"

41

"Yes, those Indian savages. The first boats back during the battle were full of tales of massacres, torture and scalping. Their wild war cries could be heard from here and there was no way that we could get the militia across the river after that. They had been happy to cross when they thought they would be raiding the property of the citizens of Queenston, but not when they heard about the Indians. A good number have now declared that they are going home.

"Surely you have Indians in America?"

"Oh we do, there is some American Iroquois territory south of us, I believe, but they have been persuaded to stay on their land. Our soldiers don't trust them, you see."

"I have some sympathy with your soldiers. One of the devils turned murderously on me when I gave an order he did not like. Then there is the scalping, which is beyond barbaric."

The major refilled my glass, smiling. "Well you can always come over to our side. Heaven knows we need some experienced officers and we have a number of British deserters already."

For a brief moment I was tempted, I have always got on well with Americans. There had been Cathcart who had assisted me and Cochrane in Tunisia and the crew of the American barque that had helped me escape France. They had all been good fellows. Even my gaoler in Boston had been kind and considerate. In contrast Canada seemed a strange, foreign land and it had been years now since I had set foot in Britain. But for all that, I could not imagine standing in battle in opposition to those dressed in red. I had seen too much blood seep into scarlet cloth for that. So I smiled and shook my head to decline his offer.

"Well you can dine with me tonight, there is some venison, and then in the morning you can take your prisoners home." He grinned. "In fact I think there are some Indians amongst them."

The major was as good as his word and after a pleasant dinner and good night's sleep I found myself back on the Lewiston dock next morning with half a dozen bedraggled redcoats, who looked like they had suffered a worse night than me, and three silent, surly Indians. Given all the talk of massacres and scalping I was surprised that the

Indians had not been killed or at least mistreated in captivity, but aside from one who had a bandage around his head, they seemed unharmed. I noticed, though, that the Americans had kept their hands tied behind their backs, while the British soldiers were not secured at all.

The major had accompanied me down to the dock and again there was no great hostility from the American soldiers and militia in the streets. The boats had already started to ply their trade back and forth across the river. So as we stood waiting for passage on the quay, I was surprised to hear sudden gunfire: there were three bangs from the British canon.

"What the devil is that? I thought there was a truce!" As I spoke I looked across the river but there were no plumes of water to indicate shot landing amongst the boats.

"Don't worry, they are just firing a salute for your General Brock." As the major stopped speaking the guns on the American shore started their own salute for the British general. I was amazed at the civility of it all, given that the Americans had tried to invade just the previous day. Yesterday we had been fighting a pitched battle and now they were saluting our fallen commander. Not that I was complaining. I thanked the major warmly for his hospitality and threw him a smart salute before climbing down into the boat with the returning prisoners.

We soon came up to Queenston where I saw that there was still a large crowd of American prisoners waiting to cross. Stepping ashore I had the Iroquois warriors untied and all of the former prisoners went off searching for their comrades. As for me, I was not sure where to go. I had no particular wish to return to the Iroquois; I had made an enemy of Black Eagle and he would have friends willing to avenge him. The invasion had been repulsed and the Americans did not look in a fit state to launch another one any time soon. Perhaps now would be a good time to seek another posting with our new commander, perhaps a comfortable billet on his staff. I made my way to the Queenston Inn, which, from the horses tied up outside, was clearly Sheaffe's current headquarters. I had barely set my foot over the threshold when I was intercepted by some staff wallah.

"Who are you and what do you want?" The rudely blunt enquiry came from an immaculately dressed major, who had a languid air about him that instantly rubbed me up the wrong way.

"Why, my compliments to you, sir, on this fine day," I responded with exaggerated politeness to show that I intended to ignore his rudeness. "I do not believe that I have had the honour of an introduction, Major…?"

The major glared at me in irritation but then saw no alternative but to give his name. "It is Major Fforbes, with two 'f's. And you are?"

"Captain Flashman, with one 'f'," I replied. "I am here to see General Sheaffe," I added.

"The general has asked me to deal with all matters that are not urgent," replied Fforbes, shuffling through some papers with a frown. "What is it you wanted?"

"Well I have completed the exchange of prisoners as requested by the general, and I wondered if he had any new duties for me."

"Ah, here it is," said Fforbes pulling a paper triumphantly from the pile. "You are the officer that escaped from France, aren't you?" Without waiting for a reply he continued, "I see General Brock detailed you to act as liaison for the Iroquois."

"Yes but now that the invasion has been repulsed…"

"That is just their first attempt," interrupted Fforbes. "There are bound to be others and we will continue to need liaison with our native allies. You should return to your duty, sir. General Brock's orders stand until they are countermanded by General Sheaffe."

"But for God's sake, man," I protested. "Some of them are murdering savages. You cannot expect me, a British officer, to live with them in some mud hut. One of them already tried to kill me when I got in his way.

Fforbes just smiled at me before replying. "Your orders stand, Captain, and you may be interested to know that Major Norton came to see me earlier, to say that he thought you would be an excellent liaison officer. I wish you well and I think that you will find living with the Iroquois an interesting experience."

Chapter 5

I found Norton and Iroquois still up on the heights where I had last seen them. Now the battle was over, most were now dressed in ornately embroidered deerskin tunics and trousers. Much of the war paint had been washed off, although on some there were still traces of where it had been. They seemed far less intimidating now, sitting around their campfires and talking. Only the sight of one man cleaning the back of a scalp with his knife gave any clue to the recent savagery. Norton stood with a crowd of men surrounding the recently recovered warriors as they recounted their experiences, but when he noticed me he broke away and came over.

"Welcome back Flashman," he called and he seemed genuinely pleased to see me. "Thank you for collecting our missing men. Are you ready to leave?"

"I suppose so. Are we going back to Fort George?" I asked hopefully. Fort George was where the Indians had been garrisoned before the battle and it was at least a soundly built structure that would keep out the weather.

"No, the men are keen to celebrate their victory on the Grand River. We are going back to our lands and there will be much feasting. Your horse is tied up over there."

I had no idea then what an Iroquois village would look like. Did they really live in mud huts or perhaps wood frames covered in bark and grass? Or possibly shelters built around fallen trees? Whichever, the prospect did not sound appealing with winter approaching. I cast around for an excuse. I spotted it sitting slumped at a nearby campfire. "I don't think he would welcome me in your camp," I said pointing to the warrior. "And I would rather not spend the next few days continually watching my back."

Norton followed my gaze and called out, "Black Eagle, come here." The big man reluctantly got to his feet as his fellows cackled over some joke, doubtless at his expense. He did indeed look as though his fighting spirit had left him, as he walked over staring miserably at the ground. "I think you owe Captain Flashman an apology," reminded Norton sternly.

Black Eagle raised his gaze to look into my face for the first time since he had faced me the previous afternoon. "Little Father, I apologise for attacking you," the warrior mumbled abjectly.

Well it was the first time I had been called that. They had called Brock the 'Great Father' and so it was clearly a term of respect. I thought a magnanimous gesture was called for, especially if I had to spend time with these warriors. So I reached to my belt and pulled out Black Eagle's tomahawk and offered it back. But the big man just shrank back a pace away from the weapon.

"No, Little Father, that is yours, you have beaten me in battle."

"I know it seems silly to you, Flashman," intervened Norton, "but many of these warriors feel that some of their fighting spirit lives in their hair and if they lose it they feel emasculated somehow."

"Perhaps this can help, then." As I spoke I reached into my pocket. I pulled out a long greasy lock of hair, still tied with a red strip of cloth and adorned with some eagle feathers. I had picked it up the previous day while I waited for Winfield Scott to approach. I had wondered if it might come in handy. As I held it out to the warrior he gave a yelp of delight and threw his arms around me, half squeezing the air out of my chest. Never have I seen such a sudden transformation from misery to delight.

"Oh well done, Flashman!" cried Norton. "For a warrior to live after losing their hair is unusual, but to receive their hair back from the man who had taken it is a very rare thing indeed. Black Eagle's spirit is restored to him."

The man himself finally let go of me and then sank to one knee and kissed the back of my hand. Before I could react to that he was off and running back to his fellows holding his hair aloft and giving his whooping war cry.

"You have made a true friend there, Flashman," exclaimed Norton, grinning. "Black Eagle will never attack you again. Now will you feel safe in our village?"

"What is an Indian village like?" I asked cautiously. "I mean do they live in caves or mud houses? What are their dwellings made of?"

"Caves and mud houses?" Norton repeated and then he roared with laughter. Wait and see, Flashman, but I promise you that you will be most comfortable.

We set off later that morning. Norton and I were the only two mounted and we rode at the front of the column while the Indians carrying bundles of their possessions followed on behind. We were just over a day's ride to the Grand River reservation. Norton explained that originally the Iroquois had lived mostly to the south, in New York State. But after the American War of Independence many had migrated north to land in Canada known as the Grand River Tract. Initially it stretched some six miles either side of the Grand River for over a hundred a fifty miles of the river's length. It was a huge strip of land but in the intervening years much of the northern half had been sold off by the Indians to white settlers.

"Are many of the Indians Christians?" I asked, remembering my conversation with Smoke Johnson under the bush.

"A growing number," Norton replied. "I do my best to encourage them; a few years ago I translated the Saint John's Gospel into Mohawk. When this war is over I will try to translate the other Gospels."

"A Bible scholar, Iroquois war chief, friend of the British aristocracy, is there no end to your talents?" I looked at my riding companion carefully. Without his war paint he was far less intimidating, and he looked older. I thought he was aged in his mid-forties and he clearly had Indian blood in him. "I take it you are half Iroquoian? Was your father a white settler who married an Indian woman?"

"You could not be more wrong. My father was a Cherokee brave from America. He was captured by the British before the Revolutionary War and later joined the British army. He went back to Britain with his regiment and there married a Scottish girl. I was born and brought up in Scotland. Later I joined the army and was eventually posted back here in Canada. I left the army and became a translator. I

47

spent a lot of time with the Iroquois. Remember I told you that the Iroquois are also known as the Six Nations as there are six tribes in that group? Well one of the chiefs formally adopted me as a Mohawk, one of the six tribes, and that is how I came to be a Mohawk war chief."

"So how did you get to meet the Duke of Northumberland and attend the English court?"

"The Six Nations sent me to London to negotiate with the British government on their behalf. I met many people there who helped me. There was a lot of interest in our people; I even had my portrait painted in London." He laughed. "The artist insisted on painting me in a romantic pose – I looked like a fortune teller in a travelling show. I think the sight of me painted for war would have frightened too many ladies."

We rode companionably for the rest of that day before making camp in a forest clearing. Some Indians had been hunting while we had marched and soon there were fires burning and meat roasting. I threw my blanket down on the ground and sat near a blaze with a roasting haunch of venison suspended above it. Norton, Black Eagle, Smoke Johnson and more Indians I was getting to know were sitting around the same flames. The other Iroquois seemed to treat me with renewed respect since I had returned Black Eagle's hair. I thought I was getting on well with the big Indian until he marched around the fire to stand in front of me.

"Little Father will not sleep on that Indian Land," he intoned with a look of concern.

I was hungry and tired and not inclined to put up with any more of his superstitious nonsense. "Is that what your Great Spirit tells you?" I asked wearily.

Black Eagle looked puzzled and turned to Smoke Johnson, saying something in Iroquoian at which Johnson roared with delight. "It is nothing to do with the Great Spirit," he gasped out between bouts of laughter. "The big lug does not know the English words to tell you, but you have put your blanket on an ants' nest!"

48

I looked down. There were hundreds of the black insects on me. As I started to brush them away I felt the first one bite and then I was up on my feet sweeping them off my clothes. Soon half the warriors there were howling with mirth at my expense. Even Norton called out something about the white man's war dance. I was not amused; the damn creatures were still biting. Some had got down my shirt and so I tore the garment off over my head. I was just shaking the insects out of the shirt over the fire when I noticed that the laughter had suddenly died away. When I looked around they were all staring at me as though they had seen a ghost.

"What the devil is it?" I asked irritably as I shook the last ants off.

"Your chest, Flashman," said Norton. "The scar on your chest."

"Oh that. It was a wound I picked up in Spain last year." If you have read my previous memoirs you will know that I was shot through the chest at the battle of Albuera. There was a small entry scar on my back but a much bigger, star-shaped exit scar on my chest.

Black Eagle came up to me with an awestruck look on his face. Slowly he put his left hand over the entry scar and then reached around to put his right hand on the big exit scar and stared at the space between his hands as though he was watching a miracle. Then he suddenly snatched both hands away and called out something in his native tongue that brought gasps from some of the watching Indians.

"What the devil is the matter with him now?" I asked.

Smoke Johnson replied. "He says that you must be most favoured by the Great Spirit to survive such a wound."

"It is remarkable," agreed Norton. "In all my time in the army I never saw anyone survive a wound such as that."

I explained that I had been lucky and been treated by a good surgeon, but then they wanted me to tell them about the battle I had been wounded in. When I told them about the casualties at Albuera they rocked and moaned in wonder. Norton explained that the dead in that battle outweighed the number of Iroquois thought to be living. Several exclaimed that this proved the white men were limitless in number to consider such losses.

When I recounted how the battle had been fought, with lines of British and French troops facing each other, they shook their heads in dismay again. Why, they asked, had we not ambushed the French on the road and drawn them into more ambushes in the forest? Given the way the battle had been fought, it was a fair question. Such tactics could hardly have been less effective than Beresford's dithering. When I tried to explain about the cavalry screens that the French used to protect their march, they then suggested slipping into the French camp at night and cutting as many throats as possible. That, they assured me, was the way to fight a war.

In exasperation I tried to claim that they simply did not understand the European style of warfare. Norton grinned and I remembered that he at least had once also served in the British army.

"I think you are forgetting," he said quietly, "that our warriors have just won the battle of Queenston for the British."

"Really?" I objected. "I think General Sheaffe would disagree. If the Americans had managed to get enough men and ammunition across the river they would have held the day."

"So why didn't they get enough men and ammunition across the river?" pressed Norton. Several of the Indians were grinning now as they followed his line of thought.

"Well the British artillery made the crossing difficult for the American boats." I saw where he was going with his argument as well, but I was too stubborn to concede the point.

"You know as well as I that boats continued to cross, and that in the afternoon the ones coming from the American shore were half empty. Why was that, do you think?"

"A lot of them were sick, they have dysentery and their rations are not getting through."

"And…" persisted Norton.

"Oh all right!" I thought back to the genial Major Cartwright when he gave me the real reason why they could not get more of the militia to cross. "They had heard your wretched war cries and were worried about being scalped when they got across the river." The Indians chuckled as I conceded the argument, but Norton was not finished.

"And do you think one of the reasons that the Americans ran out of ammunition was because they fired volley after volley into the trees we were in, to make us keep our distance?"

Before I could reply, Smoke Johnson spoke up. "And they rushed their shots, firing high." He was right about that as only five Iroquois had been killed in the battle and eight wounded. I did not know what the American casualties were, but they must have been in the hundreds.

"All right," I yielded. "I admit that you might have made a bigger contribution to the victory than I first thought."

We settled down a bit after that. The venison was good and I found a new ant-free patch of ground on which to spread my blanket. Several of the Indians were smoking and Norton showed me how to use the pipe bowl of my tomahawk. Some believed that the smoke helped them commune with the spirits. God knows what they put in with the tobacco, but it produced a richer more mellow smoke than any cigar.

"The tobacco tastes good, doesn't it?" enquired Norton.

"It is certainly the best Iroquois thing I have had so far," I agreed feeling relaxed.

"Yes, you must find lots of our ways strange, but there is a purpose to most of them." He paused for a while as though considering what to say next and then pressed on. "Take scalping, for example. I know you find it abhorrent but Queenston shows how effective it is. The Iroquois do not have the advantage of numbers and so they must use other tactics to beat their enemies. They have always relied on ambush as well as hiding their true strength and frightening their enemies into retreat or surrender. In the past they would torture prisoners so that the screams would weaken the courage of their opponents, as well as scalp the dead. They would never stand in a line in front of their enemies; it would give away their strength and location. Instead they would fight from the edge of a forest and try to draw an enemy into the trees where their men could be surrounded and slowly destroyed. A good war chief does not come back with enemy flags; he comes back having instilled fear and respect in his enemies. He also brings home most if not all of

51

the warriors he left with. When you understand that, you will begin to understand the Iroquois."

"Tell me, Norton," I asked sleepily. "On what side do you butter your crumpet?"

"What on earth do you mean?"

"Well sometimes you talk of the Iroquois as 'they' and sometimes you talk as though you are one of them. In your heart are you Iroquois or British?"

"If I knew the answer to that, my friend, I would feel much more content." Norton sighed as he considered the question. "I was brought up in Britain, although my father would tell me tales of Indian life. The Iroquois have welcomed me, formally adopted me as a Mohawk and made me a war chief. But I cannot forget what I know of the white man's world. The Iroquois are a nomadic people. They used to move their villages every twenty years or so as game became harder to find. But they have sold off too much of their original land grant to keep moving. Now they are going to have to change their way of life. They cannot remain dependent on gifts from the British as these will stop as soon as the British have no more use for the Indians. More settlers will come and there will be more pressure for land." I remember him turning to me all moist-eyed at one point and gripping my arm. "You know, Flashman," he cried, "I think it is my God given duty to help the Iroquois adapt to the modern world."

Another man might have been stirred by this all this passion and altruistic ambition but not me. I had seen too many old English villages destroyed by the enclosure of land by rich aristocrats. Money talks and when their way of life ceased to be viable, the Indians would have a simple choice: change or starve. I must have fallen asleep as he talked as I don't remember him stopping, but I do recall I had the strangest dream. I was back at Albuera before I had been shot. The French column in front of me was breaking in panic and through their ranks charged thousands of triumphant Iroquois warriors. Then they were torturing someone; I could see a British officer tied to a spit over the same fire we had cooked the deer. I remember struggling to push through the surrounding throng of men. Then as I got to the front, the spit rotated so that the victim was looking calmly at me. He spoke with icy condescension as he informed me, "The name is Fforbes, with two 'f's."

The next morning I felt surprisingly thick-headed considering we had consumed no spirits. The camp was struck and we began our march through the Grand River lands. It was still mostly forest but every now and then we came across a cleared field of crops and paths that led away into the trees. The band of warriors behind slowly shrank as men slipped away to their homes. When we finally reached the Iroquois village where Norton lived, I almost did not recognise it as an Indian settlement. It looked exactly the same as some white towns I had seen, with plank houses and log cabins. There was even a white painted church with a steeple. Crowds of women and children and old men came out to welcome the war band and the warriors excitedly told of their victories. Soon I was in the middle of a great crowd in the centre of the village and staring in bewilderment at the people about me. I had expected them all to look like…well, Indians, but there seemed all sorts of nationalities.

Amongst the women was a very pretty blonde-haired girl who was throwing her arms about Smoke Johnson. She had a blonde-haired baby tied to a device on her back. There were several brown-haired women and a girl scowling from the back of the crowd, who had bright red hair. It wasn't just hair colour. Two of the old men welcoming the warriors back were black. Another had the narrow eyes I had last seen on a merchant in India, who it was claimed had come from China. Quite a few looked to be at least half white and with my black hair and olive skin from my Spanish mother, I seemed almost as Indian as them. Only my red coat made me stand out from the crowd.

When I asked Norton about this variety of races he told me that the Iroquois would take women and children as hostages in raids and then absorb them into the tribe. They would not be treated as slaves but full members of the tribe, to marry and have Iroquois children of their own. He pointed out the two black men. "One of our foraging parties found them close to death in the woods. They were escaped slaves who had tried to survive on their own, but they had no idea how to live on this land. They were taken back to the village and, once they had recovered, invited to join the tribe."

"Did they have a real choice?" I asked.

"Certainly, anyone can leave at any time; we are not that far from white communities. But they prefer now to live as part of the tribal family in our village than somewhere else."

This tribal family was now in a mood to celebrate and as soon as we arrived preparations began for a huge feast. Norton invited me to stay with him in a house that was as comfortable as any I stayed in while in Canada. I spent much of that first afternoon sitting on a rocking chair on his porch watching as women prepared huge bowls of mysterious foods, plucked fowl and prepared joints of meat for roasting. The men seemed to do little work, but instead painted depictions of their victories and achievements on long strips of bark that would be the centrepiece of the festivities. Then they painted themselves in the war paint colours they had fought the battle in and started to gather in the centre of the village.

I felt a complete outsider, but they did their best to involve me in the celebrations. Norton introduced me to some wizened old Indian who I gathered was the village chief. He made a long rambling speech of welcome I could not understand. Then Smoke Johnson took me away to look at the bark strips. He wanted to show me a section he had painted, which depicted a stick man with a red smudge on his chest which I gathered was me in my red coat. The stick man was swiping a sword over the head of another crouching Indian whose hair was flying through the air. A crowd of villagers were gathered around the painting giggling like young children over a fart. If Black Eagle ever saw his depiction he did not react; I did not doubt he had painted himself elsewhere on the strips killing that sentry and collecting a handful of other scalps.

Shortly after that the singing and dancing started. There is a reason why Iroquois songs and dances have not become popular: they are bloody awful. Lines of men swaying and chanting, interspersed with the occasional shriek; I can honestly say that I have heard more harmony from a cow in labour. Oh don't get me wrong, it is not as bad

54

as bagpipes – what is? – but the noise somehow managed to be both dreary and disturbing. I found some corner of the clearing to sit in, out of the way. Mercifully at the same time that they started this caterwauling din they also served the food and some strong spirits. Back then I had no idea what I was actually eating, but I did know that most of it was delicious. There were corn cakes sweetened with syrup and others containing berries, some kind of apple chutney and plenty of meat, including slices of smoked venison that I particularly enjoyed. The camp women ensured I was well supplied and they also brought cups of liquor. It tasted like cheap brandy but with some berry flavour added. In no time at all I had reached a happy mellow drunkenness and singing became less jarring.

Then the chanting stopped and the warriors sat themselves in a big circle around the fire, surrounded by the other villagers to hear their stories. Norton and Smoke Johnson came and got me up from the floor and gave me a place in the circle. Tobacco was being passed now and as I still had the tomahawk in my belt, once more the pipe bowl end was filled. I soon felt even mellower than I had before. I could not understand most of the tales as they were told in Iroquoian, but several warriors got up to act how they had beaten an enemy or avoided an attack.

Suddenly I realised that I was being called to the centre of the circle. When I had staggered into the space it was clear that they wanted me to remove my shirt to show them my wound again. I did so and many of the villagers who had not seen it before crowded round to look. Then the singing started again with various warriors getting up to give a solo refrain. Norton rose and gave a Scottish lament from his childhood. When my turn came, all I could think of was a bawdy drinking song I had sung in London clubs. It was called *To Anacreon in Heaven* and it finishes with the refrain:

'*And besides I'll instruct you like to entwine;*
The Myrtle of Venus with Bacchus' Vine.'

The symbolism was lost on the Iroquois but they cheered politely as I slumped back in my place and puffed on my tomahawk.

The rest of the evening is a bit hazy. I was still bare-chested and I recall that several of the warriors, including Smoke Johnson, decided that my wound would benefit from some war paint. They outlined the big star-shaped scar in yellow and then added further outlines in red and then black so that it looked like I had a huge target on my torso. Even to my drink-fuddled brain, that seemed a rather reckless war paint design. I must have fallen asleep then before I somehow got to bed. But slumbering next to drunken Iroquois warriors with war paint is a dangerous thing to do. I discovered this the next morning when I awoke with a roaring hangover. I staggered out of the cabin to get a drink, but as I bent over the bucket of water I got the fright of my life. I actually whirled round with arms raised in defence before I realised that the fearsome face covered in red, black and yellow that I had just seen staring at me, was my own.

Chapter 6

Norton and several of the other Iroquois war chiefs took turns taking war bands back to the Niagara over the next few weeks, but they did not see any further action. The Americans did try one more crossing but that was even less successful and easily seen off by the local troops. I on the other hand stayed in the village and had to concede that it seemed a very comfortable life. With the harsh winter coming, any further campaigning would have to wait until the spring. The Indians were busy gathering food before the snows came and there seemed a bountiful harvest. Well, when I say Indians, I actually mean the Indian women, as most warriors thought it was beneath them to toil in the fields. The men viewed themselves as hunters. When I asked Black Eagle if he ever helped with the crops, he told me proudly that only women and hogs were suited to dig in the ground.

Norton did tend his own vegetable patch and one afternoon he asked me to help him.

"It might help change their opinion if they see that even a British officer is prepared to till the ground." I pottered about among his vegetables for a bit, but looking at the plots cultivated around the village it seemed that the women did not need much help. In many fields they were managing to grow three crops at once, typically corn and up those stems grew beans and below them squash plants were fruiting. Norton explained that he was trying to encourage white farmers to buy land in the area to help the Indians understand about crop rotation and other innovations. Some men did work on the land; the two former slaves had a mule and plough and hired their services out to the women to help clear their plots.

This virtuous agricultural work was all very well but I preferred to spend my time with the warriors. They filled their time with gambling, drinking, smoking, competitions of skill such as knife and tomahawk throwing and of course hunting. Hurling a tomahawk into a tree trunk from twenty paces is not nearly as easy as it looks when done by an expert. I discovered that the pipe bowl on the back of my tomahawk blade was not just there for smoking, but also for balancing the weapon when throwing. Get the timing wrong and you harmlessly clout your target with just the shaft of your axe. But it was the hunting I enjoyed most. Norton might have been right about the farming, but there is something far more manly and satisfying in bringing back a brace of rabbits or a turkey for the pot, than pulling up a carrot.

Black Eagle and Smoke Johnson would often go hunting together and sometimes I would go too. The pair of them had an uncanny knack of finding game and we rarely came home empty handed. It was on one of those hunting expeditions that I first met Magda.

We had been stalking in a line near the river. They had put me in the middle as I was the least likely to spot anything; Johnson was on my left near the bank and Black Eagle to my right. We had been moving quietly through the trees for nearly an hour when there was the sound of a women's scream to my left followed immediately by a booming gunshot. There was no sound from Johnson and I sprinted in his direction. I could hear Black Eagle crashing through the trees behind me, but as we got close to the river Johnson stepped out from behind a tree.

"Keep back or the crazy bastard might try and shoot you too."

"Who was it?" I gasped, out of breath.

"Some white woman in a boat on the river. She screamed when she saw me and then one of her servants fired a huge gun in my direction."

"Which way were they going?" asked Black Eagle.

"Up river."

There was shouting now coming from the water, the woman was yelling at someone to keep still. I decided to creep forward and see for myself. I crawled up into a thick bush at the top of a hill overlooking the river; my red coat was too conspicuous to risk standing out in the open. The small boat was drifting just twenty yards away in mid-stream. The oarsman sitting on the middle thwart was watching over his shoulder as the woman, with her back to me, tended to an injured man in the bows of the boat. There were just the three of them in the craft, and a large luggage chest by the vacant seat in the stern. The wounded man was whimpering with pain and I could see the barrel of a large blunderbuss leaning against the gunwale.

"Did you hit him with something?" I whispered to Johnson as he crawled up beside me.

"No, he saw me and snatched up that great cannon of his. Then he fired it and fell back in the boat. Missed me by yards," the warrior added grinning. The boat was slowly turning in the current and at that moment the girl stood up in the boat and looked at the shore. It was the first time I saw her face and it literally took my breath away. She was the most beautiful woman I think I ever saw. Her starched white bonnet had been dislodged and her long blonde hair moved in the gentle breeze. Even from that distance her eyes sparkled as she nervously scanned the shore. She spoke a few words to the man in the bows, who, I saw now, had his arm in a sling. Then she started to move back to her seat in the stern. The plain smock dress that she wore did nothing for her figure but its drabness only seemed to exaggerate her beauty.

"What a magnificent woman," I breathed.

"She is probably going to that foreign settlement up river," said Black Eagle. "They dress in those plain clothes."

"What foreign settlement?" I asked.

"I don't know," replied Black Eagle. "They do not mix with our people."

"I have got to meet her," I whispered.

"Their boat is in shallow water," whispered Black Eagle. "Their gun has fired; we can drag them ashore." The big warrior and Johnson were just starting to get up to do precisely that, when I hissed for them to stay still. The bush had moved as they had tried to rise and the oarsman had seen the disturbance. He was squinting in our direction and then I saw him grin before pulling once more on his oars as the woman settled back in her seat.

"Dammit, I think the oarsman has seen us."

"Don't worry," soothed Johnson. "That's old Renton. He makes his living rowing up and down the river. He often calls into our village for meat and sometimes fetches supplies. He knows we will not harm him."

"But if we are not going to drag the boat ashore," interrupted Black Eagle, "how are you going to meet the woman?"

"Ah," I grinned. "We need to engineer the right kind of introduction and I think that you are just the fellows to help."

The boat made slow progress against the current of the river and it was easy for us to get upstream and well ahead. So it was that an hour after we first saw them, Renton and his passengers came under a second Indian attack. They had just rounded a bend in the river when the air was rent with several different war cries, one slightly hoarse. Then from out of the trees burst two Indians with their muskets and tomahawks held aloft, wet river mud on their faces and screaming fit to burst. One had emerged slightly behind the little craft and the other ahead, it was looking grim for the boat occupants and a scream from the woman was almost lost in the general din. The injured man in the bows was standing and seemed to be trying to climb out. Only the oarsman looked unperturbed, a puzzled smile on his face. Cue the gallant Flashy.

"Leave that woman alone, you villains!" I roared as I emerged from the trees, holding my musket and with a pistol shoved in my belt. Black Eagle, now standing on a little promontory over the water, swung his rifle to cover me and fired. While still on the run towards the boat I pointed my musket in his direction and pulled the trigger. The gun banged with an impressive amount of gun smoke. A blood-curdling shriek came from Black Eagle as he clutched his chest and tottered unsteadily on his rock for several seconds before toppling backwards into the water. There was another splash as the man in the bow of the boat also fell in the river. But now Smoke Johnson charged towards me, determined to avenge his comrade and still shrieking his hideous cries. I pulled the pistol from my belt and when he was still twenty yards off I fired. Once again the Indian clutched his chest and gave a pitiful wail before pitching down onto his knees. He held out a hand to me in mute appeal, and then made a strange gargling noise before falling forward onto the soft river bank, his legs spasming death throes as he fell. It was possibly the worst piece of overacting I had ever seen, but we were not finished yet. I pushed the pistol back in my

60

belt, drew my sword and turned to the empty forest. "Let that be a lesson to you," I shouted, "unless any more of you want a taste of cold steel."

My threats were interrupted by another splash and I looked round to see that the woman had now jumped into the water too.

"Quickly, Lobster," whispered Smoke Johnson's 'corpse'. "Get the silly woman before she drowns."

I did not need telling twice. After all this effort to stage our charade it would be the ultimate irony if such a beauty was lost as a result. I splashed through the shallows; I could see her still bonneted head in the water. She seemed to be fighting with the other man who had jumped out of the boat. Renton was standing in his craft and had thrown the end of a rope in their direction. The boat was drifting in the current and the water was only waist deep when I reached it. I threw the musket, pistol, ammunition bag and my sword inside before plunging after the struggling couple.

The man evidently could not swim and was out of his depth. He was thrashing about and when he grabbed hold of the girl he kept pushing her under in an effort to keep himself afloat. The girl was twisting away and trying to swim up behind the man to grab him, but that was almost impossible as he was panicking and flailing about. I grabbed the rope floating on the water and swam up to them. The girl had lost her bonnet now and her gold hair splayed out in the water behind her. She was gasping for breath after another dunking from the floundering man.

"Here, take this," I shouted, offering her the rope. I heard the oars creak as Renton brought the boat up behind me. The girl turned towards the boat as the drowning man grabbed hold of my left arm. I went under the water once, but my right hand was already reaching for the tomahawk that was still in my belt. As we both emerged from the water again my right hand was gripping the shaft with the brass pipe bowl facing the water, I brought it down smartly behind the man's ear. That put a stop to his struggling and while he was still stunned I dragged him up to the boat's gunwale. Renton reached down, grabbed his arms and hauled him up over the side while the girl trod water alongside the boat. Close to and wet, she looked even more radiant. I was not sure it was just the water making me breathless.

She looked at me and then modestly lowered her gaze. "Thank you, sir, for your help," she gasped.

"Oh it was nothing, you know," I claimed offhandedly. "All in a day's work for a soldier."

"You ready to come aboard, miss?" called Renton from above, before reaching down under her arms and hauling her upwards. If the plain drab shift had done nothing for her figure when it was dry, by Christ when it was wet it could have brought a city to a standstill. I watched in wonder as her soaked form rose before me with the wet cloth clinging to her breasts and buttocks like a second skin. I floated in awe for a moment, thanking God that the water was cold enough to subdue any sign of obvious interest. As the girl settled back in her seat I swung a leg up over the side. Renton reached down and helped pull me aboard and then made room for me to sit beside him on the central thwart. The girl was quickly pulling the shift away from her body to try to make herself look less exposed.

"We must go ashore, I need to change my clothes." She spoke good English but I detected a foreign accent, perhaps Austrian. I struggled to tear my eyes away from her and glanced over my shoulder, where the other man lay almost forgotten in the bows of the boat. He was whimpering quietly and clutching his head with his good arm while he had already put the other back in the sodden sling around his neck.

I looked at Renton, who, like me, was similarly distracted. "We cannot go ashore here, miss," he protested. Those savage Indians will kill us all. You will just have to stay as you are for a while, I am afraid." I was pretty sure that he was not remotely 'afraid' at all. In fact he licked his lips with delight at the prospect.

"What about that island upstream?" The girl pointed over my shoulder and looking once more I saw a small island with a handful of trees and bushes on it in the middle of the river. "Surely there cannot be Indians on that." Renton grudgingly conceded that it was unlikely to be infested with hostile warriors. Taking an oar each, we reluctantly rowed until the little boat beached on what was little more than a mud bank with vegetation. The girl opened her trunk and rummaged for fresh, dry clothes. Renton and I had disembarked, ostensibly to pull the craft further out of the water, but we were both hoping for a chance to lift the girl out of the boat. To our disappointment she nimbly jumped out by herself and disappeared behind some thick foliage at the very far side of the island.

Renton spat some tobacco juice onto the sand. "You tell Smoke Johnson that his dying act was the worst piece of dumb play that I ever saw."

I grinned and nodded to the trees. "If things go to plan I am rather hoping that you will see Johnson before me."

"I thought that was your game," grunted Renton. "But you are wasting your time there. I am taking her up to where the river forks to meet her new husband. He is some kind of pastor and she is another religious type. She keeps reading her Bible and quoting the commandments." I hid my disappointment by asking about the third occupant of the boat. "Oh he is just some lad her father hired to keep her safe. Damn fool overloaded the gun and now his shoulder is broke." Renton glanced inside the boat where the young man was still lying grey-faced in the bow and laughed. "Damn me, but was he scared witless of your Indian friends, though."

"The girl swims well," I pointed out.

"Aye, she has courage I'll say that for her. She did not hesitate when she saw the lad could not swim." We chatted on for a while. Renton had heard that a British soldier had been staying at the Iroquois village and had spotted all three of us when we had first seen the boat. Then we heard Magda coming back through the bushes. The girl emerged wearing another of her shapeless smocks and bonnets with a bundle of wet clothes in her hand. Her figure was once more obscured, but I did not mind. The image of her being pulled from the water was still seared into my memory, indeed even now over thirty years later I can see it as clearly as if it were yesterday.

"Captain Thomas Flashman, ma'am," I saluted smartly. "I do not believe I yet have the honour of your name."

63

"It is Magdalena Dietrich," she replied smiling demurely. "But most people call me Magda." We helped her back into the boat and then Renton and I pushed off and resumed our places at the oars.

"Do I detect an accent in your English, Magda?" I asked as we started rowing again upstream. "Are your parents Austrian?"

"I come from a Mennonite community in Pennsylvania."

"Oh," I replied. It was a term I had not heard before. "So, er, where is Mennononia?"

She laughed. "It is not a place, it is a church. We are what you would probably call puritans; we observe the Ten Commandments and try to live a simple life of devotion to our Lord. Most of our families came from Holland and the neighbouring German states. I was born in Pennsylvania but we speak German within the community."

"Born here, eh?" I said. "Was that a long time ago?"

She smiled at my clumsy enquiry at her age. "I am nineteen years old, Captain."

"That is old for getting married in these parts," cried Renton with all the tact of a myopic bull in a porcelain factory.

"My mother died, and I had to help my father bring up my brothers and sisters. Pastor Johannes is an old friend of my father's and when his wife died my father betrothed me to him."

"So you have not met your new husband yet, then?" I probed.

"No, he is establishing a new community here. It does not even have a name yet."

We got to the nameless place an hour later. It seemed abandoned. There was just a rough wooden jetty, a water mill that looked like it had not been used in months, a small hut and a track leading into the forest.

"Did your husband know you were coming?" I asked.

"Yes," replied Magda, struggling and failing to hide her disappointment in her new home. "He told me the farm was down the track. I will leave the luggage here and go off to find it."

"I could not possibly leave you alone here," I told her. "There are all sorts of dangers in the forest." I turned back to the boatman and

64

winked. "Renton will have to take your companion back so that he can get his shoulder seen to, but I would be happy to stay and escort you.

"That's right, ma'am," piped up Renton. "I will need to take the lad to Brant's Ford. That is the nearest place where there is a healer." I grinned; Brant's Ford was the name of the Indian village that I was living at. I doubted the young man would find being treated by the wrinkled old medicine women there, with her pots and potions, that relaxing.

"Please don't trouble yourself, Captain, I am sure I will be fine." Magda walked hesitantly off the end of the jetty onto the grassy, overgrown track.

"Ma'am, you do not know this country. This is still Indian territory; I could not possibly leave you here undefended."

She turned to face me again, looking pale. "Sir, you are a soldier and I know you will think differently but Mennonites do not believe in violence; we do not fight and we do not kill. It says in the Bible," she added holding the book with a white-knuckled grip to her chest, "that whoever sheds human blood will have their blood shed, for in the image of God has God made mankind." She took a deep breath before adding, "If it is God's will that I die here today then so be it."

I suppressed a smile; she was obviously frightened, but trying to cling on to tenets that she had been taught in some nice safe church in Pennsylvania. "You don't understand," I said as I buckled on my sword and picked up my weapons. "If the Indians find you they will use you in the basest way and then they will take that pretty gold hair. Have you heard of scalping?"

She obviously had as she quivered deliciously with fear. Then the poor girl glanced nervously around as though a savage could be hidden behind every bush. "Perhaps your company would deter the Indians," she conceded. "But please, we must avoid any bloodshed."

"I will do my best to avoid killing any Indians," I promised her. "Now, do you know how far inland this farm is? It will be getting dark soon and we might be better spending the night in that cabin than out in the open in the forest. Campfires can be seen for miles." I was in no rush to deliver Magda to her new husband, at least not before I had spent some time with her. So as Renton pushed off down-stream, Magda and I carried her heavy trunk to the cabin and tried to make ourselves comfortable for the night. I managed to shoot a rabbit as some of the fine powder I used for hunting was still dry in the powder horn. My tobacco was wet, though, and I left that drying out near the fire that Magda built in the hearth. Near to the mill I found an apple tree and some berry bushes, so by nightfall we had meat roasting and fruit to go with it.

"How old is your husband?" I asked as I cut the meat for us to eat.

"A little older than my father – probably around fifty."

"Do you know what he looks like?"

She looked sad as she bit down on the first piece of meat. "He will have a beard and my father says that he has crinkly hair, but he has not seen Johannes for many years."

"Is an old bearded man what you were hoping for in a husband?"

She stiffened at that. "It is not seemly to discuss such things with a strange man."

We ate in silence for a while and then I spoke up. "It seems to me that now is absolutely the right time to talk about such things. Once you are married it will be too late."

"I have to marry him," she said quietly. "It is an honour to marry a pastor and if I do not my father will be shamed and I would be shunned by the community."

I gave her one of the apples and then tested my tobacco drying on the hearth. It was not bone dry but it needed some moisture to smoke well. Magda watched as I pulled my tomahawk from my belt and carefully packed the pipe bowl. Then I lit it with a spill from the fire and sat back, breathing in the fragrant smoke. "Have you been with a man before or will the pastor be your first?"

She looked shocked, "It is not seemly to discuss such things."

"I see," I replied calmly and puffed again on the tomahawk shaft. "This is an Indian tool," I told her, "an axe and a smoking pipe combined. Have you smoked a pipe?" She shook her head, staring at the smoking bowl. I passed it over to her. "Suck the smoke to flavour your mouth; don't take it down into your lungs."

She puffed hesitantly on the pipe and blew out the smoke before drawing on it more confidently again. "It tastes of flowers and mown grass and coffee and all sorts of things."

"It does," I agreed and for a few minutes we smoked companionably passing the pipe between us without saying a word.

"I have not been with a man before," she broke the long silence.

"I suspect that a fat old farmer was not who you imagined for your first time."

She looked at me and blushed a deep shade of pink before casting her eyes down again. "Please it is not…"

"Seemly, yes I know. You like that word a lot, don't you. Perhaps I should charge you an item of clothing every time you use it."

"You wouldn't!" she exclaimed. "That would be…" I cocked an eyebrow and she seemed to go even redder before finishing. "That would be most ungallant."

"Have they at least told you what to expect?" I enquired. "When you are first with your husband."

"It says in the Bible, in Ephesians, that a wife must submit in everything to her husband and so I will do what my husband asks."

"That is it? That is all you know, a quote from Ephesians?" I remembered that her mother had died and so perhaps there was no one to tell her what to do.

"Please, it is not…we should not discuss such things." As though paying the penalty she reached up and slowly removed her bonnet and placed it in her lap. I saw a tear trickle down her face. I reached out and gently held her hand. I felt a swell of affection for her, but also anger at how her community had sent her out so unprepared. "One of the women told me that the things he would want to do would hurt," she whispered and then she started to cry. I put my arm around her and pulled her towards me.

We held each other for a while and then I bent down to kiss her. At first she responded but then she pushed me away. "I can't, not with you. You are a man of violence."

"Don't be silly," I tried to comfort her.

"You killed two men this morning, have you forgotten? Does killing come so easily to you?"

I smiled and then laughed when I saw her shocked expression. "I did not kill anybody. My Indian friends and I staged the attack so that I could meet you. The guns were not loaded with ball. God, a fifty yard musket shot fired while running combined with a twenty yard pistol shot – it would never happen. Did you not see Smoke Johnson's overly dramatic death throes?"

"No, I was too busy rescuing Duncan." She paused, looking astonished. "Do you mean to say that you did all of that just to meet me?"

"Yes, you quite took my breath away the moment I first saw you, just after your man Duncan shot at Johnson."

"You were there too, and you really didn't kill them?" She reached round for her Bible and thrust it towards me. "Swear on the Bible that you have not killed anybody."

"I swear on this Bible that I did not kill those two Indians," I said staring into those clear blue eyes and carefully editing her requested pledge. But before she could notice I added, "They are both alive and well. Ask Renton next time you see him for he saw that those were impossible shots. If you like I can bring the warriors back here to visit."

I did not get any further before she threw her arms around me and started to smother me with kisses.

"I am so pleased," she sobbed as she held herself tightly against me. "I felt so alone."

By George, I thought, what a capital transformation. Kissing her back, I held her with one hand and started to undo the buttons down the front of her smock with the other. As soon as there was room I slipped a hand inside her clothes and cupped one of her splendid breasts. For a moment her body tensed and her fingers dug into my shoulder. Then her muscles relaxed and she pressed her face into my neck. "Now that," she whispered huskily in my ear, "is very unseemly."

Chapter 7

That night in the little cabin by the fork in the river was one of the best of my life, and without being one to boast, I would venture that it was for Magda too. Before that night, while she had known her Bible, when it came to the carnal act she did not know her Deuteronomy from her Leviticus. That changed as I gently initiated her into a myriad of different pleasures. The sun was high in the sky when we finally emerged, and as no one was around, we washed naked in the river.

As we splashed about I was shocked to discover that she still intended to go through with the marriage. She viewed her betrothal as a binding contract that she could not break without shaming her family. I tried to persuade her to come back to the Indian village with me but she would have none of it.

"You will go back to war," she pointed out, "and then what will become of me? You have given me a wonderful night and I am grateful, but now I must take up my responsibilities."

I argued with her for ages but she could not be shifted. At length, by early afternoon, we were dressed and walking up the cart track, holding her trunk between us. Half an hour from the river we found a large log cabin with the name 'Johannes' burnt onto a plank by the front door. There was no answer to our knock and a search of the meagre farmstead revealed no trace of the fortunate groom. I had hoped to find the bastard dead in some field, but while the place was deserted it had not been abandoned. There were still clothes and boots in the cabin and a large Bible with the names of Johannes' family written inside.

"He would not have left this behind," said Magda noting that her name had already been added beneath that of his late wife, whose grave we had already found behind the empty stable. "He must have ridden into the nearest town and been delayed."

"Well I am not leaving you by yourself," I told her. "When he comes home we will tell him that I replaced the man your father hired after he was injured."

We waited all day, fed the chickens and did other chores around the farm, but there was still no sign of the man. As darkness fell we lit lamps and went inside the cabin. I thought that he was unlikely to try and make it through the surrounding forest on horseback at night and so I took Magda once more in my arms and led her into the small bedroom at the end of the cabin. We were busy working our way through the Gospels of St Flashy when we heard the neigh of a horse right outside the front of the cabin.

"Oh my goodness, it is Johannes," gasped Magda. "He will find me in bed with you."

"Just buy me some time to get away," I whispered getting up and throwing open the little shuttered window in the bedroom.

But already I could tell that there would not be time to climb through the opening; the eager husband's footsteps could be heard thumping up the path to the front of the house. "Magda, is that you who has lit the lamps? I am so sorry I was not here to meet you." The door of the cabin banged open. He must have quickly scanned the dimly lit room for people, missing my sword and musket leaning in the corner, and turned immediately for the bedroom door. "Here I am, my darling," he called as he raised the latch and started to enter. I only just got my shoulder to the other side of the door in time. I slammed it shut and heard a surprised cry as he landed on his arse on the other side.

"Please, my husband," Magda called out. "I need to prepare myself for you. I have a specially embroidered nightdress that I want to wear when we spend our first night together."

"You are so strong, darling," muttered Johannes appreciatively from the other side of the door, before adding, "but be quick as I am anxious to see you and hold you in my arms."

Magda threw open her trunk, while I cast around for my breeches. Once those were on I dropped my boots and other clothes out of the window. I blew a farewell kiss to Magda as she struggled to pull a nightdress over her head and then I dropped silently to the ground outside. I had to get my sword and musket back and so I crept around to the front of the cabin where the door still hung open.

"You can come in now," called Magda. As I heard the door to the bedroom open I slipped into the other room of the cabin and moved swiftly and silently on bare feet to where my sword and musket were resting against the wall. Of course, I had forgotten that the first thing a randy old goat of a husband would want to do with a new young wife is to see what she looks like.

"Oh I have so looked forward to this moment," babbled Johannes. "Please come this way so that I can see you." Holding her hands in his, he backed out into the main room of the cabin, where the light from the lantern slowly illuminated the couple. I saw Magda's eyes widen in alarm as she looked over her new husband's shoulder and saw her lover standing in just his breeches in the corner of the room. I ducked down behind a high-backed wooden chair, but I doubt Johannes would have noticed if I had danced a hornpipe behind him. The effect of Magda's beauty on him was the same as it had been on me and I heard him gasp as she came into the light. Then after a moment he whispered, "You are so beautiful; God is very kind to me."

"You are kind to me also, husband," replied Magda dutifully. While I could not see, I imagined her gazing at the narrow high-backed chair I was crouching behind before she added, "Now husband, please let us go back into the bedroom."

The horny bastard did not need asking twice. "Yes, yes, if that will please you," he muttered virtually pushing Magda back towards the bed. I was up in a moment, sword and musket in hand and was out of the cabin before the bedroom door had fully closed. I had no wish to hear Magda and her husband together and so I grabbed my boots and clothes from beneath their bedroom window and sprinted off into the night before getting properly dressed.

Even though I found a comfortable bed of straw in the stable, it was a miserable night, full of sour thoughts about the honeymoon couple. The next morning at first light I made my way back down to the little jetty by the water. There was always some traffic on the river – it was the easiest way to pass through the forest – and by lunchtime I had caught a passage with two Indians in a canoe back to Brant's Ford. Returning to Norton's cabin I struggled to get Magda off my mind. I took out my frustrations on Norton's vegetable patch, providing a sterling example for the warriors as I hacked through weeds, and as it turned out, a line of plants that Norton had wanted to keep.

Over the coming weeks the weather got colder and it was clear that there would be no major campaigning until the spring. The village seemed as good a place as any to spend the dark cold months. It was well supplied and sufficiently far from the border to be immune from any cross-border raids. The Iroquois also made me feel very welcome.

If I am honest Magda was the other reason I did not want to stray far from Brant's Ford as my thoughts often drifted to that little farm just ten miles to the north. Twice that autumn and winter I travelled all the way up to see her, but I did not let her see me. The first time I went by canoe and the second, when the river was frozen, on horseback. On each occasion I watched through my telescope as she and her husband bustled about the smallholding doing chores. Seeing him properly in the daylight, Johannes did have the fuzzy hair that her father had described, but it was now half grey. He looked a grim and slightly forbidding figure. I could well imagine him shouting about hell and brimstone from the pulpit, if they had pulpits in Mennonite churches. I kept searching for any sign that Magda was happy with her new life; if she had been then I think I would have been able to forget her. After all she was right; I was a soldier and although she did not know it, I already had an estranged wife in England. But not once in the time I watched, even when they walked past each other, did I see a smile cross either of their faces.

Now, readers of my earlier memoirs might be forgiven for wondering why a man, who had enjoyed more than a few women in a lust-filled career, was getting so sentimental over some slip of a girl. Well you are right, I was getting maudlin about Magda, but if you had seen her, looked into those crystal clear blue eyes and spent a night in the cabin with her, well I rather think you would be feeling maudlin too.

To help cheer me up Norton ensured that there were plenty of Christmas festivities in the village. No more than half of the Iroquois were Christians, but it seemed that the Great Spirit was not averse to

72

celebrating the passing of mid-winter either. It was the first time I saw a Christmas tree; the custom had been learned from German immigrants to America. A large fir was cut down and installed in the church and every Christian household in the village helped decorate it with painted feathers, strips of cloth and candles. A service was held in the church at midnight on Christmas Eve with the candles lit and hymns sung. Most of the congregation, including me, were drunk and the singing was raucous, but the service was more spirited as a result. As I gazed at the decorated foliage under the church beams, I could not help but wonder if Magda with her German ancestry was looking at a similar tree. The following day instead of what, for me, was the traditional Christmas goose for dinner, we had turkey. Several large birds were cooked by the women in a big clay oven; there were even roast potatoes, which were not a traditional Iroquois staple.

As the twelve days of Christmas stretched into the New Year, I was left to reflect on what 1813 might bring. I had started the previous year in Portugal and had endured all manner of adventures since then. I had no wish to throw myself unnecessarily into the fray again and so when Norton left with a small war party to see what was happening to the west I let him go without me. He was back a couple of months later, having achieved very little, but he brought news.

He told me that an American general called Harrison had marched with a large force to try and relieve Detroit. The ground he had to cover was wild and remote; it was hard going in summer never mind in the depths of winter. Indian scouts had monitored their progress and the advance guard of this force had suffered a particularly tough time. When they had entered an area grimly known as the Black Swamp, they had struggled to get any supplies through at all. They barely made five miles a day as horses and wagons floundered in the mud. Morale was low; they had not been paid for three months and were desperately short of warm clothes, food and medicine.

Eventually this beleaguered advance guard managed to capture the British outpost at a place called Frenchtown, on the River Raisin, just twenty-six miles from Detroit. But the men were so exhausted they took no precautions against a counter attack and a few days later a

British force under its western commander, General Procter, routed them. The Americans lost nearly three hundred dead and six hundred taken prisoner. Harrison was forced to withdraw the rest of his force. What Norton omitted to mention was that after the battle Procter had neglected to provide enough guards for the wounded American prisoners. The Americans had raided several Indian villages on their march and now a group of drunken Indians murdered some eighty of the wounded prisoners in revenge.

While Norton had been away, the men from the Canadian Indian Agency had visited the village with cartloads of gifts for the Indians. These included blankets, clothing, pots, pans, weapons, gunpowder, flints and all manner of other necessaries. I had discovered that the British used the gifts as a means of controlling the Iroquois and ensuring their dependence. There was friction between Norton, who had close links with the army and who was encouraging the Indians to become more self-sufficient, and the Indian Agency, who wanted to maintain their control. This year Norton had been promised by the army extra gifts as reward for their participation in the war but only some of these were delivered. The Indian Agency also ensured that Norton and his supporters got fewer gifts than the families that were dependent on handouts. The few warriors who had joined their women in farming their own land to increase its efficiency viewed this as unfair. It was a deliberate attempt to undermine Norton's authority with the tribe and when he returned he was furious.

General Sheaffe was then in the town of York, (now known as Toronto) and Norton planned to visit him, remonstrate over the missing gifts and seek permission to lead a war party to the west. It was now March and having hidden away all winter I thought it was time I made an appearance. So I offered to accompany him. I cleaned and pressed my army coat but the regulation army britches had long since been torn and worn out. I had taken to wearing buckskin trousers instead. We set off north along well-used paths. We passed within a mile of Magda's farmstead but I resisted the urge to suggest a visit. From there we skirted around the shore of Lake Ontario until we came up on the meagre fortifications of York.

The town was the capital of the southern half of Canada. It was an isolated place with a long beach to the west of the town that would be ideal to land troops. Its only defence to such a landing was a battery containing two condemned guns clamped onto a log base. They could fire, but only in a fixed direction. Sheaffe was busy strengthening the defences and foundations for a fort had been dug but it would be months before it was complete. The only other sizeable structure was the dockyard where work was underway to build a new ship, named for General Brock.

We found Sheaffe in his office at Government House and this time I did get to meet him despite his obstructive aide, Fforbes, being on hand. As Norton informed Sheaffe of the missing gifts, the general's annoying aide turned to me. "You appear to be going native on us," he sneered when he noticed my deerskin trousers. "Surely that is not proper dress for a regular officer; it would barely be acceptable in the militia."

"Among the many gifts that the Indian Agency failed to deliver," I told him, "was a replacement officer's uniform for me." I turned to the general. "I thought buck skin would be preferable to buck naked."

"Quite so," laughed Sheaffe. "Fforbes, sort out some replacement uniform for Captain Flashman and then get a despatch written from me to the Indian Agency about these missing gifts. With the Americans set to pour over the border in all directions, now is not the time to offend our valued Indian allies."

"Yes sir," said Fforbes giving me a sour look as he left the room.

"I thought I might take a war party to help General Procter in the west, sir," suggested Norton. "Once the extra gifts have been received, the men will be keen to fight again."

"No, no," protested Sheaffe settling into a chair by the fire and gesturing for Norton and I to do the same. "Procter has enough Indian allies in the west; it is here I need the Iroquois. The Americans could come over the Niagara at any moment. I need your men at the river now."

"Sir," replied Norton diplomatically, "the ice floes on the Niagara at this time of year would make any crossing of the river by boat almost impossible. It will be at least a month, possibly two, before they could consider an attack across the Niagara. That is why I suggested to General Procter when I met him in January that we might be able to help him during the first part of the year."

"No," repeated Sheaffe. "I admire your fighting spirit, Norton, but I need your men here. My people tell me that the Americans are gathering men for an attack in the east. There are at least two thousand men at their naval base on Lake Ontario and possibly another two thousand more on the way. If they do not attack across the river they could simply sail past the river mouth on the lake and attack Fort George from the rear." Fort George guarded the British side of the Niagara River where it flowed into Lake Ontario and was a prime American target. The discussion continued but Sheaffe could not be moved and eventually Norton agreed to bring as many men as he could to Fort George.

As we started to leave, the general pulled me to one side for a word in private. "I just wanted to thank you for what you are doing, Captain. I know it cannot be easy for an English gentleman to live among those savages, but I need someone I can trust to be with them and make sure that they stay loyal."

"You are most kind, General, but I am pleased to do my duty." It was, I thought, so far possibly the easiest posting I had ever had, but then of course the general had to ruin things.

"When the Americans attack I will want the Six Nations men at the forefront of our defence. They have proved themselves excellent light troops and I will be counting on men like you and Norton to make sure that they are used to best effect. But be careful, Captain. After the unpleasantness at the River Raisin the Americans are in no mood to give quarter to white men fighting among the Indians. Their General Hull issued a proclamation at the start of the war that no white man fighting at the side of the Indian will be taken prisoner; instant destruction is to be his lot." It was then that I heard about the massacre of the American wounded at the River Raisin and the potentially fatal consequences for me. Now I was expected to help lead the Indians into attack against the strongest American positions, but to anticipate nothing less than summary execution if I was captured.

"But they are still taking Indians prisoner, we saw that at Queenston," I queried.

"Yes but the Americans think savagery is part of the Indian's nature, although I dare say they will take fewer prisoners now. On the other hand they believe that a Christian white man should know better than to fight in the Indian way. They might have been forgiving if you had been captured at Queenston, especially as you were an officer, but now their mood has turned ugly. There will be no more firing guns in salute to fallen enemy generals. You will need to be careful you do not fall into their hands when they attack."

You are damn right there, I thought. I was going to make sure I was harder to get than a flea on a skunk when the Americans came pouring over the border. But aloud I said, "Oh you can count on me, sir, I pride myself on being in the right place when an enemy attacks." The general beamed at this and patted me on the back before showing us out. I had meant what I told him, but I suspect that the general and I had very different ideas on where the 'right place' was during an enemy attack. In the swamps and forests of Canada, any battle was likely to be a confused affair and I planned to take full advantage to keep as much out of danger as possible. To me the 'right place' was in the saddle of a fast, well-fed horse that was safely out of range of the enemy.

We left York early the next morning with me wearing a less tatty officer's coat. Its condition fell far short of pristine, however, let down by patched holes and bloodstains on one sleeve and the right shoulder. I had been given two new pairs of breeches as well, but I found the buckskin trousers warmer and more comfortable on the cold spring morning.

"We will not get many warriors at this time of year," Norton confided. "They will be too busy collecting maple sap." I knew he was right as the Indians had a sweet tooth and maple syrup stocks had been running low over the winter. There had been much talk of the coming harvest. I had been amazed to discover that the sweet syrup that was used like honey came not from bees but from trees in the forest. The sap only becomes sweet after the spring thaw begins and then the Indians would cut a notch in the bark and collect the sap with a hollow reed leading into a wooden cup tied to the trunk. The sap would then be gathered and boiled to condense the flavour. If Norton struggled to get the warriors into the fields for planting, he had no such problems getting them into the forest to tap sap from the trees. This was seen as men's work, possibly because a good amount of the sweet sap never actually made it back to the village.

When we had left Brant's Ford it had been just too soon to start making syrup, but by the time we returned production was in full flow. When Norton spoke to the village elders they agreed that few warriors would want to go until the sugar was made and the extra gifts received. Iroquois society was surprisingly complex: the war chiefs like Norton and what I called the civil chiefs, were all men, but they were selected, and deselected on occasion, by a group of hereditary clan leaders, who were all women. All of the leadership were united in the view that Sheaffe was wrong; the ice around the head of the Niagara was too dangerous to allow boats to cross at this time of year. This was the time to sow crops and collect syrup, they said, and only when that was done would they help the white man. They also pointed out that the white militia regiments had not been called up and so the white farmers were busy sowing their crops. Why, they asked, should only the Iroquois be asked to serve, while surely the American militia were in their fields too.

It made sense to me and Norton agreed to take just a token number of warriors to the river, bringing the rest when they were willing to come. "If the Americans have gathered four thousand men at their naval base," he told me after the meeting with the leaders, "then they could attack anywhere around Lake Ontario. The southern shore of the lake is only twenty miles from Brant's Ford. The warriors will not want to stray far from their homes in case they have to defend them. It is probably just as well we are not travelling west." He paused thinking for a moment and then added, "I liked General Procter and I hope I have not misled him about expecting our warriors. I would really like to get a message to him, but it would need to be from someone he trusts."

The Grand River Tract where the Iroquois lived was on a relatively narrow neck of land between Lakes Ontario and Erie. It was not a good place to be trapped, especially if you were likely to be shot on sight. My mind had been turning over how I was to slip away from any fighting between the Iroquois and the Americans and now this seemed a heaven-sent opportunity. Here in the east the Americans would attack sooner or later, and Sheaffe would expect me in the thick of the fighting. But in the west, from what we had heard, the Americans were beaten and demoralised. The British general there seemed to know his business. Going west would give me more room to manoeuvre and, I naively thought, keep me safer too.

"I could take a message to Procter for you," I offered. "General Sheaffe expects me to stay here but if you were to cover for me, I am sure I would be back before the Americans attack." I smiled at him as innocently as I could, but I had no intention of returning until *after* an attack and then only if the Americans had been beaten back.

"Would you, Thomas?" Norton beamed with delight. "That would be most helpful. I can give Sheaffe an excuse if he asks for you, perhaps tell him you are ill. Take Black Eagle with you – he can act as a guide and help introduce you to the western tribes helping General Procter."

So it was that two days later I was heading west, into what I hoped was a military backwater to ride out the critical stage of the war in peace and comfort. If ever a plan was misguided it was that one. Thinking back I am amazed that I somehow managed to keep my precious hide in one piece over the following months. Instead of a safe berth to see out the campaign I found myself facing a series of disasters, massacres and misfortunes, not least a catastrophic battle that I unwittingly started.

Mine was not the only calamitous defeat that season. As it turned out Sheaffe was right about an imminent attack, but very wrong about the target. It came the following month but not near Niagara; the Americans launched a surprise attack on York. They drove Sheaffe

79

and his army out of the town, burned all the public buildings and destroyed the half-built General Brock warship. Later that year they did attack Fort George too, but I was up to my neck in problems of my own by then.

Chapter 8

The journey west was tougher going than I thought it would be, but it would have been even harder without Morag. Black Eagle had been keen to travel with me when I mentioned our mission, but counselled me to leave my horse behind. "The ground will either be frozen or bog most of the way. We would have to carry fodder and there would be little to feed it on when we arrive." He explained that the Americans had lost so many horses that they were using oxen to transport supplies, as those big beasts could forage in the woods where horses could not. "We will bring Morag to help carry supplies," he told me.

So on that first morning of our trip I prepared myself with my buckskin trousers over stout boots. On top of my patched army coat I wore a fur smock and hat to keep me warm. My sword and tomahawk were strapped around my waist; from one shoulder hung a musket and from the other a pouch for ammunition and tobacco with a roll of blanket wrapped in more deerskin. Morag, I was told, would carry everything else. I had imagined Morag to be some kind of hardy pack mule or an ox, so you can imagine my surprise when Black Eagle hove into view down the path from the centre of the village. I don't know about you, but for me the name Morag conjures up some sour-faced old trot from Perthshire with her mouth pursed in permanent disapproval. Imagine that person aged about twenty, dressed in Indian clothes and staggering under a massive bundle tied to her back, and you will have pictured the scene. I had seen her before, of course – she was the only red-haired woman in the village. With her pale skin and permanent scowl, she clearly had plenty of Celtic blood in her.

"Good God, man," I exclaimed. "I thought you were bringing a mule or an ox to carry things, not a woman."

"Morag will be easier to feed," said Black Eagle smiling happily as he bounded ahead of the creature of burden behind him. "And she can cook for us," he added, clearly pleased with his plan.

"But look at her." I pointed to the figure coming towards us, bent forward to balance her load. "She is never going to keep up with all that on her back. We are going to have to share some of it out."

"She would be insulted," objected Black Eagle, appearing puzzled at my concern. "The women are strong; they are used to working in the fields and their backs can carry heavy loads." He spoke of her as though he was a carter talking of a prized beast and for a moment I thought he might show me her teeth. Before I could respond the lady herself spoke up.

"If you fools are going to chatter all day then get off the path," she snarled as she approached. Both Black Eagle and I stepped back to leave her the compacted snow on the trail which was easier to walk on. She stomped silently past and I saw now that among various sacks and bundles tied to her back was a small cast iron cooking pot.

"See? She is a strong woman," pointed out Black Eagle with, I thought, a touch of admiration in his tone.

We marched behind Morag that morning. I thought it was best to let her set the pace and she did not falter once. When we stopped at lunchtime, while Black Eagle and I skirted around the woods in search of game for dinner, she busied herself making a fire. When we came back, empty handed, she had warm water to drink and some kind of maize porridge to eat. She barely spoke a word and the only sign of her irritation was the force with which she splatted the porridge into the wooden bowls. When I asked if she was fit to go further, she gave me a malevolent scowl and silently started to tie her bundles back together.

We set off again in the afternoon with Black Eagle and me now in front. The big Indian was still keen to find something for the pot. We detoured to a lake to look for ducks, but they flew off long before they were in range. Morag pressed on past without us and it was evening when we caught up with her, having followed her trail through the snow and mud. She had set up camp under a half-fallen tree, which provided some relief from the wind. She had then dragged other branches to make a rudimentary shelter. By the time we got there, a fire was once more heating water. She did not hide her disgust when she saw we had failed once again in our hunting and rummaged in her packs for dried meat and more maize. At sunset we put down our blankets under the branches and prepared for the night. Morag chose to

82

lie between us and we huddled together to share some warmth. Close to, I discovered that Morag stank. God knows what she had smeared on herself, but it smelt like rancid bear grease.

I was just going to sleep when I felt a hand reach for me under the blankets. It had to be Morag and for a moment I did not respond. I had not been with a woman since Magda, but any frustration I might have felt was outweighed by a number of factors. Morag seemed a permanently angry woman, which was not an attractive trait. There was also the stench; whatever she had daubed herself with was not French perfume. But most importantly, any carnal relations would involve undoing clothes and it was freezing that night. Finally we were bound to wake Black Eagle and I had begun to suspect that the big warrior had a liking for Morag himself. The last thing I needed when we awoke in the morning was for them both to be scowling at me. I reached down under my blanket and grabbed the intruding wrist before firmly evicting it back out into the cold.

The next morning Black Eagle had his food delivered from a height of three inches, whereas mine was delivered from around three feet with an accompanying growl.

"Have you upset Morag?" asked Black Eagle chuckling.

"Perhaps I snored last night," I replied coolly before catching her eye and adding, "My wife in England often complained about it." I thought knowing I was married might make her feel less rejected and indeed her expression did mellow for a brief second before Black Eagle spoke up again.

"Did that young foreign girl you bedded complain about your snoring too?"

We pressed on for another ten days. My suspicions that Black Eagle had feelings for Morag were confirmed by his enthusiasm in hunting to find meat that would impress her. He must have covered twice the distance I did in his search for prey. He came back with two rabbits and a small turkey over that time to supplement the dried meat and porridge diet. The giddy young fool even carried some of her bundles, although it was hard to gauge from her face if he was making any progress. At the end of the tenth day I decided to give love's young dream a chance and announced that I would go hunting on my own. I gave them a couple of hours, spent them mostly smoking, and then returned. I could tell instantly that something had happened while I was away by the change in their attitude. Morag was stirring the pot looking almost demure while Black Eagle strolled around in front of her like the lord of the manor.

"I have taken the woman," he announced in an overly casual tone that you might use to announce that you had taken a newspaper. I could tell he was pleased with himself, though, and it was probably just as well that he did not see the glowering look of triumph that Morag shot me over his shoulder. I was pretty certain that he'd had very little say in her seduction. That evening we all ate well on some leftover turkey and even my porridge was delivered from a height of just a few inches.

"I think she will make a good wife," said Black Eagle as we walked together the next morning. He was holding the iron cook pot while Morag, carrying the rest of her bundles, walked some hundred yards in front of us.

"If you are sure," I murmured.

"Do you not think so?" he pressed. "She is fit and strong and even though she is not a full Indian, she is pretty."

"Do you not think she is… well… a bit intimidating?" I countered.

"What is this 'intimating'? What does it mean?" When I explained what intimidating meant he roared with laughter at the very idea that a warrior would be frightened or controlled by a woman. He was Black Eagle and he was frightened of no one, he announced. But after a while he lapsed into silence and I could see that I had planted a seed of doubt in his mind.

God knows what he said to her later, but that night my porridge was delivered from such a height that it missed my bowl entirely to land in the snow!

Chapter 9

The journey from Brant's Ford to Amherstburg was some one hundred and eighty miles and at that time of year it took two weeks. The town was on the north-western shore of Lake Erie, just a short distance from Detroit across the river of the same name. We arrived in the middle of April and the place was a hive of activity. Despite the continuing cold wet weather, there was an air of excitement around the place and one word was on everyone's lips: Tecumseh.

I had heard the name before and knew he was a chief of the Shawnee tribe. The Iroquois had barely mentioned him, but I swiftly discovered that among the western tribes he seemed to be treated as some kind of living god. However, what really astonished me was that the whites seemed in awe of him too. When we arrived in the town Black Eagle had sought out some Indian friends, while I decided to spend time with my own kind in one of the taverns. There was an air of celebration about the place as news had just come in about Napoleon's retreat from Moscow. It seemed at last as though the war in Europe was turning against the French and that meant that more men and resources might find their way to Canada.

"But they will probably arrive too late," I was told by one grizzled old Canadian militia man. "Tecumseh is coming and most of the American army has gone home."

"What do you mean gone home?" I asked.

"The Americans had four thousand men building a stronghold called Fort Meigs, which was to launch their invasion of Canada. But nearly all of the men were militia and once their term of enlistment ended they all went home and left the place abandoned. Their General Harrison is searching for more men but he won't get many, not in spring time."

"Why not?" I pressed.

The man looked at me in bewilderment for a moment and then laughed. "You surely are not a farmer, are you, son. It will soon be time to sow our crops. That is why we are pleased Tecumseh is coming. That wily old Indian will wrap things up double quick so that we can get back to our land."

"He is a good fighter, then?"

"Hell yes, why when the Americans invaded last year he cut their supply line with just fifty men and kept it cut against hundreds of men sent to clear the route. Captured all the mail too so that we could see just how a-feared their general was about being overrun by Indians." The old man chuckled. "When we came up on Detroit, Tecumseh had his men pass at least three times through a gap in the trees to convince the Yankees that he had nearly two thousand Indians instead of just over five hundred. The American general soon surrendered after that."

"Five hundred is a good number of warriors," I reflected thinking back to what the Iroquois had done with just eighty.

"He is bringing a thousand this time," crowed the old veteran. "They want revenge against this General Harrison who has been fighting them in America."

I left the tavern feeling quite confident that I had done the right thing in coming west. The British had five hundred regular troops and another five hundred militia. With a further thousand Indians, I thought, that should be more than enough to beat whatever force this General Harrison would be able to scratch together.

After a night at the inn I set off the next morning to General Procter's headquarters, a large house overlooking the lake. I still had the now faded letter of introduction from the governor general that I had given Brock and I passed this to Procter's aide while I waited for Procter to see me. In a few moments the general himself emerged from one of the side rooms.

"Captain Flashman, you are most welcome, sir. I am surprised but delighted that the governor general has sent me such an experienced officer. I need as many such men as I can get."

"My compliments to you, sir," I replied, saluting. "From what I hear in town, General, your command seems very confident of victory in the coming campaign."

Instead of sharing the ebullient confidence of his men, Procter seemed to sag a little at what I had intended as a compliment to his leadership. "Not all of my command appreciates the strategic realities, Captain," he replied wearily. "Now, do you have despatches for me from the governor general?"

"I regret, sir, that I do not come from the governor; I am here on behalf of John Norton, to tell you that he will not be able to support you as he would have wished. He has been ordered to reinforce the men of General Sheaffe instead."

Procter did not hide his disappointment. "Come in, sir, take a seat at the table," he said gesturing to some furniture at the end of a long room. "I probably should have known better than to expect any reinforcement from the east." He busied himself pouring us each a glass of madeira before he sat down heavily beside me. "They expect me to perform miracles with a few hundred soldiers and the Indians."

"But surely a few Iroquois won't make that much difference when you have Tecumseh and his thousand warriors?"

Procter's initial response was a heavy sigh. "It is not the Iroquois I wanted," he admitted at last, "but Norton."

"I don't understand, sir," I replied. "From what I hear Tecumseh commands huge respect from all who have fought with him and he is a skilled war leader. Why would you need Norton as well?"

"Because Norton is half British, he knows about our ways. See here." With that he pulled across the map on the table showing Lake Erie and the surrounding territory. "At the moment our ships control the lake, but there," his finger stabbed down on a small bay on the Pennsylvania shore of the lake, "the Americans are building a new fleet of their own. It will challenge us for supremacy and if they win they can land troops behind us and cut our main lines of supply."

"Are we building new ships as well?"

"Yes, there is one new ship on the blocks here. It is half built and will not be ready until the summer. But it is the skilled sailors I need. What counts as our navy on this lake are known as the Provincial Marine; they can cross the lake but are barely equipped to fight on it. One of the captains I have just stood down was eighty-seven."

"So should you not try to destroy their fleet before it can put to sea?"

"Precisely, now the ice on the lake is clearing we could sail a force there to do just that. But the Americans expect me to do it and I would need every man I can get, including the Indians, to guarantee success."

"But Tecumseh does not agree?" I guessed.

"No, he is determined that we should attack the Americans at Fort Meigs. He wants to destroy it before the Americans can gather there in strength. He does not understand about naval warfare. That is why I wanted Norton to help explain that burning the American fleet should be the first priority."

"Is there no way he can be persuaded?"

"No, his brother is some kind of prophet for his people and Tecumseh has been working towards his vision for a confederacy of Indian nations. Some warriors treat him as an ambassador of their Great Spirit; when he toured south a few years ago a comet was seen in the sky and then last winter there were earthquakes. Many seemed to think that these events were linked to him. He has been influencing tribes as far south as Florida and is only interested in building and defending his Indian territory. Defeating Harrison is part of that dream; keeping naval superiority on Lake Erie isn't."

We talked some more and Procter appeared quite lonely in command. He only had one aide outside and judging from the mood in the town, he had clearly not shared his concerns with his officers. He seemed nervous of Tecumseh and resentful that the Indian's intransigence was effectively determining British strategy. As I stood to leave Procter ran his eye down my attire. I still had on my deerskin trousers. Most of the garrison seemed to be wearing a varied mixture of garments, but I was wearing my patched army coat to show my rank. "Be careful if you fight among the Indians Flashman, that red coat won't protect you. The Americans are in a murderous mood after that unfortunate incident at the River Raisin."

"Yes, General Sheaffe told me that they would kill any white man found fighting with the Indians."

"Hmph," grunted Procter, before adding, "they would probably hang me as well if they catch us."

"Henry," called a woman's voice sharply from the other end of the room. "Not in front of Lavinia!" I had assumed that we were alone but when I looked around to the other end of the room, I saw a middle-aged woman glaring sternly around a high-backed chair on one side of the fire and a wide-eyed girl peering around another.

"Sorry m'dear," grunted Procter before turning to me. "Perhaps Tecumseh is right. If we drive the Americans from Fort Meigs, they will not have men left to land behind our lines."

I left Procter's presence feeling a lot more sanguine about my prospects. In the east the British were deciding strategy and the Indians were supporting them but in the west the situation was almost reversed. The British did not have the numbers to fight on their own and so they were reliant on their Indian allies, who ultimately were working towards their own goals.

With the benefit of hindsight it is easy to be dismissive about Tecumseh's plans for an Indian confederation stretching from Canada to the Gulf of Mexico. But back then the idea did not seem so absurd. Just twenty years previously an Indian chief called Little Turtle had annihilated an American force of a thousand men. Now there were a similar number of Indians ready to go to war to achieve it, and if success looked likely, then I did not doubt that thousands more would find the courage to join them.

I had expected Black Eagle to be supportive of Tecumseh's plans, but to my surprise he was scornful of the idea. "You will never get that many tribes agreeing for long," he told me. "Most have been at war with each other for much longer than they have been fighting the whites."

"But the Iroquois have formed a long-lasting confederation," I pointed out. "If the Six Nations can stay together, then why not other tribes?"

"The Six Nations are not really together, at least not now. Some of us fight for the British but those living in America are keeping out of the war and some would even be willing to fight for the Americans if they were needed." He grinned and reached across to tug gently on my hair. "But one thing will always bring us together: taking white scalps!"

Over the next couple of days I saw Procter several times walking about the town, either on his own or with his wife. Apart from the occasional salute from the regular soldiers, he moved almost anonymously around the settlement. Things were rather different for his co-commander. On the third day word spread around the community like wildfire that Tecumseh was coming. His canoes had crossed the Detroit River and with a bodyguard of eighty warriors he was on his way. Within a very short while every man, woman and child of all races and creeds were gathered in the centre of town and craning their gaze towards its western end. The only person missing was Procter, who stayed aloof in his headquarters. I will admit to being more than a mite curious about this famous chief myself. When his cavalcade went riding past I was among those hanging out of an upstairs window at the inn.

I saw a portrait of Tecumseh once; in it he was wearing a British army coat, but he wasn't wearing it that day. Given what I know of him, I doubt he ever wore one as he never saw himself as a British soldier. When I first clapped eyes on him he was wearing deerskin leggings and a printed calico shirt. There was a bandana around his long hair and a small silver ornament was suspended from the skin between his nostrils. I had expected this chief, whom everyone described in almost divine terms, to be severe and forbidding, but instead he was smiling and pointing out people in the crowd. If anything he seemed amused at the scale of his welcome, especially from the white militia. As he dismounted in front of Procter's headquarters, some of the Indians set up a whooping and started brandishing their tomahawks. The militia nearby started to shrink back, gazing nervously over their shoulders. But Tecumseh just grinned again and shouted something in their language to quieten the warriors down. He certainly exuded a calm confidence and I began to understand why so many would put their faith in him. As he strolled up the steps into Procter's home, taking the salute of the sentries, he did not look the slightest bit overawed. A man with a white beard greeted the chief on Procter's porch. This I learned was Elliot from the Indian Agency, who acted as interpreter as Tecumseh spoke little English. Then the pair of them walked calmly inside to finalise the campaign plan with the British general.

The next morning there was no surprise when it was announced that the army would be embarking to attack Fort Meigs. The fort was some distance up the Maumee River, which flowed into the south-western corner of Lake Erie. The British force embarked on all the available shipping on the 23rd of April as Tecumseh led his Indians around the western end of the lake. If you have not seen it then the term 'lake' might be misleading for Lake Erie is little short of an inland sea. In the middle you cannot see any of the surrounding land and it is known for its stormy weather.

I had no horse and no wish to tramp around the lake with the Indians. So Black Eagle and I got a passage on what was then the fleet's flagship, the *Queen Charlotte*. The ship was loaded with men and supplies. Most of the crew were young boys and old men and at least fifty soldiers were detailed to help them. It took for ever to get underway as the soldiers milled around with ropes, unsure what they were doing. Compared to my time sailing with Cochrane in the Mediterranean, the level of incompetence was almost laughable. At one point I heard an exasperated bosun shouting at a line of soldiers to "pull the rope towards the pointed end of the ship," after they had failed to distinguish between the bow and the stern.

One person who thoroughly enjoyed the trip was Black Eagle. He had never been on what he called 'a white man's big canoe' before and laughed with delight as the patched sails finally started to pull us through the water. As he saw the men moving about the rigging above his head he wanted to go aloft too. I took him up the shrouds to the maintop, thinking that he would be clutching the mainmast when we got there and nervously peering over the edge – as I had when I first went aloft. Instead the man seemed to have no fear of heights at all. In the end one of the few able seamen on board took him far higher than I wanted to go, virtually to the masthead. He came down gabbling in delight at the experience, lapsing into Iroquoian when he ran out of English superlatives.

By the time we dropped anchor at the mouth of the River Maumee, Black Eagle was quite the Jack Tar, edging out on the yards and helping to reef in the sails. The *Queen Charlotte* had too deep a draught to go far up river and so the supplies and guns were winched down onto some of the smaller gunboats and transports to be sailed and kedged upstream. It was tough work, but not nearly as difficult as dragging the heavy guns over the wet muddy tracks. The fort was some twenty miles upriver but eventually we were able to land the guns just before the boats were exposed to bombardment by artillery in the fort. We had two twenty-four-pounder guns taken from Detroit, a mortar, a howitzer and three twelve-pounders; not a huge arsenal, but more than enough to deal with a half-built wooden fort. The first of the Indians started to catch up with us over those final miles as teams of oxen and lines of men struggled to move the guns forward. Then I heard a cry that the fort was in view and Black Eagle and I pushed on to get a first glimpse of Fort Meigs.

As I scanned it through the telescope my hopes soared. The fort was on a plateau on the south-eastern bank overlooking a bend in the river. A gully protected it on one side and while the river looked wide and shallow – there were several islands mid-stream – it was deep enough to slow any attack. It was a strong position but the escarpment on the opposite bank was taller. Once we had our guns mounted on the heights near the walls we would easily be able to bombard the fort. I had been dreading a long drawn out siege, but I smiled in delight as I watched a swarm of men moving like ants around what seemed quite low walls. It was clear that the fort was not yet finished. Men were dragging barrel loads of soft river mud up the slopes, evidently in a hurry to complete their work before the British and Indian forces started to surround them. I wondered if the stumpy walls were completed all the way around the rows of tents and other buildings I could just make out inside the fort. If not, I thought the siege of Fort Meigs was only likely to last a day or two. Even if the walls were complete, our guns should make short work of them.

Chapter 10

The history books will tell you that the battle for Fort Meigs was won by the American General Harrison. There are seven hundred men from Kentucky who would probably question if it was won at all, but for my money the battle was won by the engineer that Harrison left in charge of the fort while he went recruiting for a new army. His name, I later discovered, was Eleazer Wood and like most engineers he was a cunning bastard. I realised this the next day when I stood on the escarpment across the river and immediately opposite the fort. Now I could see that the walls were completed all the way around the stronghold and that they were not as short as I had first thought. Wood had guessed that we would place our batteries near where I was standing and had built a long embankment of mud just in front of the walls to protect the fortification. It was a bit like a stone glacis, built in front of stone forts to deflect cannon balls. If the mud had been dry and brittle it would have been an insignificant obstacle, but the mud was wet, indeed it was raining as I stood there that morning. The bank would be impossible to destroy with gunfire. At least we could fire over the walls into the fort, I thought. There was a tall row of tents near the wall and probably many more beyond that.

Over the next few days the British dug out gun batteries, most on the escarpment where I had stood, but also one on the southern bank. Some twelve hundred Indians had arrived now and they roamed around the fort to ensure that no one got in or out. The Americans had a number of guns of their own and did their best to disrupt our preparations, but on the 1st of May we opened the bombardment.

By the end of that day all we had achieved was to make the bank in front of the fort resemble a giant steamed pudding, with dozens of cannon balls stuck like currants in the mud. To make matters worse as our cannon opened fire the Americans pulled what we had thought was the canvas of tents away to reveal huge embankments within the fort that further protected those inside. Just before sunset Tecumseh and Procter stood on the embankment surveying the complete lack of progress made. To add insult to injury, as the light began to fail several

Americans could be seen scampering along the bank and digging out the British cannon balls, presumably to fire back to us the next day.

Procter gazed disconsolately at the scene but Tecumseh was shouting and raging at Elliot, his interpreter. I drifted over to eavesdrop on the conversation. The Indian seemed to be complaining that the Americans were fighting like groundhogs, burrowing in the mud instead of fighting in the open like men.

"I have invited them to surrender," Procter was telling the tall chief beside him. "I have even warned that I cannot guarantee their safety as prisoners if the fort is stormed by your warriors, but they have refused to consider our demand." Tecumseh growled something in his language and while Procter looked up expectantly, Elliot just shrugged, tactfully deciding that translation would not be helpful. Procter pressed on. "Our gunners will get better and tomorrow we will have a furnace heating shot. They probably have around a thousand men in there and they did not have time to stock up on supplies. We will starve them out if we have to."

The next few days were a miserable existence – cold and wet with soldiers, militia and Indians spending most of their time languishing in rudimentary shelters. The furnace took forever to heat round shot to a glowing red and invariably this just proved a very labour-intensive method of drying out a small patch of mud on one of the embankments. We out-numbered the defenders by two to one, but that was not a lot of use when they would not come out and we appeared unable to get inside their defences. Hopes of a quick victory were well and truly dashed and everyone seemed resigned to a long drawn out stalemate. Then on the sixth day everything changed.

It started like any other; I awoke in the British camp on the northern shore as the sun crept over the horizon. I was cold, my clothes were damp and my limbs stiff as I crawled out of my shelter and staggered to my feet. My hovel was at the edge of the British encampment where it joined a swathe of shelters built by the Indians. Until the previous night I had shared my bijou residence with Black Eagle, but the day before Morag had arrived, having travelled overland with many of the women who followed their men on the warpath. I buckled on my sword, tucked the tomahawk into my belt and grabbed my musket and ammunition pouch. Finally I picked up the round river stone wrapped in a patch of leather from under the collection of chopped branches and foliage that made up the roof I slept under. Then I ambled over to a much sturdier shelter that Morag had thrown up on her first day in the camp. A big moccasin-covered foot protruded from the entrance.

"Are you coming?" I asked stretching my stiff muscles. "I am cold and want to get warm."

There was a brief whispered argument inside and the rustling of some clothes being pulled on. "I am coming, Little Father," called Black Eagle as he started to emerge from the doorway. Once outside he stood up and stretched before grinning at me. "It was lovely and warm in my hut."

Morag crawled out behind him with a bundle in her hands. As she stood she glanced across at my shelter and shook her head in disgust. She had been scathingly critical when she had first seen it and the flimsy structure clearly had not grown on her. "A drunk, toothless beaver could build something stronger," she sneered.

"It is not that bad," I offered defensively. Black Eagle and I had spent half a day building it.

She thrust a small bundle to Black Eagle and to my surprise handed another similar bundle to me. "Dried meat and wheat cakes," she announced and then she turned to me with a hand on her hip. "So do you want me to build you a shelter or not?"

I glanced at her shelter and then at mine. Hers looked like it could keep out the wind and the rain whereas I knew from experience that mine did neither well and part of the roof had collapsed the previous night. "Well if it is not too much trouble, it probably could do with some improvement," I suggested brightly while Black Eagle sniggered behind me. The big warrior and I turned for the escarpment up to the guns. We had barely gone a dozen paces when I heard a crash of poles and sticks and looked around to see my shelter had already been demolished.

Black Eagle chuckled. "I told you she is a good woman. She will build you a fine shelter." He gestured at the wrapped stone under my arm "Are we going to the gunners' oven?"

The foundry that the gunners had made to heat shot had many other uses. While it appeared useless at bringing down the walls of the fort, towards the end of the day dozens of large round stones taken from the river bed were heated inside it. These were then wrapped in leather or blankets to keep people warm at night. "Yes," I replied, "and we may even be able to warm through the cakes too." A short while later and we were sitting with a group of gunners on some logs by the guns, hot stones on our laps and under our feet while we munched away on the breakfast Morag had provided.

"They are quiet this morning," observed the artillery sergeant sitting with us. "They have normally sent a few balls over by now." It was still early; there were only a hundred or so men on the cliff top and most of those were wearing the blue coats of the artillery. A handful of others wore red coats like mine and apart from some warriors setting off to hunt in the nearby woods, Black Eagle was the only Indian present.

"Hello, where has that boat come from?" said the sergeant, pointing. There was a cutter with at least twenty men on board and it was approaching the far shore of the river from the south.

I pulled my telescope from my pocket to study it. "It looks like some American reinforcements trying to reach the fort, but they will never get through. That far bank is swarming with our men." I was just about to put the glass down when the edge of the lens caught a glimpse of two more boats coming around the bend in the river. "There are more of them…" I started but I got no further, for at that moment every single gun in the fort crashed out and half a dozen cannon balls came whirring in our direction. We threw ourselves to the ground but most passed harmlessly overhead; one clipped the edge of the escarpment showering us with mud before bouncing away. There were trumpets sounding now and staring across the river I saw that some of the garrison were sallying from the fort to meet up with the reinforcements. I realised the Americans must have got some messages

96

out to plan this, for they had caught us completely by surprise. The gunners were shouting and rushing to their pieces to open fire on these new targets while Black Eagle and I hastily got out of the way. Thank God the action is all happening on the other side of the river, I thought, but no sooner was the notion in my head than the Indian hunting party came running and yelling out of the forest on the other side of the clearing.

The hunters were pointing at the south and shouting about canoes. When I looked in that direction I saw the first men climbing over the lip of the escarpment on this side of the river. At first there were just a dozen men but within seconds at least a hundred men could be seen sliding over the edge of the plateau and for all we knew they could be hundreds more behind them.

"Get that gun round, load with canister!" the officer in charge of the battery was shouting as his men threw themselves at the gun nearest the southern edge of the escarpment. I did not hang around to watch; the gunners did not need our help and while I did not realise it, the outcome of the battle depended on my next decision.

I looked back the way we had come. It had taken us over ten minutes to walk from the British camp and it would be several minutes of hard running to get back. The Americans were already starting to charge towards us and might overhaul us. They could certainly get within musket range and I did not want a well-aimed rifle bullet in the back. There were no places to hide between where we stood and the camp and, for all we knew, the Americans could be sending more men in boats to attack there as well. The alternative was to head inland for the trees. They were closer, would give us cover and as I remembered Smoke Johnson telling me, only an idiot would follow Indians into a forest. "Come on," I shouted to Black Eagle, gesturing towards the trees. "That way."

We grabbed our weapons and broke into a run, the gunners and the river behind us, the distant British camp to our right and the Americans pouring onto the plain to our left. In front I could see the Indian hunting party retreating back into the trees. After running just a few yards my tall companion was pulling ahead and I was sprinting flat out to try and keep up. The tranquillity of just a few moments ago was shattered: musket volleys were crackling on the other side of the river and cannon were now firing from the fort and the British battery, while on both river banks trumpets signalling alarm or advance were sounding in all directions. I looked over my shoulder and saw that most of the Americans were charging our guns but a score of men had seen us and were running in our direction to cut us off. Some were pointing and they were shouting something, but I could not make it out above the sound of me gasping for air as I ran.

It was close but I thought we would make the shelter of the trees before the Americans. But then I heard a crackle of fire and several musket balls whizzed over my head. Foolishly I looked over my shoulder again and the next moment my foot had caught in a hole and I was tumbling to the ground. I was stunned for a moment, but then Black Eagle was back at my side and pulling me up.

"Come on, Little Father," he urged. "A few more yards and we will be in the trees."

It was then I heard what the Americans were shouting. There had been a whoop of triumph when I had gone down and I remember hearing someone shout, "I got that Indian officer," then another voice yelling out, "Remember the Raisin." I was staggering to my feet again now and recalled with a chill what fate would befall any British officer found fighting with the Indians.

It is amazing what the fear of death will do to your stamina. I was getting a second wind and in a moment I was up and running again. The Americans were now close on our heels and I realised with despair that even if we made the trees we would not have time to find cover. I forced myself over the last few yards searching for the thickest patch of undergrowth and then the trees in front of me exploded into life. The bushes were suddenly covered in musket smoke as a volley of shots was fired at our pursuers while the air was rent with the war cries of countless warriors. I realised that it was the hunting party who had come back to give us covering fire. There were no more than a dozen of them but they made enough noise for twice that number.

We were close enough to the Americans to hear the wet smack sounds as bullets hit flesh followed by yells and the clatter of equipment as men either fell or threw themselves to the ground. As I reached the first tree I risked another look back. Our pursuers were all prone in the dirt. Some looked dead or wounded but others were aiming into the trees unsure how many enemy they faced. Gazing beyond them I could see that our gunners had already abandoned their weapons; some were surrendering and others running back to the British camp, the slower ones set to be overhauled by a crowd of Americans in pursuit. There must have been well over five hundred Americans on the plateau then, maybe a thousand. They were all militia, judging from their dress, and now they were spreading out hunting for more enemies. Many had heard shots coming from the trees and started to move in our direction. Further away I could see that the fort's guns were firing to the south, to protect those of its garrison that must have met up with the new arrivals. There was no return gunfire from the British battery and I guessed that this too must have been captured.

It took just the briefest second to take this in but in that moment a ball from one of the prone militia slammed into the tree trunk I was standing behind.

"There is a British officer with them Injuns," shouted one of the militia, while another of his comrades bawled at the men rushing towards them. "Come on, we got them on the run, remember the Raisin!" I was already darting away again before all the words were out of his mouth. The hunting party were scampering back deeper into the forest now, still making their awful war cries while Black Eagle ran with me.

"Stop behind this bush and leave your red coat," he gasped after we had run fifty yards into the trees. "You are too easy to see in that." I did not hesitate to do as he suggested. He held my gun and ammunition while I tore the garment off. I was going to throw it into a bush but Black Eagle took it off me and wrapped it around a tree stump. Gazing down, my white shirt seemed similarly striking against the green foliage, so I pulled that off over my head as well.

As I took my gun back I glanced over the warrior's shoulder. Through a gap in the trees hundreds of the militia were running across the plateau towards us. We were off again in a moment. While my mind was almost numb with fear and panic, I had just enough thought to realise that without the coat and shirt I looked much like any of the other Indians. I thanked my stars for my Spanish blood, giving me dark hair and an olive complexion. But while I might look like an Indian, I could not melt into the forest like one; when I looked to my left the hunting party seemed to have disappeared.

"Where are they?" I gasped pointing to where I had expected them to be.

"They are drawing the Americans into the trees," Black Eagle replied calmly, seeming barely out of breath. "Come on, Little Father, we will make a stand by that split tree."

For a moment I thought I had misheard. "Draw them into the trees?" I exclaimed. "But there are hundreds of them and only a dozen of us."

"Then it will be a famous victory, Little Father." Black Eagle chuckled at my dismay before adding, "You are forgetting about the hundreds of warriors in the British camp. If we can draw the Americans deep into the forest then our brothers can trap and kill them." My mind was struggling to keep up. Five minutes earlier I had been sitting warming my feet and enjoying breakfast without a care in the world; since then our siege had been blown apart. We had lost all our artillery and were reeling from multiple assaults. Now this great big oaf was suggesting that we could still snatch triumph from the jaws of defeat.

We reached the split tree and Black Eagle stopped running, turned and levelled his musket against a splinter of wood in the trunk to keep it steady. As he did so there was a distant sound of breaking twigs and undergrowth as the bulk of the militia charged into the forest behind us. Compared to the silent hunting party, it sounded like a herd of elephants entering the trees and there was certainly no attempt at stealth. Men were yelling at each other to spread out, others were shouting for men to stay in lines while some were asking how many

Indians there were and which way we had gone. Several shots were fired and one man was yelling to cease fire as someone had nearly shot him. At first they nervously edged into the trees but then there was a shot from our right, followed immediately by a war whoop, which almost drowned out the scream of pain from the person hit. There was a fusillade of fire in return, a long stuttering volley that lasted nearly a minute. It snapped branches and sent leaves falling from the canopy overhead but I caught a fleeting glimpse of two Indians pulling back on our right, unhurt.

The militia were angry now and were edging forward through the trees. There was another shot and war whoop further down the tree line, but now I could hear clearly the voices of the men coming towards us.

"I am going to kill one of those sons of bitches and scalp him," snarled one. "Let's see how they like a taste of their own medicine."

The hair on the back of my neck started to prickle. "Should we not be moving back?" I whispered to Black Eagle, but he just slowly shook his head without taking his eyes of the trees in front of us.

"I seen one!" called out a voice and a shot cracked out. Instinctively I ducked but no ball thudded into the tree or the ground around us. There was another burst of fire immediately to our front as at least twenty soldiers let fly with their guns and men rushed through the forest.

"God damn, it is just his coat," yelled a voice in disgust.

"I reckon we have frightened them off," said another man as he pushed his way through a bush. It was the last thing he ever said as Black Eagle's gun fired. I had the briefest glimpse of the militia man sinking down to his knees before I was off and running again. With Black Eagle's war whoop ringing in my ears, we bounded over fallen logs and ducked around bushes. Several shots were fired after us but many of our pursuers had not reloaded and those that did fire seemed to do so blindly. I ran as silently as I could on the balls of my feet but still I made some noise, although this was probably drowned out by the men charging behind. Suddenly there were two more of the hunting party in front of us, they grinned as we ran past. They both had muskets levelled to ambush those following in our wake. A hundred yards further on and we heard the two hunters shoot and a fusillade of return fire from the militia. Black Eagle stopped again behind a half-fallen tree with a solid trunk to protect us. I took up a position to fire but the big warrior took the gun out of my hand.

"I have seen you shoot," he said with a grin. "We cannot afford to miss. Here, reload my gun, we should not have long to wait now.

"What do you mean?" I asked taking the gun from him. "What are we waiting for?"

"Listen," he said simply. At first all I could hear was the militia crashing about in the trees, but then I understood. It was as though a distant pack of wolves were charging into the forest, a growing chorus of howls and shrieks that chilled your blood.

Chapter 11

It was not hard to imagine the horror in the trees we had run through. I leaned against a stump to catch my breath while I reloaded the gun. I could hear the awful howling getting louder and then the sound of gunfire as the Indians came up on their enemy. Single, carefully aimed shots were met with crashing volleys from the militia. I suspected that most of the American fire smashed through little more than foliage as the warriors melted away after taking their shots. I could hear men shouting to fall back and then the terrible screams of the wounded left behind.

"We should go," said Black Eagle gesturing towards the fray while taking back his loaded gun and passing me mine.

"But no scalps," I warned. "I gave you your hair back; you are not to take anyone else's."

"No scalps," agreed the big man grinning. "But now you are fighting among us you should look more like a warrior. The Shawnee shoot quickly and do not look carefully like the Iroquois." He casually looked me up and down. My skin was pale compared to his and he was a good number of inches taller and broader around the chest. "Stand still," he commanded and then he reached into his ammunition pouch and pulled out a hollowed piece of horn. Dipping his finger in it, he drew two horizontal lines on my cheeks and then did the same on his own. The red war paint smelled quite pleasant but he was not finished yet. Next he pulled out a strip of cloth and tied that around my head. Then he reached into his pouch and pulled out a feather. I recognised it; this was one he had worn in his own hair before I had cut it off. He tucked it into the strip of cloth. "Now you are ready," he announced.

The noise of battle continued in front of us and I was in no hurry to stumble across some trigger-happy Shawnee or cornered militia man. We stalked forward slowly and silently, listening as the sound of combat ebbed and flowed ahead of us. Black Eagle wanted to go faster but I made him go at my pace. I was happy for the battle to pass us by, but after a minute of silent stalking, something crashing through the undergrowth indicated that it was coming to find us.

103

They had to be militia making that noise and my suspicions were confirmed when I heard one call, "This way, Jeb." Black Eagle and I both knelt behind a large fallen tree with our muskets levelled to cover their approach. We were on one side of a small clearing, perhaps ten yards across to give us a clear field of fire. They were getting closer; I could hear them scrabbling desperately up a short bank that we had climbed earlier. Then there was an Indian war whoop close by.

"Oh Jesus," one of the men gasped and I realised that other Indians must be pursuing them through the trees. They half fell into the clearing. One was young, perhaps only twenty, and he had stumbled on a root as he had pushed through the last bush. The older one, in his forties, was reaching across to help him stay on his feet when I called out.

"Keep still!" I shouted. The older man's head whirled round to look at us, while the boy wailed in despair and slumped to the ground. "Drop your weapons, you are our prisoners."

The older man let the musket fall from his fingers, but his chin came up and he glared at me defiantly. "Kill me if you must," he growled, "but spare the boy… No, get off me." His speech was interrupted by Black Eagle, who had run forward with piece of cord. He pushed the older militia man to the ground and with a knee in the man's back was roughly tying his hands together. Then as he sprang across to the boy with the other end of the rope, two more Indians burst out of the bushes. The two warriors looked down at the scene before them and shouted angrily at Black Eagle. Having roughly tied the boy's hands he stood and shouted back to them in Iroquoian. Whatever he said did not find favour with the warriors and one of them hefted a vicious balled club with an iron spike through the business end. They had not noticed me and looked up in surprise when I cocked my musket and pointed it at the man holding the club. I stepped into the clearing still pointing the gun at the new arrivals.

"What is happening?" I asked Black Eagle

"They are angry we have claimed the prisoners that they were chasing," the warrior said calmly while reaching down for his own gun. There was a sudden burst of new war cries and whooping to my

104

right some distance off through the trees. I quickly glanced across but could not see anything. Black Eagle spoke once again to the other Indians in their language, pointing where this sound was coming from. After a sour glance at me, without another word, they both turned and ran off in that direction "They are going to try to capture some prisoners of their own," the big warrior explained.

I looked down on our captives. The older man had been pulled round onto his back as Black Eagle had hauled on his cord to tie up the younger one. "What are you going to do to us?" The older man asked hesitantly, as though he was not sure he wanted to know the answer to his question.

"We are taking you prisoner," I told him. "We are not killing and scalping either of you. So if you have any sense you will not try to run off – there are many in this wood who would not be as generous." The man sagged in relief and shut his eyes, I guessed in a silent prayer. I turned to Black Eagle, "You were a bit quick tying them up."

"This is a matunip line," he explained holding up one end of the chord, which I now saw was decorated with tassels on its end and markings along its length. "It marks ownership of the prisoners. If they were untied, the other warriors could have claimed them."

"Well tie them up properly and let's get out of here," I muttered softly as a hideous shriek to our right indicated that another militia man had not been as fortunate in his captivity.

A minute later and both men were retied. They were connected together by the cord but this time their hands were tied in front of them. There was enough of the thin rope for them to walk easily side by side and having picked up their weapons we gestured for them to start back to the clearing. They went quietly enough, although I heard the older man murmur some encouragement to the younger fellow, who looked terrified. His nerves could not have been eased over the next few minutes as we found four militia corpses as we made our way through the forest. All had been scalped and one had been smashed beyond recognition with a club. Even though they had been trying to kill me, indeed their pursuit of me into the trees might have been their downfall, I could not help but feel sorry for them. The Indians moved like murderous phantoms through the trees and I guessed that most of these men barely got a glimpse of their attacker before they were killed.

We found my coat still on its tree stump where we had left it. When I lifted it up there must have been twenty bullet holes in it and the back had been slashed by a knife.

"They have some vicious moths in these trees," I muttered putting the tattered remains of the scarlet cloth back on the tree.

"You're that Indian officer," gasped the younger militia man as realisation finally dawned.

The older man hawked and spat to show his disgust. "I bet you must be right proud of how your men are fightin'," he snarled.

"I am a British officer," I told him. "I am with my Iroquoian friend here but I have no control over the tribes." My announcement was interrupted by another piercing shriek from further in the woods, causing the younger man to shudder in horror. "Right now," I admitted, "I doubt anyone can control them."

"We heard Tecumseh was with them," said the older man truculently.

"Not with these men," I gestured into the woods. "Tecumseh was camping on the other side of the river."

There was one more horror before we got back onto the open ground of the plateau. It was as we were walking out of the woods that we heard it, a hoarse voice calling for water. When I looked, I could see the legs of the man speaking protruding from under some ferns. The limbs were trembling and I guessed that the man was badly wounded. The two militia men stepped forward to see if it was someone they knew. The older man pulled back a branch and a second later the younger one was on his knees retching up his breakfast. With a sense of trepidation I looked over the militia man's shoulder. The poor devil on the ground was covered in blood. He had been shot in the stomach, had what looked like a tomahawk wound above his right ear and had then been scalped... but he was still alive.

"It is all right, friend, we are here for you," soothed the older militia man getting down on his knees beside his wounded comrade.

The injured man turned his face to the voice, it was a mask of blood. "I can't see you," he croaked. "I am hurt right bad." As he spoke Black Eagle knelt down behind the man and pulled out his knife. He looked at the older militia man and cocked his head enquiringly.

The older militia man nodded his head and then with his voice breaking slightly spoke again to the man lying in front of him. "The pain will stop in a minute, friend." With that Black Eagle leaned forward and with a swift cut severed the blood vessel in the man's neck. There was not as much blood as I expected – much of it must have seeped out already. But the trembling in the wounded man's legs slowly stopped and then, with a deep sigh, he died.

I guess I have seen more death than most, but in the heat of battle you are too busy trying to save your own skin to worry about the recently departed. This was different; at that brief moment there seemed to be an eerie stillness in the forest and we all stared at the man for a moment. Whatever your race, creed or politics, the sight of life leaving another human being in such circumstances is always a sobering affair. It is especially the case when you know that you could have been in the dead man's shoes just a few minutes before. We paused to let the older militia man mutter a short prayer and then I led my little party back across the open plateau.

Chapter 12

Our side of the river was now firmly back under our control. The far side of the plateau was swarming with British regular troops and our militia. Many of them were guarding prisoners who they had taken when they recaptured our guns. The noise of battle across the river had now also diminished with just a sporadic crackle of fire. With nothing better to do we walked back to where we had started the battle, by the guns. I even wondered if my unfinished breakfast was where I had left it; now the danger was past I was feeling decidedly hungry.

"By Christ, I was not expecting to see you two again."

"It is good to see you too, Sergeant," I replied to the grinning artilleryman as he stepped out from behind the furnace with a steaming pewter mug in his hand.

"We were captured for all of five minutes," the man grinned. "Most of them had gone charging off after you and those Indians. There were hardly any left here when our boys came on up over the lip of the hill. Would you like a cup of tea, sir? Here have this one."

I took the cup gratefully and eased myself down on my old log seat. Black Eagle sat beside me while the prisoners slumped down at our feet. The sergeant disappeared again but was back a moment later with more cups of tea for Black Eagle and the prisoners.

"There," he announced to the prisoners, "that should make things better," as though tea was the cure for all misadventures.

"Why did so many follow us into the trees?" I asked the sergeant.

"You would be better off asking 'im, sir," replied the sergeant gesturing to the prisoner at my feet. But the militia man showed no sign of wanting to answer the question and so the sergeant continued. "All I know is that the man who seemed to be in command was yelling for them to come back, but when the Indians came over the hill he was forced to go in after them to avoid being separated from most of his men."

"We were supposed to spike the guns and then cross over to the fort," said the older militia man dully. "It was some of our men that were massacred at the Raisin; our boys saw you and the other Indians and thought they could get you."

"Spike our guns!" exclaimed the sergeant. He turned to me "Do you know, sir, they tried to do it with ramrods rather than proper spikes." He shook his head in dismay, clearly offended by this lack of professionalism in the act of sabotage. "It won't take us a moment to get those out." Perfectly on cue to prove his point, the first British cannon fired to send a ball across the river.

"What has happened over there?" I asked gesturing to where the shot must have landed.

"Oh they captured the guns over there too but if they have not spiked them properly, it will not be a problem. The Indians and our boys were swarming all around them and they were forced to retreat under heavy fire back into their fort before they could be surrounded." He paused, shaking his head again. "I reckon they got at least seven hundred men as reinforcements, caught us out good and proper they did." He looked apologetically at Black Eagle before adding, "I thought them Indians were supposed to be scouting for us, but there was no warning at all. " He laughed. "Mind you, they are as keen as mustard to get some scalps; dozens of them swam across the river to get to the action on this side, but I reckon most arrived too late."

We sat sipping our tea in a companionable silence for a while. With the possible exception of Black Eagle, we were probably all reflecting on the fact that we had received some form of lucky escape. The moment of calm contemplation was suddenly shattered by a new voice yelling in outrage.

"Sergeant, what in God's name do you think you are doing? We do not serve tea to bloody savages or Americans. This is an artillery battery not one of those liberal coffee shops!"

The sergeant sprang to his feet to address a red-faced artillery lieutenant, who seemed to be on the verge of apoplexy at the sight in front of him. The sergeant pointed at me. "But this one is an officer, sir!"

"Indian officer!" shouted the lieutenant as a vein bulged on his temple. "He will be some jumped up half-breed translator getting above himself." The lieutenant turned to me. "You might be some war chief to your own people, but that does not make you an officer to His Majesty's Royal Artillery. Now get out of here and take your wretched prisoners with you."

I smiled and got to my feet, I was going to enjoy bringing this cove down a peg or two. I saw him notice the gold-hilted sword at my hip as I stood and for the first time a flicker of doubt crossed his features. "*Captain* Thomas Flashman," I said languidly in my best British upper class drawl. "In fact *Captain Sir* Thomas Flashman," I clarified throwing in my Spanish title. "Formerly of the Buff's Regiment serving in Spain but now attached by General Sheaffe to the Iroquois."

"I do apologise, sir—" started the lieutenant.

I cut him off. "Tell me, do lieutenants in His Majesty's Royal Artillery normally insult senior officers? What was it now," I paused as though trying to remember. "Ah yes, a 'jumped up half-breed translator getting above himself'."

"Please forgive me, sir," pleaded the lieutenant jumping smartly to attention and saluting. "I had no idea who you were, my sincerest apologies."

"And you are?" I enquired coldly.

"Lieutenant Davis, sir," he replied abjectly. "And once again I do apologise." He paused and then added with feeling, "It has been a rather trying morning."

He looked so miserable I could not help myself smiling, "You can say that again," I said. "But at least now it looks like we will take the fort."

"Yes sir, they will not want to venture out in the open again." Davis seemed very eager to agree with me. "Now they have extra mouths to feed and were probably already short of supplies. We will have to starve them out as our guns are never going to take down those mud banks."

"Well carry on, then," I ordered dismissing him. The man saluted, turned, took several steps, then he hesitated a moment before returning and saluting again.

"My compliments, sir, but I thought you should know that General Procter has ordered that all prisoners be taken to that old fort near our camp." He paused, looking nervously at Black Eagle. "It still has some low ramparts, sir, and he wants to protect the prisoners from any further…unpleasantness with the Indian soldiers, sir." With that he saluted once more and turned swiftly on his heel.

I was not surprised at the news. Procter would have been reprimanded for allowing the massacre at the Raisin and he clearly did not want such atrocities repeated. I looked across the plateau towards the trees to see a steady stream of Indians emerging. To my surprise they had a large number of prisoners with them. They certainly seemed to have captured more than they had killed. Another group of prisoners, captured around the guns, was already making its way to the old fort, guarded by some regular soldiers. The old fort was below the plateau by the river. It was called Fort Miami and while its broken down walls were now barely five feet high, it could be used to gather prisoners and show that they were under British protection. My thoughts were interrupted by the younger militia man at my feet.

"Are you really an English Lord?" he asked.

"No," I grinned. "I was made a knight of an old Spanish town called Alcantara after a battle there. Now, if you have finished your tea, we had better get you to the safety of the old fort."

We set off with the militia men walking in front while Black Eagle and I ambled along behind them. There seemed no rush now; the artillery behind us crashed out occasionally and the guns in Fort Meigs gave some reply, but the effort from both sides seemed half-hearted as they recovered from the activities of earlier in the day.

"There may be trouble at Fort Miami," Black Eagle warned me as we started to walk down the edge of the escarpment towards the camp. "The Indians here will view prisoners as the property of the man who has captured them. They do not trust the white man's system of parole and many think it is better to kill prisoners during a war so that you are sure that they will not fight you again."

It was a grim warning and one that seemed borne out by our first view of Fort Miami. The party of British regulars in front of us were

111

trying to drive their prisoners through the gate of the fort but Indians stood on either side of the entrance and were hitting prisoners with sticks, ramrods and rifle butts as they went past. Some reached forward to steal possessions from the prisoners and when one objected an Indian reached forward with a pistol and simply shot the man dead. I looked around expecting the soldiers to react to this act of murder, but those nearby edged back nervously. There were only fifty soldiers and they were surrounded by some five hundred Indians, many in an ugly mood as their prisoners were taken off them and sent into the fort. Procter might have wanted to avoid another massacre but he had not sent nearly enough men to avoid one. The few soldiers that were there looked harassed and apprehensive as they were jostled and often threatened in languages they did not understand. The atmosphere was like a powder keg and it would only take a spark to set if off.

Another prisoner was shot dead running the gauntlet into the fort. It seemed to me that the Indians were trying to provoke either the prisoners or the guards into reacting so that they had an excuse to attack the unarmed men in the stockade.

"What do they hope to achieve by beating and shooting at the prisoners?" I asked Black Eagle.

"It is the old way," he replied. "When prisoners were taken they would be beaten so that people could choose who was brave and worthy of joining the tribe." We watched as two warriors pulled the corpses of the dead from the line and scalped them in full view of the other militia prisoners. Several British soldiers had tried to get between the Indians and the prisoners to protect them, but they were being jostled and pushed about as the Indians jeered at their compassion.

"Let us take our captives around the back," suggested Black Eagle. "We can push them over the walls." In the time it took us to get to the back of the fort there were at least three more gunshots from where the prisoners were being forced to run the gauntlet to enter the ruined structure. The ramparts were barely three feet tall at the back and various warriors were leaning over them and threatening the prisoners. We pushed through and made a gap. Both our militia men were pale

112

with fear and I did not blame them. But I judged that they were marginally safer within the walls than outside. Black Eagle untied them and then when he thought no one was watching, he reached into his belt and passed the older militia man a knife that he must have confiscated from him earlier. Not a word was said, but a glance was exchanged between the two men, which must have spoken volumes. Then the two militia swung their legs over the wall. It was at that moment that somebody struck the spark.

There was a tussle on the far side of the compound from us, at the gate to the fort. Three British regulars were just inside the gate, trying to make sure that no Indians came in with the Americans. Some Indians now seemed to be trying to block the passage of the militia at the gate. An old grey-haired British soldier moved forward to intervene.

"Oh nichee wah," he was shouting, which meant 'friend, stop' in Indian. It was one of the few phrases the soldiers knew in the Indian tongue and we had been hearing it a lot in the last few minutes. This time it did the soldier no good. While he succeeded in pulling an American through, one of the Indians leaning over the wall behind him levelled his musket and shot the British soldier in the back. For a brief second there was a shocked silence as everyone watched the redcoat slowly topple forward into the mud. A big line had been crossed and all those watching, inside the fort and out knew it. The moment was broken by a wild war whoop from near where the shot was fired. An Indian climbed up on the wall and as he finished his war cry he aimed his musket at the crowd of prisoners and fired.

Pandemonium broke out then. The Americans started to desperately move around inside the enclosure, but there was nowhere they could go: they were surrounded by enemies. The three or four British soldiers still inside the compound were up over the wall in a flash and running in the direction of the British camp, and from what I could see, the rest of the outnumbered guard of redcoats were joining them.

"Oh my God, they are going to kill them all," I muttered.

"There is nothing you can do, Little Father," whispered Black Eagle. "They are only ignoring you because they think you are one of us." He was right. The Indians were shouting and waving weapons all around the low walls of the old fort now, baying for blood. It was like a bear baiting contest before the dogs were released. Another gun fired into the crowd of prisoners. I could see that some had dropped to their knees to pray, sensing death was imminent, while others circled around waiting for the first Indian to charge them.

It would only have taken another few seconds for the blood bath to start but then two men galloped up on horseback. One stayed back outside the fort; the other rode straight in through the gate and I saw it was Tecumseh. The cheering Indians redoubled their noise when they saw their chief. They evidently expected him to lead them in their massacre, but he just circled his horse staring at them, his face expressionless. Then he noticed the British soldier lying face down in the mud. He dropped down from his horse and turned the old man over to check if he was alive. The noise of the crowd started to die down – this was not how the warriors had expected their leader to behave. Still the chief said nothing, but instead he climbed up on the tallest stretch of wall. Glaring around at those watching him, he waited for silence.

I have seen a few great orators in my time, Pitt the Younger, William Wilberforce and Mary Clarke amongst others, but few were as impressive as Tecumseh. I say that not understanding a single word of his speech, beyond Black Eagle's rough translation, but I judge him on the effect he had on his audience. He waited until you could have heard a pin drop before he spoke, quietly at first so that people craned forward to hear him. He pointed down at the dead British soldier and then spoke in an angry tone to his followers.

"He asks how we can expect to win our freedom if we make enemies of the British as well as the Americans," whispered Black Eagle. "He says that there is no honour in killing unarmed men, it will create more enemies and hatred." A man called out something from the crowd and whatever he shouted brought some murmurs of agreement from those watching. "The man says that we have always killed prisoners in time of war," added Black Eagle. Tecumseh waited for the noise to die down again and then he started to speak, his voice slowly rising as he spoke more passionately, jabbing his finger for emphasis at those watching.

"What is he saying?" I asked

"He says we must forget the old ways that have served us poorly. He says we need to think about how we will make a nation for our children and generations to come. Our enemies must fear us in war but respect us to live in peace beside them. Now he is telling them to go back to their camps and make no more trouble for their British allies."

From the length of time Tecumseh was talking, I don't think Black Eagle translated everything. Possibly he made comments critical of the whites or the British specifically, that Black Eagle chose to omit. But whatever he said it had a dramatic effect on his audience. From being on the verge of a catastrophic bloodletting, the hundreds of warriors turned calmly away from the little fort. As they walked back to their camp they busily debated among themselves what they had heard; those that did not speak the Shawnee tongue were probably having the words translated for them too.

The American prisoners had also watched the speech, like me, with no understanding of what points were being made, but knowing that their lives hung in the balance. As they began to realise that they were safe one of their officers stepped forward and walked up to Tecumseh. He spoke briefly to express the gratitude of the prisoners for the chief's intervention, but Tecumseh just frowned and looked round for the man who had arrived with him. I saw it was Elliot, the Indian Agency translator who now told Tecumseh what the American officer had said. The chief looked again at the officer and at the men crowded behind him. Then turning back to the officer he gave a brief nod of acknowledgement and wheeled his horse away.

Chapter 13

I have heard various stories of Tecumseh stopping that massacre: in some he tomahawked two Indians and in others he urged Procter to put on petticoats, claiming he was unfit to command. Well I was there and the originators of these tales clearly were not. Someone else who was not present at Tecumseh's speech was Procter – he would have sent more men to guard the prisoners if he had been. After the massacre at the Raisin to send just one company of soldiers to guard the Americans was a foolish mistake. Those redcoats were in an impossible position and it is probably a miracle that only one of them was killed. Around twenty Americans were killed before Tecumseh appeared. But his intervention and speech saved the lives of some eight hundred prisoners, including two hundred wounded.

During the night after the battle, the Indian end of the camp was filled with the sound of drums and whooping as the warriors celebrated their victory. While Black Eagle joined them, I had no friends among the Shawnee or other tribes and few spoke English, so I spent the evening with my new friends in the Royal Artillery. This time I was welcomed as an honoured guest and Lieutenant Davis even gave me a new shirt to replace the one I had lost in the battle. We drank and told tales and even held a sweepstake on how many days the American garrison would hold out. I don't know who held the stakes but they must have done well as no one collected on the bet.

No one thought the Americans would be able to gather another relief force in this remote part of the country before the garrison of Fort Meigs was starved into submission. Many felt that the land around the fort should be given to the Indians, to create a buffer between the Americans and Canada. Oh we spent much time that night discussing what Procter should do when he captured Fort Meigs. It was only the next morning that we discovered that we were being a mite premature.

I awoke in my new waterproof shelter a short while after dawn the next morning with a hangover. It does not matter where in the world you go and what supplies are running short, soldiers always seem able to find wine, beer or spirits; although whatever we had been drinking the previous night was the roughest sort. My head throbbed and it was not made any easier by an incessant clattering and banging from the camp outside. Why couldn't those bloody Indians just lie quietly on their blankets?

Eventually I could stand it no longer and crawled out of the low entrance to my den into an unfeasibly bright day. As I stood a little unsteadily and gazed about, I still could not understand why there was so much noise. Indians were normally quiet in the mornings, but as I gazed across the camp most of them seemed to be awake and industriously working. Then I saw that several of them were tying possessions onto horses. While I watched another tore down the wall of his shelter to search for belongings inside; he was clearly not planning to use it again. Eventually a thought began to surface in my booze-soaked brain: the Indians were leaving.

It made no sense at all. Only one Indian shelter showed no sign of demolition and that was the one on the other side of mine where Black Eagle and Morag slept. I staggered over to it, I knew they were inside because I could hear them whispering and cooing at each other. I also noticed that since the last time I had interrupted them in their den, Morag had built a door, but this was important… at least to me.

"Black Eagle," I bawled through the wooden sides of the structure. "Come out, the Indians are leaving."

Morag issued a stream of what sounded like vehement curses in Iroquoian and I was at that moment quite glad that I did not understand most of the language. Then Black Eagle chuckled and try to placate her before I heard him moving and the wooden door swung open.

"What is the problem, Little Father?" asked the huge warrior as he stretched out his muscles beside me.

"What is the problem?" I repeated astonished at his calmness. "Look, the Indians are packing up. They are preparing to leave before we have captured the fort."

"They are going back to their villages to celebrate their great victory over the Americans," he replied staring at me curiously as though it was obvious.

117

"But they can't," I exclaimed, stunned that he was not taking in the bigger picture. "You cannot leave a war halfway through, just because you have won a battle. We haven't captured the fort yet, that is why we came all this way. If they wait a bit longer then it will fall and they will have an even greater victory celebrate."

"You are thinking like a British soldier," Black Eagle told me calmly. "The warriors are not soldiers; they come and go as they please. Many have taken scalps or loot from prisoners and they are pleased to have beaten such a big force of long knives. They have seen how strong the walls of the American fort are and they do not believe that the British guns will ever batter them down. They always celebrate with their tribes after a great victory, it is our way. They want to go home now."

I stood stunned for a moment trying to take this in. It was madness, I thought. If the Indians went the Americans would outnumber the remaining British and militia forces. They could break out from the fort whenever they liked and bring in more supplies. Unless the Indians could be stopped our certain victory would turn into a defeat. That thought sobered me up more than a little. I ducked back into my shelter to get as properly dressed as I could without my officer's coat. There was only one Indian who I thought stood a chance of stopping the Indians leave: Tecumseh. I made my way into the British camp to find General Procter to see if he could persuade the chief to intervene.

Interrupting a general before his breakfast is rarely a good idea, but I could not afford to wait. The first Indians were already pulling out of the camp. I gave the sentry my name and told him that it was urgent and he disappeared inside the flap of the general's tent.

The general emerged a moment later, still in his nightshirt and with a slight frown on his face. "Well, Captain, this is most irregular. I gather you have an urgent matter to discuss that cannot wait a moment longer?"

"Yes sir," I told him bringing myself smartly to attention. "The Indians are leaving, sir."

"Don't be ridiculous," he retorted sharply before turning to re-enter his tent.

I was nonplussed for a moment. That was one response I had not expected. "If you stand here, sir, you can see the first of them moving out between that line of tents," I said pointing in the right direction.

"They cannot possibly be leaving," he replied irritably but he turned again and walked to where I was standing and gazed down the line of tents. "That must be a hunting party," he declared dismissively.

"You can see that they have their possessions on their backs or on their horses," I pointed out. "They would not take those hunting."

"But they can't leave," exploded Procter. "Not now." I had some sympathy for the old boy as my brain had made the same assumptions just moments before, but then I was not a commanding general on the cusp of my greatest ever victory. I explained to him what Black Eagle had told me and when he still expressed disbelief I told him about how the Iroquois had gone to celebrate their victory after the battle at Queenston.

"I saw how Tecumseh turned them around at Fort Miami yesterday, sir," I told Procter and watched as he paled slightly at the mention of the place. "He carries great sway with the Indians. If anyone can stop them from observing this custom it is him."

"I will speak to him," agreed Procter with what I thought was a note of reluctance. "And thank you for telling me, Captain, it is good to know that there are some officers in this army I can rely on." With that he moved back inside his tent to get dressed.

Procter struck me as a strangely isolated figure. He evidently did not get on with some of his officers, judging from his final comment, and I gauged that his relationship with Tecumseh was not close either. But I was confident that Tecumseh would persuade the Indians to stay – he, after all, was the person who had pressed for the attack on Fort Meigs in the first place.

As the day progressed it seemed that my faith was misplaced. I saw the chief moving around the Indian encampment. From what I could tell from his gestures, he was passionately arguing his case but one by one the shelters kept on coming down and the line of men moving out of the camp grew from a trickle to a long and continuous flow.

119

My fears seemed confirmed when a weary sentry tracked me down at the end of the day and told me that Procter wanted to see me.

"Do you know what it is about?" I asked.

"No sir," he replied woodenly, "the general did not say."

"And of course you do not listen to his conversations through the canvas walls of his tent," I prompted.

"Certainly not, sir," said the sentry, although he grinned as he told the lie. Having thought about it for a moment the sentry lowered his voice, "I would tread carefully with the general, sir, he is in a fearful temper, something to do with the Indians and the militia, sir."

Forearmed with that information I cautiously entered Procter's tent, but the welcome at least was civil.

"Ah, Captain Flashman, do come in and take a seat," he greeted me. The sentry had been right, he did seem tense, but he forced a smile and made an effort to be cheerful. "Can I offer you some madeira and a slice of fruit cake? My wife made the cake herself and sent it up with the latest supplies. I took a seat and accepted his offer. I guessed that Mrs Procter must have had a cook when she was growing up for she clearly had not learned the art herself. You could have used the cake to hammer in nails. When the general was not watching I dropped the inedible hard lump into my pocket.

"I wanted to thank you," he continued, "for your warning of the Indian departure this morning." He paused, gritting his teeth for a moment as though it was an effort for him to remain calm. "Unfortunately, as you will have seen, Tecumseh has only managed to persuade less than a hundred warriors to remain with us." He stopped again to take a deep breath and picked up a silver mounted glass inkwell from his small table and gazed at that while he continued. "In addition I have been informed this afternoon by the commanders of our militia regiments that in the light of the Indian withdrawal, they are also resolved to retire. Their men believe that there is still time to get some crops in and they want to get back to their farms."

"You mean we are going to abandon the siege?"

"Yes of course we are going to abandon the bloody siege!" he roared at me and with that he hurled the inkwell across the tent, to leave a dark spatter mark of ink down the canvas. Seeing the look of shock on my face as I hurriedly stood, he immediately held out his hands in supplication. "I am sorry, I do apologise, Captain, please sit down again. I should not take things out on you of all people. It is just that it is so damn frustrating."

"Indeed, sir," I agreed cautiously, not wanting to provoke another outburst.

Do you know that the prisoners we captured from the fort told us that they have less than a week's supplies and typhoid and dysentery are rife among the garrison? That bloody Indian wanted this battle and now his men are abandoning it just when we have victory in the palm of our hand. I begged him, Flashman," said Procter, his eyes starting to water in emotion. "I bloody begged him to stay and then those Judases in the militia stabbed me in the back as well." I glanced across at the decanter; there was less than half an inch of the spirit at the bottom and I guessed that Procter had consumed the rest that afternoon.

"Tecumseh did try, sir, I saw him in the Indian camp for most of the day. Can we not maintain the siege with just the regular soldiers?"

"No, they are the only regular troops I have or am likely to get. They are the backbone of my force and I cannot risking losing most of them in a battle where they would be outnumbered at least two to one." He gave a heavy sigh. "We will have to withdraw."

The next morning General Harrison must have been rubbing his eyes with disbelief as he watched his enemies retire just when it seemed he was cornered. I hope he had the sense to thank his engineer, for if the walls of Fort Meigs had shown any sign of imminent collapse then I suspect that the Indians and hence the militia would have stayed.

Travelling downstream was a lot quicker than coming up the river against the current. Two days later Black Eagle and I found ourselves once more on the deck of the *Queen Charlotte*. This time we were heading back to Amherstburg across Lake Erie, and the water of the lake was surprisingly choppy. Like most of the British fleet, the *Queen Charlotte* was an old ship that had seen much better days. In the rough swell she wallowed about like a half-filled kettle. The pumps were working around the clock as squads of soldiers took their turn at them while waves broke over the bow, filling the ship with more water.

I had been given a bunk in the officers' quarters, but at first it was virtually impossible to sleep. Every time the ship went on a westerly tack the wind and spray hurled itself against the port side of the ship. My bunk was on the port side and spray poured through a small gap in the planking. My bedding was damp and even though I tried to sleep in all my clothes, I struggled to get warm and comfortable. I remember shifting after something hard dug in my side and then I had the solution to my problem. A couple of sharp raps with the sole of my boot and the hole was plugged. I gave a murmur of thanks to Mrs Procter; while her cake might have been inedible, it made excellent caulking for gaps in a ship's side!

Chapter 14

The British force arrived back in Amherstburg in mid-May. Apart from some thirty warriors with Tecumseh, the Indians had already dispersed back to their homes. They had been given new territory to build their villages on the southern shore of Lake Erie, the land north of Fort Meigs. As soon as we docked the militia poured off the ships and then also disappeared off to their farms. Only the regular soldiers remained and they were fed up and demoralised. Many of them had spoken to American prisoners and knew how close we had been to an easy victory. They were not slow to share their frustrations, leading to anger and resentment. Lives had been lost for no good reason and having walked away from the Americans just when we had them on the verge of defeat, everyone knew that we would have to fight General Harrison and his men again.

Ironically it was General Procter that they blamed for this mismanagement. It was, I thought, a matter of presentation. Procter looked weary and depressed with an air of defeat about him. He did not share his problems with his senior officers and so most were unaware of his appeal to Tecumseh or his frustration at the retreat. He looked like a man responsible for a debacle and so most people assumed that he was. On the other hand Tecumseh's natural demeanour gave him the air of the noble savage. Here was a man with vision and courage, who had single-handedly saved the lives of all the American prisoners and whose warriors had led the charge against the enemy. While Procter was short and squat, Tecumseh was tall, slim and, judging from several women who affected to swoon in his presence, good looking. The fact that he spoke little English gave the chief an air of mystery. As a result, most of the soldiers and citizens of Amherstburg were quite happy to believe that the only reason the Indians dispersed when they did, was because Procter had failed to stop them.

The mood was not improved when news reached the town of the British defeat at York and of Americans massing for a new attack on the Niagara peninsula. I congratulated myself on my decision to move west. It sounded like the Niagara area would soon be a very unhealthy place to be. While we could not capture Fort Meigs, at least the Americans were in no position to attack the British at Amherstburg. A few days later news came that the two forts on the Canadian side of the River Niagara were both in American hands.

"Perhaps the Great Spirit has turned against the British," speculated Black Eagle. Certainly the tide of the war seemed to have changed. In the beginning with the capture of Detroit and victory at Queenston, the British were triumphant – to their own surprise as much as their enemies'. But now the difference in numbers seemed to be telling. It was also a matter of supply lines: British military stores had to be sent thousands of miles across the Atlantic and then hundreds of miles across often difficult terrain. The Americans were fighting on their own doorstep with armouries, foundries and boat yards no more than a few hundred miles from their forces.

I found out precisely how bad things were one evening when I was invited to a formal dinner at Procter's headquarters. I was by no means among the most senior officers, but I had discovered that Procter kept a coterie of trusted officers of various ranks, with whom he shared opinions; while others – including his second in command – he did not trust and kept in the dark. I am always happy to toady up to a senior officer if it keeps me informed: if the front was about to collapse, I wanted to be among the first to know so that I could plan my escape accordingly.

I managed to borrow a new captain's uniform to smarten myself up and was just leaving the inn when I found Black Eagle waiting outside in his most embroidered deerskin tunic, hair oiled and gleaming with three stripes of war paint on each cheek. "What on earth are you doing here?" I asked.

"I am coming to the dinner," he replied.

"But you can't, you have to be invited. This will be a formal affair with knives and forks, none of your normal gnawing on bones and farting. Trust me, you would not enjoy it."

124

I had expected him to look a bit disappointed but instead he smiled. "But I have been invited."

"What?"

"It is not just whites at this dinner," he said grinning at the astonishment on my face. "Tecumseh will be there, and several other chiefs. I have been invited to represent the eastern Iroquois."

He was right. When we arrived at Procter's home, which he referred to grandly as Government House, there was an array of brightly dressed individuals milling around outside. In addition to the scarlet coats of the army, there was the blue of the Royal Artillery, some civic leader in a burgundy coat and half a dozen Indians in a riot of colour. Headwear ranged from bicorns, tricorns and shakoes to an aviary of feathers and one cove, who appeared to be wearing an upturned china pot. The doors were eventually thrown open and we were invited inside where a receiving line awaited. First was Procter with a stern and serious demeanour, shaking the hand of every guest as they entered. Beside him was his wife, who twittered superficial greetings while staring nervously at the more exotically dressed guests. To a growl of disapproval from her husband, she actually dropped into a curtsey when Tecumseh's tall frame appeared in front of her as though he were royalty. Last in the line was a one-armed sailor called Barclay, as guest of honour. He had just arrived to take command of the battered naval fleet.

Most of the Indians looked out of place and awkward in the refined setting of Mrs Procter's drawing room, but Tecumseh seemed entirely at home. With Elliot his interpreter alongside, he talked to those around him with his lively eyes darting among the gathering. Like the rest of the warriors he was wearing deerskin leggings and while most of the Indians had matching tunics he wore another of his European shirts and a red cloak. Everyone was armed; officers had swords dangling at their hip but the Indians invariably had pistols, knives and even tomahawks tucked into their belts.

As we moved into the ornate dining room Tecumseh took his place on Procter's left while Barclay sat on his right. To get comfortable the Indian pulled out his pistols and put them on either side of his plate while his big hunting knife and tomahawk were placed just beyond his spoons. Other warriors followed his lead, and with a loud clatter a small armoury of weapons was deposited down the middle of the table. If that behaviour seemed unusual to the white diners present, then the array of Mrs Procter's best silver cutlery was equally incongruous for the Indians. I was sitting next to Black Eagle, who looked with bemusement at the array of knives, forks and spoons around his place setting. This was a man who normally ate with a hunting knife and his fingers or occasionally a single spoon.

A beef consommé arrived as the first course, or 'meat water' as Black Eagle dismissed it. I just about stopped him drinking from the bowl, but he soon decided that spooning the liquid was not worth the effort. Then a course of steamed lake fish was presented, which the big warrior polished off in two mouthfuls. He was relieved to learn that the meat course was next and probably expected the roasted side of an ox to be delivered. He did not bother to hide his disappointment at the few slices of beef and vegetables that did appear.

"What feast is this?" he grumbled. "There is not enough food to feed a wren never mind a man and my glass has been drier than an old crone's tit all night." Procter had wisely decided to serve one glass per course to avoid the warriors getting drunk, although I noticed that Tecumseh did not drink at all, preferring water. Glasses of custards arrived next and as I pointed out his custard spoon Black Eagle snorted in disgust. He picked up the glass, which looked tiny in his big hand, and holding it to his mouth, sucked up the dessert in a single mouthful.

As the last of the food was cleared away Procter called the gathering to order, stilling the various conversations around the table. "Gentlemen," he announced, "I invited you here to update you on events and to discuss our future strategy." He paused to allow Elliot, sitting on the other side of Tecumseh, to translate his words for the Indians present. "I must first welcome Captain Barclay, who will command our ships. I had hoped he would come with many sailors for our fleet, but despite my highlighting our urgent need of men and supplies, only a surgeon and six sailors could be spared."

126

He paused again and then proceeded to explain the precarious situation that his command was in. The American attack on York had destroyed naval stores and supplies that were desperately needed by his flotilla. But more importantly the American invasion of the Niagara peninsula was making it harder to get other supplies too. Powder and ball was already running low and food would also soon be in short supply if they could not maintain control of Lake Erie. He announced that Barclay would be sailing to the port of Presque Isle in Pennsylvania to gauge the readiness of the American fleet being built there. Then he leaned forward and gazed defiantly around the table, before once again proposing a combined attack to destroy the enemy flotilla before it could set sail. Then the British general sat back in his chair while those around the table either listened to the end of the translation or murmured among themselves at the situation Procter had outlined.

I had known things were tough, but not as bad as that. Rumour had it that the Iroquois and the British had stemmed the American advance on the Niagara, but if supplies stopped getting through then we would be forced to retreat or starve during the long winter. I thought Procter had put forward a clear and logical case for an attack on Presque Isle, but Tecumseh did not seem stirred. He listened impassively to the British commander and then after a moment's thought he started his reply.

"I too welcome the Father with the One Arm," Elliot translated. The chief looked calmly at Procter as he continued. "In a few weeks Dickson the Redhead will bring fourteen hundred warriors to Amherstburg. They come from many tribes in the west and some will bring their families. They will all need food and supplies to fight the Americans." Procter slowly shook his head in anguish at the thought of this many extra mouths to feed with his limited supplies. But Tecumseh was not finished. "Warriors who have travelled so far must not wait long to fight the enemy. My people have been given land on the southern shore of the lake, north of Fort Meigs. The Americans from the fort are raiding my villages, which must be the priority.

127

Instead of attacking the American big canoes I say that we should attack again Fort Meigs."

You could have heard a pin drop when the translator had finished, the only noise was a curious 'chink' sound, which came from Procter. He had not said a word while Elliot delivered Tecumseh's response but his face was getting steadily redder with supressed rage. Diplomacy demanded that he deal with the Indian war leader respectfully, but you got the strong impression that if left to his own devices, he would like nothing more than to bludgeon the chief's serenely calm face with one of the many tomahawks scattered down the table. After taking a deep breath Procter announced that they would hold a council meeting to discuss the matter further. As those around the table got up to take their leave, I noticed Procter gesture to one of the men waiting on the table. He opened his fist and dropped onto the man's tray two halves of the glass that he had evidently snapped in his hand as Tecumseh proposed his own objective.

Chapter 15

Over the coming weeks the relationship between Procter and Tecumseh became even more strained. In an effort to quell acts of rebellion by the American population of Detroit, Procter had several of the agitators sent to Quebec in chains. Mindful that his Indian villages would need to exist alongside Detroit, Tecumseh intervened in several cases, resulting in reprieves for those concerned. The Americans had already heard how the chief had saved the prisoners at Fort Meigs. Despite the fact that he was their enemy, Tecumseh's standing grew even further in the eyes of the Americans, while Procter was seen as a heartless oppressor.

The British general was an increasingly bitter and frustrated man. He was starved of supplies and support by the governor general in Quebec, who expected him to rely heavily on the large Indian force at his disposal. What his superiors did not appreciate was that his native allies had goals of their own, which did not always tie in with those of Britain. Even his own officers did not give him their full support, although this was partly because he took few of them into his confidence. Most of his senior commanders were not present at the dinner with Tecumseh and only found out their general's views from the few more junior officers he did trust. As a result most were openly critical of their commander, with a widely expressed view that he was incompetent and out of his depth.

Things did not improve with the council meeting Procter had promised to decide the way forward. He explained that the large cannon used in the earlier assault were no longer available. As no new ordinance was being sent from the east, these would be loaded into his new flagship the *Detroit*. He pointed out that the Americans had undoubtedly spent the time since the last siege strengthening Fort Meigs. If his larger guns could not breach the fort before, then clearly the smaller guns left to him would certainly not. Tecumseh just ignored this objection and claimed that if the British gave the Indians spades they would dig their way into the fort if necessary. Meanwhile Barclay reported from his reconnaissance voyage that the American

129

fleet looked ready to sail and would be bigger than his own, which was desperately short of skilled seamen. He joined Procter in pressing for an attack on the American anchorage, but the chief would not be moved. His villages had to be protected and he wanted to take his large Indian force to attack General Harrison, for whom he felt a particular animosity.

It was an ugly tense meeting. At one point Procter rounded on Elliot over the supplies they were providing to feed and equip the Indians. The two threatened to come to blows before they were pulled apart. In the end the general was forced to agree to Tecumseh's request, if for no other reason than he wanted the Indians away from Amherstburg. A shortage of supplies had already seen some warriors raiding local Canadian farms and the militia refused to leave their land as they had to protect their families. A further fourteen hundred warriors and their families in the town would have made the situation much worse. If he agreed to the attack then at least the Indians would join those on the southern shore of Lake Erie, formerly American territory, and away from Canadian property.

Procter's army officers were understandably outraged when they learned of the new attack. The few six-pounder cannon they had left would never breach the walls and while there would be more Indians in the attack, this time the militia refused to travel. Procter was roundly condemned by all and sundry. Most still blamed him for allowing the Indians to abandon the first siege on the cusp of victory and now this new venture was seen as the ultimate folly.

While the army descended into virtual mutiny, militia men fortified their farms against their former allies and the Indians complained that the Great Father was neglecting them with poor supplies; it seemed that the only person who was not frustrated and angry was my trusty companion - who had a growing enthusiasm in, of all things, the navy. I knew Black Eagle had spent some time at the dockyard watching the masts being raised on the new *Detroit*, but one afternoon he came up to me his eyes bright with excitement. He handed me a handbill and asked me to read it. I have the paper still, it is with my other

130

mementoes from my campaigning and so I can copy it exactly as follows:

HMS Detroit
All able-bodied seamen and sturdy
landsmen willing to serve His Majesty
and enrich themselves are invited
forthwith to enter for His Majesty's ship
Detroit, *Captain Robert Barclay commanding.*
She will be ready to sail in a few weeks and
labour will be required to help fit her out.

Those fond of pumping and hard work had better not apply – the Detroit *is as tight as a bottle, sails like a witch, scuds like a Mudian and lays like a Gannet. She has one deck to sleep under and another to dine on. Dry hammocks, regular meals and plenty of grog – the mainbrace is always spliced when it rains or blows hard.*

It went on to give details of the joining bounties available, which for landsmen – and Indians – was one pound sixteen shillings.

"Is this true about the easy life and the money?" asked Black Eagle. "Morag thinks I should join – that money would buy a lot in the village – but what is a mudian?"

I could not help but laugh at his naïve enthusiasm. "Very little of it is true," I told him. "You might get the bounty if you live and gold is sent for the pay chest, but there are bound to be deductions. As for the rest, with so few skilled seamen aboard, that ship will sail like a bucket. You heard at the dinner that if there is a battle the British fleet will be outnumbered. Trust me," I said with feeling, "you cannot hide on a small ship and in battle it is not the cannon balls that kill, but the splinters that they send scything across the decks."

The big warrior looked disappointed and went off to give Morag the bad tidings. But my curiosity was aroused and I strolled off to the dockyard to look at the new ship. The vessel was not yet afloat and it looked like there would be at least a month's work before its timbers got wet. I was turning away when a voice called out my name.

"It is Captain Flashman, is it not?" I turned and saw Barclay walking towards me with another gentleman I did not recognise. Barclay held out his remaining hand in greeting. "It is good to see you again, Captain. May I introduce John Christie, my friend and ship's surgeon." He turned to his companion. "Captain Flashman is a friend of that big Indian who was asking you about sea battles yesterday."

"Ah," replied Christie grinning. "He was most disappointed to learn that despite being in a fair few battles, I have seen very little action from my station in the bowels of the ship."

"I am sorry if he has been a nuisance," I said. "He does seem to have developed a passion for all things nautical just recently."

"Oh he is most welcome," Barclay assured me. "In fact I hope you will not mind but I gave him one of our recruitment handbills. But don't worry we will not be looking for a crew for at least a month."

"Yes he has shown it to me and I have to say it is a creative portrayal of a ship yet to taste the water."

Barclay laughed. "Yes it is a powerful description. I borrowed it from a recruitment notice for the *Tartarus* I saw in Halifax earlier this year. It seemed to work for that ship, so I thought I would try it for the *Detroit*."

"Do you think she will be finished on time?" I asked.

"Oh the American ships will almost certainly be ready first, but she should be completed in time to see action."

"It is a shame that Tecumseh will not agree to attack the American fleet in port to at least even the odds."

Barclay lowered his voice so that no one else working nearby could hear. "Even if he did it would be no easy contest. I estimate that there are some two thousand American militia guarding the anchorage and so unless we had the advantage of surprise, it would be a bloody business. I would have been willing to sacrifice one of the smaller schooners as a fire ship to burn them out, but there is a sandbank that would stop such an attack. However," he brightened, "we still have a good chance, particularly if we have the wind and can catch them at some disadvantage."

"Well I wish you good luck when you eventually put to sea, or should I say 'to lake'?"

Christie looked at me curiously, "That warrior of yours tells me that you have served in the Navy, is that right?"

"I was with Cochrane when he captured the *Gamo*," I admitted, mentioning a well-known prize-taking in the Mediterranean. "But that was a long time ago."

"Were you, by God!" exclaimed Barclay "That must have been a capital action. Look while I have some skilled gunners, I have precious few proper seamen. Your experience as one of my officers would be invaluable."

"No, no," I replied, alarmed at the direction this conversation was going. "I was a diplomatic courier then. I sailed with Cochrane for a year, but I was never more than an honorary midshipman. I have no idea of sailing or navigation."

I swiftly made my escape after that. Barclay was not getting me on that tub in some death or glory charge against a larger fleet – or at least so I thought then. Which did leave the thought: what *was* I going to do? I had been in North America for nearly a year and was still no closer to going home than when I had been pushed into the Boston gaol. No British soldier was going to be allowed to sail home unless they were seriously wounded. To the east the battle for the Niagara peninsula was in full swing with little quarter given by either side. If I went back with Black Eagle I could find myself attached to the Iroquois again and facing instant death if captured. At least here in the west, while plans for the assault on Fort Meigs looked hopeless, the Americans were on the defensive and not likely to launch an invasion of Canada. At worst if we lost control of the lake and supplies dried up, well Black Eagle and Morag were more than capable of living off the land. I knew Black Eagle would not abandon me and we could survive together in the wilderness while we worked our way to safety.

A few weeks after the council meeting, the guns of the fort at Amherstburg rang out to announce the arrival of some fifty large bark canoes carrying flags and hundreds of war-painted warriors. This was the advance party of those brought by Dickson the Redhead. If I had thought that the Iroquois were a colourful lot they were nothing to this gathering. Black Eagle told me that they represented at least eight different Indian nations. As Tecumseh welcomed them he must have felt that this combined army was the beginning of his larger Native American state.

Many of the new arrivals were not familiar with living among white communities and did not seem to distinguish greatly between the British and the American enemy. More farms had their livestock raided and in town anything of value was being stolen. A number had glared covetously at my gold-hilted sword, which looked incongruous with my Indian buckskin clothes. It was only a matter of time before some of the villains waylaid me to steal it. So I deposited my sword, watch and some papers I wanted to keep at a village store which had a strong room.

If the first siege of Fort Meigs had been a failure, the second one was a complete farce. Only some four hundred and fifty British regulars and a handful of small cannon crossed the lake from Amherstburg but Tecumseh gathered together two and a half thousand warriors, by far the largest force he commanded. Black Eagle and I found ourselves again on the *Queen Charlotte* bound for the mouth of the Maumee River, along with a lot of demoralised soldiers. No one thought that the second siege would succeed when the first had failed and there was near mutiny as the small cannon were dragged and floated up the river to take up position in the old batteries.

We reached the old campground near Fort Miami and settled on virtually the same spot as we had before. Morag had not come this time but in the warm summer evenings we could sleep out in the open and so we did not need her shelter building expertise. It was obvious from a cursory look across the river that the fort's ramparts were even stronger than they had been before. Our puny guns would never be able to smash their way in. Americans looked curiously over their walls wondering what we would do next and many of us on our side of the river were wondering the same. Procter retired to his tent and left things to Tecumseh – he had insisted on coming here and so he could work out how the fort could be taken.

After several days of inactivity it was rumoured that General Harrison was not inside the fort but coming to relieve the siege with eight hundred men. A huge war dance greeted this news and a large party of warriors set off the next day to intercept Harrison, only to return two days later having discovered the news was false. Harrison, it turned out, was many miles away at Sandusky and showing no signs of moving. He knew as well as we did that as long as his men stayed in the fort they were completely safe.

Tecumseh's next plan was to stage a mock battle on the Sandusky road just out of sight of the fort. He wanted to give the garrison the impression that a relief force was marching towards them so that they would sally out as they had in the first siege to join up with the new arrivals. A huge amount of increasingly scarce ammunition was then blazed away by hundreds of Indians running around in circles emitting whooping war cries. I did not even bother to view this fiasco but stood watching the fort. One rampart was crowded with curious spectators gazing in the direction of the noise but they showed not the slightest inclination to venture forth. They must have known that no relief force was coming as well as we did.

As Tecumseh ran out of ideas Procter suggested that they lift the siege and move a hundred miles west to attack Sandusky. If Harrison retreated then at least they could raid more livestock to alleviate the supply problem. Tecumseh, of course disagreed; by now their relationship had almost completely broken down. He insisted that he needed to keep his part of the army close to his villages but he agreed to occupy the marshy land between the Maumee and Sandusky rivers to ambush any force that might try to cross it.

A few days later and we were back aboard the *Queen Charlotte* as we sailed along the lake shore towards Sandusky. The low morale of the British force had slumped even further during the shambles at Fort Meigs and now we had been abandoned by all but around two hundred of our Indian allies. They had only stayed for the prospect of loot rather than any confidence in our commander's plan. Little was seen of

Procter; he largely shut himself away in his cabin and chose to dine alone. When, occasionally, he did emerge on deck, beyond the brief salute of the officer of the watch, he barely communicated with anyone.

Sandusky, at the mouth of the river of the same name, had already been abandoned. We went ashore and rummaged about but everything of use or value, including cattle, had been taken further inland. But the following day Indian scouts reported that twenty miles upstream Fort Stephenson was still occupied by a small force of Americans. They assured Procter that here was a fort that could be taken. It was small, isolated and with two thousand Indians in the vicinity looking for an American army, it was unlikely to be relieved. The general seemed immediately to cheer up; here at last was an enemy he could beat. He needed some success to restore his prestige with the Indians and he was all too aware of the low morale of his men. A victory, albeit a small one, would start to restore his fortunes.

Everyone seemed to sense the change in mood and there was even some singing as the five six-pounder cannon were loaded on the shallow draught gunboats with the howitzer to be towed up river. It was a twenty mile journey against the current, which took two days, but the Indians advised that the garrison remained in place and that no relieving force was on the way. I had not seen a British victory since Queenston and even I thought that our luck was about to change. That feeling was only enhanced as we rounded a bend in the river and got our first glimpse of Fort Stephenson. It seemed a small, squat and miserable affair. We did not know it then, but its commanding officer was a 21-year-old called Groghan. He had been ordered to abandon the fort by Harrison when the American general learned of our approach. Groghan had chosen to disregard the order and hold his ground – a decision for which he was to be dismissed by Harrison.

What the young garrison commander lacked in experience he made up for in pluck. We soon discovered that Groghan was in no mood to surrender when a six-pounder cannon from inside the fort banged out as our gunboats rounded the river bend. It was a poorly aimed shot and the fire soon ceased. It seemed that they were low on ammunition, which made things all the better for us. We had arrived in late afternoon and soon disembarked the guns while reconnoitring a good place to set up a battery to knock down the walls. The fort consisted of three blockhouses joined by a surrounding log wall of fifteen feet in height, with a ditch of some eight feet in front of the walls. With such relatively short walls and the small garrison, several of the Indians proposed attacking at night, with grapnels or climbing poles. They thought that they could slip silently over the walls and cut some throats before the Americans knew they were there.

Black Eagle was convinced it was the only way to attack the fort. "If you can get enough over the wall to kill the sentries without raising the alarm then you could open the gate and storm the fort. If not, you could slip away in the darkness after killing just a few. Several sleepless nights sitting scared in the dark and they would soon surrender."

Stealth and ambush was always the Indian's preferred means of attack and it might well have worked but Procter would not hear of it. "Such murderous practices would dishonour a victory," he insisted to a gathering of his senior officer officers. As well as myself a major and two other captains, Procter had gathered his second in Command Colonel Warburton and another colonel called Short. We stood on a small hill overlooking the fort, watching as our men started to dig out a battery on higher ground some two hundred and fifty yards from the fort. "Well what do you make of it, gentlemen?" Procter asked.

"How many men do they have inside?" Colonel Short enquired.

"The Indians report around a hundred and fifty, all regular soldiers," replied Procter. "And with two thousand warriors between here and Fort Meigs they are confident that no more reinforcements will get through."

"There is some two hundred yards of clear ground we will have to cross to get to the walls," mused Short.

"Perhaps we should attack at night," proposed the other Colonel, Warburton. "We would keep the element of surprise and it would suit our Indian allies better." He could not have said anything more calculated to get Procter to disagree.

137

"No gentlemen, we will attack during the day. Our guns will weaken their walls and then we will assault the fort, but simultaneously in two directions to divide their fire." The two colonels exchanged a glance; they would clearly be expected to lead an attack each and it looked like neither relished the prospect. All of a sudden this easy victory did not seem quite so easy after all.

Chapter 16

Overnight a gun battery was built and most of the cannon dragged into
it. At dawn the Americans found four of our cannon covering the
north-west corner of the fort, where there was no blockhouse, and the
remaining cannon and howitzer covering the north-east corner. Then
Procter had his British and Indian force show its numbers, beyond
musket range, to prove to the Americans that they were outnumbered
and outgunned by approximately six to one. It must have been an
intimidating sight to those inside the fort, a ring of enemies leaving no
opportunity for escape, with many of the Indians yelling war cries and
waving their weapons in the air.

"Are we going to give them the opportunity to surrender before we
start the attack, sir?" I asked Procter.

"Of course, Captain," replied Procter staring at the fort through his
glass. "Although I imagine that if they were minded to give up the fort
they would have abandoned it before we arrived." He looked at me.
"Perhaps you would be kind enough to do the honours."

A few minutes later and I was strolling towards the fort
accompanied by one soldier with a large white kerchief tied to a long
stick to show we came under a truce. We stopped halfway between our
lines and the fort, waiting for someone to come out and meet us. We
were then within musket range from the fort but I was not concerned.
It would have been madness to kill an emissary under a white flag
when surrounded by overwhelming numbers. After waiting a minute
the fort's main gate opened a yard or so. From it emerged two soldiers,
a young officer and a private with a white flag tied to the end of the
barrel of his musket. As he got closer I saw that the officer was only an
ensign, a boy of little more than sixteen or seventeen from the look of
him. He did not seem afraid, more excited at being the centre of
attention for two armies. He was staring about him at those watching
his approach.

"Ensign Shipp," the boy introduced himself. He had started to
salute and then thought better of it and converted the movement to
brush some non-existent lint off his sleeve.

I grinned at the clumsy motion. "Captain Flashman, I've come to give your garrison the chance to surrender the fort. You can retire with honour and your weapons." I gestured at the men surrounding the fort. "There is no need for any bloodshed, you can see how outnumbered you are."

"Did you say your name was Flashman?" asked the ensign frowning as though the name meant something to him.

"Yes but I am not known around here."

"Damn you, sir, but you are!" At this the little pipsqueak took a step towards me with his fists clenched at his sides.

"What the devil are you talking about? I have never been here before."

"Well we know about you, sir, and your murdering ways." The boy seemed to be working himself into quite a passion. "There will be no Indian massacre here, sir, because this fort will not be surrendered while a single man of the garrison is able to resist you." With that he turned on his heel and started to march back to the fort.

"You fool," I called after him. "You have got me confused with someone else." He did not respond and I turned to see the private staring ahead with a stony face. "Well I don't know what the deuce he was talking about," I muttered. "Come on, we had better go back." We marched towards the British lines with me trying to look unconcerned, but the ensign's outburst had unsettled me somewhat. Who the hell was I supposed to have murdered? To the best of my knowledge I had not killed anyone since I had been in North America. Quite the reverse; I had saved a boy his age at Queenston. Yet he reacted as though I had been slaughtering innocents all over the place. It made no sense but there was nothing that I could do about it and so I just continued on my way to our lines. I thought that perhaps there would be an explanation when we took the fort.

Procter had clearly expected a refusal and the first salvo from the new British battery was fired the moment the ensign was back inside the fort's walls. The barrage continued for much of the day but while the logs that made the palisade and block houses were splintered and cracked by some of the cannons, nowhere along the line was there a viable breach to allow an assault. A larger cannon would have smashed the walls down in no time, as there were no banks of mud to protect them, but the six-pounder fired balls the size of small apples and even at such short range they did not have the weight to tear a large log in two. Procter paced up and down with increasing impatience. He stood to one side of the battery so that he could see around the large cloud of gun smoke that partly obscured the fort for the gunners. After two balls missed the fort entirely he called a halt to the barrage. He told the gunners to wait for the smoke to clear and then to concentrate on the north-west corner. It would signal clearly where the attack was coming but it was the only way that he would have a sufficient gap for his men to enter the fort.

Over the next couple of hours ball after ball was carefully aimed at the corner of the squat fort. The trunks that made up the palisade at that point were slowly cracked and then broken, while the howitzer dropped shells just inside the corner to deter Americans from making any running repairs. Slowly the sturdy wall was transformed into a tangled mess of logs and splinters, but there was enough of a gap for men to get through. The Indians had watched the preparations for the attack with curiosity, many expressing the view that to charge so far over open ground against soldiers in broad daylight was foolhardy in the extreme. They had a point: as the guns continued to fire the cloud of gun smoke never covered more than half of the distance we had to cross and was quite thin as the wind gradually dispersed it. But Procter was thinking along similar lines, as I discovered when he summoned me to join him on the rise from which he was observing the bombardment.

"Ah, Captain Flashman," he called as I approached. "You will join us for the attack, I trust?" He spoke as though he were inviting me to the local hunt or some other pleasurable experience, rather than a suicidal charge towards over a hundred waiting soldiers. But I had shirked my way out of far more pressing invitations than that and I was ready for him.

"I rather think my place is with the Indians, sir, to encourage them to attack to support your assault." I gestured apologetically towards my clothing. "And as you can see, sir, I am sadly lacking in regimentals. I would let down the smart appearance of your men. I do not even have my sword with me, just a musket and tomahawk."

"Nonsense, man," Procter brushed aside my objections as of no account. "You can join me at the back of the column; no one will see what you are wearing there. We will show those warriors what the British can do, eh?" Without even waiting for a reply he continued. "Now that big Indian you travel with looks a reliable fellow, I have a job for him."

"You do, sir?" I asked still reeling from the prospect of being involved in the attack and racking my mind for another means to wriggle out.

"Yes," said Procter bending down and picking up a handful of grass. He let the blades slowly drop from his fingers, watching carefully the direction the wind blew them. "There," he pointed to a spot in the trees opposite the western rampart of the fort. "That tree with the broken trunk that looks like an 'N', do you see it?"

"Yes sir," I replied, puzzled.

"Have your man build a fire there and tell him to use damp wood and grass to make lots of smoke. I want great plumes of the stuff to blow across the north-west corner we are going to attack – that should hide our approach until we are right on top of them." I looked at the old boy with renewed respect; he did seem to know his business after all. He rubbed his hands together, eagerly anticipating the prospect of battle. It was as though he were ten years younger than the tired and frustrated old man who had watched the siege at Fort Meigs. He saw me looking at him and winked. "It is a trick I learned from the Indians years ago, but don't tell your man that. Let him believe it that it is a British tactic too."

Black Eagle went off to do the general's bidding and soon thick acrid smoke was obscuring the front of the fort. It had been decided that Colonel Warburton would lead the diversionary attack from the south. Procter told him to make the approach at precisely five-thirty and wished him well. Then Warburton led his two hundred men and set off through the tress so that the garrison would not get advance

142

warning of from where the attack would be made. Colonel Short prepared his men for the main attack; ensuring soldiers with axes were at the front, ready to cut through any obstacles. Despite assuring Colonel Short that he would not interfere and would only join the attack in the rear ranks, Procter continued to fuss about. First ensuring that the guns would fire right up to the moment that our men reached the walls, and then warning the men not to cough to alert the garrison as they went through the smoke.

It was, I thought, a meticulously planned attack, with every chance of success; not that this made me feel any more comfortable about participating in it. At least being right at the back I felt a hell of a lot safer than those at the front led by Colonel Short. As Procter's watch chimed five-thirty we looked at the smoke blocking our view and imagined the diversionary attack pouring out of the wood to the south. At least half of the garrison should be rushing to meet this new threat. No order was shouted to start the assault, instead a flag was silently raised and two hundred men started to march briskly forward. We covered the first hundred yards with the British battery on our right continuing to fire shot into the now battered corner of the fort. I also heard the 'whoomp' of the howitzer as it dropped another shell into the centre courtyard of the bastion, with a resulting crashing explosion as it went off.

"Your man is doing well with the smoke," remarked Procter as he strolled along beside me. He looked to have no more care than if he was taking a Sunday saunter in Hyde Park. Only the drawn sword which he held, resting the blade on his shoulder, gave any hint that he was marching into battle. "Can you hear musket fire yet?" he enquired. "The diversionary attack should be drawing their fire at any moment."

Black Eagle was still busy fanning flames which produced a prodigious amount of smoke. It completely obscured the fort with only the occasional glimpse of a block house roof. There was no sound of gunfire and I noticed no sound of coughing from within the fort either. I guessed that the smoke was passing just in front of the breach.

"No I can't hear a thing," I replied grimly, my stomach starting to churn as we got ever closer to the unseen fort. Why oh why, I asked myself had I not invented some drama with the Indians that I would have had to resolve. They were all sitting safely in a gully nearby awaiting the outcome of the attack and that was the place for Flashy. It was too late now, of course; Procter had been determined that every British man should be in the attack to show the warriors how civilised soldiers fought. I counted my blessings for the hundredth time in the last few minutes that I was in the rear rank. Fifty yards to go and still the attack seemed undetected by the garrison. They were not fools, I reasoned, and at any moment they would realise that our cannon had just stopped firing. I listened again for any sound of firing towards the diversionary attack. Would the Americans realise that an assault on the breach was likely to come at the same time?

Thirty yards to go and still not a hint of alarm from the fort. The first ranks must have been taking deep breaths to hold as they disappeared into the smoke. How many, I wondered, were thinking it might be their last. Still no sound of firing to the south. I began to inhale myself as I approached the bank of smoke but then all hell broke loose.

Black Eagle told me afterwards that the bank of smoke had drifted in the wind and stopped some fifteen paces from the wall. A tantalisingly short distance, but every single one of the one hundred and fifty American regulars had their weapons trained on the smoke. Inexplicably the diversionary attack had not even appeared when the first ranks of redcoats emerged. An initial crackle of musketry rang out. The first screams were heard from our forward ranks and then more fire as the Americans aimed blindly through the smoke, correctly guessing that more men would be following on behind. My eyes were just starting to sting from the smoke when I heard the first shots and I felt something pluck at my sleeve. For a second I thought it was Procter, but he was a yard away, pushing forward, waving his sword and yelling at the men to advance. Staring at the sleeve of my buckskin tunic I saw a neat round hole of a musket ball that must have missed my flesh by a fraction of an inch. I was now alone in the last rank of the attack and I did what any sensible person would do in those circumstances: I threw myself to the ground hunting for any shelter I could find.

The smoke was thinner at ground level and I saw a forest of legs moving forward ahead of me; some stumbling over prone bodies and others toppling like fallen trees as they were hit. Musket balls whirred above my head like lethal hornets and for a moment I just pressed myself into the ground. Deliverance arrived in the unlikely form of a portly corporal with half his skull shot away. He crashed to the ground just a few yards ahead. I crawled forward, grabbed his arm to pull him up on his side and then huddled in to shelter behind his lifeless corpse. I could hear Procter still bawling at the men to advance, but they could do it without me. As the American fire began to die away as men started to reload, the surviving British surged forward once more out of the smoke.

"Axe men to the front," shouted someone. Then another voice, Colonel Short, I think, yelled, "Come on, my brave boys, show the damned Yankees how the British fight." There was a full-throated roar from the men in front of me and despite the slaughter they had suffered, I heard them charging forward. I could picture them crowding into the ditch and up the other side with axes swinging to remove the last obstacles in their way. It was at this moment that the American six-pounder cannon fired. It must have been in the blockhouse overlooking the ditch, loaded with grape shot and musket balls. There was a chorus of agonising screams and yells as the lethal discharge swept through the ditch packed with soldiers trying to enter the fort.

"Oh dear God, fall back!" It was Procter's voice. He must have come out on the other side of the smoke and seen the carnage before him. It was obvious that the assault had failed; half the attackers were lying dead and wounded about him and Procter did not hesitate to order the withdrawal. "Fall back," I heard him repeat and then, "No, run back though the smoke… here let me help you." A stampede of boots started to pass my prone body, but I did not join it. I knew at any moment the soldiers would have reloaded and then another lethal hail would be fired into the smoke. I kept the corpse beside me lying on its side to give me as much cover as possible and waited. A second or two later another crackling fusillade started. It lasted nearly a minute and twice I felt the corpse next to me jerk as further balls hit it. Then the rate of fire began to slow, ironically to stop only when a shout went up that there were more British to the south. I was up then and running back the way we had come. As I left the bank of smoke I almost ran in to a man stumbling along clutching a wound in his chest, which was bleeding profusely.

Procter was there as well, encouraging the last of his men still able to retreat back towards the British camp. He glanced up when he saw me and then he cocked his head to listen. A distant crackle of musketry was now coming from the south. His mouth twisted into a bitter grimace. "Captain Flashman, I would be obliged if you would have one of your Indians inform Colonel Warburton that his diversion is no longer required.

"Right away, sir," I replied and moved swiftly on towards the edge of the trees where some Indians were watching. After several paces something made me look back at Procter. He had dropped down onto his knees, his head was in his hands and I could see that his knuckles were white as he squeezed on his own skull. He started to rock backwards and forwards, silently at first and then he started to repeat a word, getting louder and louder.

"Bastards…. Bastards…. Bastards!" he shouted. To this day I am not sure whether he meant the American garrison, the Indians who had pressed for the attack or Warburton's mistimed diversion.

Chapter 17

Colonel Short and another twenty-six men were left dead in the ditch at Fort Stephenson while another twenty-six were so badly injured they were unable to get away and were captured. Many of those died of their wounds. A further forty-four injured managed to return to the British camp although several of those later also died of their injuries. In all, half of the initial attack force were either killed or injured. Procter, while physically intact, seemed a broken man. Compared to his earlier renewed enthusiasm he plunged into the grip of depression and despair. He ordered the immediate withdrawal of the British force back to Amherstburg and once on board ship, locked himself away in his cabin.

One of the few people he did invite to see him was me. Many of his officers had been wounded and killed and he needed replacements. I venture that he chose me as he thought I was someone he could trust, and so we must add poor judgement to his many faults. I was invited to take command of the survivors from one company involved in the main attack. I accepted with ease. The general exuded an air of defeat and I could sense that he was not going to be launching any further attacks for a while. I could stay with the army if it chose to retreat north to the British centre and I thought being in the army would stop me getting dragged into any desperate action on the lake itself.

One person that Procter definitely did not want to see was Warburton. The good colonel did not reappear until the middle of the night after the battle, claiming he was pinned down by enemy fire in a ditch until he was able to escape in the dark. There was never a satisfactory explanation of why the diversionary strike was late. Warburton claimed that Procter had started his assault too soon, but some hinted that the colonel had deliberately tried to sabotage the attack. All I know is that Warburton had not been among the few that Procter had normally included in his confidence and that after Fort Stephenson Procter never trusted Warburton again.

Morale among the remnants of the British force plumbed new depths as we sailed back across Lake Erie. Blame and recrimination flew about, mostly aimed at the hidden away Procter and Warburton. Despite insisting on the second fruitless attack on Fort Meigs, Tecumseh was rarely mentioned. The few Indians travelling with us sat about and morosely complained that it was clear that the Great Spirit had abandoned the British. Privately many of the soldiers, and I suspect Procter too, would have agreed. The mood of gloom and despondency only got worse when we reached Amherstburg, for there more bad news waited. The American fleet on Lake Erie had got over the sandbar and was patrolling the lake.

If Procter thought his position was grim before, now it was truly desperate. Most of his food and ammunition was sent by boat down the lake and now the larger American fleet cut this critical supply route. With thousands of extra Indians and their families to feed, even with rationing, provisions would only last a few weeks. Ball and powder was also in short supply and unless the route could be re-opened the western Canadian force would soon be able to offer little resistance to any American attack. Procter turned to Barclay and implored him to do whatever he could to clear away the American fleet.

The new flagship *Detroit* was now afloat and the dockyard was working feverishly to get her ready to sail but they were still desperately short of materials. When Barclay had written to the governor general to highlight his urgent need for ropes, canvas, tar, cannons, gunpowder, cannonballs, pulleys and a thousand other things needed for a ship, he was told brusquely that none were available and he would have to capture what he needed from the enemy.

Copies of Barclay's recruitment handbills started to appear around the town and while they gathered some initial interest, a few days later the new American fleet appeared off Amherstburg and patrolled just out of range of the few guns left in the fort. Even the most dim-witted landsman could see that there were nine ships flying the American flag, while there were only six ships in the British fleet.

The few guns left in the Amherstburg fort fired a warning shot on the first day that the American fleet appeared to encourage them to stand off, away from the town. It was fortunate that the Americans did not press inshore to test our gunnery as what appeared to be guns in most of the gun ports were in fact painted logs. The original weapons had been rolled carefully out of the fort and down to the dockyard to be loaded aboard the *Detroit*. With them went nearly all of the cannon balls and the remaining gunpowder.

Rations for the garrison were cut again over the next few days as supplies began to run low. Something had to be done – and quickly. Procter and Barclay had no choice but to risk all on one last gamble: that they could beat the American fleet – if only they could get the men to sail it.

There was inevitability to my next summons to see Procter. I went with a sense of grim foreboding about what he would now ask of me; something that was only confirmed when I saw a grinning naval officer standing beside him.

"Barclay here tells me that you were once a naval officer involved in some famous naval victories," said Procter staring at me curiously. "Naval officer, army officer, spy and trusted emissary of the Iroquois: you are a man of many abilities, Captain."

"As I explained to Captain Barclay, my rank in the navy was an honorary one; I have no experience of sailing a ship."

"But you do have experience of fighting on one and that is more than the rest of my command," Procter pointed out, smiling. "All most of us know of life at sea is the journey in the transport to these shores."

"The general has offered to provide some soldiers to help crew my ships," interrupted Barclay. "When he asked who I wanted I remembered that you had sailed with Cochrane." I inwardly cursed my talkative nature as the sailor continued. "I need all the experience I can get and I will happily take you and your company as well as that big Indian who you travel with. He is already skilled in moving about the rigging."

"Of course, gentlemen," I answered while making up my mind that I would go nowhere near their damned ships. "I would be happy to serve wherever I can be of the most use."

"Excellent," Procter beamed at me. "Barclay thinks that he has the means to beat the Americans. If he can succeed then it will transform our situation here."

"But don't they greatly outnumber us in both ships and guns?" I asked.

"Yes but most of their guns are effective only at short range," explained Barclay. "The guns we have from the fort can be fired over a much longer distance. Most of the gunners from the fort have also joined the crews and so our fire should be accurate. If I can keep the American ships just within our range then we can batter them and take very little in reply."

Barclay sounded surprisingly upbeat for someone whose flagship had been cobbled together from bits of rope and spars found in the dockyard. Certainly our gunners were skilled, but I was not fooled. His strategy relied on having the wind advantage and that was notoriously fickle on the lakes. The Americans also had more schooners, which could sail closer to the wind and get behind us. No, I thought, the British fleet would be beaten and there was no way I was being dragged into a maelstrom of splinters in the middle of the lake.

As soon as I left Procter's headquarters instead of heading to the barracks to prepare my men for their voyage, I headed out to the Indian village to find Black Eagle. I knew the garrison was down to its last few barrels of flour: it was time to slide out.

To my surprise Morag was there and already helping the big warrior pack for a journey. "Black Eagle," I called as I walked briskly towards them. "It is time we left."

"I am prepared, Little Father. The Father with the One Arm has already found me in the town and told me about the battle he is planning."

"What? No, we are not joining the battle; we need to leave to go north." I looked around to check we could not be overheard. "The Father with the One Arm will lose the battle at sea and the garrison here is running out of food and supplies. If we do not want to starve, we need to head north now and live off the land while we travel towards safety."

Black Eagle looked puzzled but it was Morag who replied. "Black Eagle will receive one pound sixteen shillings in silver to join the Father with the One Arm. How much will he receive if he runs away?"

"He can't receive it or spend it if he is lying dead at the bottom of the lake," I retorted. "And anyway we are not running away," I added. "We are picking our fight, which is part of the Iroquois tradition."

"What do you know of Iroquois tradition?" she spat back at me. "The Father with the One Arm is the chief of the big canoes. He has fought in many of their battles and he says that he can win. He wants Black Eagle to join him and he will pay him much silver."

"I want to fight in the big canoes, confirmed Black Eagle truculently. "I want to fly over the water high in the branches of the ship and watch the Father with the One Arm beat the Americans."

For the next ten minutes I did my utmost to persuade them that this was just sheer folly, but they could not be moved. Black Eagle had always been fascinated by the ships and Morag seemed equally obsessed with the prospect of having money. I realised that I was trapped. I could not travel north on my own; with my hunting and foraging skills I would soon starve. But when I returned to town I would have no choice but to join Barclay's damn ship. I inwardly cursed the stubborn Indian and started to wonder if there were any real grounds for Barclay's hope of victory.

The next morning, along with the thirty fit men left in my company, Black Eagle and I were rowed out to the *Detroit*. To a landsmen she might have looked a sound ship, but close inspection showed that she had been built in a hurry. With a shortage of rope, there was a bare minimum of rigging. The ratline rope ladders up the shrouds seemed to have been made with scraps of cord and did not run across all the shrouds as normal. As we were rowed close to the hull, carpenters could still be heard banging away as they made final alterations.

Black Eagle was impressed, though, gazing up in wonder at what was the largest ship in the meagre British fleet. "Is it the biggest canoe you have seen?" he asked.

"No," I laughed. "When I was in Spain many years ago I sailed on a huge ship with over a hundred guns arrayed over four decks."

"A hundred guns," repeated Black Eagle in wonder. "You could capture the world with such a ship."

"Well not that one," I told him. "It lies in pieces at the bottom of the ocean now. Let's get aboard and see how many guns are on this ship." The answer turned out to be nineteen and serving them were many of the gunners I had last seen at Fort Meigs. Lieutenant Davis of the Royal Artillery made a point of giving me a warm welcome, probably still mindful of the insults at our first acquaintance.

"They are good pieces," he said gesturing to several iron barrels that currently rested on the deck. "Once the carpenters have made the gun trucks to hold them in we should be ready." The carpenters were busy making the small wheeled gun carriages that were used on board ship to help absorb the recoil of the gun. "Barclay is down below checking on stores," Davis continued. "He tells me that you have some naval experience. I don't suppose you have ever aimed a gun on board a ship before, have you?"

A memory came back of my time with Cochrane. I had wanted a chance at firing the six-pounder cannon and he had let me have a go at some Spanish merchant ships that had beached themselves to escape capture. One had been carrying oil, which having been set ablaze, had turned the whole ship into a huge lamp that could be seen for miles. Ultimately the inferno had attracted the enemy ships that had sunk us. "I did once," I told him, "but it did not end well."

"Well any experience is better than none. I don't have men to captain all the guns and the rest of the crews are soldiers only familiar with muskets. I would be most obliged, sir, if you could captain that twelve-pounder," he asked pointing to one of the barrels resting on the deck. I reluctantly agreed. If I had to spend time on the wretched ship then crouching down behind the substantial bulwarks with a huge lump of cast iron in front of me was a lot safer than prancing around the exposed quarter deck with the other officers. It would also give me something to do, and if Barclay was right, then well-aimed gunnery could make all the difference.

Once aboard, we sat on the ship without moving for over a week. The gun trucks were all completed and the crew divided into gun crews. There was not enough powder and shot to practice the gunnery but all the crews went through their paces, running out the gun, pretending to fire, bracing after the recoil, sponging out and ramming home the charges. After his enthusiasm to fight in the big canoes, I thought Black Eagle would jump at the chance to join my gun crew. But instead he preferred to spend his time aloft, particularly with the two naval seamen on board, listening to their tales of life on the high seas.

Several times Procter was rowed out to the ship. He was clearly anxious for the fleet to set sail as soon as possible, but Barclay was adamant that his strategy would only work if he had the wind advantage. Often during their discussions the two men could be seen staring aloft, where Barclay's commodore's pennant flag hung limply or flapped gently in a breeze from the wrong direction. Then on the morning of the 9th of September Barclay's luck finally changed: the wind slowly edged around to come from the west.

Black Eagle shook me awake in my bunk. "The sailors say that we will weigh anchor this morning. The wind is blowing us towards the east." He grinned, "Soon this ship will move across the water faster than a horse can run. Come on, are you going to sleep all day?"

I hurriedly dressed and went up on deck to find it a hive of activity and boats rowing to and from the shore like water beetles. Barclay stood on his quarter deck giving orders and beamed in delight when he saw me. "Captain Flashman, come and join me. At last the wind has turned in our favour."

"It is not a strong wind," I pointed out as I stood beside him.

Barclay glanced up at the flag flapping feebly above us and then checked we could not be overheard. "No, it is weak, but it is in the right direction." He lowered his voice. "Between ourselves there is not a day's flour left in the ship's stores. We cannot afford to wait for anything stronger. This wind, God willing, will blow us towards the enemy and more importantly stop the enemy closing with us too quickly."

"Do you know where the enemy is?"

153

"The last I heard it was at Put-in-Bay, this end of the lake near the mouth of the Sandusky, about forty miles away. Unless the wind strengthens it will take us a day to get there." He patted me on the back. "Sailing with Cochrane you must be well used to taking on excessive odds and winning. I know I can rely on you to help keep the men steady."

If you only knew, I thought, remembering the times that Cochrane's antics had left me quaking with terror. But aloud I said, "Of course, and it might be a good idea to have some more gun drills once we are out on the lake to keep the men occupied."

"Yes, an excellent suggestion," agreed Barclay happily, little realising that I would welcome the distraction of something to do myself.

We finally set sail at eleven that morning and the breeze wafted us gently south-east towards the American fleet. Much of the day was filled with the rumble of gun trucks as they were pushed in or out of the gun ports. Despite the fact that not a single gun had actually been fired due to the shortage of powder, I thought that the crews were shaping up pretty well. My men all knew their job and jumped to it automatically now without any orders from me. As night fell Barclay calculated that we were still only halfway across the lake. Lanterns were raised to keep the fleet together and lookouts posted in case the Americans planned any surprise attack of their own.

I did not get much sleep that night and I doubt anyone else aboard did either. Barclay had roamed the ship during the day talking to everyone and trying to instil confidence that we could beat the larger American fleet. Most seemed convinced that it was possible, but they knew that it was a huge gamble – with their lives as the stake. But they also knew just how desperate the situation was at Amherstburg; we had been on shortened rations and everyone knew that supplies were drying up. Without control of the lake the few carts that could travel overland would never be able to supply food and ammunition in the quantities needed.

No one needed help getting up next morning. Long before dawn everyone was waiting on deck. As the sun slowly crept over the eastern horizon we were all craning our necks up to the lookout at the top of the mainmast as he squinted against the light. Then came the cry we had all been waiting for: "Sail ho!"

Chapter 18

On sighting our foe Barclay immediately ordered a reduction in sail so that we were just crawling along. The Americans had been anchored behind a headland, but as the morning sun rose we saw their fleet labouring their way around it and tacking backwards and forwards to slowly close the distance with us. Barclay affected to be calm and relaxed, but from the way the fingers of his remaining hand kept drumming on the quarterdeck rail, I could see that he was as tense as a drum skin. If the wind stayed from the west then his plan would work; he would be able to pound the bigger ships in the American fleet long before their more numerous short range guns could be brought to bear. But the pennant at the top of the mast showed that the light breeze was fickle and to me it seemed to be edging south.

It had gone ten o'clock before the Americans had finally tacked their way around the headland and by then it was clear the wind was indeed shifting south. Barclay's gamble appeared to have failed. The more numerous American ships would soon have the wind behind them and then could press on towards us to make the best use of their guns.

"The breeze is still light," said Barclay staring aloft. "It will still take a while for them to close." He squinted at the opposing fleet through the powerful watch-keeping telescope and then passed the instrument to me. "They seem well spaced out. What do you think?" The British ships were arrayed in a line roughly east to west with the biggest ships such as the *Detroit* the middle. The Americans were coming from the south in a line of their own. Two small schooners were out in front but then was the first of two big ships, flying a commodore's pennant. There was a small brig behind the flagship and then a sizeable gap before the second of the larger vessels.

"The big one in front is the *Lawrence*," Barclay told me. "That is Perry's flagship. He comes from a naval family and seems to know what he is doing. The second big ship further back is the *Niagara*. They are the only two ships we really need to worry about. They are five times the size of any of the others. They both have twenty guns, but nearly all of them are thirty-two-pounder carronades. Short range, but murderous if they get close."

"Well the *Lawrence* will come into our range a long time before the *Niagara*," I pointed out. More in hope than expectation I added, "With luck we will be able to deal with them one at a time."

With a sense of trepidation I made my way down to the gun deck. My cannon was on the port side of the ship which would see action first. Gunnery at sea is a complicated matter: it is easy to line your gun on the target, especially in a calm sea; the tricky part is getting the range. I crouched for a while squinting down the barrel of the gun, timing how quickly the muzzle moved in the slow swell. The guns did not have a proper firing mechanism; I would have to spark the flint of an empty pistol over the touch hole. There would then be a split second delay before the main charge fired, and in that time the muzzle would rise several inches. To make matters harder you obviously could not look along the barrel as you set off the charge as the gun would slam back with the recoil as it fired. I gave the gun maximum elevation using wedges on the gun truck and then calculated that I had to wait two seconds from the bottom of the down roll of the boat before firing and then the ball would leave the barrel two and a half seconds from the bottom of the down roll.

There was no powder for practice shots and so we carefully loaded the gun and found the roundest of cannon balls for the truest line. The two schooners crept closer but we took no notice of them; it was the *Lawrence* we were focussing on. One of the American schooners opened fire with a large gun in her bows, but they had overloaded it and the gun exploded. We saw a flash and heard the thud of an explosion as its crew rushed forward to deal with the injured and put out a small fire. It seemed a good omen somehow for the battle to come. With what seemed like infinite slowness the *Lawrence* crept forward. Several times, requests were made to open fire but each time Barclay turned them down. We did not have ammunition to waste, but equally we had to make the most of the time when our guns were in range and the *Lawrence*'s were not. My eyes ached from staring at the ship through my telescope but eventually Barclay gave the order.

"Lieutenant Davis, I think you can try some ranging shots now." There was a cheer from those on deck as the tension felt immediately eased.

"Very good, sir," called Davis and then he turned to his row of guns and their crews. "Right, gentlemen, we will fire the guns on my order one at a time so that we can gauge the fall of shot for each gun."

The two big twenty-four-pounders went first. One shot fell well short, but the second probably went over the top of the big ship, although the gunner claimed a hit to jeers from the other gun crews. Two more guns fired and then it was my turn. I checked for the thousandth time the flint in the unloaded pistol I would use to fire the charge, took a final squint down the barrel and then stood to one side. I waited for the bottom of the down roll, counted two seconds, pulled the pistol trigger and stood smartly back. The gun crashed back on its ropes but I was already busy staring over the side, looking for the fall of shot. The cloud of gun smoke obscured my view, but those further down the deck shouted that a plume of white water had appeared just off the port bow of the *Lawrence*, the closest shot yet.

"Well done, Captain Flashman," called Barclay. "We will make a gunner of you yet."

I did not do so well with my second shot – the powder in the cannon's touch hole sputtered too long and by the time the charge actually fired the ship was rolling down again and the ball ploughed into the water a few hundred yards away. But as the *Lawrence* crept ever closer I did much better with my third. According to Barclay, my ball punched a neat hole in their foretop sail. "Good work, Flashman, that will help slow them down.

We had been ordered to 'fire at will' by that stage, although Davis kept emphasising that accuracy was much more important than the rate of fire. Gradually the range got shorter and soon I was knocking back one of the wedges in the gun truck to lower the elevation. I peered around the edge of the gun port searching for the *Niagara*, but strangely she had dropped even further back. Instead of forcing us to divide our fire between the two main threats to our fleet, the captain of the *Niagara* seemed content to let Perry and the crew of the *Lawrence* face the combined might of the British fleet alone. I could hear the *Queen Charlotte* opening fire now. She had been detailed to cover the *Niagara*, but as her foe seemed disinclined to engage, she moved forward to pour her fire into the *Lawrence* as well.

"A guinea each to the gun crew that gets the first good hit on her hull," called out Barclay. Moments later he announced that the prize had been won as one of the twenty-four-pound balls smashed into the *Lawrence*'s fo'c'sle. If my fifth ball did not hit the *Lawrence* it must have gone damn close and now all the guns seemed to have the range and the line. White spouts from falling balls appeared all around her and more holes appeared in her sails. Soon several guns were claiming hits to the hull and all the while she could offer nothing in reply.

At one point the gun smoke got so thick I struggled to see the target at all and took a few steps down the deck to squint through a gap in the haze. "I think she is three quarters of a mile off," said Davis peering over my shoulder. "We don't need to worry about her guns until it is half a mile." He grinned. "Plenty of time to knock holes in her yet, what?"

I got back to work, yelling at my men to haul on the ropes and tackles to get the gun muzzle back through the port. I could see the ship again and once more I went through my new ritual of alignment and calculation. Then I held the pistol lock over the touch hole and counted. I felt somehow that it was a good shot and ran a few paces up the deck to see around my own gun smoke while the crew started to sponge out and reload the gun. I was just in time to see the *Lawrence*'s sails quiver and back as the fore topmast was hit. With infinite slowness the mast began to slowly lean over the port side of the ship, the rate of fall increasing as various stays holding the mast up snapped. It smashed its way down through the rigging until half of the mast was in the sea. I could imagine men scurrying about the deck to cut the wreckage free as it was already dragging the ship around. Gradually the side of the *Lawrence* was exposed as the broken mast and sails acted like a giant rudder. Its guns stared impotently from the gun ports, but now there was a much larger target to aim at.

Naval warfare can be a brutal business, but when you are in the happy position of firing at an enemy that cannot shoot back, well it can be quite enjoyable. As I watched several balls smashed into the side of the ship and then my gun crew were yelling for me to get back and lay my own gun again.

Only the second schooner that had approached with the *Lawrence* was close enough to fire, but guns mounted in the bows of a ship are notoriously hard to aim. While I heard its cannon banging away I did not see a single shot hit home. The guns of the *Detroit* and *Queen Charlotte* pounded the *Lawrence*, over the next few minutes, but despite our efforts her crew gradually managed to cut away the wreckage and slowly the ship turned towards us again. We set to once more focussing on the bow of the ship coming towards us. Still the *Niagara* showed no sign of entering the fray and the other smaller American ships were also staying out of range. In contrast the British fleet stayed in a line with the *Queen Charlotte* now close behind the *Detroit*. Some of the smaller British ships, where they had guns with the range, were now also opening a carefully aimed fire at the *Lawrence*. The American ship was taking a dreadful punishment, but still it ploughed slowly towards us. Closer and closer it got until finally it was no more than half a mile away. Gradually the shape changed again as the ship turned, this time presenting her undamaged side towards us with the black muzzles glinting ominously in the gun ports.

"Now we are for it," muttered one of my gun crew. I fired our cannon and then throwing naval discipline in the scuppers, I ordered the men to lie flat on the deck. Well I could not lie down on my own with any dignity, and at any moment I expected a shattering impact and lethal splinters to scythe across the deck. I looked up and several gun crews had done the same, although Barclay and his naval lieutenant still stood proudly upright on the quarter deck. There was a dull roar as the *Lawrence* fired its first broadside, my muscles tensed waiting for the crash of iron into the ship... but there was nothing.

"He had double shotted his guns," called out Barclay. "It shortens the range." I sprang up and was just in time to see the remains of a row of water spouts falling back into the sea some hundred yards short.

Already the *Lawrence* was turning again to close the range further; I had a nasty feeling that Commodore Perry would not make the same mistake again.

We threw ourselves into the gunnery with renewed vigour, even more conscious of the need to stop the American ship before it stopped us with its huge ship-killer guns. I am sure that I hit the *Lawrence* twice in the next few minutes. Its sails were little more than a collection of holes now but still the ship kept some momentum. Then there was an almighty crashing sound and tearing noise and I looked through the gun port to see the *Lawrence*'s mainmast start to fall down the length of the ship.

Rigging and sail remnants crashed over the side, pulling the ship round again as it had with the top mast. I was relieved to see that it was the already damaged side of the *Lawrence* that would be facing us again. It was a feeling that was short-lived, though; as the first of its carronades crashed out. The *Detroit* rocked with the impact of the huge cannon ball smashing into its hull. There were screams and shouts from the deck below where the ball must have hit. My gun crew were already running our gun out again. There was no lying on the deck now; this was a duel until one side destroyed the other and everybody on that deck knew it.

My gun flew back on its traces, the smoke obscured my view but as it cleared I saw a hole in the *Lawrence*'s side near the gun port I had been aiming at. Three more of the *Lawrence*'s guns fired and this time there was a shriek of agony from the quarter deck. I looked around to see Barclay was down and his lieutenant was holding on to the mast for support, also clearly wounded.

"Keep firing," yelled Lieutenant Davis. "Aim for their gun ports." I looked along the side of the American ship for a gun that was still firing and gave orders for the gun to be shifted a point to the left. Only half of the *Lawrence*'s guns still seemed to be in action, but I knew that those gunners would also be aiming at our gun ports, possibly one lining up on mine at that very moment.

"Heave!" shouted one of the soldiers on my crew as they hauled on the rope that pushed the muzzle of our gun out of the port once more.

Carefully I lined my gun up on the gun port of the American ship. I could see flickers of movement as they completed their reloading. I had to focus, check alignment and wait for the down roll. Then I saw the muzzle of the American gun start to move forward but I was acting almost automatically now. Stand back and start to count... place the pistol over the touch hole... fire.

The next moment I was flat on my back, my left arm numb with an impact. My hearing seemed dulled for a moment and I remember gazing up and seeing Barclay being carried below with his normally white breeches crimson with blood. Shaking my head I looked around. The second gun along from mine had taken a direct hit. The ball must have hit the front of the gun truck, which had disintegrated. Splinters had killed or wounded most of the crew and some of those on the next gun. Of the heavy cannon barrel there was no sign, but judging from a smear of gore on the deck behind and a hole in the bulwark on the opposite side of the *Detroit*, it had been smashed overboard.

"Come on, men," I yelled, my voice sounding distant in my own ears. "Don't just stand there, reload!" If that sounds like Flashy being surprisingly brave in the face of the enemy, it wasn't. It was simply a matter of survival. If there is one thing that concentrates my mind, it is preserving my own precious skin. As I watched the pools of blood running into the scuppers, it was abundantly clear that we had to completely disable the *Lawrence* to survive. I felt my left arm, it was sore but nothing was broken. I flexed my fingers to get some feeling back as my hearing gradually returned and the noise around me got louder. The crew were already sponging out the gun and then a cheer went up from someone near the stern of the ship

"They have struck," called a voice. "They have only gone and bloody struck their colours." I looked up over the bulwark. The American flag was still flying from a half broken mizzen yard but the commodore's pennant was definitely being deliberately hauled down.

"Cease fire!" called Lieutenant Davis, "but keep your guns loaded until their other flag comes down." I slumped down to sit on a grating while most of the men crowded the rail to anxiously watch the American ship. Screams and yells from their wounded could clearly be heard in the relative quiet that followed such a prolonged spell of gunfire. There must have been the odd groan from our wounded too as they were carried below, but I do not recall any. We just stood and watched in silence until finally the rope holding the American flag was cut and it came fluttering down.

There was a deafening cheer then and men were embracing and slapping each other on the back. Against all the odds we had beaten one of the big American ships and our fleet should be more than a match for the remaining one. It meant that we could protect our supply route on Lake Erie once again. I wondered if Barclay was still alive. If he was, he should be told that his great gamble had paid off. I was just turning for the hatch when a voice called out in indignation.

"Look, their commodore is making a run for it."

I turned around in surprise to see a small cutter appearing behind the *Lawrence* and rowing hard for the rest of the American fleet. There were only five men aboard and judging from the pennant held by the one who was not rowing; it seemed that Commodore Perry was indeed getting away.

"He can't do that – they have struck their colours," shouted one gunner.

"Given the distance he is behind the *Lawrence*," called Davis. "I suspect he left before the ship struck."

A gun banged out from the *Queen Charlotte* behind and a water spout appeared alongside the rowing boat. Two more guns fired from the *Queen Charlotte*, both missing and then the stern most gun on the *Detroit* fired.

"Cease fire!" ordered Davis. "You could blaze all day at a target that small and not hit it." There were groans and shouts of indignation at this but Davis was not moved. He caught my eye and with a nod of his head gestured to the far side of the deck where we could talk in private. "We have used three quarters of our gunpowder," he murmured. "We cannot afford to waste it. We just have to hope that the commodore tries to preserve what is left of his fleet and takes it back to harbour."

163

"Surely he will," I offered. "He has just seen us destroy his flagship." As I spoke I looked around our deck at the damage. We still had all but one of our guns, although we had taken a fair few wounded. The area around the quarter deck was the most smashed. The first lieutenant had also been taken below for his wounds to be tended. Now a nervous midshipman from the provincial marine seemed to be the naval commander of the British flagship. He was gazing anxiously aloft where Black Eagle and a handful of other sailors were trying to repair some of the damaged rigging. One yardarm hung at an alarming angle, half pointing at the deck, but there was not too much damage to the sails as they had been side on to the enemy. "I will go down to Barclay," I told Davis. "He should know that his fleet has been victorious."

"Let's hope you are right," muttered Davis as I disappeared down the hatch.

Chapter 19

The bottom or orlop deck of a ship after a battle is a miserable and depressing place. Below the waterline it is relatively safe from gunfire, which is why the ship's surgeon has his station there, but this also means that it is damp and poorly lit. As I entered the gloomy interior, lanterns hanging from the low ceiling revealed more than a dozen wounded men waiting to be treated. Christie the surgeon was standing over a prone figure lying on an operating table made up of canvas tied over several sea chests. The lantern above this improvised stage shone dimly down on the patient: it was Barclay.

As I approached I was amazed the man was still alive. His right leg looked mangled and a huge splinter of wood was still sticking out of his left. His remaining arm had also been wounded and hung lifeless at his side. Despite his injuries, Barclay's eyes glittered with interest as I approached. "For God's sake tell me what is happening. I can't find out anything down here."

"You have a victory," I told him, smiling. "The *Lawrence* has struck."

"We did it then," gasped Barclay quietly, a satisfied smile crossing his face. "At least I have not died in vain."

"You're not dead yet," grumbled Christie. He gave a wry grin before adding, "Others would be insulted by your lack of faith in my abilities."

Barclay smiled weakly. "Well you took off my left arm so I should know what you are about." With a grunt of effort he managed to raise his head to look down at his mangled limbs. "You might as well ease up, John," he gasped. "I do not appear to have a working fin left. No point in living like that. I should go out at my moment of triumph like Nelson."

"Get away with you," growled the surgeon. "I should be able to save your left leg and I have not even properly examined your arm yet."

Barclay looked up at me, "You see, Flashman, I am destined to be buried in instalments." He tried to laugh at his own joke, but I saw a tear run down his cheek before he gritted his teeth at the pain he was suffering. "Tell them to let Perry keep his sword," he gasped. "He fought bravely. Why the *Niagara* did not keep up I will never know, but I will be forever grateful that it didn't."

I hesitated, about to tell Barclay a lie, but it just didn't seem right. "Perry escaped," I told him.

"Escaped?" Barclay's eyes were instantly open and staring sharply at me. "What do you mean escaped?"

"Before they struck, he took off in a boat with four seamen, rowing furiously for the shelter of their fleet."

Barclay closed his eyes and let out a deep sigh. "I fear then we might have been celebrating prematurely."

"He won't attack again," I proclaimed with more confidence than I was now feeling. "We smashed his first big ship and he will know that we could do the same to the other."

"He is a brave man, aiming to make his reputation," said Barclay quietly. "If he knows as much about our affairs as I have tried to learn about his, then he will know we are short of supplies. Do we have much powder left?"

"Not much," I admitted, wishing then that I had not told him about Perry after all.

"I am going to have to saw now." Christie looked down at his patient. "Do you want me to put the leather pad between your teeth?"

"No," grunted Barclay, as sweat started to glisten on his brow. "Hold my hand will, you Flashman?" he whispered, but he held up the stump of his left arm.

Unsure what to do I looked at Christie, but he just nodded and gestured at the stump before he turned his attention back to his grisly work. "I'm holding it," I told Barclay and then rested one hand on his withered arm muscle. A few seconds later and there was the awful grind of the bone saw doing its devilish work. With a slight groan Barclay fainted, slumping unconscious on the table. One glance at what Christie was doing to the captain's leg and I nearly joined him.

"Sit down on that spare chest if you are unsteady," ordered the surgeon. "I don't need you falling down and getting in my way."

"Thank you," I gasped taking the offered seat.

"Do you think the Americans will attack again?" asked Christie.

"I have no idea. I wish I had not told him about Perry now. You know, in case…." I left the sentence hanging.

"Hell's teeth!" exclaimed the surgeon. "Does no one on this damned boat think I can save him? He will be up and dancing again, you will see." I sat back and closed my eyes. Christie was mercifully quick with the saw and I felt the sense of nausea subside as he carried on with his work, humming quietly to himself. I am not sure how long I was there but when I opened my eyes again he had finished bandaging the stump of Barclay's right leg and was now working on the left.

"Did you really amputate his other arm?" I asked.

"Yes it was at Trafalgar, damn bloody day that was."

"You did not operate on Nelson as well did you?"

Christie laughed. "No I am far too junior to lay hands on an admiral. Commodores are my limit and anyway we were not on the *Victory*. There now," he declared straightening up. "That should save one of his 'fins' as long as it does not get infected. It is the arm I am worried about. There are no bones broken but he says he has lost all feeling in it. I can cut and stitch, but there is not much I can do about things like that. We will just have to hope that it comes back in time, these things often do."

"Well I suppose I had better get back on deck," I said getting to my feet. "With luck Commodore Perry is now sailing his fleet all the way back to Presque Isle." No sooner were the words out of my mouth than there was a violent crashing sound and the whole deck canted to one side. Christie threw his body over his patient to keep Barclay on the table, but I was sent sprawling to the floor.

"What on earth was that?" asked the surgeon. "Have we run aground?"

"We can't have done, we were several miles from the shore." Then I heard a crashing noise above my head, the snapping of spars and ropes. "Another ship has run into us, we have been rammed!" I called as I got to my feet and ran for the ladder leading to the deck above.

167

As I emerged onto the sunlit upper deck, blinking in the bright light it was not hard to see what had happened. The side of the *Queen Charlotte* was still embedded in the starboard rail of the *Detroit*, with the rigging of the two ships hopelessly entangled above my head. I looked to my left, struggling to get my bearings. Where the American fleet had been visible over the port side there was now only the shore of the lake a mile or so away. For a moment I breathed a heavy sigh of relief and then I heard a voice calling me from above.

"Little Father," shouted Black Eagle, "come and help me." I looked up and there was the big Indian halfway along one of the yard arms, hacking furiously at ropes with his tomahawk to try and separate the ships. He seemed in a desperate hurry and for a moment I did not understand. Then I realised that the gun crews and everyone else on deck was rushing about. It made no sense – the American fleet had gone. Then the sick realisation dawned. The impact of the *Queen Charlotte* had twisted the ship around. The port side, which had been facing south, was now facing the lake shore to the west. With a sense of foreboding I ran up the quarterdeck steps to look astern, to the south. There in the strengthening wind came the *Niagara*, white water breaking at her bow as she ploughed towards us. Gazing up I saw Perry's wretched flag flying from her masthead. Beyond the *Niagara*, the rest of the American fleet followed on behind.

A string of profanities escaped my lips. It did not matter that we had little ammunition, for most of our guns would be dismounted and wrecked long before we would have the chance to use them. The *Niagara* was already less than half a mile away but it was coming closer, much closer. Perry probably could not believe his luck: the two strongest vessels in the British fleet helpless and tangled together with their sterns pointing helpfully towards him. We were virtually begging to be raked by his big ship killer carronades. The heavy balls would smash through the stern windows and carry away everything and everyone in their path before they smashed through the bows.

"Little Father," called the familiar voice again from above, "I need your help."

I hated going aloft on a ship and rarely went higher than the sturdy maintop, but suddenly high in the rigging seemed a surprisingly safe place to be. It was certainly preferable to drowning on the orlop deck with the surgeon or being pulped on the main deck.

"I'm coming," I shouted and checking that my own tomahawk was still tucked into my belt I ran for the ratlines and started to climb. I swiftly reached the maintop but then had to climb the steeper rope ladder to the next yard arm. I knew that the *Niagara* must be getting closer but I dared not look down. Eventually the ladder stopped at a small platform, with the yard arm just in front of me. I stretched out one foot onto the rope that was suspended under the yardarm for the crew to walk along. It wobbled alarmingly as I gingerly reached out a hand for the huge wooden spar.

"Come quickly, Little Father," urged Black Eagle. He was standing on the same rope and must have felt the tremor as I put my foot on it. Instinctively I looked out to where he was standing and could not help but notice the height we were above the lake.

"Oh Jesus," I gasped as I switched my weight onto the rope and hugged the top of the yardarm like some long lost lover. Bent over, clutching the wooden spar, I looked down. The deck seemed ridiculously small beneath me, the crew moving about like insects. I raised my head to look astern and there was the *Niagara*, getting even closer and evidently planning to open fire at almost point blank range. We would all be dead if we could not separate the ships and so I edged slowly further out on the yard, hand over white-knuckled, trembling hand. It seemed to take an age but eventually Black Eagle was beside me.

"Here," he called passing me a rope as casually as if he stood on a street corner. "Hold this tight so that I can cut it." I grabbed hold of the rope and pulled it while still crouched over the yardarm. The big warrior leaned back. Keeping his balance with just one hand and grabbing his tomahawk with the other, he parted the rope in one blow. "Hold on," he said calmly as though I could actually grip any harder. "It looks like the American ship is about to fire."

I glanced down and the *Niagara* was indeed finally bracing round, its gun muzzles glinting in the sun as they pointed to the sterns of the British ships. When they fired the guns were so close you did not so much hear the cannon as feel the booming in your chest. The yard arm bucked as the ship below us was nearly torn apart by the impact of those huge thirty-two-pound balls of iron. As the ringing in my ears died away, it was replaced by the screams and shrieks of agony from the poor devils on the deck below. Mercifully the cloud of gun smoke shrouded much of the destruction.

"She's moving," shouted Black Eagle, who was pointing down at the *Queen Charlotte*. The force of the American gunnery had succeeded where our efforts had failed. The two British ships were at last slowly starting to drift apart.

"That rope is still attached," I shouted, pointing. One stuck cable would be all it would take to pull the ships back together again.

Black Eagle edged out to the very far end of the yard. "I will grab the rope, you cut it," he shouted over his shoulder. I eased out a few more steps, wondering how on earth I could cut a rope and hold on at the same time. Then the *Niagara* fired again and it ceased to matter.

To this day I am not entirely sure what happened: whether one of their guns had actually aimed at the rigging or whether it was a ball that had ricocheted from one of our cannons below. All I know is that one moment I was edging along the yard, and the next Black Eagle and I were holding on to the end of the yard arm that was falling through space. I must have let go of the spar on the way down. I don't remember yelling as I fell but I probably did. But I do recall feeling a sense of relief as I saw the sea and not the deck beneath me and then I hit the water hard, feet first. All the air was knocked out of me but as I opened my eyes underwater I got a good view of the fresh timber on the underside of the *Detroit*. I pulled hard for the surface and came up gasping for air. For a second I was alone and then Black Eagle bobbed up like a cork ten yards away. Between us floated an eight foot length of yardarm, with several ropes still attached.

"Can you swim?" I asked the warrior as I swam towards the wood.

"Yes Little Father," he gasped back. "But not as far as the shore."

I glanced around. The shore looked even further at sea level, but I remembered it was no more than a mile away and the surface of the lake did not have much of a swell. I could hear timbers still being smashed on both the *Detroit* and the *Queen Charlotte*; there would be no refuge on those ships. Beyond them I could see that the rest of the British fleet was scattering before the wind, but already the fast American schooners were chasing them down. We would either have to swim for it or be taken prisoner. I still did not trust the Americans dealing with prisoners, especially if I was found with an Indian. "Grab the wood," I told him. "We will use that as a float, so we can rest. Now help me point it to the shore and then we will start swimming."

Chapter 20

It took us two hours to swim ashore. The wooden yardarm undoubtedly slowed us down, but it gave us both comfort that we could rest when we wanted. Several times we stopped, holding on to that spar and watched as the battle reached its resolution behind us. The *Detroit* and the *Queen Charlotte* both struck their colours a short while after we had swum away. Holes gaped through the bulwarks and the two ships looked like shattered wrecks. We thought some of the smaller ships might escape, but as we watched each one was overhauled and captured. The entire British fleet had been lost.

Floating low on the surface of the lake we could not see everything, but we did notice the American flag rise once more to the top of the flag jack on the *Lawrence* and then a short while later Perry's commodore's pennant reappeared at the mast head of what was left of his flagship. It was the most complete victory. As I watched I wondered whether Barclay was still alive and I was not sure if I wished he were. We saw a few smaller boats rowing around the bigger ships picking up survivors but none of them noticed us and we certainly did not hail them. Captivity was not an enticing prospect.

The lake water was not too cold and as the ships receded behind us we scanned the shore searching for a good place to land. There was not a sign of civilisation anywhere, just mile after mile of forest. We had sailed past this land to attack Fort Stephenson. Put-in-Bay was close to the mouth of the Sandusky and that was American territory. But if we moved along the coast to the west then we would find the land that Tecumseh's people occupied and from there we could get back to Amherstburg.

We staggered out of the water exhausted. Apart from the soaked clothes we stood up in, all we had was my small telescope and my tomahawk which miraculously had stayed in my belt when I hit the water. The telescope had been in my tunic pocket, but had still cracked on impact with the water.

"We will need a fire tonight to get warm and dry our clothes," stated Black Eagle, "We would be best to go into the forest so that it cannot be seen."

"But we haven't a flint or anything to spark a fire," I pointed out, before receiving a withering look from the big Indian.

"Leave making the fire to me," he said wearily before leading the way into the trees. He found a good place to camp and sent me into the trees with my tomahawk to cut some dry wood to burn. By the time I came back a small fire was already burning on some kindling which he was feeding with dry twigs.

"I'm hungry. Is there anything around here we can eat?" I asked. Without a word Black Eagle took the tomahawk out of my hand and disappeared into the trees. I sat by the fire and slowly fed it wood, feeling pretty helpless in this environment. Once we had reached shore I had relaxed, thinking that we had only to walk to find help. But this was a hostile place without supplies or weapons. It would probably take at least two days to reach the mouth of the Maumee River, where Tecumseh's people could be found. Until then, I thought, we would struggle to feed and defend ourselves with just one tomahawk, especially if the Americans sent out patrols. Black Eagle appeared a short while later and hopes that he had found a tasty rabbit were dashed when I saw he had two washed pieces of root in his hand.

"You can eat this," he declared passing one to me and sitting beside me to gnaw on the other. You have probably not tried to eat a tightly balled roll of wool stockings soaked in sour goat's milk – neither had I – but that is what the root tasted like. I did not want to look ungrateful and so I gamely tried chewing on the thing to get some sustenance but it was foul. I looked at Black Eagle and he was clearly enjoying it as much as I. We caught each other's eye, grinned and spat the muck out. "The women normally boil this root," he explained. "Now I understand why, but we have no pot."

"We could try roasting it on a stone by the fire," I suggested.

"It will take more than a fire to make that edible," said the Indian. "I found a track when I was hunting, it looks well used. In the morning we will go along it and see what we can find. We will get something better to eat tomorrow."

We settled down resigned to hunger, but I reflected at least we were alive and free, which was more than could be claimed for the rest of the crew of the British fleet. It was just starting to get dark when we heard the unmistakeable sound of a horse whinny. Black Eagle was up in a flash and kicking dirt over the fire to put it out. "Someone is riding along that track," he whispered. "Come on." He was off moving silently through the trees so quickly that I struggled to keep up and see where I was going in the gloom under the tree canopy. Once, I stepped on a branch that snapped loudly. I could imagine Black Eagle silently cursing my clumsiness, but there was no shout of alarm. Suddenly I burst through the trees and found myself out in the open on the track. I caught a brief glimpse of some dark shadows moving away from me before I felt a hand grab my deerskin tunic and pull me back.

"There are four horsemen," Black Eagle whispered in my ear. "Americans I think, as they have two Indians with them tied up as prisoners. Look, they are going that way, heading towards Sandusky."

"Four of them, you say," I repeated nervously. I had been hoping for some solitary traveller we could rob. But if they had prisoners then these men were probably armed militia who would be on their guard. "They are heading in the wrong direction for us...." I started to deter my friend from planning any rash move, but it was already too late for that.

"They must make camp soon," growled the Indian and when they do, we will free our brothers and attack." He grinned, his teeth shining white in the darkness, "Come on. Keep to the edge of the path so that they cannot see you." I had no choice but to follow in the Indian's wake. At least with a break in the trees over the path allowing some moonlight to shine down, it was much easier to see where I was going.

As it turned out the big warrior was wrong. The Americans were not aiming to make camp; they had a far more comfortable arrangement in mind. The path crossed a much wider road through the forest and there at the crossing was a large wooden cabin. For the middle of nowhere it was quite a luxurious timber building, at least three rooms with a porch around the door. Two pitch torches illuminated a portly middle-aged matron standing at the front of the building, while two younger women peered through the doorway behind her. The militia men had dismounted and were all standing on the ground in front of the porch. One of them seemed to be trying to sell a bow, quiver of arrows and a thick necklace he had taken from the Indian prisoners.

"What are they doing?" asked Black Eagle.

"I don't know. Let's get closer so that we can hear them." We crept further forward through the trees, keeping to the darker shadows.

The militia man with the bow handed the weapon and other items to the older woman. "You can see it is quality work," I could just about hear him say. "One of these fellas is a war chief," he said gesturing to his prisoners, who were now being tied to a nearby tree. "That there necklace is made of wampum, made of tiny bits of shell. Indians really value wampum, worth more than its weight in gold, that is."

"Do I look like a god damn Indian?" the woman snorted. "She threw the bow, quiver and necklace contemptuously away into the bushes at the end of the porch. "If you want my girls it is gold or silver and not any of your god damn native beads."

The militia man who had offered the goods looked crestfallen, while his fellows hooted with laughter. I was shaking my head in amazement. "We have only gone and found ourselves a knocking shop in the middle of the woods," I whispered to Black Eagle.

"What is this 'knocking shop'?" he asked.

"A whorehouse. A brothel," I offered.

The Indian smiled and nodded in understanding. "I know what a whorehouse is. Now they will be too interested in the women to be on their guard." As we watched it looked like he was right. The first militia man had already reached reluctantly for his purse.

"Half now, half afterwards," insisted the fellow stubbornly. There is a cove familiar with the shadier practices of cat lane I thought. A second militia man stepped up with coins too and both went inside with the girls. The other two men settled themselves on chairs on the porch and yelled at their comrades not to be too long. A minute later the madam brought these two a jug of drink and then she too disappeared inside.

Black Eagle watched all this silently and then he turned to me with one of the most evil grins I have ever seen. "Now we will have some fun, Little Father. Keep your eye on the prisoners for a moment." With that he gave what I thought was an excellent impression of the call of the screech owl. The damn things had made me jump when I was first in Canada, but now I was used to them. The noise sounded good to me but something about it alerted the prisoners. If I had not been watching I would have missed it, but they both stiffened at the call and glanced at each other. While the militia men had ignored the sound completely, the prisoners evidently knew that the creature responsible was a lot bigger than an owl.

"Give me your tomahawk," whispered Black Eagle. "We need to free those Indians and I want to get that bow and an arrow." I passed him the weapon and settled down to watch, glad that he was taking all the risk.

As I watched his form melt into the shadows, I reflected that there probably was not a great deal of risk involved. A year ago and I might have been worried, but I had seen how easily the Indians disappeared into the forest. Hell if you were foolish enough to sit down among the trees, they could probably pick your pocket without you noticing, although they were just as likely to kill you and take your scalp too.

The first inkling I had of what Black Eagle was up to was a slight glint of metal in the air followed by a 'chunk' sound. Suddenly my tomahawk was embedded low in the trunk that the two Indians were tied to. A moment later and a pair of tied hands were already reaching out to grab it. I looked across to the militia. They were still chortling over some joke, apparently without a care in the world. They were not bothering to look about them; I suspected that the blazing torches illuminating the porch had already ruined their night vision.

Only by continuously watching where the arrows had been thrown did I manage to see Black Eagle again, a fleeting shadow as he grabbed what he wanted and slipped away. Then for an age nothing seemed to happen at all. I guessed we were waiting for the prisoners to

176

cut themselves free, but I became impatient. I would show Black Eagle that I could creep about too. Lowering myself down on my belly I started to wriggle forward, following the line of a shadow from a tree trunk to the shadow of a bush halfway between the trees and the house. I had nearly got there when suddenly the prisoners started grunting loudly and rocking about, still apparently with their hands behind their backs. They had been gagged as well as tied, but now they seemed to be trying to shout through the cloth.

"Shut yer damn row," called one of the militia men on the porch. The prisoners took no notice and continued to try and yell through their gags. "If you don't shut up I will shut yer up myself," shouted the same militia man. I watched lying prone in the shadows as he stood, hitched his trousers a little and after picking up his musket started striding towards the prisoners. He had covered half the distance when suddenly everything happened at once. One of the prisoners sprang to his feet. The militia man gave a surprised shout of alarm as he realised that the Indian's hands were no longer tied. He may have even glimpsed the tomahawk flying through the air before it embedded itself just above his groin. His comrade has risen at the first shout, but from out of the darkness an arrow flashed, hitting him in the arm.

"Indians!" the militia man yelled in warning. He stared in shock for a moment at the arrow protruding from his arm, unsure what to do. Then Black Eagle's war cry rent the air, followed a second later by cries from the two prisoners who had now removed their gags. The militia man recovered from his shock pretty quickly after that. In a moment he was vaulting over the porch rail with the arrow still embedded in his limb. As he disappeared into the darkness, he did not pause as he yelled, "Indian attack!" again to his friends inside the building.

I started to get up but then dropped down again. I had long since learned never to be first through a door if any enemy was waiting on the other side. I expected the militia to try to cover the doors and windows of the cabin with their guns, but instead they panicked. The shutters on both sides of the cabin were flung open. On the side nearest to me the militia man must have dropped down almost in Black

177

Eagle's lap. A shriek indicated that he would not live long to regret his mistake. On the other side of the cabin I had the briefest glimpse of a man running bare arsed in just a shirt with a musket in his hands, as he hurtled towards the cover of the trees. The two former prisoners were already standing over the man they had attacked and I saw the tomahawk rise and fall as he was despatched.

I was up and running now. With the militia men dead or running, that just left the women and I felt confident I could deal with them. It was the gallant Flashy to the rescue, to protect these damsels in distress from the savage Indian. If I played my cards right, I thought, instead of a hungry night in the forest, I could satisfy all my appetites in a nice warm bed.

It was only as I started to push open the door that I dimly remembered my golden rule about not being the first into a potential ambush. With heightened senses I heard that familiar click of a gun lock, but I was already throwing myself to the floor. In the confined space of the cabin the discharge from the gun was both blinding and deafening. I felt the disturbance of air over my neck as a hail of gunshot and assorted ironmongery disintegrated the top part of the door. As I looked up through the acrid smoke I saw the madam falling to the floor with the recoil, a big double-barrelled gun still in her hands.

"Damn your eyes, woman, I am a British officer and I am trying to save you," I roared. "Now put that gun down before someone gets hurt." I looked about me: two rooms opened off the central one; to my right a dark-haired girl stared out, part Indian from the look of her, while to the left a pretty blonde piece was kneeling on the floor, holding the trousers of her former client. She looked a very tidy indeed, but before I could say anything Black Eagle pushed in behind me, another arrow already strung to his bow.

"Little Father, are you all right?"

The madam screamed as he pointed his bow at her but I pushed the weapon down.

"I am fine. It was just a misunderstanding, wasn't it?" I asked of the madam who nodded in dumb agreement. I looked back outside; the

178

two former prisoners had picked up weapons from the dead militia and were running off in search of the two that had escaped, still whooping their dreadful cries. I gave a sigh of relief – it seemed we were safe. If the surviving militia had any sense this was the last place that they would come back to. I turned back to Black Eagle. "Keep an eye on these two, will you?" I asked pointing at the madam and the dark-skinned girl. "See if you can get them to rustle up some food. I am going to have to interrogate this other prisoner." I pointed at the blonde still kneeling on the floor.

"What is this 'integrate'?" enquired Black Eagle, but I was already walking into the blonde's room and shutting the door behind me.

"I'm five dollars if you want me," announced the girl as she continued to search the pockets of the abandoned trousers. I bent down and pulled them out of her hand. "Hey you cannot do that they are mine."

"No, they are a prize of war," I told her. "And anyway I doubt you had the chance to earn the money before your customer ran for it." I shook the trousers and a purse jingled from one of the pockets. I swiftly found it and opened it up. A handful of silver dollar coins lay inside.

"I am five dollars," repeated the girl staring first at the purse and then at me. "Are you really a British officer? You sound like one, but you don't look like one."

"Captain Thomas Flashman at your service, ma'am," I declared, formally saluting in my damp deerskin clothes. "Now I recall that your madam agreed a price of two dollars with your former client. A British gentleman never pays more than an American for a woman and so that is what I will pay you, agreed?"

The girl nodded sullenly but at that moment a shot rang out and we both heard the thud of a ball into the wall outside. I listened a moment for any more shots in case new militia soldiers had arrived on the scene. I still had no weapons and with armed men roaming about, prudence demanded going outside and finding something to defend myself with. But she was a very pretty girl and her curves reminded me how long it had been since I was last with a woman. My brain was urging me to check who was outside and arm myself, while other parts of my body were insisting that I stay and enjoy the bounties on offer. "Hell," I muttered to myself in indecision. But then I remembered that Black Eagle was outside and anyone would struggle to get past him. "All right I told the girl, three dollars but we have to make it quick."

She giggled. "Men normally pay me more to take my time, mister."

Chapter 21

Halfway through the bout with Sally, that was the name of the blonde girl, we heard the triumphant whoops of the Indians outside. I gathered that they had been successful in tracking down the remaining militia men. A few minutes later we heard two horses ride off, which hopefully meant that there were another two for us still tied up outside. I relaxed after that and told Sally to take her time after all. I was surprised that she did not seem the slightest bit bothered that the man who had very recently been warming her bed had probably just been killed and scalped in the forest.

"He was mean-spirited," she said shrugging. "I can't care about men in this line of work. You are all just customers and if you are paying cash money so much the better. We have had all sorts here lately. British soldiers and sailors, American sailors and militia, even some Indians with money and we always get people from the town." She explained that we were not far from Sandusky, but the respectable people of that community did not want a whorehouse on their streets. Husbands did not want to be seen visiting either and so a more remote location suited them. "We have had lots of Perry's boys in here recently," she told me. She raised her chin and added, "We heard the gunfire of a battle on the lake. I am guessing that as you are here in wet clothes, that means you British got your ass whipped by our boys."

I pulled her towards me and spanked her bare buttocks. "If there is to be any arse whipping to be done around here, I will be doing it." As I lay back I told her a bit about the battle and the outcome.

"What does it mean?" she asked.

"It means that there won't be any more British expeditions on this side of the lake for a while. In fact we will probably have to pull back from Amherstburg as we could be easily surrounded." The town was at the end of a neck of land that could easily be cut off by a landing further down the shore.

"The Indians won't like that. There are thousands of them living in new villages they have just built further west. Will they stay?"

"That was, I thought, a very good question. They would be loath to give up the territory that the British had given them, but they were reliant on supplies, particularly of ammunition from the British. They must already be in short supply and if the British were forced to pull back they would be cut off entirely. Unless they could raid the Americans for supplies, it seemed that they had little choice but to retreat north with the British or west on their own. My contemplation of the situation was interrupted by the sound of an amorous coupling in a nearby room.

"That will be Phoebe with that friend of yours," informed Sally. "She is partial to a big strong Indian." From the squeals of delight coming through the thin plank wall she certainly was and the sound reminded me of the opportunities I had close to hand. I reached over and grabbed Sally, determined to make sure I had my three dollars' worth.

It was dawn when we were awoken by the madam hammering on the wall. "Come on, git up, my girls have got chores to do," she yelled. It had been a much more pleasant night than I had anticipated when I was chewing on that disgusting root. But a rumbling stomach reminded me that while one appetite had been satisfied, my need for food was stronger than ever. I got dressed leaving Sally's coins on the bed and went into the central room. Black Eagle was just emerging from the far room. The girl Phoebe was visible over his shoulder, still lying on her bed appearing sated and grinning like the cat that had the cream.

"I have integrated with the other prisoner," the big Indian announced proudly.

"I think you mean interrogate," I corrected and then looked over his shoulder at the girl lying exhausted on her back. "On second thoughts, perhaps you are right. She looks like you have been trying very hard to integrate with her."

"You owe me another two dollars for Phoebe," demanded the madam, with a face so sour it could have curdled milk.

There were still plenty of coins in the purse and so I offered three if she provided breakfast. While she cooked I went outside. The former

182

Indian prisoners had left us two muskets, a good pistol and some ammunition, while a pair of horses remained tied to the rail where the militia had left them. There were two militia bodies sprawled near the house, but I did not look at those then to avoid ruining my appetite. I was hungry and soon we were sitting down to a plate of pancakes and syrup with half a dozen eggs boiling in a pan for us to take with us. It was good to have full bellies again.

"Do you know," I pronounced between mouthfuls, "that we are probably the only crew members from the entire British fleet that are still at liberty. Procter might have heard the gunfire but he will only know the battle has been lost when none of his ships return."

"Where will we go?" asked Black Eagle.

"We have no choice but to ride west along the shore of the lake. Hopefully we will not find any more militia. We must reach the Indian lands soon and then we cross the Maumee River and ride on to Detroit. We can cross the water there and ride on to Amherstburg. It will be around seventy-five miles and should take two or three days.

"I have never ridden a horse so far," mused the Indian.

"Well it will be useful to keep the horses because I suspect we will be retreating further north once we reach Amherstburg."

Having eaten our fill we went outside. Black Eagle picked up the wampum bead necklace that the American had been trying to buy the girl with and put it around his neck. I found my tomahawk still lying in the dirt next to the man it had killed. The man's pockets had already been turned out, probably by the madam hunting for more coins, and some discarded papers lay in the folds of his coat. I was just getting up again when my brain registered that the word 'Flash' had appeared at the folded edge of one. I bent down for a second look. I picked up the yellowed leaflet and unfolded it only for my blood to chill in my veins.

The paper was headed '*Criminals of War*,' and denounced four white men who were known to fight with Indians and 'indulge in their most bestial practices'. John Norton was listed together with John Brant and Dickson the Redhead, who had brought extra warriors for Tecumseh. I knew all of these men, they all had some Indian blood in them, but not the man who was given top billing.

'British officer known by the name of Flashman,' I read. *'Said to have been a chief amongst the Iroquois at Queenston, where many American prisoners murdered and scalped. Witnessed threatening American prisoners with massacre and scalping. Also to have allowed the drowning of American prisoners through overloading of boats. Justice to be meted out when apprehended.'*

It was a monstrous defamation. Yes I had threatened the prisoners with the Indians, but I would not have allowed their murder. As for the drowning, the threats had been made specifically to avoid the boats being overloaded. I sat back stunned for a moment as things began to fall into place. It certainly explained the ensign's strange reaction at Fort Stephenson. I wondered if that was why they had put up such a strong defence – perhaps they thought that only death and mutilation at the hands of the notorious Flashman awaited them.

I almost brought my breakfast back up when I thought what this meant for me. There I was behind enemy lines and I was now a marked man. Any 'justice' I could expect on capture was likely to be swift and fatal.

"Look at this!" I cried waving the paper at Black Eagle.

"I cannot read, Little Father, what does it say?" I was about to tell him when I noticed the madam staring suspiciously at me from her porch.

"Never mind, I will tell you later. Let's get rid of these bodies and get on our way."

Black Eagle picked up the two corpses that were lying outside the house and dropped them into the nearby trees so that they were out of sight. The madam was shouting that we should give them a Christian burial, but we had no the time for that.

"Get a Christian to dig them Christian graves," growled Black Eagle as he nervously eyed his horse and started to lower the stirrup straps as far as they would go.

I picked up one of the muskets and the pistol before walking my horse out to the middle of the little crossroads. Anxiously I looked up the road and the track but they were empty in all directions. I could not leave soon enough, but as Black Eagle got ready to mount up, to my surprise, both the girls seemed sorry to see us go. They ran up and threw their arms around us in farewell. I should have been more suspicious as it was hours later before I discovered the razor cut at the bottom of the empty purse tied to my belt.

We pulled free of their embraces and mounted up. Black Eagle appeared very uncomfortable on his horse, which he struggled to control.

"Have you ridden much before?" I asked, anxious now to get moving.

"Only once," he admitted, "and that was a mule, not a horse like this. They are hard to make go."

His mount, aware it had a novice on board, was being awkward. I was about to give him some pointers on horsemanship, but the big Indian solved the problem in his own way. Black Eagle leaned back in the saddle and gave the animal a tremendous slap on its haunch. It was a blow that would have stunned an ox and the startled beast sprang forward. The warrior only just managed to stay in the saddle, but after that he seemed to have little trouble 'making it go'.

We went back down the track, riding towards the west and for the first couple of miles we went at a fair pace. Partly because Black Eagle's horse was too frightened to stop and partly because I wanted to put some distance between us and that woodland brothel. As we went I told Black Eagle about the contents of the flyer I had found on the militia corpse. Then, having been caught out before by having incriminating documents on my person, I tore the thing into tiny fragments and scattered them to the wind as we rode.

"If you are caught you must give a false name," said Black Eagle. "As long we do not encounter any Americans who know you, or other prisoners who could give you away, you should be fine." He was right, very few Americans knew me by name and in my buckskin clothes I was far less recognisable as the British officer than I had been at Queenston. Still I was more than a bit relieved to find we had reached Indian territory at the end of the first day's ride, having not seen another American on our journey. We spent the night at one of the new

Indian villages, built on land Tecumseh had secured as a reward for helping the British drive the Americans back to Fort Meigs.

I had already agreed with Black Eagle that we would explain that we were scouts and not mention the fate of the British fleet. I thought that we should give that news to Procter first. While the villagers had heard the gunfire of the naval battle and asked if we had any news of the big canoes, they did not seem unduly concerned. The women were out in the fields tending the crops as though they had every expectation of still being there at harvest time.

The nearest sizeable American force was at Fort Meigs and the local warriors seemed confident that they could keep the garrison bottled up there – provided the British could keep them supplied with ammunition. I casually enquired if they had enough ball and powder at the moment, but was told that the latest shipment of gifts had been delayed. The local chief was not worried, though; he had been assured by the local Indian Agency representative that the next shipment would be double to make up for the shortfall. Whether the Indian Agency man had any understanding of the real situation or was just passing on promises made to him, it was hard to say. But as we rode through one village after another, the situation was the same in each one: complete ignorance of the precarious situation they were in.

Things were little better in Detroit. Judging from the surly looks from the American citizens, they had not received any news of Perry's victory either; nor had they heard the gunfire, being that much further west. At least the population was not hungry as supplies were getting through from farms in the area. In fact some stores were being transported over the Detroit River into Canada, where with more Indian mouths to feed, rations were now close to starvation levels. We took the ferry over the river and rode on to Amherstburg. We were halfway there when we came across two very excited warriors riding in the opposite direction.

"The British general has gone mad," they shouted at us as they rode past. "He is destroying his own fort." They were racing for the ferry, keen to bring this news to Tecumseh and the other Indians on the southern shore of the lake. I suspected that the peaceful complacency of the villages we had just ridden through was about to be rudely shattered.

"But the Americans will never be able to fight their way through Tecumseh's men," pointed out Black Eagle. "There is lots of forest. They would be ambushed every step of the way."

"They won't need to fight through them, they can go round them. They will join Perry's fleet at Sandusky and sail across the lake. Then they will have the Indian villages surrounded and can make sure that no more ammunition reaches them."

"Most of the tribes will look to make peace if that happens," said Black Eagle gloomily. "Will the big canoes take long to repair?" he asked scanning the horizon as though their top sails could appear at any moment.

"The *Lawrence* will, but the *Niagara* won't and Perry now has the British vessels to add to his fleet. He has more than enough to ship Harrison's army. They could be here in two weeks."

When we got into Amherstburg we found a group of redcoats half-heartedly working at knocking down the fortifications. They were, I saw, new, younger soldiers. These were the reinforcements that Procter had been pressing to receive for the last year. Ironically they had arrived just as retreat seemed inevitable.

I went in search of our general and discovered he was at his house in town. Having given my name to a scowling housekeeper, I was shown into his office to wait. Male and female voices could be heard arguing from the floor above and the British commander in western Canada eventually entered the room flustered and carrying three women's dresses. For a man facing impending military disaster, he seemed to have his priorities slightly out of kilter.

"Good God, Captain Flashman," he exclaimed when he saw me. "You did sail with Barclay, didn't you? Did one of our ships escape after all?"

"No sir. My Iroquois companion and I had to swim ashore. We commandeered some horses and have just ridden around the western end of the lake. I take it you have heard that the fleet was captured, then?"

187

"We heard the sound of battle and before he left Barclay assured me that he would send word after an engagement, even if he had to send a ship's boat to do it. When no word came, I assumed the worst. Now let me put these dresses down and get you a drink. Then you can tell me what happened." Procter draped the clothes over the back of a chair and poured two glasses from a nearly empty decanter. As he put the glasses down on a side table, the door burst open and Mrs Procter glared at her husband disapprovingly.

"Henry you have creased those dresses," she admonished, picking them up from where he had left them. "Now have you organised a second cart for our luggage? No, I thought not. Well you must get on," she gestured dismissively to me, "I am sure that this Indian will understand." Then she bustled out of the room without waiting for any reply.

Procter shrugged apologetically. "The women are preparing for our inevitable retreat, Captain."

"Indeed, yes sir, there is no avoiding that now." I tried to sound as though this was to be regretted but inwardly my heart soared. Ever since I had seen that wretched poster I had been harbouring the fear that Procter would choose to make some reckless last stand. "I suppose we will fall back on York?" I enquired. The headquarters of southern Canada had been re-established there after the American raid.

"Those are my orders, although it will be difficult to slip away. The Indians will view it as a great betrayal when they find out."

"Slip away?" I repeated astonished. "You surely do not think we can pull the British army back without the Indians noticing? Why, we passed two Indian messengers riding to Tecumseh on our way here. They told us that you were pulling down the fort. He will know in a couple of days and I fear he will swiftly deduce what it means."

"But we will never be able to pull back that quickly," cried Procter alarmed. "I have not told Warburton of the plan yet and he would need time to organise the withdrawal from Detroit."

"Sir I think we will need the Indians with us when we pull back. Even with your reinforcements, you will have less than a thousand men. General Harrison is rumoured to be gathering an army of three to four thousand. With those numbers they could land anywhere on the lake shore and cut us off."

"No," insisted Procter stubbornly. "I will not have that damned Indian running the show again. We will retire as ordered and the Indians will have to look out for themselves." He sat back and stared into the flames of the fire. "And anyway," he added quietly, "if the worst should happen, Harrison is an honourable fellow. He would treat the people properly."

I also sat back in my chair to consider for a moment. Without the Indians the British force would be small and vulnerable, slowed by a large retinue of civilians. It would be a very tempting target for Harrison; he was bound to do all he could to capture the whole British army of western Canada. Harrison was a politician as well as a general and he would not fail to see what that could do to his career. If the army was encircled then the identity of one 'criminal of war' would come to light. I could not afford to take that chance. On top of that if we betrayed the Indians, there was every chance that they would turn on us instead.

I look at Procter; his jaw was set in a resolute expression as he stared into space. He must have had bitter memories of being manoeuvred into doing things he did not want, but I had to manipulate him again. If I was to get the old fool to do what I wanted, I realised that I would have to gammon him – it was just a matter of finding the right levers to pull.

"I am sure that this will have no bearing on your decision, sir, but I probably should tell you that while we were making our way back from where we swam ashore, we made an unpleasant discovery." Procter looked up, his brows raised in curiosity. "We ambushed some militia men to steal their horses," I continued, "and on one of them we found some posters headed 'Criminals of War'. I am afraid to say that you that you featured on one of them."

"Good grief, what do you mean?"

The best lies were always those that have some element of truth to them. In this case I was just changing some rather important details. "The poster condemned you for the massacre at the Raisin and the prisoners killed at Fort Meigs, sir. It called for justice to be meted out to you if you were taken."

"You mean…" gasped Procter not quite able to finish the sentence.

"I fear that you will be hanged if you are taken, sir."

"The villains!" exclaimed Procter. "It is one thing to be killed or wounded in battle, but to be hung like a common criminal…." His hand went up to his neck, as though he could feel the rough hemp rope closing around his throat.

"Obviously such a matter can have no bearing on your decision," I continued, blithely ignoring the look on his face that told me that the exact opposite was true.

"Indeed, Captain," declared Procter straightening up. "We must do what we think is best for our command."

"As you say, sir," I continued, "but there is also the matter of the women and children."

"What about them?"

"Well I know that you have spent most of your career here in Canada, sir, but I have seen several military retreats in Spain. They can be particularly hard on the women and children, especially if the column is overrun." I paused for a moment to allow time for his imagination to go to work: marauding Kentucky backwoodsmen grabbing at his wife and daughters. "Without the Indians," I continued, "we will be outnumbered three or four to one. I don't need to tell you, sir, that morale is low, the men have not been paid for six months and are on half rations. Why, just on the way here I saw a poster some American sympathiser had pinned up in the street claiming that Harrison will issue arrears of pay and welcome deserters into his forces. We could end up with just a small core of loyal men, overwhelmed and surrounded in the forest by thousands of Americans baying for your blood, sir. And of course they would show little sympathy for the women."

Procter had paled as I described his possible fate, but I decided to twist the knife a little more, dropping my voice to a whisper. "It is very likely, sir, that the American officers would lose control of their men. I have seen it happen several times before with our soldiers at places like Badajoz. You would not want the women and your girls to suffer that kind of fate would you, sir?"

"No, no of course not," whispered Procter in reply. Events following the siege of Badajoz were notorious in the army. Everyone knew that even Wellington lost control of the army then, with thousands of innocent civilians raped or murdered. "But how will I persuade Tecumseh to help us when he will know I was planning to run out on him?"

I had already thought of the answer to that one. "Offer him powder and ammunition. His people are now desperately short and they will need it if they are to stand any chance of defending their homelands. Tell him he can have as much as his men can carry if he accompanies us to York. After all, there must be a stockpile there of the powder that they have not been able to send us down the lake."

"You don't know that damned Indian, Flashman. I tell you if we involve him and his Indians then he will find a way to have us dancing to his tune. He will not give up his wretched confederation that easily." Procter stared once more into the flames of his fire. "I appreciate your loyalty, Captain, and I will think on what you have said. Naturally I would be grateful if you would keep what you have told me to yourself, especially about the posters. We do not need others knowing about that."

"Of course, sir," I agreed watching the play of emotions across his face. There was fear all right, but it was hard to say if he was more frightened of Tecumseh or the Americans.

"In fact, given your experience of military retreats, it might be useful if you helped prepare for ours. It may be that we might need to send at least the women and children away with very little warning. Please include my carriage in those preparations; Mrs Procter prefers to travel in it. Oh and there is no need to keep Colonel Warburton informed. Between ourselves, I do not trust that man, I suspect he would pass on to the Indians any information he receives on our plans. Now, I must not keep you from your new duties …."

With that I was shown from the house and soon found myself standing in the street outside. Black Eagle ambled over from where he had been waiting.

"What did he say?" asked the Indian. "Why is he pulling down the fort?"

I tried to get my thoughts in order before replying. Being a craven coward myself I can easily recognise cowardice in others, but it was not that driving Procter. While I do my utmost to avoid unnecessary danger, I am mindful of protecting my reputation as well. But if I was right then Procter was planning to run and leave his command behind; protecting his neck and his family without consideration for the disgrace and ignominy that would follow. "I rather think the man's nerve has gone," I told Black Eagle. "I think he is planning to slide out on us all."

I had campaigned with some pretty rum fellows in my time, but this beat all. Dowlat Rao Scindia had gone to war high on opiates and concubines; John Downie had dressed his men like a Shakespearian theatre troupe; while General Erskine was insane, with certificates from the asylum to prove it. But all of those men had been outwardly brave leaders. Now here was Procter, a man just promoted to major general in the British army no less, who seemed determined to leave me covering his retreat while he raced ahead of his army and left most of his allies and possibly his second in command in the dark about the fact he was leaving at all.

Chapter 22

Over the next few days Amherstburg and the nearby town of Sandwich were turned into a hive of activity for at least some of the British – those who knew what was happening. Every river boat that could be found was gathered, loaded with people and supplies and sent up the Detroit River to Lake St Clair and the mouth of the Thames River. The Canadian Thames River went roughly along the route of our march and so it would be much easier to transport supplies by boat. But on the southern shore of Lake Erie the British garrison in Detroit and elsewhere was in blissful ignorance of the departure plans being made. Colonel Warburton only found out that the fort at Amherstburg was being demolished when he received enquiries from the Indians. When he wrote urgently for an explanation from Procter, he received a reply to the effect that the general had the right to issue whatever secret orders he liked.

Tecumseh could not be fobbed off so easily. Like many of his warriors, he was furious at what seemed clearly an act of treachery and betrayal. With some three hundred of his men he rode to Amherstburg and demanded a council meeting with Procter. Black Eagle mixed with the warriors and told me that he had never seen the Indians so angry with the British. Some were threatening to join the Americans and fight us instead, while others wanted nothing more to do with the treacherous white man. Ironically it was the fact that Warburton and several other British officers were also clearly in the dark about what was happening – and just as furious – which kept most of the venom directed at Procter and not the British as a whole.

For the next two days Procter kept seeking updates from me on the evacuation plans. It was two hundred and fifty miles to York and over half of the civilian population would want to join with the army when it left. Most of the local garrison was now employed in the preparations, but it would still be at least a week before sufficient boats, carts, animals and supplies had been gathered. I am not sure whether Black Eagle talked to some of his Indian friends, but Tecumseh seemed to have got the idea that Procter might depart in advance of the evacuation. Camps of warriors appeared on the roads leaving both Amherstburg and Sandwich and the Indians did not bother to hide who they were looking out for.

As the days passed, Procter's evasions began to wear thin. Some warriors threatened to drag him from his house and carry him to the council by force. Even Procter could see now that he was cornered and had little choice but agree to a meeting with Tecumseh and all of the senior British commanders and local officials. The council was held in a hall within the now partially demolished fort at Amherstburg. The half broken down walls served to remind everyone of Procter's perfidy. As the colourful Indian party gathered in the middle of the room and British officers around the outside, the mood was tenser than a drawn bowstring. I made a point of sitting well away from Procter when he arrived; it was not beyond the realms of possibility that a tomahawk or some other weapon would be thrown at him if the mood turned ugly.

The British general had been the last to enter the council chamber, to a roar of disapproval from the Indians. He was pale-faced and clearly nervous as he took his chair at the head of the room. I looked along the line of British officers present – most were not bothering to hide their amusement at their commander's discomfort. To open the meeting Tecumseh rose to his feet in a leather tunic with an ostrich feather in his head band. The warriors almost instantly stilled their noise, highlighting the commanding dignity of their chief. Tecumseh slowly let his gaze roam around the room, his dark eyes searching out those of every one of the British and Canadian officials sitting around the edge. Some looked away but when his eyes met mine, I raised my chin and looked squarely back. Finally he looked at Procter. Elliot, the old grey-haired translator, got to his feet beside him.

It was a powerful speech, reminding the British commander that the Indians had risen to support the redcoats at their request. The British had promised to protect their families and help recover their lands if the Indians fought alongside them. General Brock had promised that the British would never give up Canadian soil, but now the British were tearing down their forts and preparing to run without sight of the

194

enemy. There was no news of the battle of the big canoes on the lake and no American soldiers within a hundred miles. He looked directly at Procter when he continued. "We must compare our father's conduct to a fat animal that carries its tail upon its back, but when affrighted, drops it between its legs and runs off."

There were howls and hoots of laughter at that remark and not just by the Indians in the middle of the room. Procter sat red-faced on his chair glaring angrily back at the Indian as he finished his speech. Tecumseh declared that Procter was welcome to go provided he left the arms and ammunition sent by the King Across the Sea for his red children. He concluded by saying, "Our lives are in the hands of the Great Spirit. We are determined to defend our lands, and if it is his will, we wish to leave our bones upon them."

The Indians rose as one after that, waving their tomahawks in the air and demanding that their powder horns be filled. In the end Tecumseh had to rise to his feet again to demand silence so that Procter could make a reply. The general was a far less inspiring leader than the Indian commander, nervously licking his lips with eyes darting about for signs of any support. Clearing his throat he announced what he had known for nearly a week: that the British fleet had been completely destroyed and that the Americans had total command of the lake. Warburton looked furious that he had not been informed of this already and dashed an earthenware cup he had been drinking from to the floor in disgust. I suspected that this overly theatrical gesture was partly intended to convince the Indians that he had not been party to this secret.

Procter waited for the hubbub that followed his announcement to die down before he continued. "This council twice decided to attack Fort Meigs when we could have attacked the American fleet in its anchorage." He looked sadly at the warriors, silently reminding them that it was he who had argued for the attack on the fleet. "But now we must address the situation we find ourselves in. Each day," he told the Indians, "we eat fourteen cattle and seven thousand pounds of flour. This is more than the surrounding farms can deliver and now no more supplies will reach us down the lake. For the last few weeks ships have not been able to deliver the gunpowder and ammunition sent by the King Across the Sea – supplies are running low. The American control of the lake changes things. They will not fight their way towards us from Fort Meigs. They will come by ship and land behind us if we stay in Amherstburg."

A new burst of conversation broke out amongst both the Indians and the British and Canadians. A warrior stood up in the middle of the room. "You want to run like a frightened hen from an enemy so far away that you cannot even see it. Let the Americans come and we will kill them and take their supplies." This was greeted with a huge roar of approval from the warriors present.

Procter held up his hand for silence again. He had been weighing up the mood of his audience as he had been speaking and I think he must have judged that a retreat all the way to York would not wash with the Indians. So he looked Tecumseh squarely in the eye, holding his gaze as though that would convince the Indian of the veracity of what he was about to say. Then he told the chief what I was sure was a blatant lie. "We will just retreat a little way up the river to a point where the Americans cannot easily surround us."

"Where exactly will we make our stand?" asked Tecumseh getting to his feet again.

Procter looked momentarily alarmed at this request for detail. He had evidently not even looked at his map with a view to making a stand and had no idea where to suggest. He had no choice but to stall for time. "I will decide in the next two days," he announced before turning and leaving the council hall before any more questions could be asked.

Half an hour later Procter had ridden out of Amherstburg, heading for Sandwich while Colonel Warburton was complaining loudly of having just been handed written orders from the general. He was required to 'square things away' with the Indians. "I will be damned if I will," he fumed. "How can I convince Tecumseh of a plan our general has not even had the decency to share with me?"

The next two days were not any easier as the last supplies and the few guns left in the fort were transported by boat to the mouth of the

Thames. The Indians watched their abandonment with growing discontent, while messengers rode back and forth from their villages reporting that there was no sign of Americans marching towards us. It was not just the Indians that were verging on open revolt. Warburton and others openly questioned Procter's plan, with some astutely voicing the opinion that beyond headlong flight he had no strategy at all.

I kept my own council, although some looked suspiciously at me, thinking I was one of the few in Procter's inner circle of cronies that did know what was happening. I just went about my business of ensuring that we took with us everything that we might need on the retreat and left nothing of value for the Americans. I had been several days at this work when I suddenly remembered that my gold-hilted sword was still in the town store vault. I had spent so long dressed in buckskin with my tomahawk in my belt, that it seemed strange to have the weapon back at my hip.

While others moaned about retreat and dishonour and abandoning territory and allies, it seemed clear to me that surrounded by a lake controlled by the enemy, Amherstburg would soon be a very unpleasant place to be. This was especially the case if you were deemed by that enemy to be a criminal requiring immediate execution. We were leaving a place of imminent danger and if we could keep ahead of the Americans all the way to a place of safety, then that was just fine for me. Indians and their supporters wrung their hands and dashed hats to the ground, complaining that separating an Indian army from their traditional homelands on American soil would be the end of Tecumseh's federation. I did not give two pins for that; it had always seemed the most optimistic of ambitions. Individual Indians, never mind the tribes, were far too used to being free spirits. I thought that they could never be aligned and ruled as a single state.

But as time passed it was clear that everyone, myself included, wanted to know a bit more about precisely what Procter was planning, or at least have some reassurance that there was a plan. If the warriors under Tecumseh could not be convinced that it was worth remaining with the British during the retreat, then my earlier doom-mongering

197

with Procter, about desertions and massacres, could come true after all. A second council was organised two days after the first one to force our commander to talk.

When Procter arrived in Amherstburg for this second meeting he went immediately to his now sparsely furnished house and summoned me to report on the progress of the evacuation. I had just finished telling him of the supplies sent up river when there was a knock at the door. It was Elliot, Tecumseh's interpreter. His normally ruddy complexion was pale, nearly matching the pallor of the greasy locks of hair that reached down to his shoulders.

"I need to talk to you urgently, General."

"Ah, Colonel Elliot, do come in." Procter viewed the visitor with suspicion. I knew that Elliot had been in the territory for well over twenty years and Procter suspected that his allegiance was now more with the Indians than with the British.

"They are gonna break with us, General," warned Elliot without preamble. "I have never seen 'em so mad. One of them even threatened me with a tomahawk earlier and talked about taking my scalp." He paused and pointed to a large map of the territory that Procter had laid out on a table, "If you don't give them some hope of keepin' their confederation together then you ain't gonna have an army to retreat with."

"You mean they might attack us?" Procter looked shocked. "I cannot believe that they would be capable of such treachery."

Elliot gave a snort of derision. "Treachery is exactly what they accuse you of. I would not have believed it either a week ago, but now...." He took a deep breath. "For the first time in my life, General, I don't feel safe among some of them Indians. Tecumseh now, he will not turn on us, but he will struggle to control some of the wilder ones if you don't give him something to work with."

Procter licked his lips and stared down at the map, obviously considering his options. Then he looked up. "Gentlemen, rest assured that I have a plan and I will present it to Tecumseh and my other officers when we meet later this morning. And now if you will both excuse me...."

198

With that Elliot and I were dismissed. I had not had much dealing with the translator before, in fact I had been surprised when Procter had addressed him as a colonel, not realising he had a military rank.

"Do you think Procter has a plan that will work with the Indians?" he asked me quietly as we emerged back into the sunlight.

"I'll be dammed if I know," I told him. "He has not told me if he has."

Two hours later and we were back for the planned council meeting. I had brought Black Eagle with me so that he could listen in to the Indian conversations, but this turned out to be a waste of time as most of the warriors had refused to attend to show their contempt for the proceedings. Tecumseh brought just three of his warrior chiefs with him and Elliot, while Warburton also appeared with three of his officers, determined not to be left out of the discussions.

Procter opened the meeting by reminding everyone again of the implications of Perry's victory on the lake.

"How can we be sure that Perry has enough big canoes left to transport the American army?" asked Elliot after a whispered conversation with Tecumseh. "The Father with the One Arm could have sunk many before he was captured."

Procter turned to Black Eagle and me. "Because these two gentlemen were on Barclay's flagship during the battle. Flashman, perhaps you would explain what you saw."

I briefly summarised the battle and Tecumseh nodded several times as Elliot translated. "The Father with the One Arm was a brave warrior," he announced at last.

"Now gentlemen," called Procter directing everyone's attention back to the map. "I propose that we make our stand here." He pointed to a place on the map called Chatham. It was where a tributary flowed into the Thames forming a fork in the river. The Americans would be obliged to approach up the 'handle' of the fork if they were using boats, while the land between the two rivers would be protected on two sides by water. "It is far enough up steam to avoid us being trapped or encircled by landings further up the coast and is, I think you will agree, an excellent defensive position."

199

There were several glances around the room. Procter had surprised them with what seemed a sound approach and people began to nod in approval.

Tecumseh listened intently to the translation and then said something in reply. "Tecumseh approves," announced Elliot with I thought a sense of relief about him. He added, "It is also far enough to stretch American supply lines. The Indians will be able to ambush them, take supplies we need and leave them without."

"If you cannot take their ammunition, then blow it up," suggested Colonel Warburton rubbing his hands together with sudden enthusiasm. "We can hold them at Chatham and then wear them down until we are ready to push them all the way back here."

Elliot spoke quietly to Tecumseh, who beamed in delight. He turned to Procter, "I have explained that this means that he will be able to maintain links to the tribal homelands and that there is still hope for his confederation. Indeed, sir, you have given us all hope."

I have never seen the mood of a meeting change so radically and so quickly. At the start Procter was seen as a lost cause, disliked or reviled by almost everyone around the table. At the end of it he had given them hope of victory and the fulfilment of other more ambitious dreams. I smiled with the rest of them, but thought that making a stand in the way he had described was a wild departure from his earlier plan.

I was still not convinced that he had really changed his mind at all and so I stayed back at the end of the meeting until I could speak to him alone. He was just rolling up his map when I walked back to the table.

"Sir if I am to help manage our retreat I am going to need to know what our ultimate goal is. When we talked alone before you were aiming to retreat all the way to York, but now you have laid out plans to make a stand at Chatham." I took one final glance around to ensure no one else had entered the room. "Sir, are we really going to make a stand at Chatham?"

Procter beamed at me and put a hand on my shoulder. Then he looked me firmly in the eye and said, "Of course we are making a stand at Chatham. You can forget about retreating to York; we will make our stand and with our Indian allies and we will beat the Americans."

"I am pleased to hear it, sir," I said turning away. I had my answer. Procter had held my gaze just a second or two longer than normal. He had done exactly the same when he had spoken to Tecumseh at that first council meeting. I was sure the bastard was lying.

Chapter 23

Within hours of the council meeting with Procter, Tecumseh had confirmed that he would join the retreat and bring twelve hundred warriors with him. That second council meeting had taken place on the 20th September and by the 24th, unwanted supplies were being burned at Detroit. Trudging past the flames was a long line of Indian families, forced to abandon their new villages, heading for the ferry over the Detroit River to join the warriors heading north.

Our gallant commander, having secured Indian support for his retreat, had already departed Amherstburg. Soldiers wearing patched blankets and tattered greatcoats to keep out the growing winter chill reported seeing their general draped in fur rugs riding in his carriage up the road that went towards Chatham. He was doubtless aiming to meet up with his family that he had sent on ahead. By then just about every craft that could float with a shallow draught had been loaded with supplies and then rowed, sailed or towed around Lake St Clair towards the mouth of the Thames.

Most of the army marched after them the next day, mixing with a stream of warriors that were still coming over on the ferry from Detroit. Black Eagle had sent Morag to join the other Indian women and children as they trudged north. Instead of joining her he remained with me. I had been detailed to stay with the rear guard. This detachment had some two hundred soldiers and a similar number of warriors, with Warburton in command. We were not expected to engage the enemy, or you could be sure I would have been elsewhere, but instead to watch for their arrival and burn the empty buildings of the town.

I thought we would probably have another week before the Americans arrived, but they were in a hurry. They wanted to make as much progress as possible before the winter snows arrived and the very next day Perry's fleet appeared. But instead of landing in Amherstburg, they sailed straight past.

"They will be going to Detroit," announced Warburton confidently. "They will want to tell its people of their new dominance on the lake and leave a sizeable garrison there to deter any raids by the Indians still on the American shore." It turned out Warburton was right and the lookout we posted reported that the American fleet was showing no sign of movement as darkness fell. We spent a final night in Amherstburg and then the next morning soldiers and warriors roamed the town putting all the empty buildings to the torch.

It reminded me of the burning of the Portuguese villages during our retreat to Torres Vedras, but our general then had a clear plan to return and I was pretty sure that things were not the same this time. As the Union Jack came down the flagstaff in the already burning fort, I think all who saw it must have wondered if it would ever rise to the peak there again. The old dry timbers burned easily and soon spirals of thick dark smoke were rising into the air to mark the destruction of most of the town. The wind, I noticed, was blowing the smoke to the east, perfect to bring Perry's fleet back towards us from Detroit. It was not too long before the lookout reported that sails were approaching.

We rode out of town, Black Eagle and I, still on our stolen horses, while the warriors and soldiers marched along the track beside us. A steady cold rain had started as we began the march, which was already dampening the fires we had left behind. Those who had greatcoats pulled up the collars and turned their faces away from the wind. The weather made what was a miserable experience even more desolate. I remember feeling quite sorry for myself, wondering what this wretched conflict had in store for me now and if I would ever see the shores of Britain again.

Four miles along the road after a steady climb we came upon a hilltop. I glanced up and saw a knot of horsemen staring back at the town we had just left. Tecumseh, tall and erect on his mount, was unmistakable as was Elliot alongside him. Warburton and one of his officers were also with the group and he called me over.

"Captain Flashman, do you still have your glass?"

"One lens is cracked," I told him, "but it still serves to a degree."

"Well mine was smashed at Fort Stephenson; could you lend yours to Tecumseh so that he can view the Americans landing?" I rode across and passed over the instrument. Staring through the murky weather I could just make out several ships now tied up at the dock and long snaking lines of men as they marched ashore. Tecumseh scanned the men briefly with the glass and then raised it a few degrees to scan the distant horizon.

"He is trying to get one last glimpse of the American shore," muttered Elliot riding up beside me. "Probably wondering if he will ever see it again. Do you know where our commander is? I have not seen him since the council meeting and I would have thought his place was here."

"From what I have heard, he is at the front of the column with his wife and daughters," I responded in a deliberately neutral tone. To change the subject I asked "Tell me, sir, you know more about the Indians than most white people. Do you think that this Indian confederation could ever work? My Iroquois friend," I gestured to Black Eagle who had got off his horse to let it crop some grass a few yards away, "tells me that they struggle to align six small Indian nations spread over a few hundred miles.. He thinks that there is no chance of making all of the tribes cooperate as a single nation."

"Your Iroquois friend is probably right," admitted Elliot. "Two tribes further south are warring with each other as we speak. But he has to try. You know how things are in Britain and Europe. More and more will come here to seek their fortune and they will all need land. Unless Tecumseh succeeds, the Indian way of life will be lost." He gave a heavy sigh before adding, "And now it all rests on General Procter and what happens at Chatham."

He looked at me expectantly as though I would give him some words of reassurance, but I said nothing. Procter's nerves were shot and I had terrified the man further with talk of him being hung and his wife and daughters being ravished if the Americans caught up with them. I had succeeded in getting him to retreat with the Indians, but now I suspected that he would not stop for anything. The Indian confederation, the British hold on western Canada and a good number of soldiers and Indians would all be sacrificed. Procter thought it was to enable him to save his neck and his family, but in reality it was all to save the neck of one Thomas Flashman.

As I had not responded, Elliot lowered his voice and asked the question that he had really wanted to ask all along. "People tell me that Procter trusts you and he invited you to all of the council meetings. You must know him reasonably well. Do you think he will make a stand at Chatham?"

What could I say? If I revealed my suspicions Procter would deny it and probably send me on some suicidal mission as punishment. At the end of the day Procter was also doing what I wanted – taking me to safety. "All I can tell you, sir," I told him, "is that I asked the general that very question when we were alone and he looked me in the eye and assured me that he would make a stand at Chatham."

Elliot grunted his acknowledgement before adding, "It says something about your trust in the man that you thought it necessary to ask." He was going to say more but then Tecumseh uttered something in his native tongue and Elliot smiled. He turned to me and explained. "Tecumseh says he is surprised that they have not got their American flag flying already – the flagpole still stands."

"They would have a job using that now," I told him. "I had the flag halyard removed and two men greased the bottom of the pole as far as they could reach with a broom to stop them fitting another."

Tecumseh laughed when Elliot translated my reply and then looked at me directly. "No horsemen," he pronounced as he reached across Elliot to give me back the glass. "No horsemen," he repeated pointing down at the distant Americans.

It was the first time I had heard him speak any English and I was not sure how much of a reply he would understand. "Foot soldiers will be slower," I pointed out miming walking with my fingers. Tecumseh nodded and then stared at me frowning. His piercing dark eyes seemed to bore into mine. He said something to Elliot in his native tongue and the grey-haired man looked at me.

"He thinks he saw you at Fort Meigs?"

"Yes, I was there. At the first siege I fought with the Indians in the woods and I watched him stop the massacre of prisoners at the old fort. But I was dressed as an Indian then."

205

Tecumseh listened to Elliot translate my reply and then looked across at Black Eagle. The big warrior was now sitting looking bored on a tree trunk, stropping the blade of his knife on the leather scabbard. The chief muttered something to Elliot and then held out his hand to me. I was surprised but put out my paw and gave his a firm shake. Tecumseh nodded, smiling, and then wheeled his horse around and rode off after his men.

"He says you are a good friend to the Indians," Elliot told me grinning. "There are not many white men he says that about." Elliot pulled his horse around after the chief and left me sitting there, feeling a total fraud.

My feeling of guilt eased over the next two days as the manner of our retreat turned into a farce. If it was any indication of our effectiveness as a fighting force then the sooner we reached York the better. On the first night fifty of the British soldiers in the rear guard deserted. While they might not have believed American promises of back pay, they were disillusioned and in no mood for a long retreat only to fight elsewhere. During that first day's march we must have passed half a dozen carts and wagons, most with broken wheels which had just been abandoned rather than repaired. The situation was little better on the water. I saw a boat half sunk in the shallows, the muzzle of one of our few precious cannon now pointing harmlessly at the reeds.

By the end of the second day, Indians alone made up the rear guard but we then discovered that they were not destroying the bridges as we crossed them. Warburton had been given orders to take down all bridges after we had crossed them to slow down the enemy. But to the Indians this made no sense. Surely, they argued, we want the Americans to come with their loaded wagons over these bridges so that we can take their supplies? We do not want to wait for ever to beat them at Chatham.

They appeared a little less sanguine the next day when we discovered that some five hundred Kentucky horsemen had joined Harrison's army and that Perry had sent a flotilla of boats up the Thames in pursuit of our own. The pace of the retreat suddenly increased now and more and more equipment was abandoned along the way. Still the Indians would not destroy the bridges. Warburton had sent several messages up the line telling Procter what was happening and asking him to intervene with Tecumseh to slow the American advance. According to the messengers, Procter was travelling in his carriage with his family and declared he would reply in due course. No reply was ever forthcoming.

The following day the head of the column was due to reach Chatham. This I thought was when we would be certain if Procter was serious about making a stand or not. The line of the retreat by then straggled over several miles and the Americans were close on our heels. Late that morning a crackle of gunfire was heard on the opposite bank. A small detachment of British soldiers had been marching on that side of the river and we soon got messages back from scouts that they had been captured. Warburton and Tecumseh were sending scouts up and down the column gauging how far behind the Americans were and how soon we would reach Chatham.

At the next bridge, after pleading from Warburton, the Indians finally agreed to cut the supports and let it fall. It would not delay the Americans for long, especially their horsemen, but Warburton hoped it would give his men time to set up their defensive positions. The Americans were too close for comfort and I told Black Eagle that we had spent long enough in the rear guard. It was time to ride on ahead and see what was happening at the fork in the river. We rode our horses steadily through the throng of people on the track; I did not want to wear the mounts out if a more desperate retreat was required later in the day. Weary civilians parted down the road as they heard us coming. Many it seemed had panicked earlier when they heard the gunfire across the river, as even more possessions had just been abandoned in the grass scrub at the edge of the trail. Eventually we rounded a bend and there was Chatham laid out before us. The land in the fork of the two rivers was indeed a strong defensive position – which made it all the more regrettable that there was not a single person defending it.

Instead of soldiers digging trenches and gun emplacements on the triangle of land, two squirrels watched curiously from the trees as hundreds of people milled about on our side of the river. Many of the civilians who had jettisoned their belongings in their rush to get the protection of the British defensive line now slumped exhausted and confused on the ground, unclear what to do next. The biggest crowd was around four very harassed soldiers, who seemed to be trying in vain to get people to continue further along the riverside path. I rode my horse towards them and one, recognising me as an officer, pushed forward.

"General Procter has given orders for everyone to carry on up the river, sir."

"Why the devil did he not stop here as planned?" I asked.

"He heard the gunfire on the other side of the river, sir, and he did not think that he would have enough time to set up a defensive position before the Americans arrived."

"Do you know where he plans to stop now?"

"I am not sure he is, sir." The soldier looked over his shoulder to check people were not listening to our conversation and then added in a lower voice, "He set off at some pace in his carriage, sir."

Was I responsible for this? I wondered as I looked at the chaos all around me. I had wanted the army to pull back to safety with me in its midst, but not like this. This retreat had disaster written all over it. I was going to make damn sure I was not still around when the Americans inevitably over ran it. An angry woman with two young children was already pulling at the soldier's sleeve and demanding to know where civilian camp was.

"Good luck, Corporal," I called to him. "I think you are going to need it," I added as I wheeled my horse away.

"Is there a better defensive position further up the path?" asked Black Eagle after I had explained what had happened.

"No, this was the best one, but I am not sure that Procter was ever serious about making a stand here. He may have just said that to keep the Indians on board. Rations are sparse now; every step we take

208

further along the path will see our men get weaker and more equipment will be abandoned on the way."

"We will lose more than a few men now," warned Black Eagle. "Tecumseh only got the tribes this far by promising a battle. When the tribes learn that Procter has gone on, most will leave to work their way around the Americans and go back to their homelands."

No sooner had he finished speaking than there was a shout of alarm from back down the path and half a dozen horsemen could be seen thundering at full tilt into the clearing. As they reined up in the middle of the crowds I saw it was Tecumseh, four other Indians and Elliot. They were all staring at the empty land in the middle of the river in disbelief. Then Tecumseh stood in his stirrups and stared up at the sky while emitting the most despairing howl I have ever heard. There was a lot of shouting and raging then. Tecumseh hurled his tomahawk so hard into the trunk of a nearby tree in fury that an Indian had to use both hands to wrench it free. They would have cut the British general to pieces had he appeared at that moment and I was grateful to be wearing buckskin instead of the British red. Even Elliot was jostled by the Indians and seeing us sitting to one side of the clearing, he rode over.

"I will not, by God, sacrifice myself to their fury," he spluttered pointing up the track, "when that villain rides safely along in his carriage." He turned to me, "You knew he would not stop here, didn't you!"

"I was not sure, that is why I asked him and he told me that he would. I told you that, remember?"

Elliot cuffed a tear away from his eye. "It is the end, you know. There is no chance for the confederation now." He pointed at Tecumseh. "That man has been let down by British promises time and again, but still he worked with us, expecting only honour and decency in return." He turned away so that we could not see the tears of frustration running down his face.

I felt sorry for the old man, but he was making Tecumseh out to be some kind of saint when in fact the chief had always been working towards his own goals. "I think you will find that he wanted powder and ball in return," I corrected him. "No one else will give it to them and you said yourself that the Indian confederation was an impossible dream."

Elliot's face whirled back to face mine, his eyes blazing in anger. "You bastard! You did not want Procter to stop here at all did you?"

"I honestly don't know what would have been for the best," I told him. "If we had stopped here, well we have abandoned half our supplies on the way and could not have lasted long. Even if the Indians could have ambushed some American wagons, they could not have got the food through the American lines. The Americans would not have needed to attack; they could have starved us out. And you have seen our soldiers; half of them would have deserted if there was any kind of siege." What I did not add was that I would almost certainly have been captured, identified and hung. "At least going on," I continued, "we delay encirclement and stretch American supply lines further. But ultimately I think the Americans will win either way."

Elliot nodded slowly in understanding and then looked me in the eye. "Well I can tell you, sir, that Tecumseh will fight with us until the very end." With that he turned his horse and walked it slowly up the path, heading further north.

"Will we fight until the very end, Little Father?" asked Black Eagle.

"No, my friend," I told him. "I have other plans for us." We were interrupted by renewed shouts of rage from the Indians as more warriors arrived. One of the Indians had ridden his horse across the river and up onto the triangle of land. It turned out that it was not completely empty. Procter had left three of his precious cannon there, just the barrels, lying uselessly in the grass. As the new warriors vented their anger at British treachery, most of the white civilians decided that it would be timely to continue their retreat along the path. They were not the only ones. There seemed little benefit in staying at Chatham now and Black Eagle and I joined the slowly moving throng.

Chapter 24

Over the next few days the number of people on the march must have almost halved. There was a big difference between a retreat of fifty miles in the wilderness to an anticipated British stronghold, and a long aimless trek of two hundred and fifty miles, with little or no supplies. The Indians continued to mount a rear guard and fought several vigorous engagements, but their numbers dropped as first one war band and then another decided to leave. After three days the number of Indians had dropped from around twelve hundred to five hundred. But it was not just the Indians; many of the civilians, especially those with children or people unlikely to survive the longer journey, decided to take their chances with the Americans. They turned around and started to trudge slowly back the way they had come, perhaps hoping to recover things that they had abandoned days before. More than a handful of the British soldiers came to similar decisions and slipped away during the night. Not all were successful; two were caught by the Indians and brought back, badly beaten.

By then the boats that Perry had sent up the river were overhauling ours. Several boats were sunk or captured, including the ones carrying most of the spare ammunition. The American soldiers were pressing hard on the rear guard too now. It was only a matter of time before they overran the straggling column.

"Tomorrow we reach a settlement called Moraviantown," I told Black Eagle as we walked our horses past two carts loaded with sick or injured soldiers. "I have seen it on a map and there is a track from there that heads east, back to the Grand River lands."

"It would be good to go home," stated Black Eagle with feeling.

"Yes, from what I hear the British and Iroquois to the east have kept the Americans bottled up on the eastern end of the Niagara peninsula, so we should be safe on the Grand River." I thought it would be a brave or foolish American that would take on the Iroquois on their home territory. They knew the woods like the back of their hands and would ambush invaders every step of the way. "Speak to

Morag," I told Black Eagle, "and make sure she is ready to leave. We will go tomorrow night."

"Yes Little Father," agreed Black Eagle beaming with delight as he swung up onto the saddle and galloped off.

I knew he would spend the night with Morag in the Indian camp and so as the sun went down I found a group of soldiers with a good fire going and fell in with them. You know morale is bad in an army when the soldiers are too tired to even moan. Word was passed that an ox was being killed for food, but then they discovered that all the butchery saws and cooking pots had been sent on ahead and were already in Moraviantown. Normally there would be voluble cursing among the men at incompetent officers and venal quartermasters, but this time many men just seemed content to slump down quiet and hungry. We had a more resourceful corporal around my fire. He knew that it would be difficult to butcher an ox with a bayonet or a clasp knife, but as he looked around the fire he saw me, with a tomahawk stuck in my belt.

"Could I borrow your axe, sir?" he asked. I passed it across. A short while later he returned it, still covered in ox blood, not that I minded as he also brought with him a large joint of meat that was soon roasting over the fire. We heard several bursts of sporadic fire among the rear guard that night, but they all seemed some distance off. When I awoke I silently rejoiced that this was my last day on the march. My fireside comrades were ordered into line by a sergeant and resumed their weary progress north, while I went down to the river to wash the blood off my tomahawk. I was just dipping it into the water when I heard a horse ride up behind me.

"Flashman, is that you?" I turned and there was Colonel Warburton staring down at me. He saw what I was doing and grinned. "Have you been fighting with your Indian friends in the rear guard? From the gore on that tomahawk you must have taught at least one of our American friends a lesson in manners, eh?"

"Well I do what I can," I said diffidently. "I am not the sort to run without putting up some kind of a fight, you know."

"Yes I heard you had a fighting reputation while you were in Spain and then you fought with the Indians at Queenston and Fort Meigs. You and your Indian friend were the only ones to return from Barclay's battle on the water too. I can easily imagine how wretched you are finding this retreat." He peered around to check we were alone. "Some have urged me to take command from Procter, but between ourselves we are in such a pickle I think it is too late to save the situation."

"You may be right," I told him washing the last of the blood from the tomahawk. As I straightened up I lifted my chin and tried to look like a man brave enough to fight with Indians all night and march all day. "But I have never before been in a British army that has run headlong from the enemy without putting up a fight."

Warburton puffed himself up at that – whether he thought I was criticising him as well as Procter I am not sure. "You are right, Captain Flashman, by God you are right indeed!" With that the colonel spurred his horse forward along the track. I grinned as I watched him go. He was doubtless off to harangue Procter about the need to protect Britain's military reputation or some such call to patriotism. But if Procter would not stand at Chatham, his ability to stand was infinitely worse now. No, I thought, they could struggle on, but they would do so without me. A few hours more and then I would be long gone. I would reappear in a few months with some tale of struggling through the wilderness to escape whatever fate befell the column. I took my time getting ready to move and the first of the rear guard was just appearing down the track when I finally mounted up and rode off. I had barely covered half a mile when Warburton was back beaming with delight.

Captain Flashman, your wish has been granted," shouted Warburton. "We are finally making a stand, just a few miles ahead at a place called Moraviantown." He laughed. "You should see your face. It is the very picture of astonishment and surprise. But it is true and it is largely down to you. I spoke to Procter after our discussion earlier and he has agreed."

Heaven knows what the fool Warburton had told Procter or what possessed Procter to agree, but I am pretty sure that the look on my face would have been worth seeing. I was beyond dumbfounded. I was stupefied in my astonishment, my mind struggling to take in what had happened. Of all the damned luck, just as I was about to make my move. To add insult to injury it seemed I was the catalyst for an uncharacteristic show of backbone by our commander. Well I wasn't done for yet, I thought, I could still slide away. But Warburton was not going to let me go that easily. "Come, Captain, the general wants to see you. We will need everyone to help prepare our defence."

If I had been depressed about our prospects for success at Chatham, I was positively appalled when I saw the battleground Procter had deemed suitable. It was mile or so before the town and instead of a fork in the river, Procter had chosen some open land on the north-west bank of the Thames. He planned to defend a narrow strip of boggy ground bordered by the river on his left flank and a large swamp to his right. There were no Indians in sight and just four hundred redcoats being drawn up in two loose ranks on either side of a waterlogged patch of ground in the middle of this strategic masterpiece.

"Captain Flashman," called Procter when he saw me. "I hear from Warburton that you have called us to our duty. You are quite right and I am grateful to you. It is here we will make our stand," he announced sweeping his arm around his pathetic defences.

"But sir where are the rest of our men?"

"Apart from a few stragglers still coming in, this is all we have left fit to fight. The others are sick or wounded and some have been captured. I don't need to tell you that we have also lost some to desertion." He looked at me. "Oh I know it is a meagre force but for Britain's honour we must make some defence and look, we still have a cannon." He pointed to a solitary six-pounder in the middle of the line being lashed to a platform made of logs.

"But this is madness, sir. I know I said something about making a stand but I had no idea how few men we had." I was desperate now, I had inadvertently talked us into this mess and now I had to get us out of it. "There are three thousand infantry and some five hundred cavalry

214

coming towards us. We cannot possibly hope to win." I looked around to check we were alone before I played my trump card. "And sir, think of what will happen to you and your family if we are caught. I have been foolish, sir, in suggesting a stand and I sincerely apologise. I could not bear to have your life and particularly the fate of your wife and daughters on my conscience."

"Calm yourself, Captain. I know you are a man of honour and integrity and I do not hold you accountable for my family's fate, which is my responsibility alone. They are back at Moraviantown and have guards who will help them get away should the worst happen. As for myself, I am prepared for whatever fate awaits me." Subconsciously he moved his hand up to loosen the collar about his neck. "We will try to check the Americans here. Their supply lines are stretched and if we can hold them, perhaps they will settle for the territory they have gained to date and let us retire in peace."

Procter looked away as he spoke and I don't think that even he thought that this was a remote possibility.

"Where are the Indians, sir? Are they not joining us?"

"Oh they are to our right in the woods behind the swamp; they form a line at right angles to our own. They refuse to fight out here in the open and so will attack the flank of the Americans if Harrison comes for us first. If he goes for the Indians, we will attack the American flank. Now," he beamed at me, "we should find a position for you to command: my left flank or my right?"

I gazed about aghast at how I was being embroiled in this suicidal scheme. The left flank was opposite the track that led to Moraviantown, which was the only way I was likely to leave this field alive. "The left flank—" I started to suggest before Procter interrupted.

"No, the right flank I think. I need a good man there and it is close to the Indian position. You will be able to liaise with our allies." He laughed. "Warburton tells me that you were out fighting with the Indians last night and that he found you washing the blood off your tomahawk. He thinks you are more a warrior than a soldier." He held out his hand. "Whatever you are, Captain, you are an example to us all. You are a good man and a brave one. It takes courage to call a superior officer to his duty and you have earned my everlasting gratitude."

I automatically took his hand and gave a wan smile while inside my mind was screaming, 'You bloody fool; you should never have listened to me. I was only playing a part and now we are all going to die.'

I rode across the battlefield – an imminent field of slaughter seemed a more likely description – feeling like a drowning man being dragged into the depths. Every step took me further away from the road to Moraviantown, which was the only slender chance of escape. It seemed certain now that the Americans would capture us all. Some fool would blurt out my name and then I would spend my final conscious seconds dancing the Tyburn jig, dangling from a hangman's rope. Desperate to find some cause for hope I called out to the gun crew as I passed them still tying their cannon to their improvised gun carriage.

"Do you have canister or round shot?"

"We have neither, sir," called out an artilleryman, still bent over the gun. "No ammunition at all."

"Then what the deuce are you doing setting up the gun?" I exclaimed.

Wearily the man dropped the rope he had been trying to tie and turned to face me. I saw to my surprise it was the artillery sergeant I had sat with at Fort Meigs. As we recognised each other a grin spread across his face. "You again, sir? There is always trouble when you are about. This day I think will be no different."

"I wish I could say it is good to see you, Sergeant," I called, "but I suspect that we would both rather be somewhere else, anywhere else in fact. So tell me, why are you wasting your time with that gun if you have no ammunition?"

"The general thought the sight of it might intimidate the enemy, sir." The sergeant shook his head in weary disbelief before brightening slightly. "We do have some powder and Aldridge here is trying to carve us a cannon ball out of wood." He gestured to a soldier attempting to carve a lump of tree trunk with a knife.

"A wooden cannonball?" I repeated wondering if this situation could possibly get any worse.

"Well it will probably splinter in the barrel, sir," declared the sergeant, "so I would not raise your hopes."

"Don't worry, sir," said the soldier called Aldridge. "If this doesn't work we have another plan. We will pretend to load the gun and then we will all shout 'Bang!' at the same time." Several of his mates guffawed with laughter as he added, "That should scare the shit out of them."

"Bill!" shouted the sergeant to Aldridge. "You know better than to talk like that in front of an officer."

"Oh it is all right, Sergeant," I replied. "I think I can honestly say that his idea was the best one I have heard so far today."

When I reached them, the morale of the men I was supposed to be commanding on the right flank was no better than that of the gunners. The sergeant morosely informed me that most of his men had no more than three rounds of ammunition each. "But don't worry, sir," he added gloomily, "their cavalry will be in among us long before we run out."

I looked at the ground in front of us which was interspersed with a score of trees between our line and the edge of the forest. As their officer I thought I had to think of something positive to say, to encourage them to make a stand. Not least, because I did not want them getting in my way when I tried to get back to the road. "Surely," I suggested, "those trees will break up any cavalry charge and cause some confusion. They may even get that cannon to fire," I offered, snatching at straws of hope.

The sergeant just laughed. "You're that officer who was fighting in Spain, aren't you?" Without waiting for a reply he continued. "Those Kentucky horsemen don't ride knee to knee in neat lines like the French. They will swarm around those trees like rats with their tails on fire and just as vicious."

Well that was just the uplifting news I needed. I stopped trying to cheer the men up before I got too depressed myself. Instead I studied the ground between where I stood and the road and tried to imagine how long it would take to cross it. My contemplation was interrupted by a murmur of interest among my new command. When I turned round I saw two men emerging from the trees to our right. The tall slim warrior in the patterned shirt and deerskin leggings was unmistakably Tecumseh even without the white ostrich feather he wore in his headband. Beside him was the familiar figure of Elliot. As the pair slowly approached I saw the chief's eyes gazing around the British position. There was almost an air of pity on his face; he must have been bemused by Procter's insistence to fight out in the open rather than behind cover like the Indians.

"Flash-man," called Tecumseh, holding out his hand in greeting. Then he said something in his native tongue to Elliot.

"He says he is pleased to see you." Elliot paused before adding, "And so am I. I am sorry I was short with you before. You were just quicker than me to accept that our friend here's dreams are over."

"Think nothing of it. You have not seen that big warrior I have travelled with, have you?" I had assumed that Black Eagle would fight with the Indians, but I had not seen him since the previous day.

"Yes he is back there in the trees," confirmed Elliot gesturing behind him. He lowered his voice. "Tell me, do you think this line will stand?"

"Not a chance," I whispered in reply. "Tell Black Eagle for me that I will ride down the road to Moraviantown if I get the chance and meet him there." Elliot nodded and then we both turned as one of the soldiers asked Tecumseh the question on everybody's mind.

"We are going to die here, sir, aren't we?" It was a young soldier who spoke, little more than twenty. Tecumseh had been riding down the line of men, as though inspecting them, but making sure that he looked each man in the eye. As the young man spoke to him he looked across at Elliot for a translation. When he heard the question Tecumseh slipped easily down from his horse and gripped the young man by the shoulder, staring into his face as he spoke his reply.

Elliot rode around to stand beside him. "Tecumseh says that the Great Spirit will decide who lives and who dies. But he thinks it is better to die bravely as a warrior on a day that history-keepers in your tribe and his will remember for generations to come than to die old and forgotten in some winter lodge. He tells you to trust in the Great Spirit to decide what is best for you."

Tecumseh got back on his horse as the lad who had spoken gazed in a kind of awe at this famous warrior leader. Given how many times he had been disappointed and with his vision now in tatters, I was surprised that he had any faith left at all in a Great Spirit. Well the young soldier might have been impressed with the speech, but I wasn't. Dying an old man peacefully at home in a bed, sounded infinitely preferable to being brutally killed on some godforsaken bog at the arse end of the world. He could trust to the Great Spirit if he wanted, but I was putting my faith into my sword, the militia pistol and most especially, my fast horse.

The chief continued his progression down the entire British line, looking every man in the eye, shaking hands with every officer and even sharing a few words with Procter when he reached him. It was as though we were fighting for Tecumseh rather than futilely wasting our lives in a pointless gesture. Having examined his ally's position Tecumseh and Elliot rode back to the forest-covered swamp on our right where the Indian force was hidden.

The last of the British stragglers had by now joined the two wavering lines of men dressed in red on either side of the useless cannon. Several claimed to have seen American scouts peering out from the trees at the far side of the clearing. Certainly the Americans must have realised that we were finally waiting for them and I imagined Harrison pulling his various units into some kind of order before he launched the attack. There was nothing to do but sit on my horse behind the line of my men and wait for the inevitable.

Chapter 25

It was without doubt one of the shortest battles I have ever been in. It was also the most shameful performance of British soldiers under arms that I have ever witnessed, not that I am in any position to criticise. A chorus of bugles signified the engagement was about to start. For a moment nothing happened and then I heard the distant drumming of hooves. The American cavalry burst out of the trees on the far side of the clearing in a single mass. By Christ there seemed no end to them as they poured out of the forest, hundreds and hundreds of the devils.

Many of my men turned to look at me over their shoulders, their eyes white with fear. Normally a man who looks to me for leadership in time of battle is destined to be disappointed, but I did not want my own escape obstructed. I drew my sword and called out in a loud voice, "Stand, men, stand. Take aim and wait for the command." Then I glanced over to my left. The line held for now; muskets were being levelled. For the thousandth time I gauged the distance to the road – some three hundred yards but on horseback I would cover that quicker than most of the infantry. I would order one volley and then I would be gone. Those damned Yankees were not getting a noose around my neck. I turned back and out of the corner of my eye saw that the gun crew were already abandoning their useless weapon. Closest to the charging horsemen, they were the first to break but now one or two shots were fired in panic along the line.

"Stand still!" roared the sergeant at one soldier who looked about to run. By Satan's beard the horsemen were getting close. Then they let out some unintelligible roar of a challenge and I saw more men look round at me, little less than terror in their eyes. It is now or never, I thought. If they do not fire now, they will run anyway.

I raised my sword and brought it sweeping down. "Fire!" I shouted and a fusillade of shots rang out. I did not bother waiting to see their effect for I was already wheeling my horse to the left … and discovering I had left it a second too late. The company to the left of mine was already breaking and streaming across my path. Looking over their heads, it was as though Procter and the mounted officers about him were re-enacting the start of the derby. Every one of them was racing their horse to the track leading away from the battleground and behind them hundreds of men were running in their wake. I tried spurring my horse after them but it was useless, the throng was far too intent on its own survival to get out of my way. One wretch even tried to pull me from the saddle to take my horse and I had to beat him down with the flat of my blade.

There was another fusillade of shots and when I looked up I saw that the American cavalry were barely a hundred yards off, now firing over their horses' heads into the throng. A man near me went down clutching his face, with blood streaming through his fingers. It was hopeless. I would never get to the road and in any event that was where the American riders were now concentrating their charge. They wanted to kill or take as many prisoners as possible. I yanked again on the reins; there was only one possible escape now: into the forest with the Indians.

Two more shots from passing horsemen whistled past and I dropped low, my head down by my horse's neck. My heels raked back and the mount sprang forward. I glanced over my shoulder; most of the American troopers were ploughing into the fleeing throng but one had seen me and was wheeling his horse in my direction. There was just a fifty yards to the edge of the trees. One bewildered British soldier got in the way but just managed to throw himself clear as my mount thundered past. Another shot rang out close by. I looked behind again; the trooper was on my tail. He was putting his carbine into the holster and as I turned to watch the ground ahead I knew he would be drawing his sabre next. Well he had to catch me first, but now there was splashing under my horse's hooves as we began to enter the swamp area. The horse was slowing; it could not gallop through thick mud. I heard a cry of triumph from the man behind but then there was the sound of another shot. Peering back I saw that he had pulled a pistol rather than a sword and I thanked my lucky stars he was a poor shot, missing both horse and rider. But as my horse struggled forward a few more paces, I saw over my pursuer's shoulder that two more of the troopers were heading my way.

My screw was sinking past its fetlocks in the mud now and was struggling to make any progress at all. With three of the bastards on my tail I dropped from the saddle and into the thick ooze. I managed to run forward three paces, trying to move before my boots sunk into the mud but then I heard hooves to my right. The first pursuer had found a ridge of firmer ground and was rounding on me to cut me off, his two comrades fast approaching to cut off any escape.

"Yield, you devil," he shouted. This time he did have his sabre in his hand and he hauled it up above his head for a killing stroke.

If there was anything better than a hangman's noose awaiting me, I would have yielded then, but the fear of death kept me going. I twisted away, getting my own blade up just in time to block his blow. As the trooper wheeled his horse around for a clearer swing, I remembered something I had learned years ago from an old East India Company cavalryman. With all my remaining strength I swung my left hand to punch the animal on the nose. The horse, not surprisingly, reared up at this rough treatment and with a yell of alarm its rider was pitched out of the saddle.

For the briefest of seconds I thought I would get away. I pulled my boot out of the mud and tried to take another step forward. But then I heard a yell of rage behind and a bullet smacked into the muddy hole my foot had just vacated. I turned and there were the two other riders, sensibly staying clear of the mud. The first had rushed his shot but the second was taking his time while his comrade reloaded. The man aiming grinned as he squinted down the barrel; the muzzle looked like a black eye of death as it pointed directly at me. I swear I could see the light glint on the rifling grooves inside the muzzle. From that distance the man could not miss. I tore my other boot out of the mud but the first was already sinking again. I would never get away this time, I was done for. I shut my eyes my body tensed for the impact of the ball in my flesh. There was the sound of the shot, but remarkably no pain. Half in disbelief, I opened my eyes to look back at the trooper who had been aiming at me. I was just in time to see him topple lifeless from the saddle. Then I heard a voice ahead of me

"Flash-man."

I turned and there was Tecumseh at the edge of the trees, a rifle in his hand with a trail of gun smoke to show that it had just been fired. A handful of other warriors were also appearing and the two surviving troopers were quick to make their escape as two more shots rang out.

"Flash-man," repeated Tecumseh, "come." He pointed into the trees and I did not need telling twice. As I struggled forward through the mud he pointed to a cluster of blue flowers growing to my right. "There," he shouted. It seemed a strange time for a botanical observation, but then I realised that the ground was dryer under those flowers. The trooper who had overhauled me must have seen them and known that. I hauled my feet out of the mire until I stood on the little blue blooms, panting with the exertion of the last few moments. I turned back. The two surviving troopers who had chased me were now both mounted and racing back to their fellows. In the distance I could see redcoats being herded like sheep and almost queuing to surrender.

The troopers must have been yelling that the woods beyond the swamp were packed with Indians as I saw several heads turn and look our way. But if they were in any doubt, Tecumseh now issued a challenge of his own. He was still standing in plain view in front of the trees, his white ostrich feather marking him out as a chief. He raised his rifle in one hand above his head and lifting his chin he gave a long ululating war cry. Within a moment this was taken up by every Indian in the forest. It sounded as though there were thousands of the painted warriors in those trees, which of course was the point.

The American cavalry commander must have known who it was with the white feather and he did not hesitate. I saw him wave his sword and give the order to charge, spurring his horse towards us. Only around twenty of his nearest men came with him. The rest were still in a disordered group, trying to disentangle themselves from hapless British prisoners. I reached Tecumseh and he slapped me on the shoulder and turned to re-join his men. As we entered the trees he was laughing and shouting something to his warriors, while he seemed to be miming me punching the horse. Whatever he said his warriors guffawed, apparently unconcerned at the horsemen charging towards us. I looked over my shoulder at the approaching Americans. The twenty men were still out in front, but now a much larger body of men was charging along behind.

I'll say this for that cavalry commander; he was a brave man as his small advance party acted like a mounted 'forlorn hope' as they approached the wood. As I pushed on through the trees desperate to get as far from the coming carnage as possible, I saw hundreds of muskets levelled at their approach. There was a rippling crash of musket fire and when I looked again virtually all of the twenty men were down and horses were thrashing wounded in the wet mud. But now at least half of the nearby Indians were unloaded and the smoke gave away their positions. The much larger group of horsemen hurtled on and more than a few seemed to be heading for the dryer ground marked by the blue flowers. The Americans crashed through the outer trees of the swamp and the Indians gave way, falling back. More guns fired and musket smoke marked the edge of the swamp as Indians either screamed in agony or victory, as they were either hit or took down an enemy. I heard orders to dismount and saw the first of the Americans emerging from the smoke behind me and firing through the trees.

I was already pressing on, I had been through enough. The Indians could hold the Americans and buy me time to get away. The cacophony of battle echoing through the trees was deafening. If I needed any more encouragement to move quickly, I got it when a musket ball slammed into a tree just a yard from my side. Staring around I saw a slight incline and headed for it; the ground must be dryer there, I thought, as I slipped in another muddy pool.

"Little Father!" It was amazing I heard him above the noise of battle, but my head whipped around and there was Black Eagle reloading behind a tree twenty yards away. I pointed to the higher ground and beckoned him to follow. As I started to run up the slope I took a glance back. Like the Indians before them, most of the Americans had fired and now they were more vulnerable. Groups of warriors were charging forward to regain their lost ground. One group was led by a tall slim Indian with a white ostrich feather in his hair. He was halfway across a small clearing when he went down, clutching his side. There was so much gunfire you could not have made out the sound of the shot, but I saw a dark stain begin to spread across his shirt as he tried to pull himself up on one knee. The warriors he was with let up a terrible whooping. They pushed forward again to rescue their chief, but a ferocious fire from the Americans forced them back. I watched as the battle raged just fifty yards away, transfixed by that slim figure in the middle of the clearing. I could not see who had shot him, but he seemed done for to me. The bullet must have smashed though his ribs. Finally he toppled over to his side, his limbs relaxed and I knew he had gone.

"Little Father, are you all right?" Black Eagle was shaking my arm. "Come we must get away." It says something about my feelings for Tecumseh that for a brief moment I forgot about my own self-preservation. I barely knew the man and had seen for myself that he could be blinkered about achieving his own goals. But he had natural nobility to him, a leadership that impressed even those who could not understand him; and most importantly of all, he had just saved my life. I shook myself from my reverie and turned to continue running up the slope towards safety. As we reached the crest of the hill I had one last look back. The battle was still raging near where Tecumseh fell. Warriors were whooping and darting backwards and forwards, but I could make out other warriors who were slipping back in the same direction as us. "They won't stand for long when they learn that their chief is dead," warned Black Eagle. "Come, we must get on our way. Morag is waiting further down the track.

We ran on down the track for nearly half a mile before a voice barked out, "This way." Black Eagle smiled endearingly at his woman while she gave me her normal pinch-faced glare of disapproval. Her red hair was mostly hidden by a deerskin bonnet and she had a blanket over the top of her deerskin clothes to keep out the cold. But instead of being a beast of burden, this time she had Black Eagle's horse laden with her possessions. As we ran over she untied the creature and led it deeper into the forest.

I glanced up into the sky, looking for the sun. I had lost my bearings over the last few minutes, but the low light shining through the trees confirmed my suspicion that we were heading north-west when we should have been heading north-east. "Aren't we going the wrong way?" I asked hesitantly, pointing in what I thought was the right direction.

"Fool," Morag glared at me. "Every British soldier will be running for Moraviantown and beyond with all of the American army chasing them. Do you think we can pass through two armies without being seen and killed or robbed?

"Where are we going then?" I asked.

"We are going to a hidden place to wait for the armies to go away." What she said made some sense. We would need our supplies to make our way to the Grand River lands; the first snows would be coming soon. Black Eagle just grinned and shrugged his shoulders as he set off after his woman and I had little choice but to follow.

We spent the next three days in a small hidden glade that Morag must have found before as she led us straight to it. There were three other Indian families there already and several warriors joined us during the late afternoon. The battle, they claimed, had been lost and the Indians were dispersing. When I asked about Elliot one of them said that they had seen him leading Tecumseh's son away from the battle. No one lit a fire until it was dark and then we sat warming ourselves, listening to the occasional crackle of musket fire from what I judged to be the direction of Moraviantown. At dawn the fire was doused and we stayed restlessly in the camp. Black Eagle managed to climb high up a tree and called me to join him. "It is easier than a big canoe mast," he shouted before being hissed to silence by Morag. I had not climbed a tree since I was a boy, but with nothing else to do I scrabbled up as high as I could. We could see for miles but with most of the ground covered by forest we could spot little of interest. I got out the glass from my pocket and scanned the land around. I could just make out the clearing of the battlefield which the Americans now seemed to be camped on. Moving the glass to the left I found some bluffs which marked the settlement of Moraviantown. I could not see much, but a smudge of smoke indicated that at least one building had been burned. The only gunfire we heard now was the occasional single shot. Those in the British force had either escaped or been captured. There was no sign of any further pursuit among the Americans. They had beaten their enemy. I just hoped it would not take them long to decide to go back south.

We were not to be disappointed for when we climbed the tree on the second day we could see the Americans striking camp and watched as their wagons started to head back in the direction they had come. Later we observed a long column of men being marched south. I could not make out uniforms at that distance but as they seemed to have a heavy mounted guard I guessed that those poor devils were British prisoners. Dawn on the third day showed that the field was clear and Morag finally agreed that it was time to head east.

Chapter 26

We made our way cautiously at first, skirting around to the north of
Moraviantown. When we crossed the road that headed towards York
we found it littered with the detritus of a fleeing army. There were
empty pouches and packs, an abandoned shako and, in a ditch, a near
naked corpse that some wild animal had already feasted on. I searched
around for a musket – with just my sword, pistol and tomahawk I
missed having a weapon I could hunt with or use to help see off an
intruder. There were none of those to be found and even if I had
discovered one, there was no ammunition left behind either.

We pressed on and soon lapsed into a similar routine to that with
which we had headed out west in the first place. Morag cooked from
some supplies she had tied to the horse, while I tagged along with
Black Eagle as he hunted, usually without success. After about a week
we struck the Grand River and travelled along it for a while. There
were normally plenty of people travelling up and down the river before
it froze. We kept an eye out for boatmen, but ominously none were to
be seen. The last we had heard the Americans had been pushed to the
far eastern end of the Niagara peninsula and I hoped that the lack of
river traffic did not indicate a new assault. The Grand River after all
fed into Lake Erie, which was now dominated by Perry's fleet.

On our third day down the river we came across a small jetty and I
almost walked past it when I realised I had seen it before. I looked
around and there was the little cabin in which Magda and I had spent
that first magical night together.

"Do you mind if we stop for a while?" I suggested. "There is
someone who lives nearby that I would like to see.

Black Eagle grinned, guessing who it was. He must have already
told the story to Morag for she looked up and said, "If it is that
Christian woman, her husband will not want you sniffing around like
an autumn buck."

"Well I want to see her anyway," I replied stiffly before turning
towards the overgrown path. "You can go on – I can find my own way
from here." I strolled off but when I looked back I saw that Black

Eagle and his woman were following. Morag had a rare soft expression on her face as she led the horse with one hand and had her other arm linked in with the warrior's. I wondered if Magda now walked arm in arm with her husband. They could have a child now, I speculated. I regretted coming with Black Eagle and Morag in tow now, for if Magda looked happy I would not want to disturb her. Then Black Eagle would mock me for coming all that way without even saying hello. But I remembered my previous secret visits over a year ago now and the unsmiling faces as Magda and her husband went about their business on the farm. Call me a sentimental old fool, but I just wanted to know that she was now happy.

I reached the edge of the trees that surrounded their fields and ducked down behind a bush.

"What, are you not going down to see the woman?" queried Morag.

"No, I just want to look to check that she is content with her new life," I replied somewhat embarrassed. Morag gave a snort of derision at the white man's strange ways while I took out my glass and slowly focussed on a figure wearing the plain grey smock dress in the far field. It had to be Magda but because of her bonnet I could not see her features as she was facing away from me. She was bent over the handles of a plough and from the way she stood, she looked almost as exhausted as the poor donkey that was in the harness in front of her.

My muscles tensed in anger, but then I heard Black Eagle say behind me, "There is the preacher." I took my eye away from the glass for a wider view and there, riding away from the farmhouse, was Johannes. He was riding a fine horse and wearing what must have been his Sunday best clothes. I put my eye to the glass again. It was him all right. I could see his strange grey fuzzy hair poking out beneath the wide-brimmed black hat. He was riding towards his wife.

If I thought he was there to offer any comfort I soon realised that I was to be disappointed. As she heard him approach she looked round. She was too far away to make out her expression clearly, but I saw a flash of her blonde hair beneath the bonnet. Seeing her husband she picked up a long-handled whip and, cracking it in the air, tried to encourage the donkey forward. It managed a few steps before

229

Johannes appeared in the glass again. He sat glaring down at his wife and gesturing to the field. She in turn gestured to the exhausted donkey. They seemed to be arguing over how much ground she had covered with the plough. He reached down and at first I thought he was going to strike her. So it seemed did she as she flinched away. Instead he grabbed the whip from her hand and raised it high in the air before bringing the lash down on her back.

I was up and running before Magda's body had hit the floor, not that her husband cared; he had already spurred his horse to ride away. I shouted at him but he was too far away to hear and just rode off without a backwards glance. I kept on running. I remember that I had my sword in my hand then; God knows why I had drawn it, but I do know that I had not wanted to kill someone as badly as I wanted to kill Johannes for a very very long time.

Magda looked up puzzled when I called her name. She had last seen me clean-shaven in a British officer's coat and now a bearded wild man in buckskin was charging wildly across the fields towards her, followed by two rather intimidating Indians.

"Thomas," she shouted at last when she recognised me. Then she was on her feet and a moment later her thin body was pressed into my arms. We hugged and kissed and then I realised that my hands were wet. When I looked they were covered in blood from a vicious cut across her back.

"Let me see her," insisted Morag pushing me out of the way and then without waiting to be invited she swiftly unbuttoned the top of Magda's smock.

"It is all right now," I told Magda as Morag pulled the top of the smock open to look at the cut and then gave a snarl of anger.

"If a man beat me like this he would die with his balls in his mouth!" Morag exclaimed and then she turned to Black Eagle. "Go and bring the horse down to the house. There are some ointments I need." As she spoke I moved round to look at Magda's back. It had been beautifully smooth before but now it was criss-crossed with a series of scars, some old and others quite fresh. "Bring her to the house," Magda barked at me before striding off in that direction herself. I swept my arms around Magda, careful to hold her below her latest wound to avoid stretching it and then swept her up. She was much lighter than I expected and I could feel her ribs easily through her smock.

"What has that devil done to you?" I asked but she did not reply. She just sobbed and pressed her face into my chest. I carried her into the little cabin and turned into the bedroom. The big bed was still there and I laid her gently on it. Then I saw that there was another thin straw mattress on the floor in the corner of the room. Compared to the embroidered coverlet on the main bed this looked a meagre affair, but needlework present there too. The rough sacking blanket had the word 'harlot' sewn into it. I felt my blood boil with fury. When I got my hands on Johannes I was going to thrash him to within an inch of his life. I heard Black Eagle arrive with the horse outside and Morag went out to get her potions. She was gone a couple of minutes and Magda tried to pull herself together.

"Who are these people, Thomas?"

"They are friends, good friends," I grinned. "That big warrior was the one who threw himself into the river when we first met." She smiled but in her eyes there was a look of infinite sadness as she remembered that day. Before I could say more Morag bustled into the room with some cloth and several jars and I got up to leave.

"Thomas, please stay with me." Magda held out her hand and I gripped it, settling down on a chair by the side of the bed. Morag poured her a draught of poppy juice to start with and watched as it slowly started to take effect. Before Magda got too drowsy Morag made her roll over onto her front and then started working her ointments into the scars. The most recent one was still bleeding and its edges were wide apart. Morag dug in her bag for a needle and thread and made six quick stitches along its length. It was as good a job as I had seen done by an army surgeon and I told her so.

"I learned to do it while stitching my brother up," she told me. "He was always getting cut in fights and falling out of trees."

"I did not know you had a brother, you have never mentioned him before."

231

"He died of the wasting sickness before you came here," she told me and I got the distinct impression that she did not want to talk about it. I watched as she made a poultice and spread it over the new wound and then carefully bandaged it. By now Magda was fast asleep and snoring quietly. I stayed with her when Morag left the room. Even in sleep Magda's hand gripped mine and I was content to stare at her still beautiful face. I must have slept a little myself, for I was awoken by cooking smells from the next room. Looking at the window it was getting dark. I disentangled my fingers from Magda's and got up to stare out across the farm. There was no sign of Johannes returning and so I closed the shutters to keep out the cold.

Magda stirred at the noise. "Who is there?" she called out.

"It is me, Thomas. Do you remember we found you after Johannes cut you across the back?"

The mere mention of her husband made her half sit up in alarm. "Johannes will be back at any moment, you must go. He cannot know that you were here."

"Don't you worry about Johannes," I told her grimly. "I will be wanting a word with him when he gets here."

"You don't understand. It is not his fault it is mine. If he finds you here it will only make things worse."

"What on earth happened between you?" I asked. "He looked delighted to see you when you first met."

"You did," she replied glumly. After a moment's silence she continued softly, "Johannes was not like you in bed, he hurt me and seemed to want to do things as quickly as possible. When I suggested that we do things differently, I thought it would bring him pleasure, but instead he flew into a rage. He demanded to know if I had been with another man. I could not lie to my husband and so I told him of you and his anger got even worse. He calls me a harlot and a whore and lots of other words and makes me stay here on the farm, instead of going with him to church. I have to sleep on the floor unless he wants to…." Her voice tailed off.

"Well you won't have to worry about him any more," I told her.

"But he is still my husband," she replied tearfully, "I must stay with him, I have taken vows of marriage. If only I had not been with you, I would not have known any better and none of this would have happened."

"A vicious swine like him would have just found some other excuse to beat you," I told her.

"You must not hurt him, Thomas, he is my husband and I have a duty to look after him. Promise me you will not hurt him." I stayed silent; that was one promise I was not willing to make. "Please, Thomas, promise me," she begged.

I remembered her telling me of how her people abhorred violence and her fear that I had shot Black Eagle and Smoke Johnson when we first met. It was a shame Johannes did not detest beating his wife to the same degree. "I promise you that I will not kill him," I declared at last. But, I thought, by the time I have finished with him, he will probably wish I had.

Morag's voice called from the other room. "If you two are awake, come in and get some food." We went through and sat at the table. Morag served us from an iron pot over the fire. There was a quarter of a fowl each, potatoes and a rich gravy.

Magda looked fearfully at the plate. "Johannes does not like me killing the birds without his permission."

Morag snorted. "Don't worry about that, you need feeding up."

I had forgotten how hungry I was and tucked in with relish. Hesitantly at first, Magda joined in, until she was sucking the bones clean as though it was the first good meal she had enjoyed in months. From the look of her, it probably was.

I was just sitting back in my chair when the door to the cabin opened. Magda gave a startled shriek and sprang to her feet, knocking her stool over and shrinking back from the door. But instead of her husband it was Black Eagle. He exchanged a glance with Morag that seemed full of meaning and then stepped into the cabin and shut the door behind him.

"Have you seen my husband?" asked Magda.

Black Eagle glanced again at Morag before replying. "I have, lady. I found his body along the track. He had fallen off his horse and his head must have hit a rock."

"Is he…?" started Magda.

"Dead?" finished Black Eagle. "Yes, lady, I am afraid he is." The big warrior was trying to look solemn but I was sure he was lying. I sniffed – there was a strange smell that had entered the cabin with him.

"We must take him to the chapel," whispered Magda. "The congregation will want to prepare his body and bury their preacher there."

Black Eagle hesitated a second before replying. "I have already done it. The people are preparing the body now." I knew he was lying then. He was scornful of Christians; he would never have taken the preacher to their chapel. He probably wanted to thrash the man almost as much as I did.

Magda put her hand to her mouth and started to tremble as the implications of what had happened began to sink in.

"Come, girl," ordered Morag, picking up her bottle of poppy juice. "It is time you rested again. Come back to bed and drink some of this." Morag started to lead Magda away. The new widow looked over her shoulder to see if I was following, but I just smiled encouragingly at her and stayed where I was. I wanted to hear what had really happened to Johannes.

As soon as Morag closed the door behind them I whispered at Black Eagle, "Quick tell me, is he really dead? How did he die?"

He just grinned, held a finger to his lips and gestured at the door. "Patience, Little Father, we must wait for Morag so that I only tell the tale once."

I was beside myself with curiosity, but the big warrior would say nothing more. We heard Morag talking soothingly to Magda and I paced up and down the room with Black Eagle chuckling at me until we heard low regular snores from the bedroom. The door opened quietly and Morag came out. "All right, now tell us everything," I demanded.

"I took the horse and rode out on the track to the village to catch him on his return," Black Eagle told us. "On the way I picked up the whip that he had used on his wife; I knew you would not want him to die too quickly. I caught him easily, he was an old man, and I tied him to a tree. I told him that he was going to be whipped for what he did to his wife, but he kept shouting that he was a man of the Christian God and that I could not do that. He was wrong. I had given him about twenty lashes when he slumped down with some sort of seizure. He would not come round even after I slapped him and when I checked his heart I found he was already dead.

"Did you cut off his balls as I asked?" Morag enquired.

"There was not time before he died," replied Black Eagle and I realised that the two of them must have planned this while I was sitting with Magda.

"What about his body?" I asked. "Where is it really and what is that awful smell?"

"I buried him in the dung heap," said Black Eagle, answering both questions at once. "It seemed the best place for him and it was soft to dig while the ground is cold and hard." He looked at the plates on the table. "Now where is my dinner?" As Morag went to the pot over the fire Black Eagle passed me a small deerskin-wrapped bundle. "You can have that if you want," he whispered. I opened it up and felt a mixture of revulsion and delight. There on my lap was a patch of skin covered in grey and strangely fuzzy hair: it was Johannes' scalp.

"Put that away," scolded Morag when she saw it. "Listen to me carefully, both of you." She glared at us sternly. "That girl will question the story when the poppy juice has worn off, but she must never know what really happened, do you understand?" We both nodded sheepishly. Morag looked at me. "You Christians like to suffer for your faith – you worship a man tortured to death and this girl thinks she is a good Christian. I know you have feelings for her and so you had better heed what I am telling you. If she ever finds out what really happened here tonight, then she will never forgive you, but more importantly she will never forgive herself."

I realised that Morag was right, she usually was. That evening I went outside and with the handle of a rake I pushed the scalp deep into the dung heap with the rest of its owner.

Chapter 27

Magda must have wondered about Black Eagle's story as she lay in bed the next morning, but the lie we told was what she wanted to believe. While we all stuck to our story she did not have to face an unwelcome truth. She got up and pointedly did not mention Johannes at all. In fact in all the time I knew her, she did not speak of him ever again.

The farm was hers now, but she did not want it. She prepared to leave with us, taking just a handful of possessions and clothes. Then just before we departed, she asked us to burn the farm house. She did not explain but we all understood that it marked the end to an unhappy time of her life. Black Eagle found some lamp oil and splashed that around the little cabin. Then Magda stepped forward with a burning torch in her hand and tossed it through the door. The fire took hold quickly and a plume of smoke was soon rising high into the air. We watched for a while and then turned and headed east towards the Indian village.

It was strange being back in Brant's Ford again and it gave me very mixed feelings. On the one hand it was good to be welcomed by old friends such as Norton, Smoke Johnson and others I had spent the previous winter with, but on the other it reminded me that I was no closer to getting home to Britain. The war still raged on in Canada and in Europe, so no fit British soldiers would be allowed to leave North America. Even if I wanted to risk deserting under some disguise, the first snows of the winter had already begun to fall as we arrived in the little settlement. The only major seaport that would be open was Halifax, and that was eight hundred miles away.

There was a different mood about the village now as well. When I had first come to Brant's Ford I had arrived with a group of triumphant warriors and British arms were at the peak of their success. Now there had been a string of defeats and humiliations. Many of the Grand River people had recently abandoned their homes and moved nearer the main British garrison at Burlington for protection. They knew of the Moraviantown defeat and were worried that Harrison would bring his army to attack them. We could, at least, reassure those that were left on that score, as we had seen Harrison start his withdrawal back to Amherstburg.

Norton told me that Iroquois loyalty for the British could no longer be guaranteed. "The Americans have recruited the Iroquois in New York State to fight for them. We have already skirmished with them several times and I suspect that the Americans have sent some of their Iroquois to persuade the Grand River people to stop fighting or to change sides and turn on the British."

"What do you mean, 'you suspect'?" I queried. "Don't you know? You are still one of the war chiefs, aren't you?"

"Oh now I am seen as too close to the British to be trusted by many, but I still have a war band of loyal warriors." Norton then introduced me to a young girl called Catherine, who had been busy cleaning his cabin. I thought he had hired her as a domestic but it turned out he had married her. She was not more than fifteen years old while Norton was well into his forties. This may have explained why Norton's ardour for the war seemed to have cooled over the previous few months. He told me of the American invasion of the eastern end of the Niagara peninsula and how the Iroquois had been used as light troops to keep it contained. It had been a long and bloody business with massacres on both sides. A British fleet still contested Lake Ontario with a larger American flotilla and supplies had become scarce. With fewer gifts, some warriors had resorted to raids on white farms and relations between the two communities were becoming strained. When I told him of what had happened to Magda, he suggested that the burning of the farm and disappearance of the occupants would probably be attributed to an Iroquois raid as the farm was close to the Grand River.

Magda and I were given an empty lodge in the village to make our home during the winter and gradually many of the other villagers drifted back when word spread that Harrison's army was not coming. Magda spent much of her time with the healer of the village, who helped ensure that her back did not get infected. Magda became fascinated with the medicine woman and her work. The old woman's English name was Spotty Pots. Her lodge was lined with jars of ointments and dried herbs, seeds and powders. She was illiterate, but each pot was marked with a code of spots to help her identify the contents. She was certainly an effective healer; once, when I badly burned my hand she had treated it with one of her potions, and within three days it was as good as new.

During that long winter while Black Eagle and I would go out hunting, Magda would spend time with Spotty Pots. Soon she was learning Iroquoian and throwing herself into the heart of the village's activities. With the Iroquoian culture of integrating outsiders she was welcomed by most with open arms and was soon keeping me updated with news and gossip. At first I was puzzled by her enthusiasm to get involved with what was for her an alien culture. Then I realised that she had been brought up as part of a tightly knit church congregation and had missed that with Johannes' forced isolation. Now she saw the village of Brant's Ford as her new community. Not only that, her past life was full of prohibitions and strictures, while the Iroquois made very few demands. Christian and pagan practices were practised happily side by side. She relished the freedom her new life offered and while she attended the little church every Sunday, she was also happy to learn about medicines and treatments that owed much to beliefs surrounding the Great Spirit.

As the snows fell the war continued on around us and at last the British forces saw some success. Harrison's men remained in Amherstburg while the Americans in the east, after another push, were forced to retreat to Fort George, their last foothold on our side of the Niagara River. Norton led his war band east again to join a British attack on Fort George. He asked me if I wanted to come but I used Magda as an excuse to cry off.

It should have been an idyllic winter: a beautiful woman to share my cabin; plentiful food and drink from the village harvest; good friends to chat with around the fire and the war being fought too far away to disturb my peace. In truth it was a good winter, but it had something missing, which gnawed away at me. At first I was unsure what it was. It was certainly not the call of battle; during the final months of 1813 the war went well for the British. They pushed the

Americans back over the Niagara and even carried out some raids on their shore. The British generals seem to have forgotten I existed and Norton told me that they had long since stopped asking about my whereabouts. Magda was a willing lover but she had lost her enthusiasm for the two-backed game and there was a worldly sadness to her sometimes. I am no expert but while she never mentioned him, I think Johannes still inflicted a dark influence to stop her enjoying herself in bed. I asked her once if she ever thought about going back to her family in Pennsylvania but she shook head.

"My father would just try to find me a new husband to obey. I like my life here. I have the freedom to do what I want and I am learning ways to do God's work as a healer. I feel more at home here in just a few weeks than I think I have ever felt before." Her eyes sparkled and she leaned over and kissed me. "You know I will always be grateful to you for what you did to help me get here. But what about you, don't you want to go home? Spotty Pots says your spirit is pining for your own lands and people."

"Does she indeed," I grumbled, annoyed that they had evidently been discussing me as they made their potions. "Well she does not know what she is talking about. The day I take advice from someone who thinks burning feathers is a cure for a headache, hell will freeze over."

It took me several days to admit to myself that the healer was right; I was missing home more and more and the passage of a whole year in this wilderness just made the feelings worse. What wouldn't I give to stroll down Piccadilly in London and listen to the civilised conversation of a coffee shop? Even the high-blown drivel spouted at one of Byron's poetry evenings seemed appealing then – at least it would not include hunting, scalping or the extraordinary boils on a warrior called Little Feather's bottom – topics which seemed to dominate village conversations at that time.

A few days later Magda tried again. "Norton has been talking in the village about how Napoleon lost a million men in the attack on Russia last year. He gave up trying to explain the amount of men to some in the council because they could not envisage such a huge number, never mind that they were all dead. He says that the French will not be able to replace such an army and that the other European countries will force the French to stop the war."

"It could happen," I agreed.

"If it does then the British will send their soldiers to Canada." She paused before continuing. "Which means that they might now let soldiers who have already been here too long go home."

"They might," I conceded again. It was a delicious prospect but I did not want to raise my hopes. On the other hand I had to remind the British commanders that I still existed or I would never be considered for leave. The main command was still at Burlington, only thirty miles away, less than two days on horseback.

"If you want to go, it would be best to go now before the spring thaw turns the roads into a quagmire," said Magda, grinning as though she could read my thoughts. "Shall I get Spotty Pots to burn you some more feathers? You will probably get another headache if you have to cope with hell frozen over."

Chapter 28

Two days later and I was riding into Burlington. I knew that Sheaffe had been relieved of command in the east the previous year, but I knew little about the new general. It would have been foolish to seek out an interview unprepared, so I retired to the nearest tavern and fell into conversation with two young army lieutenants. If I had been apprehensive about the meeting before, I soon relaxed as all the news they told me was good. General Drummond was in overall command in the east but the man in charge of the Niagara peninsula was an Irish general called Phineas Riall. By all accounts friend Riall was a short, stout, naive character who relied heavily on the advice of junior officers. He had largely bought his rank and had little battle experience apart from putting down some revolts in the Caribbean. He sounded just the sort that would be impressed by tales of my heroics in Spain, Portugal and Paris before my latest adventures in North America. I was soon convinced that by the time I had finished piling it on with a trowel, I would have him piping his eye and wishing me *bon voyage*.

After a final brandy to help hone my performance I tooled round to Government House to seek an audience with my new commander. It seemed I could see him immediately and I was shown into a grand office. Immediately my spirits dropped for instead of the general there was a vaguely familiar figure bent over some papers at a desk on the far side of the room. He heard the door close behind me and without taking his eyes from his work announced, "Major Fforbes, with two 'f's. What can I do for you?"

"I was hoping to speak to General Riall," I asked hesitantly.

Still without looking up Fforbes continued in a bored tone, "The general does not see anyone unless I have approved the interview. So what is it you want?"

"I would like to go home," I stated simply.

"Wouldn't we all," said the adjutant as he gave a flourishing signature to the bottom of the document he had been reading. Then at last he raised his head. There was no sign of recognition on his face. I had grown a winter beard and my buckskin tunic had seen better days.

Only the gold sword at my hip gave any clue as to my military background. A look of irritation crossed Fforbes' face as he surveyed me. "I only deal with army matters here. You would probably be best to speak to your militia commander or perhaps the Indian Agency?"

Fforbes had already returned his attention to the papers on his desk when I replied, "But I am military. I am Captain Flashman. We met once before, just after Queenston." The man could not have looked more surprised if I had just dropped a venomous scorpion on his desk. His head whipped back up and he stared at me open-mouthed, trying to make out the face behind the beard.

"It is you! My God, sir, you have a nerve turning up here." His face was flushing with anger as his voice rose. "And to ask for passage home too, as if His Majesty's government is at the whim of cowards and deserters."

Now it was my turn to be shocked and my jaw dropped in astonishment. Oh, he had me bang to rights on both points, but I thought I had hidden it pretty well. In India, Spain and I thought in Canada too, I had gained the reputation of a brave and resourceful officer, but now Fforbes was calling me out. Well I wasn't duelling with the bastard in case he shot straight, which only left one response: outraged bluster.

"How dare you, sir, impugn my honour! I have fought with courage at virtually every major engagement of this campaign and I will not have my reputation tarnished by some jumped up desk monkey." His eyes bulged at that but I was just getting into my stride. "Where were you at Queenston when I and eighty Iroquois held down over one thousand Americans? You, sir, were not with me at Fort Meigs to repel an American surprise attack, nor were you with me when I stood on Barclay's flagship fighting the American fleet, or at Moraviantown where I commanded the right flank of Procter's line. Yet now you dare stand before me and accuse me of cowardice and desertion. I demand to see the general and report you for your insolence."

I had expected Fforbes to show some surprise or alarm at that, but instead he just laughed. "A pretty speech, sir, but with as much truth as your earlier tales. For your information all of Barclay's crew are still prisoners. But don't worry, I will make sure that you will see the general, at your court martial and perhaps again when you face a firing squad."

"Court martial… firing squad," I repeated in stunned astonishment.

"You didn't think you would get away with it, did you? I sent you to liaise with the Iroquois, but while they have fought with us hard during the campaign, you were never to be seen. When I asked Norton, he came out with a string of excuses until he seemed too embarrassed to reply to my enquiries." He gave a sneering laugh before continuing. "So I looked at the letter of introduction that came from the governor general, based on details you provided. It is patently absurd, spying on the French in Paris and escaping in an American ship. You knew full well that we could not check on those facts with the enemy. I suspect that you deserted the army in Spain and hoped to make a new life in America before this war caught you out. Since then you have been hiding, but it is getting too hot for you and so you thought you would try to bluff your way back to England."

"That is absurd, sir." I began to realise that my story did sound far-fetched, but it was true all the same. Bluster was clearly not going to work with this character; I needed some supporting witnesses. "Speak to General Procter, sir, he will confirm that I was at Fort Meigs, with Barclay and at Moraviantown."

"General Procter has suffered some form of breakdown," declared Fforbes ringing a small bell on his desk. "And when he recovers he will be facing a court martial of his own for his conduct at Moraviantown, so perhaps not an ideal character witness." I heard a door open behind me as Fforbes continued. "Ah, guards, kindly relieve Mr Flashman of his sword and escort him to the cells. He is under arrest."

"But you can't do this!" I shouted as I felt hands firmly grip my arms. "I was there, in Paris, Fort Meigs, on the *Detroit*, Moraviantown, the whole bloody lot."

"Come along, sir," said a guard's voice in my ear as I was hauled up off my feet. "You just come along quietly."

"What the deuce…?" I shouted. "Fforbes, you damn fool, every word I told you was true. Let me go, you great oafs or I will have you horsewhipped. Put me down… Fforbes, tell them to let me go!" Fforbes just laughed at my final appeal and gestured again at the guards to take me away.

I spent two weeks in those damn cells at Burlington, fuming at the irony of my situation. Oh many a time I have lied about my conduct on a campaign and invariably I have got away with it. But this time every word of my implausible tale was the truth, yet it could cost me disgrace and court martial. Surely, I wondered, Procter's wits could not be that addled. If he was asked he must be able to confirm my tale. I had no idea what other officers had survived the Moraviantown disaster, but there must be some who could confirm that a Captain Flashman had at least been there on the retreat.

At first I did not take the threat of a firing squad seriously. If no one could confirm my presence at Moraviantown, then I would insist that they write to Wellington. He would be able to confirm my Peninsular War service and that I was sent after that fool Grant all the way to Paris. But as the days passed I began to wonder if Fforbes had just left me to rot in the gaol instead of making any enquiries at all. Your mind plays tricks on you when you have been left on your own and after a while I was beginning to doubt my story myself. The only thing I was sure about was the passage of time as there was a barred window high in the cell wall. It showed the passing of night and day and I used to mark each day on the cell wall. Actually, thinking back, I was not even certain of the passage of time as I remember having arguments with myself as to whether I had yet made that day's mark or not. The guards, who brought food and changed the bucket, were clearly under orders to say nothing. They took a sadistic delight in ignoring my increasingly desperate pleas for information. I could have cried with relief with the cell door was eventually opened and a grim-faced sergeant actually spoke to me.

"This way, sir," he said gesturing back up the corridor I had arrived through. "Major Fforbes would like to see you." I shambled after the man, noting that he had called me 'sir' and hoped that this first act of respect heralded some good news. Soon I was in the rarefied atmosphere of the officer's quarters and gathering curious glances from those I passed. Then a door was opened and I was back in Fforbes' office from where I had started my recent sojourn.

The man himself was behind his desk and he looked up, wrinkling his nose in distaste when he saw me. I must have looked and smelt pretty ripe after that long in the cells. But then he forced a smile across his face, stood and walked towards me. "Ah, Captain Flashman, do come in and take a seat, here by the fire, while I get you some brandy."

"So you have found out that I was telling the truth, then?" I asked truculently, standing in the middle of the room. If the bastard thought he could just blithely brush away my incarceration he could think again. "I have been in those bloody cells for two weeks because you refused to believe the word of a British officer and gentleman," I fumed. "I should call you out and bloody thrash you."

"I offer you my most sincere apologies," said Fforbes holding out a large brandy. "Please take this and a seat by the fire." I allowed myself to be guided to a large chair as he continued. "As you must know your tale is quite remarkable; I am sure no other officer has had an experience quite like it. I wrote at once to General Procter seeking confirmation that you were at Moraviantown. To test his sanity I asked if he could verify that I was at the battle too. He attested that we were both present. So I sent a message to Colonel Warburton, but he was away on the Niagara frontier and it took some time to receive his reply."

"And he proved my story," I offered more as a statement than a question.

"Not only that, he informed me that it was you who helped him call Procter to account and to make a stand to defend the honour of British arms. He also confirmed that you and an Indian were the only ones to escape capture when Barclay's fleet was taken."

I took a sip of the brandy. "I hope this means that you will now help me to get a berth on a ship to Britain. You must see that I have done my duty here."

"I do indeed," agreed Fforbes putting down his glass and giving me what he probably hoped was his most earnest expression. He looked more like a sermonising parson with wind and I realised that bad news was coming. "But I regret that if I were to give you leave it would be revoked by the standing orders from the governor general: no fit soldiers are to be allowed home. You would then be placed on new duties of the governor's choosing. But I do have some good news for you."

"I hope so," I growled while I took in what he had told me. I had a pretty comfortable billet with Magda and the Iroquois. The last thing I needed was the governor general putting me where he was most pressed for reinforcements, which was bound to be some near-suicidal posting.

"Yes the news from Europe is excellent. You will have heard of Bonaparte's defeat in Russia last winter, well now the allies are pressing him from all directions. As well as the Russians, Prussia, and Austria are fighting the French in the east and Lord Wellington is at the Pyrenees. There is talk of peace terms – the war there cannot last much longer."

"But how does that help me?" I asked irritably.

"Soon some of Wellington's troops will be spared for this theatre, which will change the balance here too. Peninsular veterans will go through their militia like a hot knife through butter." I opened my mouth to repeat my question but Fforbes held up a hand to forestall me. "Which means," he continued, "that as the war turns in our favour some of the deserving troops here can be released to return home. I have already put your name at the top of the list of those overdue for leave."

It was something, but it was not enough. "You mean you want me to just sit around waiting for the tide to turn? That could take years. I want to speak to the general. There must be some quicker way off this wretched continent." I glared at Fforbes. "And I will be telling him how you have treated me too."

For the first time Fforbes looked alarmed. I guessed that the general knew nothing about my detention and would not be best pleased when

247

he did find out about it. "I have already told you that even if the general did grant you leave, it would only be overruled by the governor general's standing order. There are no exceptions to that. But if you are willing to go back to the Iroquois and wait just a little longer then I can offer you something else. I could get the general to sign off your promotion to the rank of major. Given what you have achieved so far, it would be well deserved."

I sat back and considered the offer. I had often thought that I was overdue advancement, but with most promotions being purchased, a rise in rank to major would have cost a small fortune. Now I could have one for nothing. If there really was no way around the governor general's edict, then warming Magda's bed a little longer was not a bad way to wait out the war. Naively, I did not see the yawning chasm of danger that was opening up in front of me. Instead as Fforbes looked anxiously at me I decided to try to take him for every penny I could. "If the promotion and pay is backdated to when I arrived in Canada, then I accept."

"Agreed," he cried a little too easily and I wondered what more I could have got out of him.

Fforbes disappeared for a while after that to make the arrangements, but he was as good as his word. After giving me some time to wash, shave and change into a fresh uniform, Major Thomas Flashman was introduced to General Riall, who congratulated me on my promotion. My new commission was in the 41st regiment but Riall had clearly been briefed that I had been fighting with the Indians.

"Fforbes here tells me that you have been doing an excellent job," boomed the general as he pumped my hand. "Well with those new fellows coming from Spain we will show those Americans a real fight, eh?"

"Indeed, General," I agreed, "and with reinforcements we can allow some leave; I have not been home in four years." It was clumsily done but I wanted to make sure that Fforbes really had put me on the list for leave. But it seemed the adjutant was keeping true to his promise.

"Ah yes, Fforbes has told me of your extraordinary adventures. Rest assured that I will let you go when I can. But in the meantime what do you make of that Norton fellow? He is half Indian, ain't he? He fought well with me on the raids over the river, but the Indian Agency says he is not reliable."

"He is a good man, sir," I replied. "He may be seen by some warriors as too close to us but I would trust him.

"Mmm," mused Riall. "Well in case he does become tempted to show that his loyalties lie elsewhere, Fforbes here has cleverly backdated your commission before his so that you are the senior man." Fforbes smiled encouragingly behind the general – this was evidently how he had persuaded Riall to sign off on the backdated promotion. "I will look to you to keep those warriors ready and bring them when I need them. Come the summer we will all go on the warpath again, what?"

"You can count on me, sir." I could not help grinning slightly at the thought that Iroquois warriors would take any notice of a date on a commission. They chose their own war chiefs, not Riall, it just showed the British lack of understanding of their ways. But I was not concerned as I was sure that Norton would do exactly what they wanted anyway.

"I am sure I can," agreed Riall showing me to the door. "Good luck to you now."

So there I was walking back through Burlington in a smart new uniform, with my old buckskins tucked under my arm. 'Major Flashman' had a nice ring to it. But as I headed back to the stables for my horse I began to reflect that with rewards come responsibility. Norton would remain the war chief as far as the Iroquois were concerned, but Riall would look for me to take some responsibility for their actions. I needed to keep the general's favour if I wanted to remain on the list for early leave. That meant at least giving the appearance of leadership. So the next time the Iroquois went campaigning I could not sit things out in Magda's bed. I would have to go too.

Chapter 29

Norton congratulated me warmly on the second epaulet for my uniform. I never did tell him that my promotion was backdated, as far as he was concerned, he was still the undisputed leader of the Iroquois war band. For a day or two I paraded myself around the village in my new duds, but marks of rank meant little to warriors who judged each other on deeds. So soon the red cloth was put away and I returned to my buckskin. I resumed my place in Magda's bed too, explaining to her that I would now be one of the first to get leave home. She seemed pleased to have me back, but I sensed that she would be equally happy to see me head for Britain's shores.

For a while it looked like I would not have long to wait. As winter turned into spring, crops were sown and the news from Europe was as sweet as the maple syrup harvest. The French were being beaten on all fronts and then as spring turned into summer news came that allied armies were entering Paris and then that the French emperor had abdicated. The war in Europe was over and the first advance parties of Wellington's Peninsular War veterans were already crossing the Atlantic.

I thought that there could be only one outcome to Madison's war now and if the man had any sense he would be suing for peace before it was too late. Every time a rider came from Burlington I would seek out information on what was happening in Europe and check if they carried a letter for me containing orders for my leave. All I got for my trouble was one two-month-old newspaper. In fact the only current news came indirectly from Morag. One morning, beaming with delight, Black Eagle called for me to go on one of our regular hunting trips. He announced that his woman had just told him she was with child. I did my best to feign surprise as Magda had given me this gossip a week earlier with a warning not to tell the big warrior before Morag broke the news to him. Black Eagle was full of himself, sure that the child would be a boy and even talking about us teaching him to hunt in the years ahead. I was beginning to wonder if I would indeed still be at Brant's Ford when the lad was old enough to shoot.

Finally at the end of June a message from Riall did arrive. For a moment I almost cried with relief – after four long years I would at last head home. Then I really did cry, not from joy but frustration. For it was not the long promised leave at all, but a request to bring the Iroquois war band to the Niagara. American forces had been seen gathering on their bank of the river and another invasion of the Niagara peninsula was anticipated.

I have always found the Americans to be a stubborn breed. Later in my career I had the privilege of hiding behind mud battlements with some of the best of them, and no matter what the odds, they all struggled to abandon a lost cause. Madison must have been no different, for despite the fact that the balance of the war seemed to be turning against him, he seemed determined to continue the conflict.

"Why the devil won't they just give up?" I fumed at Norton. "They must see that they cannot succeed now. All they will achieve is killing hundreds of their people and ours."

"They will probably want to take as much territory as they can before the veterans arrive," suggested Norton. "Then they will be in the best position when negotiations start to end the war. By the way, why do you think Riall wrote to you about this rather than me?"

"Oh it was probably because he saw me most recently," I said airily. Then to change the subject, "When do you think we should leave?"

"We will need a couple of days to gather the war band and supplies. We should be able to attract around three hundred warriors and there will be some women and other camp followers that will want to come along. We will want Spotty Pots with us; do you think Magda will come too?"

"I doubt it. She is still something of a pacifist from her Mennonite upbringing." I was right, Magda wanted no part of the war and with Spotty Pots away she had a chance to use her fast growing healing skills with those that remained. But she did help me pack. I travelled in my buckskin clothes but took the new uniform as well. She even hung a charm around my neck of shells and a piece of rabbit skin that she insisted the old women thought would protect my spirit. I preferred to put my faith in cold steel but I was grateful and kissed her fondly farewell. She was certainly very different now from the fervent Christian I had first seen on that boat.

It took two days to reach Queenston. We had to travel at a slow pace as there were so many mules and even some oxen bringing supplies with us. One, I noticed with surprise, was being led by Morag, with the proud father-to-be walking alongside.

"Shouldn't you be resting rather than going to war?" I asked her.

She actually smiled; motherhood was changing her as well. "And leave you two fools on your own? I want to make sure that my child still has a father when it is born."

Black Eagle grinned indulgently at her. "She forgets we are both great warriors, Little Father, who have vanquished many enemies."

Morag gave a snort of derision. "You would both starve if there was no game and neither of you can build a shelter that could withstand the wag of a dog's tail."

"It is summer," I cried gesturing to the sky, which had at least patches of blue visible between the clouds. "We don't need shelters and we can find game anywhere."

"I have seen you hunt, remember?" And at this she actually laughed along with others in the column. "You could not find a bear if it broke wind behind you!"

I spurred my horse down the path and realised that I felt strangely comfortable with this band of warriors and their followers. You know you are accepted into a group when they can laugh and banter with you. Oh, don't get me wrong, I still wanted to go home, desperately. But I knew I would miss those hunting trips with Black Eagle and Smoke Johnson and the evenings smoking our pipes by the fire while talking of the big deer that got away.

The following day I was feeling more melancholy as I stood on the Queenston Heights looking over the river to the American shore. There was not much activity to be seen; the American army was thought to be further south, but for me the war seemed to have come full circle. We stayed on the heights for a day and then headed south to camp near the majestic falls, with me fervently hoping that even at this late hour the Americans would see sense and call off their invasion. Then on the morning of the 3rd of July we heard distant cannon fire from the south and I realised that my hopes were dashed.

At either end of the Niagara River there are two forts, one on the British shore and one on the American one. At the southern end of the river the Americans had a fort at Buffalo while on the British bank we had Fort Erie. Word soon came that the Americans were crossing the river at its southern end in a determined attack on Fort Erie.

Everyone seemed to think that the British garrison would hold out for at least a few days and so General Riall summoned his forces to march south to relieve it. Riall had around two thousand regular soldiers, but they were scattered all over the peninsula. He gathered them together by the Chippawa River, which was the first major obstacle that the Americans would face if they headed north from Fort Erie.

The meeting point was the bridge over the Chippawa River, it was just a couple of miles south from our camp and so we were one of the first ones there. A small village had grown up around the bridge and soon it was filling with members of the three regiments that made up Riall's command. None of these were Peninsular War veterans; instead they were regiments that had been fighting in Canada since the outbreak of hostilities – which meant that they had considerably more experience than their commander. Riall arrived early the next morning with a large body of men that included a group of Indians from the western tribes. While Norton went off to meet this other war band, I slipped on my officer's uniform and went to report to Riall.

He had ridden over the bridge and with several of his staff officers had gone to survey a large expanse of clear land bordered by the Niagara River on the left and thick forest to the right.

"Ah, Major Flashman, it is good to see you," he called as I rode up. "Are your warriors here and ready for battle?"

"My compliments, General and yes they most certainly are. Are we expecting a battle here, sir? I thought we were to march to relieve Fort Erie?"

"Ah, we may have to fight here first." Riall beamed at the prospect and seemed in an ebullient mood. "Some of their fellows seem to have marched north to head us off. Look you can see some of the rascals at the far end of the clearing. They probably wanted to capture the bridge before we got here."

I gazed across the clearing and saw perhaps a hundred men moving about in front of the trees. They were wearing short light grey jackets instead of the long navy coats of the regular army. I had not seen soldiers in grey before. I raised my glass just in time to see another file of these strange troops appear. With immaculate precision they wheeled around to their left to form up in a line facing us. "They are wearing strange coats; do we know what kind of troops they are?"

"Well they are not wearing blue, so they must be militia," stated Riall firmly. "They will put up little resistance to our regulars. I suspect that most of their best troops will still be trying to capture Fort Erie, so we should have the advantage of numbers as well."

"Well they march as well as any guardsman in London," I pointed out. "Their drilling would not be out of place on the parade ground at Horseguards."

"They threw our advance guard back pretty smartly too, according to its commander," commented a familiar voice from behind. When I looked around I saw Fforbes still watching the grey troops though his own glass.

"Perhaps the advance guard are just making excuses to cover their own tardy performance," responded Riall tartly. "I tell you, gentlemen, that these are militia, they have to be, dressed like that. I have seen militia march very smartly in the West Indies. They will probably have some rich colonel who likes his men well turned out. You should be grateful that he has spent his money on their uniforms and drilling rather than cannon, for I have yet to see any artillery."

"With respect, sir," started Fforbes, "we don't know precisely who they are or how many troops the enemy has. It would be prudent to wait until our scouts can get more information."

The general wheeled his horse around so that he could glare at the knot of officers behind him. "I sometimes wonder how you ever won a

254

battle before I got here," he sneered. "You are like a huddle of timid old women. I tell you again, their best troops will be surrounding Fort Erie. This is just a regiment of some hick militia trying to get in our way. It seems that I have to remind you that our duty is to sweep this enemy away so that we can march on the fort to relieve the siege without delay."

"Yes sir," we all chorused awkwardly.

Riall snapped his glass closed to signal that the discussion was over. Then he turned to me. "Now, Major, whoever those troops are, I would like you to take your warriors down the edge of the forest so that you can attack their flank. Fforbes here tells me that is how your warriors like to fight."

"Yes sir," I confirmed smartly. Then remembering the debacle of Moraviantown I thought I would risk his ire by asking a further question. "Do we know if the Americans have any cavalry?"

Evidently Riall was not sure and so he just glared at Fforbes for an answer.

"No, those watching the river reported that they have brought hardly any horsemen across the Niagara so far."

"Excellent," I sighed with relief. Turning to Riall I added, "Rest assured, sir, that my men will do an excellent job of ambushing those soldiers. Whoever they are, I doubt that they would be foolish enough to follow the warriors into the trees."

"Well said, Major. That is the kind of positive response I expect from all my commanders." Riall glared pointedly at his other staff officers before adding, "I am sending the other Indians and some militia light troops down there as well. We will see how the Americans cope with you attacking their left flank and the rest of our force attacking their front." He rubbed his hands together enthusiastically. "I think we can confidently anticipate a solid victory, gentlemen."

I rode away feeling well pleased with myself. Riall had placed the Iroquois exactly where I would have chosen. If those strange grey-jacketed soldiers were militia, they would never stand a chance when attacked on two fronts and even regulars would struggle. Either way any infantry would know better than to chase Indians into a forest and besides, there was a huge expanse of woodland to retreat back into if necessary. I just needed to tell Norton but I could not see how he could possibly object. But when I galloped back to the Indian camp there was no sign of our Iroquois war chief. Several people told me that they had seen him riding into the woods with some scouts, but an hour later he had still not reappeared. The first of the militia and men from the western tribes were already making their way into position down the edge of the forest. I doubted that the Iroquois warriors would obey my command – I was not one of their chiefs – but if we did not advance soon Riall would be sending messages to ask why.

I was just on the verge of asking Black Eagle who the tribe would view as second in command when Norton came galloping out from the trees looking worried.

"Where have you been?" I called. "The general wants the Iroquois down at the edge of the forest with the western tribesmen."

"That is the last place we should be," announced Norton quietly, checking over his shoulder to make sure that we were not being overheard. "I have just been talking to a friend among the American Iroquois. Five hundred of them came across the river with the Americans and at least three hundred and fifty of those are with the Americans in front of us."

"Will they attack us?" I asked feeling a sudden chill in the air.

"Tell me, Flashman, if you were the American commander, where would you send your Iroquois warriors in the coming battle?"

The answer was obvious; the warriors would never stand in line like other troops and no one would be better at chasing skirmishers away from the edge of the forest than other Indians. "I would send them into the trees to come up behind those shooting from the edge of the forest," I told him. "Then those poor devils at the edge of the trees would be trapped between American warriors behind and American regular troops in front."

"Exactly," agreed Norton, "and their leader Red Jacket is no fool. That is precisely what he is bound to do. So we will have to give him a taste of his own medicine."

"What do you mean? And anyway, most of the militia and the Indians from the western tribes are already moving down to the forest edge. Should we call them back?"

"No, leave them," said Norton, grinning now. "We will go into the forest, but deeper into the trees. With luck we will come up behind Red Jacket's men. Then they will be trapped between our warriors and our skirmishers at the edge of the battleground." He turned to go and organise the war band for the attack, but after a couple of paces he looked back, frowning. "You are not planning to wear that uniform in the woods, are you? That scarlet will be easily spotted and there is still a price on your head, remember." With that he walked off leaving me staring after him with a growing sense of horror.

I had been planning to fight in uniform because I had thought it would be perfectly safe. Riall was confident of victory and that had rubbed off on me. I had imagined us blazing away from the edge of the trees, with boundless forest to run through at the first sign of danger. Now that the forest was potentially full of hostile warriors, it put rather a different light on things. Suddenly the last place I wanted to be was in that woodland and I racked my brains for an excuse to get out of the venture altogether. I was skewered by my new rank: I had to keep Riall on side to get home and he saw me as commander of the Iroquois. He would therefore expect me to be with the warriors when they emerged, hopefully triumphant, from the trees. I had no choice but to follow the war band, but I would make damn sure I was not at the front of any attack.

A short while later I reappeared dressed in my buckskin trousers and tunic, only to discover that I still fell far short of the sartorial standards required of an Iroquois warrior . A group of them surveyed me with the steely disapproval of a dowager duchess at a debutantes' ball.

"You still look like a white man," declared Morag critically. To make sure she had my full attention she added, "If you are caught they will hang you if they still have those wanted posters."

"Yes, you should look more like me," agreed Black Eagle. That seemed unlikely; the giant was a foot taller and broader than I was, covered in war paint and weapons, and it would be the deuce of a hot day before I went to war dressed in just a leather loin cloth.

"Well I am not taking off my trousers," I insisted emphatically and possibly for the first time.

"At least lose the tunic," ordered Morag, "and we will need to do something with your face and hair." Within a moment there were several of them round me, pulling and primping to their hearts' content while the object of their endeavours had very little say in what was happening. My tunic was pulled off and as I only just managed to stop them shaving me a top knot, they relented with a scarf around my head. Several feathers were tucked into it while Black Eagle got to work on my war paint. Soon I had a wide red stripe over my eyes and a black one over my jaw, like the other warriors. Mine, though, were probably crooked as I was not exactly a willing canvas. Morag and the others got involved painting swirls on my body, which, apart from making me squirm as they went on, were supposed to make me harder to spot in the trees. They wanted me to leave my sword behind too as it was not a typical warrior's weapon but I dug my heels in there. My sword was a lucky talisman that had been with me many years – and it was a damn good job I did. I was not the only one to be carrying additional weapons; while we all had muskets or rifles and tomahawks, a few also carried bows and arrows as they had at Queenston. More than a handful had vicious spears for close quarter fighting. None of the warriors carried bayonets as most used their tomahawks in hand to hand combat.

Soon the war band was ready with warrior Flashy to the fore.

"That is much better," claimed Norton when he saw me, failing to hide his amusement at my appearance. "Be silent and watchful," he shouted as he led the way into the trees. "Let's show them how the Grand River warriors fight!"

Chapter 30

We advanced through the trees in a single column for about half a mile. I was at its head with Norton, Black Eagle and Smoke Johnson, while the rest of the warriors trailed silently behind us. Compared to my clumsy approach through the woods at Queenston over a year before, I had now become quite competent at stalking quietly through the trees; but even with my best efforts, the trees were not silent. There was the distant crackle of small arms from the warriors and troops at the edge of the forest. I pitied the poor devils who were still ignorant of the horrors creeping up behind them, not that I was in any rush to find those horrors myself. When Norton signalled a halt the whole line turned to its left and began to move towards the edge of the trees in a long extended line. We had barely gone a hundred yards in the new direction when we heard distant war whoops and a cacophony of screams and yells.

"That will be the American tribesmen attacking those at the forest edge," whispered Norton. Some of the warriors began to go faster then, anxious to find the enemy, but I was content to continue my slow cautious approach. To my surprise, Norton and around thirty warriors at my end of the line, kept to my pace. I wondered if he and some of the others were simply reluctant to spill Indian blood. I did not care as long as all the fighting had finished by the time I got to the clearing.

I was feeling surprisingly relaxed until Norton whispered again. "It is good of you to stay back with me, Flashman."

I felt a prickle of alarm at that. I had thought I was shirking my place in an attack but Norton, a notoriously brave warrior, seemed to think I was doing him some favour. "Yes, err, why are we going slowly then?" I asked, not entirely sure I wanted to hear the answer.

"I told you that Red Jacket is no fool. I am worried that he will have sent out his own flank guard of warriors. Certainly now most of our warriors have run forward to attack; he will know a war band was here."

"You mean that there could be another band of American Iroquois hunting us at this very moment?" I hissed at him feeling my heart rate quicken.

"Almost certainly, he replied calmly. "But your guess is as good as mine as to how many there are in it. There could be a dozen or a hundred. I have sent two scouts ahead so we should have some warning." His painted face gave me a grotesque grin before he added, "But don't worry I am sure we will be able to handle them."

Don't worry? My mind screamed the words in disbelief as I stared wildly around, suspecting every tree trunk to be hiding an enemy. We could be being tracked by a hundred hostile warriors, which seemed every reason to worry to me. For a second I considered whether now might be a good time to make an excuse and run for it. But there was one thing more terrifying than being part of a group in a forest of hostile Iroquois, and that is being *alone* in a forest of hostile Iroquois. When I looked around the enemy could be anywhere. It would be just my luck to blunder into them on my own. I looked down our shortened line of thirty warriors and prayed that by some miracle we would miss the American war bands.

I noticed that the noise of battle had increased now. Instead of a crackle of fire there was now the steady crash of musket volleys and from the frequency, both sides were putting up a stout rate of fire. We were getting closer to the edge of the forest and if there was going to be an attack it would be soon. I felt a bead of sweat run down my brow despite the cool shade under the trees. Twice I had jumped and snatched my gun round on what I had thought was a hidden warrior, only to find it was just a dappled shadow of leaves as the sun shone through the canopy above. My nerves were as frayed as a pauper's shawl when Black Eagle reached out from my right and grabbed my arm.

"Down, Little Father," he whispered. "That is the signal from our scouts." I had not heard a thing but I dropped to one knee and then edged forward until I was crouched behind a knot of ferns. Norton moved away down the line and I saw Smoke Johnson on my left edging into cover while he scanned the trees ahead. We must have

260

crouched silently for no more than a minute, but it seemed a lifetime. Every eye was probing the undergrowth in front of us for any sign of movement. I don't know about the others but I did not see a damn thing. In fact it was as I leaned my head towards Black Eagle to whisper that I thought no one was there, that the nightmare finally arrived. I had not yet uttered a sound but as I bent towards the big warrior I heard a slight 'thock' sound behind me and saw his eyes widen in alarm. I twisted round just in time to see the feathers still vibrating at the end of an arrow, now embedded in a tree trunk behind where my head had been a moment before.

A lot happened in the next few seconds. I flung myself to the ground so that I was out of sight of the unseen bowman. Any hope that there might have been just a few warriors was dashed by what could only be described as a wall of sound coming from the trees ahead. It sounded like there were thousands of the devils all yelling their fearsome war whoops from just yards away. Some of the Grand River warriors responded in kind, but all your correspondent could manage was a rather more Anglo-Saxon string of profanities, interspersed with pleas to the Almighty to preserve my cringing carcass. As the war cry contest subsided, the musket fire began. I saw both Smoke Johnson and Black Eagle take aim and fire through the trees, but I did not even dare look up through the ferns, never mind take aim. I don't think I have ever been so scared, and I speak from considerable experience. The dreadful war cries seared through to my very soul, turning my blood to ice and my guts to water. I was frozen in terror, unable to think or act. Then I heard the running feet and knew that they were coming towards us.

It is hard to remember now, everything happened so quickly, but I was vaguely aware that Smoke Johnson was wrestling with two of the devils to my left and Black Eagle had two facing him to my right. The American tribesmen had run right through our line like a wave, chasing and hunting down those behind. I am sure that two ran right past me without noticing the body lying prone in the ferns, or perhaps they just assumed I was dead. My imagination was filled with an image of my broken and scalped body lying among the undergrowth

261

and then it seemed as though the thought was a premonition. I looked up to see a warrior running towards me. He was looking directly at my horror-struck face and he was grinning wolfishly. He must have already fired his gun as he was gripping it by the barrel and raising the butt over his head. For a moment I remained transfixed by the awful vision of my impending death, but as he started to bring the brass bound butt of the gun down to dash out my brains, the spell that bound me was finally broken.

My assailant must have assumed that, like the others, I had already fired my gun as he showed little alarm when I jerked up the barrel and cocked it. His chest was just inches from the muzzle when I pulled the trigger. His gun flew harmlessly over my head while his body dropped backwards, snatched away by the impact of the ball. I glanced over my shoulder as I got up on one knee. Everywhere I looked there were fighting Indians, in pairs or groups, with no quarter being shown by either side. The warriors fighting Smoke Johnson and Black Eagle were concentrating on their own battles and now Johnson gave a cry of alarm as one of his opponents tripped him. The man sprang forward over my friend as Johnson tried to twist away. Without thinking I dropped the musket and pulled the pistol from my belt, thumbed back the flint and, aiming for the enemy warrior's groin, I pulled the trigger. As I had anticipated the gun kicked up and the ball passed through the man's side. He screamed as he went down, distracting his comrade just long enough for Johnson to tomahawk him in the leg, damn near taking his foot off. With both assailants down, Johnson was back on his feet and plunging into a melee to his left.

I got to my feet too and drew my sword. There was no escape here and I had a dim memory of an old Danish sailor exhorting me to die with a weapon in my hand. The familiar grip felt good and I reached down with my left hand to pull my tomahawk from my belt. With no alternative, it was time to fight. I turned towards Black Eagle, who was still fending off two men with a tomahawk and his musket. The big man's muscles flexed as he scythed the gun butt through the air to keep his opponents at bay, but he was slowing and now the nearest adversary darted towards him. The attacker was concentrating on his foe as Black Eagle desperately tried to reverse his swing in time. Neither of them noticed me until my sword blade sliced up under the enemy warrior's ribs.

"Thank you, Little Father," gasped Black Eagle as he concentrated his attention on his remaining enemy, who had darted back out of both of our reach. The man I had struck made a mewing sound as he sank to his knees, one of his hands clawing at his wounded side. I had to twist the blade to free it, which caused him to scream before he collapsed to the floor. The remaining attacker let out another war whoop and glanced desperately around the trees for reinforcements. I saw now that he had a strip of white cloth tied to one arm and so did the other American warriors that lay in the clearing. Indeed, staring about me the ground was littered with the dead and dying. Some had the white arm bands but while I could still see Norton and Johnson fighting in the distance, there were several nearby that I recognised from Brant's Ford. The battle was more spread out now, with dozens of figures running to and fro through the trees.

There seemed only the one American warrior near us, who was still gazing around for help rather than attacking. For a brief moment I thought we might have a chance of getting away, but that hope was dashed when another volley of shots rang out from the trees in front of us. One of the balls was close enough for me to hear it buzz past my ear, but Black Eagle was not so fortunate. I heard him give a grunt as his musket clattered to the ground. Turning to him I saw that he had a jagged hole at the top of his left arm, which now hung loosely at his side. He still had a tomahawk in his right fist, however, and as we heard more warriors crashing through the trees towards us, we both took a step towards each other so that we were standing side by side.

We cannot have been a particularly awe-inspiring sight to the three new warriors that appeared on the scene. The newcomers gazed at us and gave a new whoop of triumph, in no rush to finish us off. Their painted faces split into grins as they spread out with the earlier attacker, to make sure we did not escape. Black Eagle did not even bother to reply with a cry of his own. He just stood there watching them through eyes half closed in pain as I stood next to him, covering his wounded side.

"It seems the Great Spirit has decided our time is up," he whispered to me.

"No," I replied and I think I even managed to grin. "Not yet." For at that moment I had a strong feeling, no, a certainty, that I was not going to die. It was strange and I cannot explain it. Perhaps I had overdosed on fear and found my courage, or perhaps the Great Spirit had spoken to me after all. I don't know, but I felt a new strength course through my limbs and I tensed myself for what would be the fight of my life. I stood with my tomahawk raised in my left hand but I kept my sword down by my side, half hidden behind my legs. It was my only advantage and I needed to make the most of it. I watched the two men circling to our left while Black Eagle watched the two to our right.

If there was a signal between them I did not see it, but in the blink of an eye they were shrieking and charging forward. I knew what I had to do. Instead of standing still or backing away, I sprang towards them. The man on my extreme left was caught off guard and had to check his run but it was the man next to him I was concentrating on. His tomahawk was raised above his head and he had no defence to the razor sharp Damascus steel blade that suddenly appeared before him. The sharpened reverse edge eviscerated him before he realised what was happening. I heard him shriek but I did not see him fall for I was already twisting away to my right. I remember hearing the swish of my blade through the air and seeing a spray of fine blood droplets fly of its tip. Then it was biting deep into flesh again, this time the neck of one of the men facing Black Eagle. I wrenched the steel free and turned again, looking for the first man I had caught off guard. It was too late; he was already behind me and then, out of the corner of my eye I saw the vicious axe head swinging towards me. I hurled myself to one side and swung the sword wildly in his direction. Then I heard rather than felt the crack of steel on bone and the world went black.

I can only have been out for a second or two but when I came round I was lying on my back with two evil painted villains staring down on me in a blurry world. I blinked and shook my head and the two warriors merged into one, the bastard who had hit me. He had put his tomahawk back in his belt and I saw him draw a knife instead, standing over me grinning.

"Oh Christ," I murmured for I knew what the knife was for: the swine was going to scalp me with it. The devil laughed when he saw the realisation cross my face. I had no idea if he planned to kill me before taking my hair and no great wish to find out. "No, please," I held out my hand to fend him off. "I am a British officer." He had to understand English, but he showed no interest in my pleading. I looked around for one of my weapons and winced as a shooting pain shot down my neck as I turned it. My tomahawk was just out of reach but the warrior kicked it further away. There was no pity in that painted face. He was enjoying the terror he was inflicting and was in no rush to end it. "Please," I repeated desperately, but then his expression did change.

His mouth opened in a silent look of surprise and then he dropped down on one knee. I tried to shuffle back away from him thinking he was going to reach forward with his knife, but he made no effort to stop me. Then over his shoulder I saw Morag looking down at me.

"Wait here," she said curtly as though there was a chance I might take an afternoon stroll.

There are times, especially when your head has been hit with a tomahawk, when your brain struggles to keep up with events. That was one for me. I could not understand what Morag was doing there. For an insane moment I wondered why she was helping the American warrior. Then she moved away. As I slumped back on the ground, out of the corner of my eye I saw her picking up an abandoned musket by the barrel and start to swing it. A moment later there was a sickening crunch as several pounds of English oak bound in brass connected with a skull, like a spoon going through a boiled egg.

The next thing I remember was Black Eagle lifting me up into a half-sitting position with his good arm. "Are you all right, Little Father?"

As I stared about me again I noticed my former scalper now lying on his side. It was only then that I saw the end of the spear protruding

265

out of his back. I was still feeling bewildered and struggled to understand what was happening. But I managed to mutter, "My head hurts and I feel sick. Are there any more of them?"

There was still the sound of fighting in the forest, shouts, whoops and screams, but they were more distant now. When I looked through the trees I only saw one figure running between the trunks and that was away from us. The clearing we were in was a different matter; it was littered with the dead and dying. I realised with a touch of pride that I must have accounted for at least four of them myself.

I felt fingers touching the back of my head. "It is just a deep cut, nothing more," reassured Morag over my shoulder. "Now we should get away from here, before some of those warriors come back."

"Go towards the clearing," I ordered. "Once we are out of these trees and with the soldiers, they will protect us from any more Indian attacks." Never had I wanted more to be out of a forest. Any tree or bush could have hidden an attacker. I yearned for some open land.

Black Eagle looked doubtful. "The sound of battle is moving northwards," he declared cocking his ear to listen. "I think the British are losing."

"Fools," muttered Morag. "The edge of the forest is where the Americans will be. They will be taking their prisoners for the white soldiers to see and celebrating their victory. We need to go deeper into the forest to hide. Now, can you stand?"

Between them they hauled me to my feet. I took a few unsteady steps but the forest seemed to spin around me. Black Eagle stooped and with his good arm picked me up and rested me over his shoulder. Morag picked up our fallen weapons and we made our way deeper into the woods. As I bounced away hanging down Black Eagle's back, I looked up and saw Morag following on behind. The normally stern and disapproving face was softer and she had tears in her eyes. Despite everything that had happened, it was possibly the most surprising thing I had seen that day. When she saw me watching her she reached forward and squeezed my hand.

"Thank you for saving him," she whispered.

"Thank you for saving me," I answered. I thought again that she seemed more mellow than normal somehow, as though being with child had changed this fearsome woman. But then I remembered that she had just killed a man with a spear and dashed out the brains of another with a musket butt, so perhaps it had not changed her that much after all.

Chapter 31

In the end we found a dry stream bed which formed a shallow gorge through the forest and then we hid under an overhang. We were invisible to anyone who was not walking along the stream. Morag searched in her bag for a poultice and first bandaged Black Eagle's shoulder and then wrapped another strip of cloth around my head.

"Where did you come from?" I asked her as she tied off the end of the bandage. "I thought you had stayed in the camp."

"No, a few of us women followed the war band into the trees. When we heard the Americans attack I ran through the trees – I was not having my child born fatherless. None of their warriors thought a woman was worth killing. Then I saw you, waving that big knife of yours around."

"Well I am glad you did," I said with feeling. Morag offered me some dried meat but I did not feel like eating. We just sat quietly, having reloaded our weapons, and waited for the day to pass. Twice we heard war bands moving through the trees. They were talking loudly about their victories and there was the odd groan either from their wounded or prisoners, but none came close enough to discover us. We also heard the noise of battle continue to recede in the distance and it seemed like Black Eagle was right about the outcome.

I discovered later that the grey-jacketed troops were not militia, but regular soldiers who had been given intensive training by my old friend from Queenston, Winfield Scott. He had prepared them for battle in every respect but one. When he ordered new uniforms it was discovered that there was no blue cloth available and so they had to have the short grey jackets instead. Riall discovered the hard way that he was up against regulars when his attack was firmly rebuffed. He also learned then that Fort Erie had surrendered without putting up a fight, enabling the Americans to bring over three thousand men to Chippawa and not the few hundred men that Riall had been expecting.

I dozed a little that afternoon but as the sun went down Black Eagle shook me awake: it was time to head north. If the forest had been a frightening place in the daytime, it was little better at night. Every hoot from an owl seemed to be some enemy signal that would cause my muscles to tense. But we saw no one as we silently made our way through the trees. Eventually we hit the Chippawa River. It was nearly seventy yards wide, but calm and we managed to wade and swim across. Once on the far shore I felt a little safer. The Americans were unlikely to have crossed to the other side after the battle. There was only one bridge near the town of Chippawa. Even a commander as inexperienced as Riall was bound to have left a rear guard covering it, or perhaps he had destroyed it. We continued our way north and eventually came across a British patrol. Taking in our appearance they directed us to the Indian camp, but I asked them to give me directions to Riall's headquarters.

"I need to report to the general," I told Black Eagle. "In case Norton did not make it back." Riall would certainly expect the man he viewed as his Indian force commander to update him on what had happened in the forest. I also thought it would do no harm for him to see me in my battle-weary state. It would remind him of the risks I had taken and how deserving I was of leave. Black Eagle insisted he would come with me, but Morag decided to press on to the Indian camp and rest before what seemed an inevitable further retreat.

It was dawn by the time Black Eagle and I emerged from the trees into the camp of the regular army. There was an avenue of tents leading to a larger bivouac in the middle, which I guessed must be Riall's headquarters. Around those was a collection of other tents, some obviously home made from canvas or leather and all manner of other makeshift shelters. We made our way down the main thoroughfare leading towards the centre of the camp. We must have looked a disreputable pair– our war paint was smudged from sweat and the river crossing, we both sported blood-stained bandages and we were festooned with weapons. We both had our muskets and tomahawks while I had my sword and a pistol stuck in my belt too. We had got halfway to Riall's tent before someone tried to stop us.

"Oi, you two," shouted a burley sergeant marching across the path to cut us off. "The Indian camp is a mile in that direction," he said pointing. "So sling your 'ook and get out of 'ere."

I was tired and weary and while I would normally have enjoyed putting the man in his place, this time I did not have the energy. I was just considering the easiest way to make the man stand down when a voice spoke out to my right.

"Steady on, Sergeant, they look like they have been in the wars too."

It was a tall sandy-haired officer sitting outside his tent shaving, with his face covered in a soapy lather. I smiled my gratitude to him, but the sergeant was not prepared to let the matter drop.

"With respect, you don't know 'em, sir. Thievin' bastards the lot of them. You would be lucky to keep that silver razor if they got in the camp, sir, like bloody magpies for a bit o' glitter, they are." He turned to me and added, "Now shove off before I kick your sorry arse out of the camp."

That was it, I really lost my temper. "Damn your eyes, man, I am a British officer, a bloody major and you will stand to attention and salute me or I will have the hide flogged off you."

"An officer?" repeated the sergeant in astonishment as several heads popped out of nearby tents to look curiously on the scene.

"Yes, a bloody officer," I fumed as I wrenched my sword half out of its scabbard. "Since when have you seen an Indian with one of these?"

The sergeant stood to attention and saluted stiffly to guffaws of amusement from several of the onlookers.

"Where did you get that sword?" It was the officer whose face was covered in soap. He was standing now and his eyes glared angrily over the suds. "Tell me where you got that sword. I knew the man who used to own it."

"Do I know you?" I asked. "I have had this sword since I killed its owner in India."

The officer stared at me then as though he had seen a ghost. "No it can't be… Flashman, is that really you?"

I stared at the man. I knew the voice then but my mind struggled to comprehend that he could be here of all places. Then he started to wipe away the soap and I immediately recognised that lantern jaw. "Campbell!"

We threw our arms around each other and hugged. Campbell was one of my oldest friends. We had known each other in India and throughout my time on the Spanish peninsula.

"My God," cried Campbell gripping my shoulders and pushing me back a pace. "Let me look at you. Why, I thought you were killed chasing after that fool Grant in Spain and now I find you alive and well on the other side of the world. However did you get here?"

"Didn't Grant mention that I was in Paris with him or that I had escaped France on an American ship?"

"You were in Paris?" repeated Campbell astonished. "No, he never mentioned you at all. We all thought you were dead."

"The bastard," I said with feeling, although given the circumstances of my parting with Grant, I could hardly expect him to do me any favours.

"And who is this?" asked Campbell gazing at the big man who stood awkwardly to one side watching our exchange.

"Ah, Campbell let me introduce to you Black Eagle. Never mind the war paint, he is fine fellow. In fact the pair of you have a lot in common."

"We do?" queried Campbell looking sceptically at the painted warrior.

"Of course." I turned to Black Eagle. "Campbell here is Scottish. They have groups called clans instead of tribes and the Campbells are some of the worst cutthroats and cattle raiders in Scotland. They instil fear in all the neighbouring clans." Campbell laughed at my description while Black Eagle looked at him with new respect. "Yes," I continued warming to my theme and noticing several nearby officers looking on with amusement. "They howl as they go into battle, do war dances over their swords and their taste in music is even worse than the Iroquois."

"And do they worship the Great Spirit in Scotland?" asked Black Eagle sensing the presence of a fellow warrior.

"Oh aye," agreed Campbell dropping into a broad Scots accent and winking at me. Black Eagle beamed with delight, but before he could say anything Campbell continued, "We call it whisky. I have some in my tent and I cannot think of a better occasion to drink it than now."

While Black Eagle was initially a little confused as to what was happening, expecting some form of religious ceremony, he soon came to appreciate the Scottish 'great spirit'. Within a few minutes he had learned the Gaelic toast of 'slàinte' and was enjoying the sensation of the amber fluid warming his insides.

"I still can't believe it," Campbell kept saying as he looked at me. "To find you alive, and here of all places."

"What brings you to Canada so soon?" I asked. "I thought the first peninsular regiments were not due to arrive for another month or two."

"They aren't but Wellington sent me on ahead to judge which units would be the most useful. For example, I see you don't have much cavalry here."

"The forests are too thick to give them room to manoeuvre and they would be easy to ambush," I told him. "Mind you, the Americans have got some militia regiments that fight well in a loose formation. Some dragoons might be useful with their carbines, but nothing that relies on charging in a straight line."

"That is exactly the information I need!" cried Campbell. "You know how we fought on the peninsula and how they have been fighting here."

"Well if you can get me posted home," I told him, "I would be happy to tell the army commanders all about it." I looked around for Campbell's coat to see what rank he held. We had both been captains in Spain, but if he held sway with army command then maybe he could overrule the governor general's standing orders.

"I am a major now," said Campbell following my gaze. "What about you."

"Oh I have been promoted too," I confirmed casually. "Major in the 41st and deputy war chief to the Iroquois, although Riall thinks I am the man in charge."

"Well you certainly look the part," stated Campbell, gazing at my painted face and grinning.

"Little Father," interrupted Black Eagle, "should we not go now and tell the general about the battle in the woods?"

"Yes I suppose we should." I started to get up from my stool in Campbell's tent but he suddenly howled with laughter.

"Little Father, why on earth do they call you that?"

"It is a long story; I will tell you later when I am back from the general."

"I shall look forward to it. By the way I saw the other person that calls you Father in England just before I came to Canada."

"What?" I asked turning back to Campbell. "Who do you mean?"

"Why your son, of course, Thomas Junior. I saw him in town with Louisa who was sorting out her father's estate. Oh God," Campbell paused and went pale at some thought, "I'm sorry, Flashman, but when we talked we both thought you were dead. She was asking if there was any hope for your survival and I am afraid that I did not give her any."

My mind was whirling. I had not thought about Louisa for months. We had been estranged for years after her aristocratic father had decided I was not good enough for his daughter. But one thought rattled through my brain louder than all the others. "I have a son?"

"You didn't know?" gasped Campbell astonished.

"I have not seen Louisa for six years. I tried writing once but Lord Berkeley replied and told me never to try to contact his daughter again. The old bastard was intercepting her letters."

"Well you are the father of a bonny boy of around five. He looks the image of you in miniature. Hey wait, with Berkeley dead you are a rich man, Thomas, for Louisa has inherited the estate and she is still your wife."

Black Eagle gave me one of his rib-cracking slaps on the back. "See soon we will both be fathers," he boomed in delight. "You must bring your boy to the Grand River and we will teach him to hunt with my son."

I sat back down on the stool in a state of shock, still trying to take everything in. "I think I am going to need another glass of whisky."

Chapter 32

That afternoon I sat down to write a note to Louisa. It was not easy –
what on earth do you say to someone in those circumstances? After
several long and rambling attempts I decided brevity would be best.
After all I had no idea how she felt about me given the years that had
passed. I told her that I was in Canada and why I had been trapped
there for over a year. I also mentioned that I had met Campbell, the
news he had given me and that I would look to come home as soon as I
could. The letter would then be sent by horse and boat to Quebec and
down the St Lawrence to the coast before finally it would be sailed
across the Atlantic. I was sincerely hoping that I would not be far
behind it.

Campbell also wrote a letter to General Drummond, the overall
army commander in Canada, insisting that my experience of battles in
both Spain and Canada would be invaluable to the war office. He came
as close as he could to demanding on behalf of Wellington that I be
released to travel back to Britain with him. He had met both the
governor general and Drummond on his way south, and was sure that
the former would waive his rule if Drummond recommended it.
Unfortunately Drummond was miles away and it would take at least
two weeks to get a reply.

Having been stuck in Canada for over a year this did not seem long
to wait in normal circumstances, but with an American invasion in full
swing, the times were far from normal. By the time a response came
we could be swept from the Niagara peninsula entirely. Indeed, if the
American army managed to link up with their fleet on Lake Ontario,
the British position would be fatally weakened before the veterans of
the Spanish campaign had a chance to make a difference.

After our letter writing Black Eagle and I stayed in Campbell's tent
that night, drinking, telling tales and catching up over old times. We
did not get a lot of sleep. The next morning the scouts reported that the
American army was showing no signs of moving. I think both sides
were still licking their wounds after the battle. As I had only my
buckskin trousers and a borrowed shirt to wear, I was keen to go with

Black Eagle back to the Indian camp. Campbell insisted on coming too so that he could see the warriors he had just heard many stories about.

I was shocked when we finally reached the land the Indians had built their shelters on, which I had last seen two days before. Then the clearing had been full of warriors and other followers. As well as the three hundred Iroquois there had been natives from the western tribes and even some white militia units. Now there were barely more than a hundred warriors left, most of whom were wounded, but judging from a collection of empty bottles, a number were also drunk.

While Black Eagle took Campbell off to introduce him to Morag, I looked for Norton. I found him in the corner of the clearing leaning against a tree. This normally energetic man looked more depressed and defeated than I had ever seen before.

"Surely these are not all that are left?" I asked when he saw me.

"No, many of the able-bodied warriors left yesterday. The Americans at the southern end of the peninsula are close to the mouth of the Grand River, so they want to go and protect their homes." He gestured at a nearby group of warriors snoring loudly surrounded by empty bottles. "Most are fairly demoralised by having to fight their Indian brothers and by a British defeat so close to their villages." He gave a heavy sigh before adding, "Many blame me for the disaster and not just the warriors. Have you seen Riall?"

"No, I was going to yesterday but after I finished catching up with an old friend from Spain," I gestured at Campbell across the clearing, "Fforbes told me that you had already seen him. He did not think it would be a good idea for me to see him as well; I gather that the general has not taken this reverse well."

"No, he was in a foul temper when I saw him, Fforbes was right to put you off. I told him that I had guided the warriors deeper into the forest to ambush the Americans and he seems to have decided that I caused his defeat. If I had lined the edge of the forest as he ordered then he thinks he would have won the battle, even though we would have been attacked from in front and behind."

"We will have to pull back in the next few days. Do you think we will get many Iroquois to re-join the army."

Norton gave a bitter laugh. "Now we will do well if many of them do not join the Americans to protect their homes." He saw my look of surprise and then added, "Don't worry, I will bring a few of my most loyal men, but I will struggle to get much more than a dozen now." He pointed across the clearing. "By the way, Magda is here. She rode in this morning with more medicines for Spotty Pots, who was running out."

I looked over and noticed for the first time the golden hair as Magda bent over some injured warrior with the medicine woman. "I will go over and see her but in the meantime, if those warriors have left any, you should have a drink. You look like you need one."

As I walked over Magda got up and Black Eagle called her over to introduce her to Campbell, who blushed furiously, as he always did in the presence of a pretty woman. "What is this?" I called out as I reached them, "All of my favourite people in one place." Magda gave me one of her dazzling smiles and I fervently hoped that Black Eagle would be discrete about the information he had learned last night. I swiftly discovered he had no idea of the concept.

"Little Father has just discovered that he has a son living in England," he blurted out as soon as I had spoken.

"Really?" Magda stared at me curiously. "Have you got a girl into trouble or is there a wife you have never mentioned before as well?"

"He has a wife too," cried out Black Eagle excitedly before I could open my mouth. "And she is rich and they have a big cabin made of stone and lands to hunt in and… ouch, what did you do that for?"

"I think," said Morag wearily, "that there are things that the Little Father wanted to tell Magda himself, in his own way."

"It is all right," laughed Magda. "I have always known that Thomas wanted to go home and I am pleased that he has a lot to go home to."

"I was estranged from my wife. I have not seen here in six years, that is why I did not mention her." I knew the concept of marriage was sacred to Magda and suddenly it was important to me that she did not think that I was some cynical, married seducer of women.

"It is all right, Thomas," Magda repeated. "Spotty Pots told me long ago that you had a woman you loved back home."

276

"What?" I asked in irritation. "That toothless old biddy does not know the first thing about it…" I started before realising that if it got me out of trouble, it might be wise to concede that the crone with the colourful crockery may indeed have some powers. "Well I don't see how she could have known," I concluded weakly.

"There are a lot of things we don't understand about Iroquois ways," Magda insisted soothingly. "But I do know that a head wound that leaves that much blood on your bandage probably needs cleaning and some stitches. Why don't you come with me and let that 'toothless old biddy' take a look at it."

I spent most of the day in the Indian camp and during that time virtually all of its occupants left. Norton went with them, looking as disconsolate as ever, with just a handful of loyal followers. With his wound properly dressed, Black Eagle decided to stay with me and once I was back in my British uniform, we returned to the British camp with Campbell.

I tried to keep away from Riall for the next few days; a defeated general is always casting around for excuses and scapegoats and it seemed Riall was blaming everyone but himself for the defeat. I caught up again with Fforbes who was being blamed for not knowing that the grey-jacketed men were regulars, even though we had both warned Riall that they seemed too well drilled for militia. The whole Fort Erie garrison was being blamed for surrendering too quickly, while scouts had been reprimanded for not warning Riall that the enemy force was much larger than he expected, regardless of the fact that the enemy had been shielded by a huge expanse of forest. Finally Norton and I were being blamed for disobeying orders and going too deep into the trees. Normally I would not have given a damn but Fforbes had other disturbing news. Drummond, he said, was far too busy gathering men to repel the new invasion to worry about Campbell's request. As Drummond had never met me, he was almost certain to forward the letter on to Riall to approve.

I fumed as I realised that the incompetent puffed-up popinjay held my fate in his hands. Campbell was due to leave the Niagara area at the end of the month. I was determined to leave with him, even if I had to desert the army to do it. It would be much easier with Riall's signature, though, and so I resigned myself to some serious toadying. Fforbes suggested that I waited a while to give the general time to calm down, but as time passed he warned that Riall's temper was not showing any sign of diminishing.

So it was that four days after the battle I staggered a little unsteadily into the general's tent. I still had a bandage around my head, which had a large bloodstain on it. My wound was actually healing well and Riall was not to know that the gore on the cloth and sticking in my hair had actually come from a dead chicken.

"Ah, Major Flashman, I wondered when you would have the nerve to show your face." The general glared at me with his small piggy eyes. "Your failure to follow the simplest order has cost me and your country dearly."

"I am sorry, sir, I was wounded in the battle," I croaked, weakly gesturing to my bandaged and bloody head.

"Battle!" shouted Riall. "You were not in the battle. You were hiding in the woods when you should have been protecting my flank." I was swiftly realising that Fforbes was not exaggerating about Riall's temper. If anything he had only wound himself up further over the perceived failings of his command.

"I can assure you, sir that the battle did extend into the forest. There were hundreds of enemy warriors in the trees who we had to engage with. I killed four myself before I took this wound."

"Hmph," grunted Riall barely bothering to hide his disbelief at my claim. "Norton told me the same story, but I saw no sign of a battle in those trees."

"With respect, sir, you could not see far into the forest...."

"Did I or did I not give you an order to take your command to line the forest edge?" interrupted Riall.

"You did, sir, but then we discovered that the enemy had hundreds of warriors who would have ambushed us from behind."

"Stuff and nonsense," roared Riall. "And where is your command now, Major? From what I hear the whole bloody lot of them have gone home."

"Many have gone to protect their lands on the Grand River – the Americans are close to their territory," I started to explain, but I got no further.

"It is outrageous!" Riall barked. "I would not let any other regiment go home when they chose, so why should I let your command do what it likes? Go and get them back, Major and that is an order. An order I expect to be obeyed, do you understand?"

"Yes sir," I replied swiftly taking my leave before I angered him any further. God knows how I was supposed to get the Iroquois back for him. It seemed that achieving this task was the only thing likely to placate him and get him to sign my release. But from what Norton had told me, if the Iroquois were to return to the war at all, there was every chance that they would be lining up in the American ranks against Riall rather than for him.

I passed Fforbes on the way back to Campbell's tent. "How was he?" Fforbes asked.

"Completely unreasonable. He does not understand at all that the Iroquois see themselves as a separate nation. He seems to think that they are just another regiment."

"At least you can get away back to that Indian village; I am stuck with him." Fforbes grinned ruefully. "And you can guess who is to blame when any element of his retreat goes wrong." Despite our earlier encounters, I was beginning to like Fforbes, particularly when I saw what he had to put up with.

"How is the retreat going?" I asked. "As he wants the Iroquois back I am guessing our general is planning to make another stand?"

"Oh the general has never been defeated before, but then he had not fought a proper battle before either. I think he is terrified of damaging his reputation with a second defeat. So he is likely to keep pulling back until he thinks he has a clear advantage. General Drummond is our best hope. He is bringing reinforcements and will take overall command when he gets here, but that is likely to be at least two weeks away. We are lucky that the Americans are not pushing forward with greater vigour."

I sat morosely in Campbell's tent for a while wondering what to do next. I did not really have a choice; I had to go back to Brant's Ford. If Norton could persuade at least a hundred warriors to re-join the British, we could explain that a lot of the rest were wounded. Any fewer than that and Riall would be convinced that both Norton and I had betrayed him.

Chapter 33

A day later and Black Eagle and I were riding into Brant's Ford. Luckily we called in first at Black Eagle's cabin on the outskirts of the village.

"What are you doing here?" Morag asked, looking slightly alarmed, as we entered.

"Is that a way for a wife to greet her man when he comes home after a long journey?" asked Black Eagle sweeping her up into his arms.

"Not you, you great lump, him, in that uniform," she said pointing at me.

"Am I no longer welcome, then?" I asked feeling slightly hurt. For a moment I wondered if the Iroquois had changed sides already, but surely Norton would have sent word.

"Of course you are," assured Morag squeezing my hand in greeting. "But not in that uniform, not today. She turned to Black Eagle. "Go and fetch his buckskins from his pack and make sure no one is watching the cabin.

"What on earth is going on?" I asked.

"There is a grand council meeting of the Iroquois here today. They are deciding what to do about the war. Some would be alarmed to see a British officer roaming around the village."

"But I am supposed to be persuading them to go back to the army and anyway, they all know that I am a British officer."

"The American warriors don't," stated Morag simply.

"You mean there are enemy warriors here in Brant's Ford now?" I was stunned. I had no idea that they would move so quickly, especially after they had been trying to kill each other just a week before. "Are the Iroquois changing sides?"

"That is what they are going to discuss. No one wants to see our people fighting each other again." At this Black Eagle re-entered the cabin with a bundle of buckskins under his arm. "Put those on," Morag continued, "and go and see John Norton, he will know much more than me."

I hurriedly changed. If the tribe was determined to switch sides then I thought that there would be little that Norton or I could do to change their minds. Norton had lost nearly all of his supporters after the battle at Chippawa. For a moment I wondered if I would be safe in the village if they did decide to switch their allegiance, but then I remembered that Norton had told me once about strict rules they had to protect delegates attending council meetings. Certainly the American warriors must have thought that they would be safe visiting the home of their very recent enemies. I had lived in the village for a good while now and I thought I had enough friends here to at least guarantee that I would not be harmed. Mind you, I did gather some curious stares from those who knew me as I walked down the main street. A number looked disapproving and I guessed that they did not think that a British soldier, even out of uniform, should be in the village at a time like this.

There were several warriors I did not know sitting outside Norton's cabin but they did not stop me as I strolled up the path and entered. Norton was sitting on the floor opposite an older grey-haired man I did not know. They were both deep in conversation and the stranger appeared mildly irritated as I interrupted them. His look was nothing, though, to Norton's gaze of shock and surprise.

"Ah, Flash-man," he called giving my name a strange Indian intonation. "Could you wait outside for a moment?"

Before I could reply the stranger started to get up. "It is all right," he said. "I have told you everything that I came to say. We should make our way to the council meeting." He got to his feet smoothly despite his age and as he did so I noticed what looked to be a big silver plate hanging from a chain beneath his coat.

"Yes indeed," agreed Norton also getting to his feet and giving me a slight shake of the head in warning. I was unsure what he was warning me about but he solved that a moment later when he introduced me. "This is Flash-man, one of my best warriors. Flash-man, meet Red Jacket."

My jaw must have dropped in surprise. This was the veteran war chief of the American warriors. I was so shocked I acted without

282

thinking and held out my hand in the European manner. "I am delighted to make your acquaintance, sir."

Norton looked appalled and hurriedly tried to cover up for me. "Flash-man is half Spanish; he has not lived with the Iroquois for that long and does not know our ways." The explanation was true as far as it went; it just neglected to mention that my other half was British. But judging from the amused twinkle that appeared in Red Jacket's eye, I don't think we fooled this canny warrior for a moment. His glance dropped to the sword at my hip and he gave a slow nod as though remembering something.

"I have heard my warriors talk about a fearsome Iroquois who stayed hidden when we first attacked and then killed many with a long knife." He reached out and shook my hand that had stayed frozen in the air when I realised my mistake. "Not all of your victims died straight away and one told of how you refused to take any scalps. For that I am grateful to you." He turned to Norton. "Several of us have also heard of a British officer that lives here with a gold-handled long knife like this one Flash-man wears. It would be better, I think, if this warrior leaves his knife in your cabin if he is attending the council."

"You don't mind if he attends?" asked Norton surprised.

"Provided he does not try to interfere in the debate," confirmed Red Jacket giving me a warning glance, "then I would welcome it. He can report to his generals on the strength of feeling of our people."

Red Jacket turned towards the door. I started to step back to give him room but to my surprise he took me by the arm and led me outside with him. He stopped on the porch and spoke quietly while staring out at the villagers bustling around preparing food and getting ready for the council meeting. "My name comes from a red coat that the British gave me when I fought for them. This silver you see around my neck was a gift from George Washington; it shows the two of us shaking hands. I tell you this to prove that I know about the white man on both sides of this war. Neither really cares about the Iroquois, they each see us as a tool to attack the other. That is why the Iroquois must choose to do what is best for them." Several more unfamiliar warriors were standing outside of the cabin as we had appeared on the porch. They were big ugly brutes and when one of them saw the sword at my hip he started for me, reaching for his tomahawk before his comrades called him back.

Red Jacket spoke sharply to the man and then turned to me. "One of the men you killed was his brother. But do not worry, my men will not harm you. It would dishonour all of us if the truce was broken." With that the chief gripped my shoulder in friendship and then walked away towards the council hall in the centre of the village, followed by his men.

"Good God, Flashman," Norton whispered behind me. "What are you doing here?"

"I live here, remember, and why didn't you tell me about this council?"

"Because I did not want you here," Norton answered honestly. "Many think I am more the servant of the British than the Iroquois. I did not want a British officer here appearing to be overseeing what I was saying in the council. Now come inside and take that sword off before you cause any more trouble."

"Are things that bad? Will they change sides?"

"I don't know, it will be a close call and much will depend on Red Jacket. He is a powerful speaker – he once gave a speech to the US Senate. I was trying to find out which way he was leaning when you came in."

"I am sorry. I had wanted to speak to you before this council to find out what was happening."

"Well we will both find out soon enough. I have to go. Speak to Black Eagle, he will show you where to sit. But for God's sake, Flashman, keep quiet. If word gets out that a British officer is interfering then it will work against us."

The council chamber was organised much like the one at Amherstburg with the important people sitting around the edge of the room and the audience in the middle. Black Eagle and I managed to find some space at the back of the room where few people noticed us. Staring around I could see the women who headed the various Iroquois clans along one wall. Amongst them I was surprised to see Spotty

Potts – she clearly had far more influence than I had realised. Then there were village chiefs and finally war chiefs, among them Red Jacket and Norton.

I would like to be able to give you a detailed account of the debate that took place over the next hour or so, but as it was nearly all in Iroquoian, I understood very little. There were various speeches of welcome, which I half followed with my limited knowledge of the tongue. Then a hush fell over the room and I sensed that business of the day was about to begin in earnest. The first to put forward their case was a tall one-eyed warrior I had not seen before. He spoke with all the fervour of one of those Methodist preachers who stand outside taverns and implore people to turn to a life of temperance. But while those sanctimonious fools were normally pelted with insults, mud and worse, I saw an increasing number of heads nodding in agreement as his one eye roved about the audience.

"He is one of the American warriors," whispered Black Eagle. "He says that the Americans will win this war as they did the last time they fought the British for their independence. The Iroquois who supported the British then lost much of their land to the Americans and he says that the same will happen again if we continue to support the British in this war. He is urging them to support the Americans to protect their land." As the man sat down there was shouts from his supporters and quite a few from the audience; they were clearly impressed with what he had said.

Then Norton got up and waited while the hubbub died down. He looked tired and while he spoke clearly it was without the passion of his predecessor. I did not need Black Eagle to translate for I could guess what he was saying. He would be telling them how the British had given them the Grand River land, how the peninsular veterans would soon be there to change the balance of the war and how the Grand River Iroquois had a treaty of friendship with the British. One of the audience shouted out something. I did not understand it all but I caught the word for 'gifts'. Supply problems meant that many of the gifts promised by the British for the Iroquois had not been received. Norton answered as best as he could, but it was clear that he was not carrying his audience as the first speaker had done. Many looked suspicious at his words and I noticed several now looking through the crowd at me, with similarly cynical expressions. As Norton sat down there was another rumble of debate from the floor, this time with much shaking of heads. That's it I thought, they will change sides. Rather than bringing my 'regiment' back to Riall, he will see it lined up against him. Then silence fell over the floor again as Red Jacket got up to speak.

The old chief slowly surveyed the room as the hubbub died down, in no hurry to start speaking. When he had their attention he started, not shouting, but speaking calmly and continuing to gaze across the audience as though he wanted to look everyone in the eye. It was a statesmanlike performance and even though I only followed about half of it, I felt myself warming to his argument.

"He says the white man can come in limitless numbers from across the sea, while we are few," summarised Black Eagle. "He says we must never fight each other as at Chippawa again, for it does not matter if the British or Americans win, the Iroquois will lose." He obviously said much more, which Black Eagle chose not to translate. From what little I could understand, he was saying that the white men on both sides were using the Iroquois as a weapon to attack their enemies. He claimed that British and Americans asked the Iroquois to take the risks of war but offered little in the way of fruits of victory. Finally he reached a rousing conclusion which was greeted with universal acclaim from those present. "He says that we should stay out of the white man's war," shouted Black Eagle over the noise. "He says that we should preserve our strength so that the white man respects us and to fight for what matters to us." It was clear from the acclaim as Red Jacket sat down that his argument had carried the day.

It was a better outcome than I had expected. At Chippawa there had been more warriors fighting for the Americans than the British, so neutrality would hurt the Americans more than us. However I did not think that Riall would see it that way and I was in no rush to tell him.

There was a feast on the night of the council meeting but I spent the evening alone in my cabin. I did not want to meet any vengeful

286

American warriors; there was always a chance that drunkenness could outweigh the diplomatic restraint of the truce. Red Jacket's party returned home the next morning and I felt safer, but I still attracted curious stares from some who evidently thought it was time for me to leave the village. I was in full agreement with them there. Word came through that the Americans were advancing past Queenston and it looked like the British would be trapped at Fort George in the corner of the Niagara peninsula. I was damned if that was going to happen to me. I was not going to be taken prisoner, especially if I was still a wanted man. I was going to go home and see my son, whatever the cost. So instead I hatched a plan to travel north as a civilian. If necessary I would work my passage in a merchantman across the Atlantic and then appeal to Wellington for help when I was back in Britain.

Several more days passed and then came news that the Americans were retreating again, back towards Chippawa, due to a shortage of supplies. General Drummond the British commander, ordered Riall to follow the Americans while he brought up a fresh army of his own. They were all to meet on a muddy little track known as Lundy's Lane. The place is forgotten by most today, but anyone who was there will never forget it. With the sound of the Niagara Falls roaring in our ears, blood was spilt, reputations were made and scores were settled.

Chapter 34

"What is that you say?" General Riall asked Norton, his eyes boggling in disbelief. Norton looked at me to see if I could explain the situation more clearly.

"The Iroquois have had a council and have agreed to stay out of the war, on both sides," I confirmed. "We have only brought a handful of loyal warriors with us today, but as there were more Iroquois fighting for the Americans at Chippawa than for the British, this will hurt the Americans more."

Norton had asked me to come with him to see Riall. He wanted me to help him confirm the strength of feeling among the Iroquois. We both had known it would be a difficult discussion, but Riall was struggling to comprehend even the basic facts.

"Are you both telling me," he croaked, struggling to get his thoughts together, "that you have had a meeting with enemy forces and agreed a truce with them?"

"It was not our meeting, it was an Iroquois council," Norton tried to patiently explain again. "Our people live on both sides of the border and—"

"Do you mean to say that you have been in the same room as emissaries from their notorious chief, what is his name," he paused as he searched among papers on his desk, "ah here it is, Red Jacket and you have not arrested them?"

"Red Jacket came himself, sir," announced Norton as I winced at this unhelpful honesty. "I had a meeting with him, but we could not arrest him as we were all covered by a truce for the council."

"This is infamy," roared Riall. "It is more than that, it is treason. Red Jacket's warriors have been raiding our towns and you had him in your power on British soil and you let him get away. By God you will pay for this, the pair of you."

"It was Iroquois soil," Norton corrected, "and as I explained we were covered by a truce."

"Truce be damned," thundered Riall. "If I did not need every last man I would arrest the pair of you now. But rest assured I will raise your conduct with General Drummond when he gets here." He gave us an ominous smile before adding, "He knows how to deal with traitors: he hangs them. Now get out of my sight." We had both started to march out of Riall's campaign tent when he called me back. "Oh, Flashman, I have here a paper from Drummond seeking your release to Britain. You can rest assured that the only way you will see Britain again is in chains!"

"Well I think that went pretty well, don't you?" I said sarcastically to Norton as I stepped out into the sunshine. "I am not sure he really cared that much about the strength of feeling amongst the Iroquois." I kicked at a stone in frustration. "Why is everyone on this wretched continent so keen on getting a rope around my neck?"

"Don't worry, Flashman, I have met Drummond and while he is harsh, he is fair. More importantly he was born in Canada and understands the Iroquois. He will be pleased that Red Jacket and his men are going home."

"Well I do not care any more. I have my bags packed and as soon as Campbell is ready to leave I am going with him. I will damn well stow away on the ship if I have to."

Over the next couple of days both Campbell and Fforbes tried to convince me to put my faith in Drummond. Both offered to speak to him on my behalf and were confident that with their joint testimony of my service in Spain and in Canada, they could outweigh any vitriol from Riall. I was not so sure; generals were inclined to support each other and Drummond would surely think twice before antagonising his second in command. But I agreed to stay with the army for a while longer as Campbell was not due to leave before the end of the month.

The Americans were still south of the Chippawa River and Riall had taken a position a mile or two north on the crest of a hill. We were very close to the Niagara Falls and a couple of times I rode over to look at them. While others commented on their majesty and power, I used to imagine pitching Riall into the rapids at the top and watching as he was drawn over the edge – it would be nothing more than the bastard deserved. But instead of loitering dangerously close to the edge of the river, Riall spent his time gathering men to form a defensive position should the Americans start to move north again.

Properly defended, the hill he had chosen would form a significant obstacle. The land in front of it was largely clear of trees for some six hundred yards, with just a few patches of scrub. A track, called Lundy's Lane ran east to west along the top of the hill. This joined with a portage road running along the river bank, forming a crossroads on the left flank of the British position. At the very top of the hill was a small cemetery, which seemed somewhat ironic given that the ground was being prepared as a battlefield.

Riall rushed about issuing orders left, right and centre. He wanted his five cannon on the forward slope of the hill so that they had a clear field of fire and planned for his infantry to form a line just in front of Lundy's Lane and behind his guns. He had amassed around eleven hundred men and we knew Drummond was marching towards us with more reinforcements. Norton and I kept well out of his way. Norton had only managed to persuade fifteen warriors to accompany him back to the Niagara and they came more out of a sense of loyalty to him rather than a desire to fight. Black Eagle had insisted on accompanying me, but with his arm still bandaged, Morag had issued dire threats to both of us as to what she would do if he got hurt again. Most of the Indians that were there came from the western tribes and they now viewed the Iroquois with suspicion, having heard of the truce. We all just loafed about waiting for Drummond to arrive and hoping that he would come before any Americans appeared at the far end of the clearing.

In the end it was a close run thing. In the early evening of the 25th of July 1814 the first American troops started threading their way through the trees at the bottom of the slope. They came marching into view in a neat column and this time the short grey jackets did not fool anyone. Norton and I made our way to stand with the men at the crest of the hill to count the approaching men. There were no more than a thousand of them, less than the force Riall commanded, but he was pacing about anxiously and giving orders for ever more scouts to give him more information.

We had a well prepared position on the hilltop and I had seen
Wellington beat far bigger odds from the top of a ridge, but Riall's
confidence seemed to disappear faster than a midshipman's coins in a
brothel. He had been beaten by these men before and the hurt to his
pride was still raw. But instead of wanting to avenge that defeat he
seemed far more concerned with avoiding another.

"Gentlemen," he finally announced as he snapped his glass shut,
"we will retire back towards Queenston until General Drummond can
join us with reinforcements."

There was a stunned silence among his staff officers who had spent
the last hours making sure all was in order to defend the hill. "But sir,"
Fforbes spoke at last, on behalf of the rest, "we have done everything
that we can to make this hill a tough place for the enemy to capture.
General Drummond is probably no more than an hour away with
another five hundred men and at least another thousand are also on
their way."

"Damn you, sir," roared Riall, "I will not have my orders
questioned. That could be the advance guard for their whole army." He
glared around at his silent staff and mercifully missed me smirking
with delight at the back of the crowd. "Give the order to retreat
without delay." With that he stalked back to his tent.

"He is mad giving up a position like this," whispered Norton. "Even
if the rest of the American army is out there, that is only around two
and a half thousand men. We will have sixteen hundred within the
hour and probably close to three thousand by nightfall."

I laughed "Well I am happy to retreat. I am not getting myself
killed for that buffoon and if he shows himself to be a poor general
then Drummond is less likely to believe any claims he makes about
us."

Winfield Scot probably could not believe his luck when he saw
teams of horses come over the top of the hill and start to limber up the
guns that had yet to fire a shot at him. But he did not have long to
celebrate as most of the guns had barely moved an inch when the
orders were cancelled and the guns left where they were. Drummond
had arrived just in time to see the first regiments marching away from

the hill and he swiftly had them turnabout. The two British generals then had what seemed to be a heated conversation before Drummond assumed overall command and continued the preparations for defending the hill.

It was then the Americans' turn to be indecisive. Winfield Scott had arrayed his men into line for an assault up the hill and they started the advance when they saw the gun limbers appear. But when the horses were sent away again the American line came to a halt. Perhaps Winfield Scott caught a glimpse of the two British generals as they sat on their horses reviewing the battlefield and feared the whole British army awaited him just over the hill. Whatever the reason, the American line stood some four hundred yards in front of the British guns, apparently unsure whether to retreat or attack.

The British gunners knew what to do, though, and opened fire on a target that was almost impossible to miss. The gun barrels were soon warm and pitching balls just in front of the American line so that they would bounce up and crash through the ranks at body height. When I had faced similar fire in India I had ordered my men to lie flat and Wellington had done the same in Spain. But these soldiers were determined to prove their new professionalism and so stood resolutely in lines as one gory hole after another was punched through their ranks. A few times the Americans replied with musket volleys but the range was far too long for them to be effective and they merely succeeded in shrouding their men in smoke. There were only three American cannon returning fire and they barely had the range to get anywhere near our artillery and they certainly could not reach the ranks of redcoats standing behind.

I could not understand why the Americans did not retreat as they did not seem to be achieving anything apart from getting killed. Norton offered to take what Indians he could gather and some militia through the woods around the edge of the field to attack the American left flank. He asked me if I wanted to go too but I refused. The whole venture sounded far too similar to Chippawa for my liking. If some of our warriors were willing to continue the fight perhaps some of theirs were too. I was not going through that nightmare again. With Morag's threats ringing in our ears, Black Eagle and I stayed on the hilltop, safely out of range of the Americans and waited for what seemed their inevitable withdrawal.

As dusk fell a stand of Congreve rockets was set up by our cannon to join the artillery barrage. There are not many moments of any battle I can honestly say I have enjoyed but that was one of them – not least because I was completely safe. I remember standing on that hilltop as the first stars appeared and hearing the distant thunder of the falls interspersed with the sporadic crash of cannon fire, the occasional crackle of musketry and the whoosh of rockets as their fiery tails veered randomly across the night sky. The Congreves were completely useless, of course, and at best will only have succeeded in frightening some horses, but against a starry sky they looked very impressive.

All good things come to an end and the start of a new phase in this battle was signalled by a sudden burst of firing on our left flank, near where the road that runs parallel with the river crossed Lundy's Lane. It turned out that not all of Winfield Scott's men had been standing and dying. Some on his right flank had taken advantage of the growing darkness to find an unseen path enabling a surprise attack on our left.

Suddenly our generals had things to do. It was too dark to see who was winning the distant fire fight and Drummond sent officers out to report for him while Riall snarled at Fforbes to get some of the gunners to swing their aim to the left. The noise of battle and from the waterfall was far too loud to yell the order to the gunners. Fforbes had barely time to call for a messenger, when Riall shouted irritably that he would take the message himself. Most of us sighed with relief to see the back of him as he had been snapping at everyone ever since he had lost command of the British force.

He disappeared into the darkness and – three cheers and a cigar to the American artillery – they only managed to hit him. My biggest regret is that I did not see it, but five minutes later Riall was being carried back on a stretcher, squealing like a stuck pig with what looked like a metal shell fragment in his arm.

"I will have to get him escorted and carried to the rear," said Fforbes wearily. "I cannot have him here screaming in front of the men."

"I will do it," I volunteered.

"Are you sure?" persisted Fforbes. "I doubt it will make much difference to how he feels about you."

I looked out into the darkness and grinned. "On the contrary, I think my circumstances are just about to improve."

"You are not going to do anything stupid are you, Flashman?" whispered Fforbes as he stood close beside me. "If he is killed there will be an inquiry."

"Don't worry," I told him. "I am not going to lay a finger on our general. Now, Black Eagle, are you ready to move? We have work to do."

Chapter 35

A short while later Black Eagle and I were walking east along Lundy's Lane, heading for the crossroads and the portage road that would take us to Queenston. A steady crackle of musket fire was continuing ahead on the right hand side of the road, while our cannon continued to bombard a now largely unseen enemy line in the darkness to their front. Between whining, Riall had decided that a stretcher was not a dignified or fast way for a general to travel and had insisted on being helped onto his horse. He was using his good arm to hold his injured one against his chest while I walked beside his mount and led it by the reins.

"Dammit, Flashman," called out Riall as a new bust of firing broke out on the right hand side of the road. "Why do we have to travel this way? Surely we should go cross country over the hill?"

"Because we need to find that portage road," I explained for the second time. "If we go cross country we will probably blunder into some forest first, which will slow us down. You don't want to bleed to death, do you?" Riall had not lost that much blood, but from the fuss he was making it was obvious that he had not been seriously wounded before. He was frightened of dying, as any man would be with a lump of metal stuck in their arm, but the fear was making him even more irritable than usual.

"Well keep that bloody Indian away from me," he snarled, "I don't trust the brute."

The 'brute' in question leaned across to me to whisper, "Why are we helping the general? I thought he was planning to have you arrested."

"You will see soon," I told him.

"Are we going to kill him?" Black Eagle's white teeth gleamed in the darkness as he grinned at the prospect.

"No we are going to deal with him in a way that will not get me in any more trouble." I smiled in the darkness for my plan was evolving. Until then I had not realised quite how frightened Riall was of the Iroquois. He was used to plantation workers in the West Indies who had largely been beaten into submission. They were very different from these proud and independent warriors, with their reputation for savage cruelty. Twice now Riall had insisted that Black Eagle move away from him, as though the Indian was an angry scorpion who could strike at any moment. I thought it would be a shocking waste not to exploit his fear for my own benefit.

"What are you two muttering about?" demanded Riall. "I am telling you, Flashman, that if you think this is going to persuade me to forget your treachery you are mistaken. I am still not convinced that you and your damn warriors did much fighting at all at Chippawa. For all I know you could have been sitting in a ditch smoking those damn pipes of yours."

"We were just wondering if many of the American warriors have broken the truce," I replied casually. "I thought I heard one of their screech owl signals, but it could have been a real owl, I suppose."

"Are you saying that we could be being tracked by enemy warriors at this moment?" whispered Riall, the whites of his eyes gleaming in the night.

"Oh they would like to fight in cover like this," I told him gesturing at the scrub and trees that lined either side of the road. It was hard to suppress a smile. Of course I knew no Indians would have considered crossing the wide expanse of open land that lay beyond the strip of scrub and besides, from what we had heard all of the American warriors were observing the truce.

"Some warriors will still be looking for scalps," added Black Eagle sensing the fun to be had and joining in. He looked at the horror that was now plainly showing on Riall's face and drew his scalping knife, testing the edge with his thumb. "You really want to be dead before they scalp you," he warned ominously.

"Good God, Flashman," cried Riall, "we need to go faster; I cannot be taken by those damn savages."

At that moment a new burst of firing broke out ahead. We could see the muzzle flashes through the branches and this time it seemed even closer to the road. It was just what I was hoping for.

"Black Eagle," I called, scout for me down the scrub on the right hand side of the road and let me know how close the American soldiers are." The big warrior disappeared into the bushes while I continued to lead the general's horse forward down the road. "If the Americans have reached the road they may ambush anyone travelling down it," I warned the general. "But we have to risk it to get you to a surgeon."

"Better the Americans than the savages," muttered Riall. At that moment a real owl hooted – unless it was Black Eagle playing tricks – and Riall nearly jumped out of the saddle in alarm. "Faster, Flashman," he cried, "for the love of God faster." With that he kicked his heels under the horse and went forward at a trot, forcing me to jog alongside with the reins. We must have covered some two hundred yards then and all the while I could hear Riall muttering to himself what seemed to be a prayer as he constantly scanned both sides of the path. "Look out!" he shouted as a dark figure stepped out into the path ahead of us.

I hauled on the horse's rein. "It's all right, it is Black Eagle," I told him before going forward to speak to the warrior. A moment later I was back with Riall as Black Eagle disappeared once more into the trees. "It is not good news, sir. The Americans are up close to the road some three hundred yards ahead of us. But there are also some Indians tracking behind us, on both sides of the road. Black Eagle does not think that there are more than a dozen and they may not even attack."

"A dozen of the devils," gasped Riall. "We can't go forward and we cannot go back, what are we going to do?"

"Don't worry," I assured him supressing a grin. "Black Eagle has gone forward to distract the Americans as we get close. We should get past in the darkness. If the Indians attack I will try to hold them off. Most will already have taken scalps at Chippawa." I paused before adding hesitantly, "Although I suppose a general's hair would be highly valued."

We started to move forward again. Riall was positively shaking with fear now. "I still have my pistol, Flashman," he whispered. "Do you think I should save it for myself, you know… at the last?"

297

The poor fool could not bring himself to finish the sentence and I almost felt sorry for him then. "Only if they have surrounded you and have their knives out," I replied. The last thing I wanted was him blowing his brains out as I knew what was going to happen next.

The night air was suddenly rent with a cacophony of screams, howls and whoops from behind us. It did not really sound like as many as a dozen Indians, but Riall was not counting. With a shriek of terror he dug in his heels and the mount sprang forward. I let go of the reins and shouted after him. "Ride, General, ride for your life and I will try and hold them off!" I fired my pistol in the air then and shouted loudly, "Come on, you devils, I will give you a taste of cold steel."

Another shot came from the Americans further down the track and staring in their direction I could see dark shapes moving onto the road to intercept the single horseman charging towards them.

"Don't shoot!" I heard Riall shout. "Don't shoot, I am a British general. Don't let those savages get me." The Americans brought his horse to a halt and I saw some reach up and haul him down from the saddle, only for him to shriek in pain as his arm was moved.

Black Eagle stepped out on the track behind me and gave one final war whoop before guffawing with laughter.

"Shut up, you fool; we don't want to give the game away now." I doubted Riall was listening, though, as he was being half pulled and half carried into the scrub along the south side of the road to start his journey to captivity. He was still shouting and yelling, but his captors were also exclaiming and hooting in delight when they saw the rank of their prisoner. I saw several of the shadows stand in the middle of the path and guessed that they must have been staring at our shapes in the gloom. They were probably trying to figure out what had frightened a British general into their ambush as they must have known there were no American Indians there. One even fired a shot at us, but at over a hundred and fifty yards, we were out of effective range for a musket. They showed no sign of wanting to pursue us, but I was confident we could lose them in the scrub to the north of the road if they had.

"Did you see his face when he looked over his shoulder at my whoops?" asked Black Eagle chuckling again. "He probably pissed himself with fear when he rode away."

I was struggling to stop laughing myself. I had always planned to engineer Riall's capture by the enemy, but to have him voluntarily give himself up was the cherry on the cake. Especially as he thought Black Eagle and I were doing all we could to save him. It could not have worked out any better, but there were still things to do. "Quickly, this way," I called stepping off the road into the scrub on its northern edge.

"Where are we going now?" asked Black Eagle.

"To Riall's tent in the British camp," I told him. "There is some paperwork I need to attend to while everyone is distracted elsewhere.

Chapter 36

By the time I got back to the top of the ridge I was in an ebullient mood. My release letter now bore Riall's signature, and the man was in no position to point out that it was a forgery. Fforbes might suspect it was faked, but as Riall was not likely to be exchanged for months, if not years, I thought he would go along with it. No one would blame him for taking the signature at face value and anyway he still owed me for my imprisonment the previous year. To make things even better, there had been no sound of battle for over half an hour. The glow of sunset in the western sky had disappeared while I was in Riall's tent and it was now virtually pitch dark. It seemed that the Americans had retired back to their camp for the night. With the battle apparently over, I suggested to Black Eagle that he should go to our tent in the camp. I would need to report the loss of Riall and I had to make it sound a dreadful misfortune. The last thing I needed was the big oaf chuckling in delight as I told the story.

Soon I was feeling my way across the top of the hill in the darkness. I could hardly see a yard or two in front of me but I could hear a rumble of voices not far away and so headed towards them.

"God damn it," I cursed as I barked my shin on a jagged lump of stone sticking up from the ground. Reaching down I realised that it was a tombstone; I was in the graveyard on the hilltop.

"Who goes there? Friend or foe?" called out a voice ahead, accompanied by the ominous sound of a weapon being cocked.

"Friend," I called back shaking my head in bemusement. This challenge worked well in Spain as there were different languages and accents. But here there was very little difference between the accent of the British, Americans or Canadians.

"Friend to who?" called out the voice suspiciously.

"King George," I replied. "It's Major Flashman."

"Flashman," Fforbes' voice rang out from the darkness. "What are you doing here? You were supposed to be taking General Riall to Queenston."

Walking towards the direction he seemed to be speaking from I replied, "I regret to advise that General Riall has been captured by the enemy. We were ambushed near the crossroads and his wound prevented him from making an escape." I had been expecting some admonishment at this, but instead of exclamations of dismay there was just silence.

"Don't worry, Major," called out another voice as I approached the huddle of men I could now see in the gloom. "We have lost two of my staff officers who were trying to report on the state of that track too." I saw a glint of gold braid on the uniform of the speaker and deduced it was General Drummond. The man did not seem at all concerned at losing the second in command, who he had argued heatedly with when he had arrived at Lundy's Lane.

"Is the battle over, sir?" I asked.

"I think so, replied the general. "The first of our reinforcements arrived a while ago and the men cheered them as they joined the line. That has probably deterred the Americans from starting another attack." The words were barely out of his mouth when there was a shout of alarm to our front, followed by a crackle of small arms fire. "What the devil is that?" shouted Drummond irritably staring forward. He was answered by the rolling discharge of our cannon. It was not the fact that they were firing that answered his enquiry, but what was revealed in the flashes of light from their muzzles. Lines of American troops could be seen charging towards our guns.

"Good God," shouted Drummond as he realised that the Americans had not gone away after all. "Forward, drive our line forward to meet them, we cannot lose the guns." I was just starting to back away into the darkness when his hand shot out and grabbed me by the shoulder. "Flashman, isn't it." Without waiting for an answer he yelled at me over the increasing noise of battle, "Go forward with the men in front of us, man." Then he was yelling at Fforbes to take forward the men on our left while I staggered away cursing my luck. How the devil was I supposed to command a force I could not even see? And I was damned if I was going to put myself at risk when I was so close to going home and seeing my wife and son. "Flashman, hold your men steady to advance with the rest," shouted Drummond over my shoulder.

"Yes sir," I shouted back realising forlornly that I would have to make at least a show of effort or my careful work of earlier in the evening would be undone. Drummond could still countermand my release if he chose.

I stumbled forward, blundering and cursing over another damn gravestone before a voice called out from just yards away, "Over here, sir."

"Who are you?" I asked of the looming figure just ahead of me.

"Sergeant Dawson, second battalion, 89th regiment, sir. The men are just in front of you, sir." I took two steps forward and nearly walked into one of them. Now I could make out a line of tall men with their shakoes blocking out some of the few stars in the night sky.

The sound of fighting was still centred on our guns to our left, but I could hear shouts and movement from not too far away in front of us too. "How far ahead are the enemy?" I found myself whispering to the sergeant as though the Americans could be close enough to listen in on our conversation.

"I don't know, sir," Dawson replied

I looked along the line as I heard a commotion to our left. There was the whinny of a horse and for a second I wondered if the Americans had cavalry, but a series of crashes and curses told me that it was an artillery horse with a limber attached fleeing through our line.

"Here they come, sir," shouted out one of the soldiers in front. Without orders, the few soldiers I could see in the gloom were raising their muskets to their shoulders and preparing to fire.

"Don't shoot," called out a voice from not more than ten yards away. "We are gunners, we are on your side," added another voice.

"Advance with your hands raised," shouted the sergeant as he stepped forward to meet three dark shadows that I saw emerging just in front of us. A moment later Dawson called out, "They are British, sir, I can feel the crowns on their buttons."

"What the hell, Sergeant, this is madness!" I exploded. "We are not going to get close enough to the enemy to feel their damn buttons." But before I could say any more I heard Drummond's voice behind me.

"Advance, the British line is to advance."

The sergeant repeated the order and the line of men in front of me began to move. To our front I heard an order given for other men to halt – it seemed horribly close. I started to follow behind my men. I had to stay close with them but I was sick with fear. I could see no more than a yard or two in any direction, there was sporadic fire from left and right and I knew that the enemy lay in wait, probably just yards away.

"Take aim," the voice came again from our front. It was so close that several of my men began to obey before they realised that they were listening to an enemy command. I looked behind us to check we were not silhouetted against the night sky, but it was pitch dark. The Americans would not see us before we could see them, which meant we would literally have to walk right up to the enemy to find them. You must have wandered into an unlit room and had to feel your way around the furniture; imagine walking through an unlit ballroom with a line of infantry waiting at the end to shoot you on sight.

We had only taken a dozen paces when my nerve failed me. At every step I had stared ahead expecting to see a line of flashes as the Americans fired their volley at what could have been point blank range.

"Halt," I shouted. The men in front of me stopped but I had no means of knowing if those further down the line had heard my orders. I put my hand on the shoulder of the soldier in front of me. "Raise your musket and fire straight ahead," I whispered. "Let's see if you hit anyone."

As the soldier moved to obey the sergeant murmured, "This is irregular, sir, the rest of the line is still marching forwards."

"I don't care," I started but then I was interrupted by a single shot and a scream of pain that seemed to come from just a few yards in front of us. "Oh God, I thought they will be firing back at any second. "All of the 89th," I shouted, "take aim…. Fire!"

The volley crashed out to be met with a chorus of screams and cries of agony from what sounded like a very short distance away. I stared into the darkness trying to gauge how far ahead the enemy were as the musket smoke stung my eyes reducing visibility even further. I could hear the rattle of ramrods along the British line as men fell automatically into the drill of reloading, something that they could all do blindfolded. Surely, I thought, firing first we must have annihilated the men standing against us. At that range nearly every ball would have found a target. But then a voice called out from the darkness in front of me.

"Steady, my boys, take aim…."

"Get down!" I shouted and led by example, throwing myself to the ground just before the command to fire was given. God knows how many of the devils there were out there, but suddenly a hail of lead was passing through our ranks. Judging from the shrieks and yells all about me, many had been slow to react to my command.

The next few minutes were complete and utter chaos. Volleys disintegrated into independent fire, lines of men became clusters. Through it all was the distant rumble of the falls on the Niagara overlaid with the shouts, screams and yells of the wounded. I stayed pressed into the ground behind a cluster of men that had formed just in front of me. I doubt that they could have seen me and I served no useful purpose standing up, armed with just a sword and pistol.

Sergeant Dawson kept giving orders to reload but we could hear equally clearly the American sergeant giving identical commands. When Dawson gave the order to fire, more often than not there was a crackle of fire from the enemy too as their soldiers obeyed our sergeant instead of their own. I dare say further down the line, our soldiers were following the drill commands of the Americans.

It was hard to gauge in the darkness but as I listened to the firing I guessed that the Americans were no more than thirty yards away and probably closer. I could hear British soldiers lying on the ground and groaning right in front of me and they gave me some cover as the

Americans were firing up the hill. I kept an ear to the ground, listening for any sign that the Americans were about to charge, but they showed no sign of movement.

In the end it was the British that withdrew. Bugles sounded and then the call went out. "Retreat to the road but no further." My men were so keen to get back that two tripped over me before I could get to my feet. I was forced to hurry back up the slope behind them. I literally ran into General Drummond at the summit of the hill as he loomed out of the darkness. He gave a gasp of pain as I blundered into his side and I saw that he had a wound in his neck that was bleeding profusely.

"Ah, Flashman, isn't it?" he said squinting at me in the gloom. "Gather your men on the road so that we can reform a straight line and then we will advance again. We must recapture those guns."

"Yes sir," I replied hurrying on to the rough track that made up Lundy's Lane. I easily found my command in the darkness; there was a babble of voices as men called out for friends and tried to work out who was missing.

"We have quite a few men missing, sir." Sergeant Dawson was at my elbow. "Possibly as many as half the company although some of them could be lost in the dark." He lowered his voice even further and added, "I saw at least two running on into the camp to hide out from the battle in the dark."

"Disgraceful," I agreed, trying to sound scandalised although it seemed like an excellent idea to me. But before I had any opportunity to do the same, bugles were sounding the advance and the sergeant looked expectantly at me to take forward the men.

Knowing the general was nearby and listening I thought a rousing speech was in order. "Men, this is Major Flashman. We must retake those guns and restore honour to British arms. I know I can rely on the men of the er…"

"Eighty ninth regiment, sir," offered Dawson helpfully.

"Indeed, the eighty ninth," I continued, "to ensure that our comrades have not fallen in vain. Come on, men, follow me to glory!"

With that I waved my sword in the air, an act that could only be seen by the half dozen men around me, and stepped off into the darkness.

Apart from a sycophantic cheer from the dutiful sergeant and a "Well done, Major" from the unseen general, my efforts received little acclaim from the men. They did, though, move forward, I heard their boot steps marching over the ground either side of me. Those brave men may have been a little less dutiful if they could have seen their commanding officer as he felt his way around the graveyard, hunting for a good place to hide. I found three tombstones all together, presumably a family grave, and ducked down on the enemy side of them, just in time before my men trudged past on either side.

The stones, crosses and other memorials stuck in the ground every few yards, soon broke up the advance of my men. They started to call out to each other as they lost touch with the men on either side, which gave the Americans plenty of warning of their approach. This time our opponents did not wait to let us fire first. A crackle of fire opened up in front of us as pin pricks of light from muzzle flashes gave away their position. Deadly balls of lead soon buzzed over the graveyard. I moved forward, but only to try to find something substantial to put between me and the enemy fire. The family grave markers had been made of wood, but I knew from walking into some before that there were also ones of stone.

The man's name was Elias – I traced that much out with my finger. He must have done well for himself as his family had been able to afford a substantial gravestone. It was at least three inches thick and chest height. I slumped gratefully behind it as I heard the battle rage on around me. I have no idea how close we came to recapturing those guns, all I could see was some three yards around that stone. I crouched there reading the markings on the stone with my fingertips and listening to the shouts and yells from the soldiers. The noise indicated that neither side was pressing forward or giving way. Further down the line, nearer the guns, occasionally there would be crashes of volleys and more noise to indicate that one side or another was attacking, but my men stayed where they were among grave markers and the enemy did the same.

306

The battle must have raged for at least another two hours. At one point Drummond tried to reform his line for a third attack but most of my men stayed put. At times it was hard to believe that the battle was real. I am sure that I heard Drummond talking to the regiment to the right of ours, the 103rd, and during a lull in the fighting he *asked* them if they would charge rather than order them to do so. They turned him down flat too. In the end the battle just gradually stopped, there were no victories or defeats, the crackle of fire just slowly stopped as men were too exhausted to continue. Perhaps some ran out of ammunition or tired of firing blindly into the dark, but gradually an eerie quiet grew over the battlefield.

I could hear men whispering and moving about near me and we could even hear the Americans talking among themselves and tending to their wounded. Judging it safe, I emerged from behind my stone and moved among the men. I congratulated them for their good work and gave the impression that I had been fighting just a few yards away. Eventually we heard the jingle of equipment and movement from the enemy lines but instead of coming towards us, they were moving away. We listened until there was silence in front of us, broken only by the whimper or cry of a wounded man that had been left behind.

Then came word that we too were retiring back to our camp. Tired men pulled themselves to their feet and taking their walking wounded with them, they started to make their way back over Lundy's Lane to the British camp.

It all seemed surreal, like no other battle I had been in. I stared blindly to where I knew the guns must be. Thousands of men had been fighting and dying to capture those lumps of metal for the last few hours. Now they had been abandoned by both armies and were guarded by just the dead and dying. Suddenly I did not want to blunder around looking for my tent. I went back to where I had spent most of the battle, to lie down on top of Elias. There I stretched out with my hands behind my head, staring up at a handful of stars and listening to the distant rumble of the falls and the occasional shout from the men left behind. I tried to make sense of what it had all been for, but I was damned if I could.

Epilogue

Anyone who tells you that they know how the battle of Lundy's Lane was fought is a damn liar. I was there and I have no idea how half of it went because most of it was fought at night. As I write this memoir Winfield Scott is head of the American army and I got to meet him a few years back. Naturally we fell to jawing about the war and it was only then that I discovered that part way through the battle he had launched his men towards the British line in a column to punch through our ranks. Until that moment I had thought that the generals on both sides had shown little imagination, relying just on frontal attacks in line.

When I said this to Winfield Scott he just laughed. "I have not told you what became of my attack yet," he replied. Then he proceeded to recount how as they advanced into the centre of the battle, his soldiers were fired on not just by the British but also by American troops who had seen a column of men loom out of the darkness beside them. Despite shouting out their allegiance, Winfield Scott's troops were caught in a withering crossfire and were eventually forced to withdraw.

I remember walking across that bloody hillside on the morning after the battle with Black Eagle, who was appalled at the slaughter.

"You once told me that the Iroquois way of fighting was savage," he reminded me. "But this is much worse than anything we have done." As I looked at row upon row of corpses that had been marched towards their enemies at virtually point blank range in the darkness, I struggled to disagree with him. In fact I never saw such short range slaughter like it, not in the peninsula or India, and I say that taking into account that I found myself near a little Belgian village called Waterloo the following year.

Lundy's Lane was to be the bloodiest battle of the whole war and for me it seems to summarise the whole conflict: huge numbers of men killed for no good purpose. At the end of the fighting, both sides returned exhausted to the camps in which they had started the battle. In the morning the Americans sent some men to try to carry the guns off,

308

but as they were British guns and nearer the British camp, we had our men there first. The Americans withdrew without any shots fired and then sent men under a flag of truce to help with their wounded.

It was clear that neither side had the appetite for further fighting just then. Black Eagle and Norton returned to the Grand River the day after the battle. I remember Black Eagle embracing me in one of his great bear hugs for the final time. He reminded me that I had to bring my son to Canada to learn to hunt with his son. Then he took off the wampum necklace that he had found at the American brothel and draped it around my neck to remember him by. I still have that band of shell beads; it is in a casket on my desk as I write this account, along with other treasures from my adventures. My slightly rusted tomahawk is also on the wall here in my study.

I did go back to Canada many years later and tried to find Black Eagle. Brant's Ford had become 'Brantsford' by then and looked much like any other town in the province. I spoke to a few old-timers and one remembered my friend. He thought Black Eagle, Morag and their family had headed west. In the churchyard I found what I was sure was Magda's grave. The year of birth was right but she had a new surname and so had evidently remarried. She had died in her forties and lay with her husband. Judging from the sentiments on the tombstone, her second marriage had been a much happier one.

When I said goodbye to Norton I thought it would be the last time I would see him too, but fate plays some strange tricks. I saw him twice more over the years. He came to Britain a year later with his young wife and a son from a previous marriage. Both were enrolled in his old school while he caught up with his British friends. He was still full of enthusiasm for helping the Iroquois adapt to the changing world, but it was not to be. A few years later he got into a fight with a man he thought had been cuckolding him and he killed the rascal. He left Canada then and headed south to the Cherokee lands of his father. He must have kept on going south, for the last letter he sent me was from Mexico in around 1827. Like most of his friends I thought he must have died when nothing more was heard from him, but I was to see him once more – in 1836 near a little mission station called the Alamo.

Two days after the battle at Lundy's Lane Campbell found me wandering through the hilltop graveyard which had more than tripled in size since I had fought among its markers. Only officers had their own plot; enlisted men were buried in mass graves by either company or regiment.

"What are you doing wandering around the battlefield gazette?" he asked. I smiled weakly at the joke for the *Gazette* in London published the names of all officers killed in service.

"Oh, just seeing who is here," I replied before adding, "why are you so cheerful?"

"Ah you would be more cheerful too if you knew what was in my hand," he replied waving a piece of paper.

"What is it?" I asked although I had already recognised the document.

"It is your release," he replied with a smug expression. "And you will never guess who signed it – General Riall. He must have done it before he was captured. I knew he could not have been as bad as Norton and you were claiming."

I smiled, largely with relief. I had been waiting impatiently for the paper to come to light, but I could hardly go chasing it. Campbell was my oldest friend, but he was burdened by a strict Calvinist upbringing that forbade lying amongst many other things. I could not confide what I had done to him; it would have tormented his Christian soul. So instead I mustered my best look of astonishment and started towards him. "Well I am truly amazed; the man must have had some humanity after all. Are we leaving today?"

"Yes, I have a man getting us a horse for luggage… What is the matter? You look like you have seen a ghost."

"Oh, I have just found the grave I was looking for." I looked down at the rough wooden marker with its engraved name and felt a pang of sadness. "Do you still carry that folding fruit knife? Could I borrow it?"

"Of course," said Campbell handing over the small sharp blade. He then stood beside me as I crouched down and started to carve a second 'f'.

Historical Notes

I am indebted to a range of sources for confirming much of the detail in Flashman's account of this extraordinary conflict. These include *The Incredible War of 1812* by J Mackay Hitsman, *1812 War with America* by Jon Latimer, *Tecumseh, A Life* by John Sugden and *The Iroquois in the War of 1812* by Carl Benn. Another immensely valuable first-hand source to some of the events covered was the *Journal of Major John Norton*, which was finished in 1816 and held in the Duke of Northumberland's library until it was published in 1970 by the Champlain Society. A copy of this can be found freely online.

War of 1812

This conflict is now rarely remembered but the background to it is largely as Flashman describes in the second chapter of this book. There was no single cause for the war and at the end, both sides claimed victory.

This account does not cover the full conflict. Significant events after Flashman departs North America include the British burning the public buildings of Washington and General Andrew Jackson defeating a British army in New Orleans. When a peace was finally agreed, the border between the United States and Canada remained exactly as it had been at the outset of hostilities.

Flashman's view that the war was a pointless waste of life was doubtless influenced by his personal experience and those he knew who were killed. But from a longer perspective the conflict may have served some purpose. Certainly both sides learned a new respect for their opponents and this may be a significant reason why the border between Canada and the United States is now the longest and most peaceful in the world.

John Norton

John Norton's background is described pretty accurately by Flashman in the book. His father was a Cherokee taken as a boy from his village and later recruited into the British army. His father returned to Britain with his regiment and subsequently married and lived in Scotland. John Norton was brought up in Dunfermline, where, judging from his journal and translation work, he had a good education. He then joined the army himself and was posted to Canada where he eventually ended up as a translator before being formally adopted into the Mohawk tribe.

His unique perspective of being a Mohawk who was brought up in Britain enabled him to represent the Six Nations or Iroquois during negotiations in London, where he made a number of influential friends including William Wilberforce and the Duke of Northumberland. It also gave him an insight into how the North American tribes would need to adapt their ways to live alongside a growing population of settlers from Europe. He promoted Christianity with his Bible translations and changes to agricultural practices, but it is perhaps for his war leadership that he was best known. Queenston was probably the pinnacle of his military career. As the tide of war turned against the British, many of the Iroquois began to suspect he held Britain's interests before theirs. Consequently in 1813 he began to lose influence in the tribe and his position was further undermined by the Indian Agency, who resented his direct links with army commanders. Ironically the British began to distrust him because they felt he put his role as an Iroquois chief above that of a British officer. Generals Drummond and Riall both lost confidence in him after learning of the truce and council meeting with the Iroquois warriors that had fought for The United States.

After the war Norton returned briefly to Britain as Flashman described. He went back to Canada with his family a year later and started farming in the Grand River lands. He lived peacefully until 1823 when he killed a man in a fight. His opponent was a man who he suspected was his much younger wife's lover. He was convicted of manslaughter and fined £25. He then decided to leave the Grand River and head back to his father's Cherokee lands that he had visited once before – that earlier tour is covered in detail in his journal. He evidently kept on travelling south and the last letters from him were dated November 1825 from Laredo, then in Mexico. Flashman is the only source for the fact that he might have lived on in that region for another ten years; he would then be aged around seventy.

Battle of Queenston

Flashman's account of the Iroquois at the battle of Queenston accords closely with the only other first-hand account, the journal of John Norton. The small number of warriors who reached the heights used classic Iroquois tactics of shock, ambush and disguising their true numbers to achieve an impact in the battle that was out of all proportion to the size of their force.

As Flashman records, as well as disrupting and demoralising the Americans on the heights and persuading many of the militia to flee the field, they were also instrumental in dissuading further militia forces from crossing the river as reinforcements. Their tactics also enticed the American force into expending large quantities of ammunition to very little effect, which was to be a crucial factor in the final stages of the battle.

Incidental details such as the presence of Captain Runchey's Company of Coloured Men, the conditions of the American army at Lewiston and the American guns joining in the salute for General Brock are all confirmed by contemporary sources.

Life with the Iroquois

Many of the details that Flashman provides of life with the Iroquois are confirmed by contemporary sources. These include details of Brant's Ford at that time, depictions painted on bark of battle achievements, preferred battle tactics and the description of tomahawks with a pipe opposite the blade. Even some of the Indians Flashman mentions have been confirmed. While no record can be found of Black Eagle and Morag, I am delighted to be able to include a photograph of John Smoke Johnson at the end of these notes. Johnson did have a half Dutch wife and took part in the battle of Queenston. His disapproval of the practice of scalping at that time has also been recorded.

There is also a record of a Magdalena Dietrich amongst the Mennonite community in Pennsylvania, although whether she was the one who travelled to Canada cannot be proved. The place at the fork of the river, which had no name in Flashman's time, became Blair, Ontario. It did have a growing Mennonite population, which was established around 1800. Blair was later absorbed into the town of Cambridge, Ontario.

It is interesting to note that Black Eagle had no fear of heights as he climbed about in the rigging of ships. Later, Iroquois were employed to help build skyscrapers in New York as they seemed fearless as they moved about on steel girders high above the ground.

One final curiosity is Flashman's choice of song when invited to sing around the Brant's Ford campfire on his first night in the village. His choice of an old London club drinking song, *To Anacreon in Heaven*, was to have particular significance for the United States. He does not mention singing it at any other time but someone in America certainly heard it. A man called Francis Scott Key used the tune for a poem, which later became the national anthem of the United States of America.

The Sieges of Fort Meigs
The somewhat bizarre sieges of Fort Meigs took place largely as Flashman described them. Most of the militia garrison of the fort had abandoned the site in early 1813 when their enlistment period had expired. The winter and landscape had been harsh and unforgiving with stories of sentries being frozen to death on duty. Many of the militia felt that they had done enough and wanted to go home. General Harrison, knowing that a British attack was likely, was then forced to recruit a new garrison, which he did leaving the fort under the command of his engineer, Eleazer Wood. It was an inspired choice as Wood greatly strengthened the defences of the fort to thwart any attack.

The first siege began on the 1st of May 1813 when the British started a bombardment of the fort. As described in this account, the guns had little effect but on the 5th of May the British force was surprised by the arrival of a twelve hundred man relief force. Of these, Colonel William Dudley, landed over eight hundred and fifty men on the British side of the river, where they allowed themselves to be drawn deep into a forest. These soldiers would have been well aware of the fighting abilities of Indians in such cover. Flashman's account gives some explanation of why they might have been lured into danger, instead of spiking the guns and retiring back to the fort as planned. Over five hundred of Dudley's men were captured; most of the rest were killed but a few managed to swim across the river to join the rest of the relief force in the fort.

Tecumseh did stop the massacre of the American prisoners, although there are no reliable accounts of what he said. Procter had sent far too few men to guard his prisoners and he had clearly not learned his lesson after the massacre at the River Raisin. In his defence much of his command was scattered and disorganised on both banks of the river after the battle, but at least one grey-haired British soldier was killed by the Indians while trying to defend the prisoners.

Most of the Indian force and subsequently the militia did abandon the siege after the battle on the 5th of May for the reasons highlighted by Flashman. A few more days would have seen the fort's surrender as they were already short of rations before the arrival of the relief force, and disease was rife in the tightly packed garrison. Procter's frustration at this point can only be imagined.

Fort Meigs was under the command of General Clay for the second siege, which seemed doomed to failure from the outset. The two six-pounder cannon the British brought with them might have punched a hole through planking or splintered a tree trunk, but they would have done little damage to a major fort. Clay probably had a good idea where his commander, General Harrison, was during the siege and so the Indian plan to lure out the garrison with their mock battle was at best a longshot.

Assault of Fort Stephenson

The assault on Fort Stephenson may well have been the turning point for General Procter's mental health as indicated by Flashman. After a long series of frustrations and defeats, to have the promise of victory offered and then snatched away by another brutal defeat would have tested the confidence of any commander.

Procter did produce a sound plan to attack the fort, which might have worked if the diversionary assault had been made on time. However the fort's defenders were well prepared and waiting for the main assault, with their one cannon used to devastating effect. Over half the assault party was killed or injured for the loss of one American soldier killed and seven wounded.

George Groghan was relieved of his command by General Harrison when he refused to evacuate the fort, although Groghan did not receive this news until after his victory. When Harrison learned of the defence of the fort, he had little alternative but to reinstate its commander.

Battle of Lake Erie
This extraordinary engagement saw the advantage swing from one side to another. Barclay's British fleet was outnumbered, out gunned and desperately lacking in skilled seamen and virtually every form of naval supply. Under immense pressure to regain control of the lake, Barclay risked all on his one advantage: longer range guns. Forced to sail in light and variable winds, the first part of the battle went well for the British. Inexplicably the second large American ship, the *Niagara* under a Captain Elliot stayed out of effective range allowing the British to concentrate all their fire on the *Lawrence* commanded by Perry. This lack of support was a cause of friction between Perry and Elliot for years to come. When the *Lawrence* was finally battered to a standstill the British thought the battle was won, but Perry was rowed away with his flag before the *Lawrence* struck her colours.

Reaching the *Niagara*, Perry sent Elliot in a small boat to round up the smaller vessels while he took the *Niagara* once more into the attack. He was hugely aided by the fact that all of the senior officers on both the *Detroit* and *Queen Charlotte* and been killed or injured. As a result, the inexperienced men then commanding the vessels allowed them to collide. This most complete victory made Perry's reputation and he became a hero in the United States. After the war he continued

316

in the navy but during a mission to Venezuela in 1819 he contracted yellow fever and died aged just thirty-four.

Barclay did survive the battle with just one leg and only limited sensation in his remaining arm. In the following court martial for the loss of his command he was completely exonerated and granted a pension. In 1815 he married and later had several children. He died in Scotland in 1837.

General Procter

Procter is a figure who has been universally condemned by history. To Americans he is still seen as something of a war criminal, while the Canadians view him as a coward. Flashman's account gives a more rounded view of a man, placed in what seemed an impossible position, who allowed himself to be manipulated by those around him, including Tecumseh and not least Flashman himself.

Procter had no battle experience before the war, but showed he had some drive with his swift counter-attack at Frenchtown. He did, however, give away the element of surprise in that engagement, resulting in higher casualties than necessary. Thereafter he struggled to maintain control of his theatre of operations. He clashed with Tecumseh who was working towards his own goals and received very little in the way of support or supplies from the governor general. He did not help his cause by alienating many of his senior officers, preferring instead the company of cronies and 'yes-men'.

He was married with a son and four daughters. It is unclear how many of his daughters accompanied him to Amherstburg, but he was evidently very much a family man. While he had shown personal courage in some of his earlier engagements, it was clear after the failed assault on Fort Stephenson that his nerve was beginning to fail. Procter found he was openly reviled both by the Indians and some of his own officers as he planned the retreat.

The withdrawal from Amherstburg was a poorly organised shambles. Procter spent most of it in his carriage with his family and was rarely seen giving any sense of command. Whether he ever intended to make a stand at Chatham and what possessed him to finally stand at Moraviantown, will never be known. By then he was in a very precarious mental state and he may not have been entirely sure himself. He was at the forefront of the subsequent rout and consequently escaped capture.

In December 1814 he was tried by court martial, which concluded the following month. He was found guilty of misconduct. In addition to demotion and suspension from duty, the Prince Regent directed that his own 'high disapprobation' be conveyed and included in the general orders to be read to the entire British army. Procter returned to England in 1815 and unsurprisingly was never given a command again. He died in 1822.

Tecumseh
Much of the information provided by Flashman on Tecumseh is confirmed by contemporary sources. This includes his insistence on attacking Fort Meigs, the saving of the American prisoners, the council meetings at Amherstburg and his conduct on the retreat and at Moraviantown. Incidental details are corroborated too such as his removing weapons at Procter's dining table and carrying out an inspection of the British troops before Moraviantown. Some of the words and phrases used by Tecumseh at the council meetings were also recorded by those present and these include him referring to Procter as a creature that 'drops his tail between his legs and runs off' and his demands for the ammunition 'sent by the King Across the Sea for his red children.'

Flashman's account of Tecumseh's death also matches key accounts although there was subsequently much debate on who had fired the lethal shot. The American cavalry commander Richard Johnson claimed that he had shot Tecumseh as a part of his campaign to be elected Vice President 1836/7. While Johnson was undoubtedly brave, leading the forlorn hope cavalry group against the Indians in the swamp – during which he was wounded by four musket balls – it is by no means certain he killed Tecumseh.

Chippawa

To this day many accounts of the battle of Chippawa barely mention the battle that took place in the forest between the militia and Indians on both sides. Instead they concentrate on the battle that took place in the open where an overconfident Riall swiftly discovered that the men in grey jackets were not militia after all. The British regulars advanced and found themselves facing well-trained American troops to their front and one flank with further canister fire from nearby artillery. Eventually they were forced to retreat in good order.

The battle in the forest took place largely as Flashman described, with Riall criticising Norton for leading the Iroquois too deep into the trees before making his attack. There is no accurate record of Indian casualties but American statistics, partly based on scalps presented after the battle, indicate that the Grand River and western tribesmen fighting for the British lost eighty-seven killed, five taken prisoner and an unknown number wounded. These were similar losses to the eighty five British dead, but this number was devastating for the much smaller Iroquois community.

Lundy's Lane

The battle of Lundy's Lane was the bloodiest battle of the whole war, with much of it fought in darkness and confusion. The early part, when there was still some light, was fought as Flashman describes. General Riall did order a retreat from Lundy's Lane but this order was countermanded when General Drummond arrived. Riall was later wounded and inexplicably captured when those escorting him to the rear took him too close to the crossroads, which were under an American attack.

The subsequent fighting which took place in near pitch darkness was a confused, short-range brutal affair. According to witnesses, General Drummond did *ask* the 103rd regiment to charge the enemy. They refused the request and fired volleys instead. As Flashman describes, in the end the guns that the battle had been fought over were abandoned by both sides.

Photograph of three Iroquois veterans who fought for the British during the war of 1812.
The man on the right is John Smoke Johnson, then aged around ninety - you can just make out the pipe bowl on the back of his tomahawk.

Thank you for reading this book and I hoped you enjoyed it. If so I would be grateful for any positive reviews on websites that you use to choose books. As there is no major publisher promoting this book, any recommendations to friends and family that you think would enjoy it would also be appreciated.

There is now a Thomas Flashman Books Facebook page to keep you updated on future books in the series. It also includes portraits, pictures and further information on characters and events featured in the books.

Also by this author

Flashman and the Seawolf

This first book in the Thomas
Flashman series covers his
adventures with Thomas Cochrane,
one of the most extraordinary
naval commanders of all time.

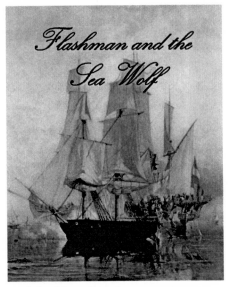

From the brothels and gambling
dens of London, through political
intrigues and espionage, the action
moves to the Mediterranean and
the real life character of Thomas
Cochrane. This book covers the
start of Cochrane's career including
the most astounding single ship action of the Napoleonic war.

Thomas Flashman provides a unique insight as danger stalks him like
a persistent bailiff through a series of adventures that prove history
really is stranger than fiction.

Flashman and the Cobra

This book takes Thomas to
territory familiar to readers of
his nephew's adventures, India,
during the second Mahratta war.
It also includes an illuminating
visit to Paris during the Peace
of Amiens in 1802.

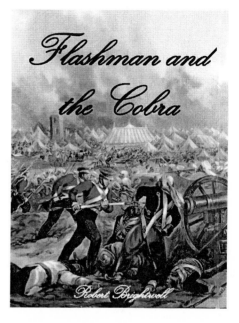

As you might expect Flashman
is embroiled in treachery and
scandal from the outset and,
despite his very best
endeavours, is often in the thick
of the action. He intrigues with
generals, warlords, fearless
warriors, nomadic bandit tribes, highland soldiers and not least a four-
foot-tall former nautch dancer, who led the only Mahratta troops to
leave the battlefield of Assaye in good order.

Flashman gives an illuminating account with a unique perspective. It
details feats of incredible courage (not his, obviously) reckless folly
and sheer good luck that were to change the future of India and the
career of a general who would later win a war in Europe.

Flashman in the Peninsula

While many people have written books and novels on the Peninsular War, Flashman's memoirs offer a unique perspective. They include new accounts of famous battles, but also incredible incidents and characters almost forgotten by history. Flashman is revealed as the catalyst to one of the greatest royal scandals of the nineteenth century which disgraced a prince and ultimately produced one of our greatest novelists. In Spain and Portugal he witnesses catastrophic incompetence and incredible courage in equal measure. He is present at an extraordinary action where a small group of men stopped the army of a French marshal in its tracks. His flatulent horse may well have routed a Spanish regiment, while his cowardice and poltroonery certainly saved the British army from a French trap.

Accompanied by Lord Byron's dog, Flashman faces death from Polish lancers and a vengeful Spanish midget, not to mention finding time to perform a blasphemous act with the famous Maid of Zaragoza. This is an account made more astonishing as the key facts are confirmed by various historical sources.

Flashman's Escape

This book covers the second half of Thomas Flashman's experiences in the Peninsular War and follows on from *Flashman in the Peninsula.*

Having lost his role as a staff officer, Flashman finds himself commanding a company in an infantry battalion. In between cuckolding his soldiers and annoying his superiors, he finds himself at the heart of the two bloodiest actions of the war. With drama and disaster in equal measure, he provides a first-hand account of not only the horror of battle but also the bloody aftermath.

Hopes for a quieter life backfire horribly when he is sent behind enemy lines to help recover an important British prisoner, who also happens to be a hated rival. His adventures take him the length of Spain and all the way to Paris on one of the most audacious wartime journeys ever undertaken. With the future of the French empire briefly placed in his quaking hands, Flashman dodges lovers, angry fathers, conspirators and ministers of state in a desperate effort to keep his cowardly carcass in one piece. It is a historical roller-coaster ride that brings together various extraordinary events, while also giving a disturbing insight into the creation of a French literary classic!

CPSIA information can be obtained
at www.ICGtesting.com
Printed in the USA
FSOW01n1317280715
9336FS